FRACTURE

THE COLOR ALCHEMIST BOOK TWO

NINA WALKER

ADDISON & GRAY PRESS
WWW.NINAWALKERBOOKS.COM

ISBN# 978-0-9992876-3-7

For Travis

ONE

JESSA

I bit my lip and rested my forehead on the large oak door. My first test in color alchemy waited on the other side. Nervous energy poured down my body in electric currents, setting me on edge. This was the beginning of my new life. I tapped my foot, ignoring the conversation that buzzed around me. I was surrounded by people who were taking bets—not on *if* I would fail, but *how fast* it would happen.

The other alchemists wanted me gone because I wasn't like them. They'd grown up together, and I was the new girl, reminding them of everything they'd missed out on. Not to mention, a typical alchemist spent years honing their magic before initiation. So it came as no surprise that my quick rise into magic wasn't well received. Of course, the king loved it. Everyone else? Not so much. Perhaps it was only natural for them to dislike the person who changed the way things were done—who cut in line. Because if I was initiated so quickly, then what else would change?

Ugh, this is so not how I thought my life would turn out.

As a prima ballerina, I'd been on the perfect track to living my dream. Sure, at times it isolated me from my peers. My single-minded passion wasn't relatable to the average teenager. Dance was my world, and I loved it. But everything had been taken away from me the day my alchemy was discovered. The last few months had been torture. But, as devastating as it was, I'd finally accepted that my life was bigger than the stage: I had a king to take down.

I ignored the cold glares and hostile mutterings of the many guardians lining the corridor outside the testing room while we waited. Guardians. That's what we called alchemists after they initiated into the Guardians of Color—GC for short. It was the elite organization, ruled by New Colony's royal family. The GC kept our kingdom powerful and prosperous.

Or so they liked to think. I knew better.

"She's going to crash and burn," someone snickered from behind. A chorus of laugher broke out.

Back straight, head up; I couldn't let them get to me. Still, an unwanted twinge of longing burned inside. Okay, if I was honest with myself, I shouldn't care about their approval, but part of me did anyway. I hated that. I had a mission to complete. Getting initiated was the first step. Once that was done, King Richard would put me to work on GC assignments and heaven knows what else. The plan was to become stronger. I would get close enough to him to use my red alchemy against him, ultimately ending his corruption.

I shuddered as I let out an overdue breath. Defeating the king and his many loyal, some even magical, subjects was a big mission for anyone to accomplish, let alone for a new alchemist. If caught, I'd undoubtedly be killed for treason. The worried thoughts crossed my mind on more than one occasion. *Is it really worth the risk? Maybe I should have stayed with my parents and the Resistance...*

I cut off the thoughts right there. No regrets.

I focused again on the door in front of me. On the other side, my first test would either end in success or disaster. I sucked in a breath, hoping for the former. I straightened my spine and turned around to face the crowd. A sea of faces glared back at me. Faulk and a couple of her officers approached, arms crossed, brows furrowed in skeptical lines. They took their jobs *very* seriously. It was almost comical, except they had the power to ruin me and we all knew it.

Stand tall, Jessa. Don't let them win.

"How's it going, Faulk? What's new in Officer Land?" I smiled inwardly at my sarcasm, knowing it would drive her nuts.

"Don't be cute," she replied curtly. Her eyes strained as she sized me up. I assumed the death of the queen and subsequent revelation that her own right-hand man, Thomas, had been the one to do it, were weighing on her career. I refused to feel sorry for her. At every turn, Faulk had made it clear that she wanted me locked up. Ever since the day she first met me, she'd hated my very existence. I was a dark stain on her otherwise shining record, the alchemist girl she'd missed.

The one who got away—kind of.

"We'll be watching you from the observation room," she continued, jabbing her finger at me as she spoke. "Don't try anything stupid. You're to get in and out as quickly as possible, obviously using alchemy to do it."

"I'll be fine," I said, keeping my voice level.

Of course they chose to keep the details of the tests a secret. If I knew what I was walking into, I wouldn't feel so unsettled.

"Good luck," Faulk said bitterly. Then she and her underlings marched away and through a door farther down

3

the hallway, slamming it behind them. The observation room, no doubt.

"Are you scared?" a voice snickered.

"You should be," another called from the group.

These lame alchemists apparently had nothing better to do.

"She's not ready," another added with a chuckle.

I didn't bother to reply because I sort of agreed with them. Since when had I ever been ready for this? *Ready* was of little consequence. The king wouldn't wait for *ready*. Neither would I.

I pushed open the heavy metallic door, anxious to discover what color I'd be working with first. I had to show strong proficiency in at least three colors to make it to initiation. I knew red and white weren't on that list, as those magics weren't accessible to the typical alchemist. In fact, I was one of the only known alchemists able to access red. And white? That was unchartered territory as well, though Lucas had his own closely hidden ability with it. That left me with purple, blue, green, yellow, and orange. There would be tests for all of those. Three was doable. However, uncertainty burned in my body.

I stepped inside.

The room was dark. As I moved in farther, a rush of humid air kicked my senses into awareness. A large space, bigger than my old dance studio. A gymnasium, I guessed. Harsh chemicals assaulted my lungs. Chlorine?

I took another tentative step forward. Blazing lights shot through my vision, and I stumbled back. *Of course...*

I exhaled slowly. It was only a swimming pool, nothing to worry about. And *yellow*.

Yellow flowers, plants, and stones lined the edge of the pool. My gaze rapidly raced across the room, assessing the

4

situation. They wanted me to perform yellow alchemy, but what was the test? What did yellow have *anything* to do with swimming?

A digital clock illuminated red numbers on a black square screen across from the pool. A countdown: 20:00.

19:59…

Twenty minutes! Only twenty minutes to accomplish what exactly?

The door slammed. A loud click echoed through the room. Panic threatened to tear me apart. I was locked in here. *Why?*

Breathing deeply, I peered over the edge of the pool. Hundreds of keys twinkled in a layer of scattered gold across the cobalt blue tiles, at least fifteen feet under water, like spilled treasure. The purpose of the test tumbled into place in my mind. It was so obvious.

I wasn't a good swimmer, but I needed to get to those keys. Fast.

I wracked my brain, drawing upon all my studies. What did I know about yellow? It was connected to energy and willpower, and, most importantly, it was an amplifier. Yellow alchemy had given me the strength to break through the wall surrounding the palace. Of course, I'd *wanted* to break through that wall. That was critical. Still, it was solid stone, and I'd been able to crumble it with superhuman strength. It was just one of the many miraculous things alchemy could do. At the time, I was convinced Lacey's survival depended on me getting to the other side of that wall.

Could I draw upon the same inner willpower again?

This time, it was *my* survival at stake. I had to pass this test. Although I was a dancer and quite athletic, I wasn't fond of water. I was a terrible swimmer. Finding the right key to open the door would take time, and the eighteen minutes I had left wouldn't cut it under normal circumstances.

I inhaled a deep breath. *You can do this. No more analyzing.*

I ripped a flower from its stem and crushed it between two fingers. It only took a moment for the yellow to lift from the broken petals and rise into the air. Another moment and the color drifted into my body. I closed my eyes, breathing in the magic, willing the yellow to enter my lungs, my bloodstream, anything to make me a faster, stronger, and better swimmer. A burst of adrenaline pulsed through my veins. The magic ignited.

I dove into the water.

Swimming down, I ignored the immediate sweep of ice that attacked my body. The water was frigid! The biting sensation cut across my skin like a million needles, stinging. I fought the distraction, the instinct to flee, and swam deeper. I refused to be bothered by the black uniform that weighed me down. Determination raced through every cell of my body. I would *not* fail.

If I ever wanted to see my family again, to help Lacey, to save New Colony from the manipulation of the GC and the king, then I had to keep swimming. And I wasn't alone. Knowing an entire resistance of people was out there somewhere bolstered my spirits. I didn't know them all yet, but I felt their solidarity with every stroke.

Settling on the bottom of the pool, the water pushed me down, even colder than before. It oppressed all my senses, caging me in. A thread of panic stitched its way into my burning chest, binding me. I forced myself to focus on the yellow magic supporting me and allowed it to strengthen my resolve. I grabbed as many keys as I could, pulling them into a makeshift pocket by tugging my shirt up around my torso. The keys were slippery and harder to pick up than I'd anticipated. I was running out of breath. I needed to move.

The urge to breathe overpowered me. My eyeballs twitched, and the weight of the water caused panic to rip through my body. I positioned my feet on the bottom, pushed off, and rocketed to the surface. I flew out of the water, yelping in surprise, and landed with a thud on the concrete.

Wet keys clattered in a golden arc around me.

I patted my body frantically, expecting pain. There was none. Nothing was broken either. I couldn't say the same for the concrete floor. A crack had formed where my body had taken the biggest hit.

Whoa... turns out I can control yellow alchemy. I paused for a momentary happy dance. *Go me!* Faulk was probably gritting her teeth in irritation by now. I grinned at the crushed floor, not hiding my gleeful smirk. I was going to own this test, and she was going to watch me.

I moved to pick keys up off the floor, my pace infinitely faster with the magic pulsing through me. With every handful, I sprinted to the door and tried to maneuver the lock into position with the different keys. None worked. Once I'd exhausted them all, I took another deep breath and dove back into the frosty water.

It wasn't just *possible* that I wouldn't make it out in twenty minutes; it was *probable*. Everywhere I looked, more keys reflected back at me. I swam anyway. As I got closer, it was as if they were mocking me and multiplying. Just how many were down here? Worry snaked through my thoughts, twisting me up and threatening to slow me down. Despite everything, the yellow energy kept me focused, moving quickly. I drew on it, the magic igniting confidence in me. And with each key I scooped up, I felt closer to my goal.

A few more flowers and three more trips into the pool, and I was starting to feel the magic wane. I was tired. The keys were beginning to slip through my fingers. I let out a frustrated yelp as yet another key proved incompatible with the lock. I shook away the urge to give up and pushed yet another into the keyhole. It clicked into the lock and turned with ease. My jaw dropped. This was it! I peered back—still ten minutes on the clock. I couldn't believe my luck. The tension in my body was immediately washed away.

"Take that," I muttered, "stupid lock."

I pushed open the door and stepped into the crowd. Their conversations silenced as shock filled their stupid faces. No doubt they didn't understand how a novice like me could complete such a difficult task.

"What? She didn't fail?" a female voice blurted, disbelieving, as the group stared.

"Nope," I boldly responded. "I didn't even lose my breath."

Then I glanced around at the thirty or so people, mostly teenagers, and winked. Okay, a little immature of me to rub it in their faces. But what did they expect? Just because I wasn't as trained as they were, I wasn't as powerful? Alchemy was still scary to me, but like it or not, it came naturally. I'd tried to fight my magic for so long, but I couldn't anymore. I was hell-bent on learning to control it so I wouldn't end up hurting someone again. I needed to be here for my own good. I needed to learn. And I wanted the chance.

A flip of silky yellow hair caught my attention. The flawless complexion behind them was familiar. Brooke. She'd made it clear she didn't like me, so I wasn't surprised to see she'd come to watch me fail. Too bad she hadn't gotten her wish. She leaned into Reed, whispering. She flipped her shiny hair back *again* and sneered at me. "You think you're something special, don't you?"

I was dang tired of her nasty comments. I'd mostly kept my mouth shut, trying to take the higher road, but I couldn't stand it any longer. "I don't know what your problem is with me, Brooke, but get over yourself and accept that I'm good enough for the GC." I glanced at Reed, my former friend. "That goes for both of you."

She laughed. "Being a guardian is about more than alchemy. It's about loyalty. We all know about your pathetic attempt to run away."

I glanced at the other alchemists, noting the interest rippling through the crowd. This was a dangerous topic. I needed to end it here and now. Of course, I didn't. "What's your point?"

"Loyal alchemists don't run away from the palace. They're honored to be here! You broke the rules. And we want to know why."

I held back a response. I couldn't give anything away. My secrets were more important than my ego, and even though I badly wanted to set Brooke straight, I didn't know how many of these alchemists were here to spy on me. I had to assume their loyalty was to Richard and Faulk.

It was possible some of them could be Resistance members, but I couldn't trust anyone until I knew for sure. Shaking my head, I pushed past her and through the hostile crowd. I held off the impulse to shiver, eager to get to my room. The adrenaline from the yellow was fading fast, and I needed to get out of my wet clothes and into a hot shower as quickly as possible.

"Jessa, fortunately for you, you've proven proficient in yellow."

I turned to the agitated voice, my internal guard on red alert. Faulk stood at the edge of the crowd, surrounded by her officers.

"If I didn't know you better, I'd think you were giving me a compliment."

She was the head of the royal officers, and their number

9

one job was to keep the alchemists in line. In her mind, I wasn't an asset. I was a liability. I didn't have as much control over my alchemy as she would have preferred—not to mention, I wasn't easily controlled. And that's what really bothered her.

Complimenting me? Never.

She frowned, studying me. "Brooke is right about the importance of loyalty in a guardian. I guess we'll see how loyal you are during your next test."

I could recognize a threat when I heard one. My brain scanned through everything I knew about alchemy and loyalty, but I found no definite link.

"Report to my office tomorrow morning for your second test."

Tomorrow? A ripple of exhaustion pulsed through my muscles at the thought. I couldn't imagine being ready for another test so quickly. "I'll be there." I nodded with a slow grin. I needed her to believe I was on her side. I had to gain her trust, as impossible as that seemed to me now. Passing these tests would be the first step.

She turned to go. "Oh, and Jessa, make sure to eat a good breakfast first. You'll need the energy." She smiled coolly and left me to my doubts.

●

I sat, soaking in the shower, allowing the hot steam from the water to thaw my frozen body, the adrenaline melting away. In the heat of the moment, I hadn't allowed myself to fully consider the ramifications of my first test. The water had been frigid, nearly icy. And those cursed keys had been *everywhere*. If I hadn't gotten control over the yellow alchemy so quickly, I would have failed. True, I only had to prove myself in three colors, and I had five chances. But I couldn't afford any mistakes. And that cold water? It was dangerous! If the first test was that hard, *that dangerous*, how bad would the second one be?

The water began to lose its warmth; I peeled my exhausted butt off the floor and practically crawled out of the shower. I forced myself to dry off and dress in the black guardian uniform. Although I wasn't technically one of them yet, I'd been allowed to wear the clothing for training. It was customary, and I'd found I actually *liked* it. The black material was surprisingly comfortable and easy to move in. And since it was black, it didn't interfere with my magic. Alchemy required that I physically touch color, and more than once, I'd inadvertently used the color of my clothing. It was rare to be able to manipulate synthetics, but I could do it. The whole reason I'd blown my cover so easily to the royals in the first place had been because I'd turned my lavender ballet costume into a ball of volatile energy. I sucked in a breath. I couldn't allow myself to think about ballet anymore. It used to be my life, but I needed to forget about it.

Peering around, I took in my newly acquired surroundings. I still had my own space, thankfully, but I wasn't near the royal wing any longer. The luxurious room Lucas had set me up in upon my arrival to the palace was long gone. Now, I was housed in enemy territory: a small dorm located in the GC wing. The room was stark white and boxlike, with a bathroom and closet attached. Not that I was complaining. It was nice, but living in a box, surrounded by a bunch of less-than-trustworthy alchemists, bothered me to no end.

That didn't change the fact that I was lucky to be here instead of in the prison below the palace. At least this way, I would be right where I needed to be.

I needed to become a guardian.

I didn't fit in with them, true. But I was trying, wasn't I? My mind flashed to the scene earlier with Brooke. *Okay, I will try harder.* But more importantly, the king wanted me initiated. Faulk had insisted I pass the required alchemy tests first, but when push came to shove, I was sure Richard would have his way. He was our *king* after all. He wanted me for nefarious reasons. It wouldn't be long before he'd be calling on me to use my red alchemy.

I shuddered at the thought. It was like a stain I couldn't wipe from my mind.

I quickly applied my usual amount of light makeup and pulled a hairbrush through my unruly locks. My hair was always a mess, especially wet, and despite the thick curls, I had what my mom called a "tender head". I seriously hated to brush it after showering, and *especially* after swimming. All those chemicals wreaked havoc with it. I tried to focus on the task, but the pain of the movements did little to distract me from my anxiety.

Red alchemy was mostly unknown. I was only one of two alchemists in King Richard's possession who had access to the magic. The other was the imprisoned officer, Thomas. Red was the color of tribe, family, and passion. I didn't know everything it was capable of, but one thing I knew for sure, it could be used to control someone's mind—pulling the red from their blood to complete the horrifying task—and I'd done it three times now. First with Lacey by accident, second with an unknowing Reed, and the last time was to an officer in training who'd attacked me. *That* time had been on purpose. Once I connected with her blood, it was easy. I told her to sit down and begin counting so I could get away. She'd done exactly what I'd said, trance-like.

Thinking about that moment brought out a dark side in me, a shadow self. Because, although I hated what I'd done, a small part was excited by the power. And thirsty for more. It left me breathless.

I shook the feeling away, reminding myself of the truth. Manipulating the color from blood had deadly consequences.

Thomas had used red alchemy to the point of utter destruction. Alchemists weren't allowed to be officers, but he'd kept his magic hidden, using red to manipulate Queen Natasha. To get her to influence the king. Thomas went too far one too many times with red alchemy and killed Natasha. I'd seen it myself. The way she'd buckled under her own weight, the gray blood dripping from her eyes and ears. Being pulled away from the scene, watching the horrified look on Lucas's face, it had rocked me to my core. Luckily, Lucas had quickly discovered the truth. Thomas was now locked up, awaiting execution.

Again and again, the "what if" scenarios haunted me. What if Lucas hadn't figured it out? What if he still thought I'd killed his mother? My eyes burned.

And now here I was, training with the guardians to use my alchemy in service of the crown. The very crown that was killing its own people. That was the other startling reason I'd decided to join the GC—to help the Resistance take him down. King Richard was using the alchemists to interrogate people, control them, and in many instances, drain the color right out from their land and kill them. The memory of the shadow lands sent a chill through my body. It was wrong to utterly destroy like that. I didn't care what Richard's reasons were.

He had to be stopped, and I had to do it.

A soft knock on the door startled me from my thoughts. I quickly attempted to brush through my wet hair one last time. The brush literally got stuck. I cringed and pulled it out. Giving up, I moved to answer the door. Lucas stood in the entrance with his hands buried deeply in his pockets. He rocked back on his heels and stared at me, his signature smirk tugging at his lips.

"I heard you made quite the splash," he said.

"Oh, shut up." I laughed and opened the door wider. I adored that about him—his corny jokes *and* signature smirk. But I'd never tell. His ego would probably suffocate us all.

He peered around the hallway, making sure he wasn't being watched by any guards, and stepped into the room. He usually had a few with him, but it was his palace, so he had a way of extending his freedom to be alone when he needed it. Lately, he'd been using that freedom a lot.

Closing the door soundlessly, he pulled me into his arms.

"You smell amazing." He sighed. I snuggled into his broad chest. His own heady smell was equally intoxicating.

Since his mother's death, he'd been coming to see me daily. We never talked about the Resistance, or her untimely murder. Instead, we spent most of our time kissing, pushing our nagging thoughts to the furthest corners of our minds as we got lost in each other. I had to admit, I felt guilty knowing that my feelings for him were so convoluted. It shouldn't be so easy for me to want him.

I couldn't seem to help myself. I wanted Lucas. The knowledge terrified me. But also thrilled me.

We had a deeper connection than anything I'd experienced. He attracted me into his world like a magnet. It certainly didn't bother me that he was the most gorgeous man I'd ever seen. But he was also much kinder than he appeared on the gossip feeds. I didn't know how to explain it, but he was just so different from what I'd expected. And Jasmine, my handler with the Resistance, wanted us together. So that made it even easier to justify my growing feelings.

It also made them more complicated...

I couldn't forget *who* he was, no matter how hard I tried. He was a member of the Heart family. A prince. And his father was my sworn enemy. Could I still trust him? That was the question that kept twisting inside. It was no secret between us that Lucas wanted me to distance myself from the Resistance. He believed we could stop his father without them. He'd hated how the Resistance had used him. They brought him in without fully trusting him or giving him the information he needed, and in the end, it had backfired on them. They lost his loyalty. I was supposed to get it back.

I gripped his cotton shirt in my fingers, biting my lip. True, I felt a little guilty about that one.

And then there was the hard fact that his father had forbidden him from dating alchemists. After his relationship with Sasha, albeit fake, Richard had put his foot down. Richard believed that alchemists had no business wearing a crown. They were meant to serve the crown only, and the officers who swarmed the palace made sure that happened. Little did Richard know, his own son was an alchemist. Few people knew Lucas's secret.

"What are you thinking?" he asked.

I didn't know what to say.

He held me like I was a life raft and he was stranded at sea. And I longed for it, despite my better judgment. Lucas wasn't supposed to touch me, nor be alone in my bedroom with me. Holding me. Kissing me.

It was all so confusing!

Yet here we were again, wrapped up in each other. He pushed me against the door and bit down on my bottom lip. A rush of adrenaline pulsed through my veins. His hands moved to hold my hips, his fingers brushing against the exposed skin under my shirt, his body flush against mine.

I sighed and inched back, staring into his hooded eyes.

Sometimes I needed to put some distance between us, unable to handle the heat. I needed to clear my head—to stay in control. "How are you?" I asked, stepping back fully this time. I felt the distance like a knife.

A pang of sadness flashed through his eyes, and he ran his hands through his dark hair. God, I loved his hair. Even that movement attracted me to him, his hands so different from my own, so entirely…masculine.

Yup, I had it bad.

"I'm doing better. *You* make everything better."

And I thought he did too.

I smiled, shyly. "You know I'm here for you if you ever need to talk."

He nodded and paced to the window, visibly shutting down. I followed, a step behind. I wanted to comfort him, to ease his pain and the worry I had for him. He was using our relationship as his escape, and as much as I enjoyed our time together—maybe too much—I didn't want him to feel alone in this. I wanted to help.

"I don't know a whole lot about grieving," I continued carefully, "but I don't think you're wrong for not wanting to talk about it. I just want you to know, you can, if you want. Talk to me, that is. About…everything, or anything. Or nothing…" I gritted my teeth, annoyed with my rambling. *Right about now would be a good time to shut your mouth, Jessa.*

"I just want to get the execution over with. Thomas needs to pay for what he did." He turned and locked eyes with me. I let the words sink in.

That wouldn't bring Natasha back. I sucked in a breath. We both knew the execution wouldn't change what happened. And I highly doubted it would even make him feel better. Still, I was sure if it had been my mother, I'd want retribution too. I needed to support him, even if the idea of an execution made me want to hide under my blankets.

"He will," I said. "He'll die, because *he* was the one who did this. He's the one who did that to her blood. He pushed her too far, nobody else."

Lucas shook his head and moved further away. "I shouldn't have been so naïve. It was right in front of my face, in my own home." He slammed his palm against the window frame. "And I didn't catch it."

"Don't do this to yourself."

"I can't talk about this with you," he replied.

"Okay. That's okay. But let me just say one thing and then I'll shut up, okay?" He didn't move. "This. Is. Not. Your. Fault. And if you decide you need someone to talk to, all I am saying is I'm here."

Did he blame *me* for what happened? I'd wanted to ask, but was too afraid of what it would do to our relationship. Had I been too much of a distraction for him? If he hadn't been so wrapped up in my drama, in saving me from Faulk that day, maybe he really would have been able to save his mother. I sucked in a breath and pushed those thoughts deep into my soul.

He finally looked at me, his expression melting. "I know what you're thinking. It's written all over your face." He strode across the small room in his usual swagger, placing his hands on my shoulders. The warmth of them automatically sent a wave of comfort through my body. I leaned in. "But if anyone's to blame, it's me, not you. If I had been honest with you from the start, you wouldn't have left like that. You were only trying to help your family."

The guilt attacked me then. I felt my chin quiver as I fought the urge to turn away. Honesty?

How honest was it for me to be with him when it was

the Resistance who'd ordered it? When Jasmine had told me to be with him, I'd been upset with him at the time. I wasn't mad anymore. So much had happened between then and now, and anger had left my heart. Still, how would he react if he knew our relationship was somehow part of the Resistance's plans? No doubt he'd end it.

Only a few weeks ago, I was convinced he'd been too close with Sasha for my comfort. I swallowed, grimacing at my behavior. I'd always thought boys were confusing but maybe it was us girls who were the source of the trouble. It wasn't long ago that I wanted nothing to do with him. Now, every time he sought me out, I easily allowed him to sweep me into his world, his arms, his scent, his mouth…

I met his pewter eyes and caught the flash that turned them dark. Unable to resist any longer, I pressed my lips to his.

●

The next morning came too quickly. I squared my shoulders and strode into the officers' headquarters, central in the GC wing. I ignored the furtive glances of the underlings and stalked up to Faulk's lair. Technically it was her office, but since I considered her the predator and me the prey, *lair* had a nice ring to it. There was little I could do to prepare today. Could they really judge loyalty using an alchemy test? No matter what faced me, I wouldn't let them break me.

Upon entering the office, I bristled at the occupants waiting for me. Faulk stood along the back wall with two hulking officers. Reed lounged next to Lucas. And none other than King Richard sat on Faulk's desk, his eyes trained on me.

"We usually leave blue for the end of the trials, but Faulk

18

thinks we ought to get it taken care of quickly with your... situation," Richard said. He looked the part of a handsome businessman, in charge and decisive. And most importantly, at the moment, he had the power.

His eyes narrowed further as I held his gaze. *Show no fear. Show no fear. Show no fear...* He had to believe I was under his control, but that didn't mean I had to cower. He wielded his power darkly and would stop at nothing to gain more. But he couldn't hold it forever. Eventually his people would see him for what he was, and he would lose everything.

I peeked at Lucas, who stood in the corner of the room. Somehow he fit in well with the surroundings, all glass and steel and modern. His expression was one of cool interest. It was an act, since the true nature of our relationship was a secret. Or maybe I was reading the situation all wrong. Maybe he knew any chance of my passing today was hopeless.

"Blue is an unlikely color for most alchemists to control. We don't expect you to be able to do much with it." Richard smiled. He spoke smoothly, unruffled by the situation.

"So why am I here?" I cocked my head.

"When we already know an alchemist can't manipulate blue, we don't just drop it altogether. How fair would that be? No, we test it in a *different* way."

"I don't understand."

Reed stepped forward, smirking, and I suddenly understood. I understood all too well. He raised an eyebrow, and I groaned.

Blue was the color of communication. It was used to spy on conversations, to make arguments extremely persuasive, and it was incredibly useful for one other thing. My mind flashed to the memory of Reed in my bedroom, drilling me for information, and how easily I'd almost given it to him.

The magic had gotten a hold of me, and I'd *wanted* to tell him everything. I'd been persuaded to open my big mouth and spill all my secrets. Luckily I'd been strong enough to hold off, and he'd gotten spooked and left without getting what he'd wanted.

But this time he wasn't going anywhere.

This time the interrogation wasn't a secret to anyone, least of all me. Could I convince them I was loyal? Icy fear prickled up my spine. This blue alchemy test was more than just a test of skill; it was a test to see if I deserved to keep my life.

"Have a seat, Jessa," Richard said. "Let's get started."

TWO

SASHA

We had the same eyes, the three of us. Eyes an indecisive blue that shifted shades depending on arbitrary things like the light or clothing or if our hair was down. Bright, cheery sky blue one minute, dark, angry ocean the next. Every time I worked with Lacey, I stared at her eyes, those six-year-old versions of my own. So innocent. I'd search them out, and before long, I'd be analyzing our similarities and differences. Her hair was lighter than my golden blonde locks, also tamed like mine. Jessa's hair had taken a different turn, raven dark and unruly. And yet we all had identical blue eyes and the same pale complexion. Traits that came from our father. Well, *their* father. I refused to consider him family.

"Are you ready to try again?" I asked Lacey. *I'm here to do a job. I'm her teacher and that's it. No more gawking.*

"You promise it's not going to hurt them?" She peered at the smattering of wildflowers growing at our feet.

"No, come here." I sat in front of the flowers and patted the space next to me. She joined, tentative at first, legs crossed, eyes still etched with worry. "I'll show you how to do it."

21

I grabbed hold of a tall, green blade of grass. It was wild, scratchy, and dry between my fingertips. Without much effort, I maneuvered the color out. Green alchemy was as natural as breathing, but I was careful not to take too much and risk killing the grass completely. Once the perfect amount of emerald energy danced in the air, I turned my attention to the overgrowth. Winter was coming, and naturally the flowers were dying off. For the purposes of this exercise, I set my intention and used the green to heal a few of the neighboring flowers. They perked up, visibly rising, restored to perfect health.

Lacey smiled with the kind of fascination that only young children could pull off. "See? That wasn't so bad," I said. "Are you ready to try?" I'd taken hardly any green from the plant, leaving only a small patch of gray. Not enough to kill it, but I also knew it would never be the same.

They never were.

"Why does it look like that?" Lacey asked. She was nearly seven and observant enough to notice the trace of gray.

"There's a price to pay for everything, kid." I smirked at my dry humor. She didn't get it. *All right then, let's try again.* "In order to give to something, like making these flowers feel healthy again, we have to take from something else. This grass gave a little bit of its life so that the flowers can keep living. Do you understand?"

"Does it have to be that way?" She bit her lip, her small face pinched. Her worry over one blade of grass was so ridiculously cute; I had to hold back a laugh. I didn't want to hurt her tender feelings, as innocent as they were.

"For what we do, yes. Alchemy is magic. And magic is never free. Taking color is the payment. But we can always try our best to make sure we don't kill anything completely. And the grass doesn't feel like we feel. It doesn't hurt. Sound

22

okay?"

"Okay." She wrinkled her nose, not convinced. "But what if it does hurt?"

Okay, she was adorable, but we had to move on.

"It won't hurt you and the grass doesn't have feelings. Now, you try. In your mind, and with *your* feelings, I want you to ask the grass to give you a little bit of its color. Do you think you can do that?"

She nodded and reached her hand out to gently caress the wild stalks. I could hardly believe someone so young could hold so much power. It wasn't fair that alchemy came on so strong in kids. It was too much responsibility. But I was just as young when I'd been discovered and taken to the guardians for training. I understood the daunting emotions she faced.

"Look, you're doing it." I pointed to the emerald strands of magic that twisted above Lacey's hand. "Now move it to some of the dying flowers," I told her before she could get frightened and lose focus. All it would take was her intention if the ability was there. Luckily, green was one of the easiest colors to manipulate. And with a use like healing, that had come in handy on more than one occasion. Just as mine had done, her flowers perked up the instant they received the green alchemy. As she giggled something in my heart cracked open.

"How's it going over here?"

I prickled at the voice of the woman who approached. It appeared she still didn't know who I was. I planned to keep it that way. Placing a false smile on my face, I looked up and greeted Lara Loxley like I cared what she had to say.

"We're making progress. Lacey just healed these flowers."

"Mom, it was magic! They're pretty, don't you think?"

"Beautiful," Lara replied. I noticed the family resemblance, despite my annoyance. Jessa's dark curly hair and height obviously came from Lara, but her sense of style was entirely different. Lara was all-colorful, each article of clothing a bright hue not matching the next. I found it odd. She didn't match the picture I'd had in my head of a cold, calculating person.

"It turns out Lacey is a natural alchemist. Like Jessa. You have talented daughters, Mrs. Loxley," I said. "Magic must run in the family." She averted her gaze; I probably shouldn't have added that last bit. Sometimes my mouth ran away with me, no matter how much I tried to keep out of trouble. Something else Jessa and I had in common. The last thing I needed was for Lara to figure out who I was. I couldn't pretend some happy family reunion with that woman or her husband, even if they were, technically, my parents.

"Well, I think that's enough for today."

Wait, what? "But we're just getting started."

"I don't want Lacey to get too tired."

I stood and brushed the dirt from my pants. "I assure you that took very little effort on her part. Like I said, she's a natural. We have a lot of work to do and not much time."

"What do you mean, not much time?"

Oh, oops. Maybe I shouldn't have said that either...

It was likely that Lacey would be needed. The Resistance had big plans to take down the monarchy, and alchemy was an integral part of that. But Lacey's parents had only agreed to her training so that she didn't accidently hurt herself. They didn't actually want—and I'll admit, neither did I— Lacey anywhere near the Resistance or New Colony.

I backpedaled. "I just meant to say there's not much time before we move on to the next color. I want to make sure she's fully comfortable with green first."

"Please, Momma." Lacey grasped her hands together in a

praying motion. "It's so much fun! I want to try some more."

"Really, I'll take care of her. The first sign of fatigue and I'll make her stop."

And it was true, I would. No one gave me that luxury when I was a kid, and while the Resistance would possibly need Lacey's help later, at least for now I certainly wasn't going to treat her like a workhorse.

"Okay, fine." Lara smiled fondly at Lacey before turning on me. "But I mean it. You stop the second she gets tired. You have to remember, she's only a child. She's my *baby*. And I want her safe at all times."

I nodded vigorously. Anything to get this woman to leave. I watched her retreat to the cropping of trees, no doubt to supervise from a close distance. Her momma-bear instinct drove an angry blade right down my center, fileting me wide open. The hot anger of rejection charred so painfully, I lost my breath. More than *anything*, I wanted to run over there and give that woman a piece of my mind. How could she now have such care for Lacey, her *baby*, when she'd had so little regard for me?

I had been her child too.

And while she didn't know who I was now, she'd certainly done nothing to protect me back then. Lara and Christopher didn't even try to hide me, like so many other New Colony parents often did. No. The second these so-called parents discovered my alchemy, they'd sent me straight to the wolves. I'd spent years burying that memory into the deepest recesses of my soul. But it flashed through my mind anyway, like nails on a chalkboard.

"Give me a hug, okay," Mommy says. I wrap my arms around her. She smells like sugar and roses. She pulls me in so tight that I squeal. She doesn't normally hug this way, but I like it. I laugh. She doesn't.

25

"What's wrong?" I ask. She's kneeling in front of me. Her eyes are all watery and blinking. She just shakes her head. Daddy comes into the room.

"Jessa's finally asleep," he says. She goes to bed before me because she's only three so she's still really little. But I'm a grown girl. I get to stay up later with Mommy and Daddy.

"Are you sure they know? They're coming?"

"I'm positive. Kareth Jackson saw her do it, Lara. You know how that woman is. She would never keep something like that secret."

Mrs. Jackson's our next-door neighbor. She isn't very nice to us. But she has kids our age that we sometimes get to play with. Mom says it's better that we play alone. She says my magic is a dangerous secret. But it doesn't feel dangerous. It's fun. Jessa loves it, too!

But since it's our family secret, I'm not supposed to do magic in front of anyone else. It's okay. I am really smart.

"What do we do?" Mommy stands now, whispering to Daddy. They think I can't hear. But that's silly thinking. Kids always hear.

"I don't know," Daddy replies. "Where would we even go?"

"Maybe we could get out."

"I have no idea how we would do that, Lara. We could all be killed."

"So what do we do?"

"Maybe they'll give her a good life. Better than we can."

"No."

"They'll train her. She'll learn how to control it."

"No."

"We'll see her again. Maybe we can work something out with them."

There's a long pause then. My heart begins to summersault through my body, like when we play tag and Daddy is just

26

about to get me. Something is bad, and Mommy is crying. But they're both nodding. And hugging. So it can't be all-bad. Mommy and Daddy always know how to fix the bad things.

"We love you very much," Daddy says, pulling me into their hug. It's my favorite kind of hug, a Frankie-sandwich. But something about it isn't right.

"I love you too."

There's a knock on the door.

●

I trusted them. Loved them. They were my protectors. So surely they would have at least put up a fight, right?

Wrong.

●

I tucked my head under the hood of my sweatshirt as I began my evening run around the perimeter of the camp. Newly fallen leaves crunched under my shoes as I focused on the trail.

Our Resistance camp was located in a remote Canadian mountain range. It worked well enough, small and isolated, even though the winters were brutal. We said "camp", but it was basically a small village of log cabins. Mostly abandoned, our people had moved in one by one. Some were fleeing prosecution from New Colony, too fearful to go anywhere else, and others were looking for a place to hide out before moving on.

Canada didn't have much government left to care about us, even if they did know we were here. Plus, there were little villages like this all over the country. It was a nation of refugees and misfits, people happy to be left alone and willing to take care of themselves. West America was a big unknown, so no one wanted to try his or her luck there, and anything south was so poverty stricken and overrun with drugs, it was downright dangerous.

I headed around the edge of camp, behind the mess hall where they were still cleaning up from dinner. We all took turns, spreading the work out evenly. I didn't stop to chat. Not that anyone expected me to. Since returning from New Colony, I'd been less than talkative. Then again, I'd never been the friendliest of the bunch.

Nobody cared.

Our community was filled with rejects. We were a mix of alchemists and their families who'd run away in order to stay together, political dissenters who'd joined the Resistance, and social outcasts looking for a better life. Because of the shadow lands, it was nearly impossible to survive a trek out of New Colony by foot. Everyone had been smuggled here either through one of the Resistance's helicopters, or, more likely, by boat on the Atlantic Ocean. Plenty of the people who lived here met the Resistance with weariness, because as much as we stood for what they believed, they feared King Richard more. But, over the years, we'd figured out how to live amicably. We worked together in a commune of sorts, growing our food, raising livestock, and sharing it all with each other. Of course, it helped that the few alchemists we did have used magic to grow healthy crops, heal the sick and injured, and just generally make life easier for everyone. Alchemy could do a lot of good things for the world, given the opportunity.

I increased my speed for the next stretch, zooming past a group practicing combat. That was something that could be seen during all daylight hours lately. We were training for something big, even if we didn't know the logistics yet.

I wasn't in the mood to join them. I would later, but running was my salvation and I needed it after my day training Lacey. Part of me wanted to forgive Lara and Christopher. It wasn't their fault. And had I been born somewhere else, I probably would have been murdered. Most countries imprisoned or executed alchemists out of ignorance and fear of the unknown.

Then the image of gray things infiltrated my mind. No. What I'd endured, being forced to harm innocent people as a child, was worse than death. The smell of decay haunted me. The cries of agonizing death terrorized my dreams. My actions as a child were something I'd live with forever, because of *them*.

My parents.

The officers.

And the royal family.

The kings of New Colony were all the same. Power hungry. Fear mongering. Strategic. Each one worse than the last. Richard used magic to keep the kingdom protected by the uncrossable shadow lands—lands that grew larger every time we flew over them. He used alchemy to keep the people in line, just comfortable enough not to question the cage. And they used alchemy to keep their own royal family living in luxury.

Worst of all, they used magic to kill.

Needless to say, after my own painful experiences with the GC, I was more than grateful to be out of there. And also more than ready to take down the royals the second I got the chance. I'd thought Lucas was different, and part of me still held out hope that he was. But reports had come back that although he was helping Jessa, he was refusing to work with the Resistance. He foolishly blamed us for the queen's death, as if we knew who was doing that to her. He admonished us for putting Jessa back in the palace, but that was the most logical course of action to gain an upper hand against Richard. And he hated that he hadn't ever been let into the inner-circle—even though we'd planned for that to happen soon. He'd ruined it, and I hoped he wouldn't get killed for it. Every day Richard continued on his path, the likelihood of a peaceful rebellion grew smaller. We would succeed, no matter what, and if that meant removing Lucas from the equation, my superiors wouldn't blink an eye. Especially now that he'd left the alliance.

Stupid boy. Why does he always have to be so difficult?

I stopped to catch my breath, bent over.

I was just outside Hank's cabin. He usually spent his evenings alone, but I heard the sound of muffled voices coming from within. Someone jogged up the front steps and entered without even knocking. Tristan. What was he doing here? I knew it had to be Resistance business, and I wanted in on that.

I took a deep breath, squared my shoulders, and pushed open the door to Hank's cabin. Sure, I might have been dripping with sweat and red-faced from the run, but I didn't care.

"Frankie, girl, always a pleasure to see your smiling face," Hank said, clearly joking at the stoic expression I so carefully wore. "I was just going to send Tristan here to fetch you."

Anyone else, and I would have called bull. But Hank didn't lie.

"Thanks for thinking of me, old man," I said. "And don't call me *Frankie*; we already talked about this. It's Sasha."

"That's right, sorry, Sasha. Old habits die hard for this *old man*." He winked. Trying to be funny, no doubt.

I scoffed and shuffled into the cozy cabin. Three other occupants filled the space. I'd spent numerous hours here and considered Hank to be the closest thing I had to a father figure. I lived in a cabin with the other single girls, though I didn't connect with anyone very well. I struggled with relationships. Can we say, abandonment issues? But Hank had never treated me like the orphan I felt I was. I loved him for it, and I owed him everything. He'd saved me from the GC and taken me under his wing. And while I'd begged him for years to let me get more involved with the Resistance, he'd only agreed when they'd needed someone young on the inside. I'd started off at a few of the distant outposts, finally working my way to the palace to monitor Lucas.

Technically, my mission there was to get the prince to fall in love with me, to get him to turn from his father and join us beyond any doubt. And technically, I'd failed. Jessa had come along, and my long lost sister had easily stolen his heart. She didn't have to try. Just the way they looked at each other wasn't something I'd ever experienced, so I didn't blame her. Since I'd recruited her to our side, I still considered the mission a win. If anyone could turn him for good, it was Jessa.

And Jessa was one of us now.

"She's the alchemist?" One of Hank's guests stepped forward. I didn't recognize him. In fact, I only recognized one of the other three. This man had a different air about him, unfamiliar and almost hostile. He was clean-shaven and dressed well—he wasn't a regular in our camp. He was an outsider.

"What business is it of yours?" I quipped back.

Hank rested a hand on my shoulder. I instantly felt protected, and the hostility inside began to defuse. I looked up at the grizzly-bear of a man: mid-fifties, hair beginning to gray, and a scruffy beard to match. I smiled.

"We didn't expect to be working directly with your

alchemists," the man pressured in a clipped tone.

"I assure you," Hank said calmly, "Sasha is an asset. She's here to help us, and we can't do this without alchemists on our side."

"And why not?"

Who is this guy? I wasn't used to people being so volatile against alchemy. In New Colony, while it was a crime to hide it, it certainly wasn't anything to be ashamed of. I was proud of who I was because I'd fought hard to become her.

"Ever heard of the phrase *fight fire with fire*?" I barked at the man. He raised an eyebrow, less than impressed. I didn't care. Whoever he was, he needed to back off. I'd proven myself time and time again, and I refused to let anyone doubt me. I studied him further and guessed he had some kind of military background. His cold eyes sparked with calculated intelligence as we faced each other.

"Sasha's right," Hank interceded. "The king has an arsenal of alchemists at his disposal. We need to take whatever magic we can get. And I promise, I've known Sasha nearly all her life. She can be trusted."

The man glared for a minute longer, then smoothly returned to his seat at the table. I followed and dropped into a vacant chair. I wouldn't shrink because of this man's opinion. He knew nothing of what I'd sacrificed for this cause.

"Sasha, this is Jacob Cole." Hank waved a hand at the jerk. "And you already know Tristan." Hank nodded to the guy sitting next to me. Oh yes, I knew Tristan all right. Before I'd left the camp, he'd been the closest thing I had to a best friend. He'd helped get me out of New Colony in the first place. And we'd spent countless hours together over the years since. He was one of those people who always had the best jokes and could diffuse any situation with his smile. Since returning, I'd worried things would be awkward between us.

I hadn't had a lot of time to catch up.

"Hey, girl." Tristan grinned. "I heard you made out with the prince."

I nearly died.

Blood rushed to my face, and I rolled my eyes. "Shut up! You're just jealous. When was the last time you got any action around here?"

Tristan only laughed and nodded. "Too true. I need a girlfriend. I also heard the prince dumped your butt. So what do you say, want to go out with me?" He waggled his eyebrows and blew me a kiss. There were no feelings between us. He was more like an older brother, since he was twenty-five and I was nineteen.

We were just friends. Not that the thought hadn't crossed my mind on occasion—because it had, especially since I'd gotten back. He had smooth Asian skin and dark eyes that always seemed to ground me. He was tall, insanely ripped, and above all else, he had a wonderful personality. It was who he *was* that I loved most.

"You wish," I laughed.

"So this teen girl, this girl making jokes about fraternizing with our sworn enemy, this is the *alchemist* you're letting in on our plans?" A fifth member of our little party stepped out from the shadowed corner. Where had he come from? I couldn't believe I hadn't zeroed in on him immediately. He said "alchemist" like it was the dirtiest of dirty words in the English language.

Oh, this should be fun.

Like Cole, he also had that outsider look: clean-cut with buzzed hair. He moved like a predator as he stalked closer. His boots clomped on the wooden floor, and then he was standing to attention. Definitely military. My eyes traveled up his tall frame, noticing the way his khakis clung to corded muscles. I swallowed, unsure of what to make of him. And then I found his eyes. They bored into mine, and my brow creased, taking in their piercing green. I gripped my hands together under the table, and swallowed again. This man was dangerous. I shook myself to alertness and gritted my teeth

"For your information, Soldier-boy, I'm nineteen. And I only fraternized with Lucas because the Resistance ordered me to. I was doing my job."

"An alchemist and a whore."

I exploded from my seat. Tristan beat me to it, launching himself at the guy with a primitive growl. Unfortunately, Cole was too fast and held him back. Hank couldn't get to me in time. Not that he wanted to stop me. Knowing Hank, he was next in line.

I rushed forward and slapped Soldier-boy across the face. My hand burned with satisfaction. "Don't ever call me that again or I'll do worse."

Before I registered what was happening, he grabbed hold of me, twisted my body, and swung me around. He had my arms locked against my sides, my back to his hard chest. One arm held me so I couldn't move, the other wrapped around my neck in a loose chokehold. Anger rippled through me.

"Like what?" he whispered into my ear.

Anger swept through my body. *Arrogant idiot! I'm an alchemist!*

He may have had me in a chokehold, but my beloved stone necklace still hung intact, filled with a myriad of colors for me to pick my poison. All it took was one second to connect with the yellow, and I had the strength I needed. I slammed him to the ground with a crack. His stunned expression only made me smile. From my peripheral vision, I saw Tristan smirk, before he doubled over with laughter.

"Like using alchemy to teach you never to touch a woman

without her permission!"

"Lady has a point," Tristan added between fits of laughter.

"You slapped me first," Soldier-boy growled.

"You called me a *whore!*"

He relented, hands up. "Okay, I'll admit I shouldn't have said that." His face reddened at that. I wasn't sure if he was still angry, or embarrassed, or both.

"You're right. You shouldn't have." A voice grumbled. I swung my head around to see Cole's deadly gaze on his man. Huh? "That's no way for my top pupil to behave toward a woman, even if she is an alchemist," he finished.

And there it is, ladies and gentlemen…

"Why do you have such a problem with alchemy?" I turned on Cole, staring him down. Who did these people think they were?

"All right, everyone settle down. That's enough fighting for now," Hank interjected. The power of his voice immediately defused the situation, as if he had blue alchemy at work. But nope, that was just Hank. We all returned to our seats, though a fair amount of hostility still hung in the room.

Hank introduced us. "Sasha and Tristan are Resistance members. Tristan may be a joker, but he's smart as a whip. Sasha is our best alchemist and loyal to a fault."

The two men stiffened. I couldn't help it; I smiled with pride and narrowed my eyes at the younger one, meeting his glare head on. "Cole and Mastin are very special guests and new members of our Resistance. They are *valued* members and we're *lucky* to have them." Hank directed those words— "valued" and "lucky"—at me.

Whatever.

I still didn't get why I had to play nice with people who so clearly hated me. I bit my lip and stiffened.

"They're the beginning of our alliance with West America."

My eyes shot to Hank. He was serious.

"Why would we want that?" The question slipped from my mouth. West America wasn't part of our cause. They hated New Colony, sure. But we didn't work with them because they also hated alchemists. They imprisoned them and sometimes even killed them. "And you expect me to trust these two?" I continued. "Alchemy is illegal in West America. I can't work with them!"

"You can and you will," Hank said, his tone final.

"Don't worry, they may be jerks, but they can be trusted," Tristan added. "They want to take down New Colony as much as we do."

"And then what? Execute me?" I asked Cole, figuring he was the authority over that Mastin guy.

"We already signed an agreement. Everything is in place. Alchemy is still illegal in West America as of today. But we won't hurt *any* cooperative citizens of New Colony if we succeed with what we set out to do."

"And what's that exactly?" I asked.

"It's quite obvious, don't you think?" Mastin said, studying his fingernails in boredom. "We're going to take back what's rightfully ours. We're going to take back New Colony and unite America again."

My mouth usually ran away with me, but, this time, I was lost for words. This was *never* what the Resistance had been about. This was *not* okay! We knew practically nothing about West America. They were a democracy still, that was true, but they hated alchemists. How could we possibly trust them with this?

"Let me just ask you one question," I said, gathering my thoughts. I glanced between the two men before settling on Mastin. He drew me to him, like a moth to the flame. A moth he probably wanted to smash under his shoe. "What is your honest opinion of alchemy?"

He didn't hesitate. "It's an abomination."

I stood, body shaking, stomach clenched in a sickening knot. I caught Hank's pained expression. He'd been an officer when he'd left New Colony and taken me and Tristan with him. He wasn't an alchemist. Tristan wasn't. Most of the Resistance weren't. The vast population wasn't.

But I was.

I was, and he'd made an alliance with people who hated my very existence. Who hated my family—Lacey and Jessa. Even if they didn't know I was their older sister, I still felt a primal need to protect them. I barely had them in my life again, and somehow, despite all logic, I wanted it to stay that way. And Hank, he was supposed to be my family too. He was the only adult who'd ever really cared about me more than my magic. And now he'd done this.

"I can't believe you'd risk my life and the lives of all the alchemists we've been trying to save. What about Jasmine? What about Jessa? Lacey? And all the others?"

"Sit down and let me explain," Hank said, his voice filled with some kind of fatherly concern, like he knew what was better for me than I did.

He doesn't get it and he never will.

I shook my head. "Mastin said enough. Alchemy is an abomination, right? Well, until these two can prove to me without a doubt that West America won't *ever* hurt innocent alchemists, I'm out." I strode from the room, out the door, and didn't look back.

THREE

LUCAS

I was useless. I just stood there, watching, knowing there was nothing I could do. And Jessa knew it too. Her curly hair was wilder than normal, her eyes wide with anxiety, as she chewed on her lip—her nervous tic. I believed she would pass this test, but there was a possibility she wouldn't. And that scared the hell out of me. If she failed today, it wasn't just her secrets that would unravel, but mine as well.

I was an alchemist. That was my secret—and my burden.

I fidgeted uncomfortably against the wall as I studied the back of my father's head, boring holes into it. What was he going to do to Jessa?

My father, Richard, had a love-hate relationship with alchemy. He wasn't an alchemist, probably much to his frustration. No one in our line before me had the magic. Still, he used alchemy to keep the royal family powerful and New Colony isolated and controlled. He surrounded himself with an army of skilled alchemists, indoctrinated from a young age, and then used intimidating officers to keep everybody in line. But that couldn't last forever: sooner or later, the alchemists would rise up. He knew it. I knew it. Faulk knew it.

And everyone in the Resistance was committed to it.

Pained, I watched him gaze at Jessa like she was the key to winning whatever sick and twisted game he was playing. She shifted in her seat, waiting for whatever was coming. Whatever it was, knowing him, it wasn't good. I'd learned all about his experiments, and he'd even tried to get my involvement with a few when I first found out. He would use his lowest level citizens, or those who were acting out for whatever reason, and would test magic on them. Sometimes torturing them. Many times killing them.

And I couldn't forget. I'd seen the shadow lands with my own eyes, the miles of dead, rotted, colorless earth where alchemists had stripped all color. The people didn't know about it. In fact, most of them loved him and treated our royal family like we were handed down from God himself. Of course it helped that Richard's Guardians of Color used blue to spy and persuade, yellow for physical strength and agility, and green to heal those deemed worthy. Purple shades were useful to my father, though also extremely hard to manipulate. They could be used for telepathy and even for predicting the future.

And now that he had Jessa, he finally had red.

When an alchemist could pull red from someone's blood, they could control that person's mind. Make them do anything. We knew this because he'd had an alchemist in the past, Jessa's older sister, who'd been able to do it. But then she'd disappeared. She'd returned years later as Sasha, much older and unrecognizable, and somehow infiltrated the GC on behalf of the Resistance. Faulk had figured that one out too late in the game, and I was still annoyed with myself for not seeing the connection sooner.

The officers had figured it out once she'd disappeared. Sasha had shown up at an outpost with a false identity, then slowly worked her way to the palace. The Resistance had to have someone on the inside because they'd also added her cover story into the files.

Richard was livid about it, and I hoped he didn't take it out on Jessa.

Jessa.

The girl who not only could access red, but who could separate colors into their primary counterparts, another remarkable talent. One she hadn't been able to replicate; but eventually, she would. There was no telling what that magic could do. If Richard could unlock her power, and worse yet, duplicate it in other alchemists, he'd be unstoppable. And if that happened, I had no doubt this girl, the one person who was capable of breathing life into my broken heart, would be lost in the crossfire.

She sat across from my father, her chin lifted and eyes narrowed in an expression that could either be interpreted as defiant or focused.

I knew better than to assume the latter.

"Let me guess? We're testing blue today?" she asked.

"That's right, but I'll be the one testing blue on you." Reed smirked. That smirk just gave me one more reason to hate him. Reed had befriended Jessa when she was the most vulnerable she'd ever been in her life, only to use and manipulate her for Faulk. He was a lackey. Another brown-nosing, ladder-climbing GC prick. But he'd failed.

And for all our sakes, he'd better fail again. Or I swear, I will beat him to a pulp. The angry threats tumbled through my mind, but I still managed to keep my expression apathetic. I'd had a lot of practice in that department over the years.

"And how is that a fair test?" Jessa asked. "Aren't I supposed to get a chance to actually *use* blue?"

"We thought you'd ask that," Faulk said, sighing heavily. "And don't worry, you will. But first, we have some questions." With a sharp tap of her pointed boot on the concrete floor, she glided forward, her hair slicked and scraped back more harshly than I'd ever seen. A repulsive creature, who basked in the enjoyment of making Jessa squirm at every opportunity. She gripped her hands behind her back and set her lips in a thin line. I attempted to relax my shoulders, aware of how tense this woman made me. When Jessa was in her sights, there was no knowing how far this monster would go—it was no wonder she and Richard worked so well together.

"I guess I don't have a choice in the matter," Jessa said, her eyes darting between Faulk and Richard. She rolled her eyes and settled farther into her chair. Reed ran his hands through his blond hair. I noticed a slight grimace as he positioned himself behind her and placed his hands on her shoulders. A pulse of anger rolled through me. He had to touch her for this, but, logical or not, it still bugged the hell out of me.

The blue angular stone was about the size of my thumb and hung from a thick, black cord around Reed's neck. It gleamed in the morning light that poured through the office windows. It only took a moment of Reed's concentration for the color to begin rising from the rock. The blue tendrils swirled in rotations of menacing magic, before they shot around the room. A slice of the magic went into Jessa, with the intention of making her susceptible to persuasion. And more of the magic went directly into Richard, doing the exact opposite, making him the one with the persuasion. Even one thread of this magic had a powerful effect, but this was double time. My entire body went cold. Reed finally removed his hands from Jessa and stepped back. I ignored his wink in her direction.

"Great work, Reed." Faulk smiled at her little alchemist protégé. And even I had to admit it *was* great work. Which made me sick. I held my jaw still, resisting the urge to groan. Jessa was in a lot of trouble.

"Are you ready to begin?" Richard asked, holding her gaze. He sat on the edge of his seat. Jessa nodded eagerly and smiled. In the short time between being affected by Reed's blue alchemy to now, she'd visibly changed. Her eyes were no longer guarded, her expression open and vulnerable.

I bit back my anger. I'd wished I'd been informed in advance of this test today so I could've warned her. But it wasn't until breakfast that *Father Dearest* had decided to let me in on what was going to happen.

This test had clearly been twisted to suit Faulk's need to sniff out any disloyalty in Jessa. It was true that we could test blue alchemy by not only asking someone to perform it, which they usually failed, but by also seeing how resistant they were to someone else using the magic on them. Also, that usually resulted in failure. Blue was one of the hardest and rarest colors to control in alchemy. There was a reason the initiates *only* had to pass three of the five main colors to be accepted into the Guardians of Color. People simply didn't have the ability to master all the colors.

"Is your allegiance to the crown?" Richard asked.

"No," Jessa replied.

No? No? She answered honestly. Can't she fight it at all? A bead of sweat ran down the back of my neck. If she didn't hide some of her deeper secrets, we were both at risk for punishment.

"Why do you say that?" Richard countered.

"I lied."

"Lied about what?" he spat.

On the outside, Faulk was an attractive woman. But that only made her more frightening. Her single-minded obsession was showing now as sneers at Jessa's answer. But I knew my father well enough. This new development would cause problems for him. He was desperate to control Jessa. But I wondered, what would happen if Jessa failed? Would he demand her initiation anyway? Would he just store her away for special occasions?

"I lied about being an alchemist. To Faulk, when she first came to see me. I'm loyal to my family more than I'm loyal to the crown. You won't let me see them." The words Jessa spoke came out in an air of honesty and calm, like she was having a normal conversation with a trusted friend.

And it was true. She wasn't lying. What else would she be honest about?

"Okay, but are you loyal to the crown *now*?" Richard asked.

"Not completely. Why would I trust the ones who have my family locked away? I'm loyal to you only as long as you can reunite us. They are my true objective."

Now I knew she was lying. Pride rippled through me, and I stood a little straighter. She and I were both fully aware of where her family really was. Richard and Faulk were only pretending to have them under lock and key. Her family was with the Resistance, safe and hidden. And as it stood, there was nothing that anyone could do about that.

Richard shifted the conversation. "And you'll do anything to make that happen? You'll do anything I ask of you?"

Jessa paused, and I ground my feet into the floor. *Please, answer correctly.*

"I don't know," she said. "I don't want to hurt anyone."

Good girl! I exhaled a slow, shuddering breath. She needed to *sound* honest, not like she was saying exactly what Richard wanted to hear. That was the only way they'd believe Reed's magic was doing its job.

"Are you hiding any more secrets from me?" Richard asked. It was a tough question. Of course, she was hiding mountains of information from him. And he suspected it. If she said no, she'd likely pass the test. Pass, because everyone would know she'd been lying and they wouldn't trust her. If she said yes, she would have to divulge some information. And it was likely she would fail this color. I wanted her to fail. For her own safety. She had to fail.

"Yes," she said simply, calmly. "I do have one more secret."

"And what's that, little alchemist?" Richard asked. The room froze with anticipation. All eyes were intense on Jessa. She swallowed before speaking easily, with an open smile.

"I know you didn't like it when your son was dating that other alchemist girl. The one who disappeared?"

"And what's your point," Faulk spat, unrestrained. She stalked behind Richard, pacing, her eyes narrowed into slits. If the woman wasn't careful, she was going to give herself a headache.

Jessa didn't bother to acknowledge Faulk; her eyes stayed locked on my father. "I know you look down on the idea of an alchemist and a royal dating. You don't want an alchemist anywhere near that crown. Lucas told me as much. But you see, I think you don't have as much control over your son as you think you do."

"And why is that?" Richard folded his arms before turning back to look at me. Actually, there was an audible shuffle as everyone in the room turned to me.

"Your son wants me."

My mouth fell into a hard line. This was so not good for us, for whatever our relationship was growing into. I wanted to keep it secret until I could find a way to get Richard to agree to it.

"Is that true?" Richard faced me now, anger dripped from the question. And a fair mix of fatherly disappointment, which didn't actually mean anything to me. I didn't care what he thought anymore.

I let out a breath. If I lied, suspicion would be sent right back on Jessa. The questions would continue until she eventually gave too much away. But if I told the truth about my relationship with her, Richard would lecture me mercilessly, and I might lose my only lifeline. Still, I had no choice.

"Her observation of me might have some truth to it," I conceded.

Reed laughed, Faulk clicked her tongue, and Richard glowered. We both knew what memory was on replay in his mind. After Richard found Sasha in my room, he'd forbidden me to fraternize with alchemists. Richard had been livid, but things had gotten so out of hand that day—and then Mom had died. We hadn't had the conversation again.

"Everybody, get out," Richard said, ice piercing every word.

"But what about the rest of the test?" Faulk asked.

"She failed," Richard spat. "Now get *out!*"

They scurried from the room like frightened mice, not a backbone in sight. Jessa followed with a dazed expression. I had to admit, I was proud of her. Everything she did made me like her even more. She'd managed to act as if she was completely under Reed's magical spell, when really, she wasn't. Her power was growing stronger every day. And turning the attention to our relationship? While it caused a problem for me, it took my father's attention off the deeper secrets we shared. It was actually kind of brilliant.

Richard stood slowly from the chair, scratching it on the

polished concrete floor. He stalked toward me until he stood only inches away. We were so similar in our physicality, it was almost uncanny. But we couldn't be more different. I stared back at the man who was my physical mirror. He was the "thirty years older" version. White peppered his dark hair. Storms brewed in his gray eyes. Deep lines pulled at his masculine face.

"Are you purposely trying to disappoint me?"

"No, sir."

"Was I not clear before? With that other…*thing*?"

"Yes, sir."

"Why are you interested in Jessa? She is a pawn. *My pawn!*" he challenged. "Alchemists are not to be trusted. *Ever.* They are too powerful to be anything other than our slaves. We have a duty to protect our *royal* bloodline. Do I make myself clear?"

I nodded, meeting the darkness in his eyes with my own. He knew nothing, absolutely nothing.

Your own son is an alchemist!

"You know we tracked that fake back to her, right?"

I paused. "What do you mean?"

"I mean that Sasha and Jessa have more in common than just alchemy."

So they'd combed through everything and figured out who Sasha really was– Francesca Loxley. The long lost alchemist, turned rebel spy.

"Stay away from Jessa," he continued. "You're no longer needed to oversee her training. She's fine to train like all the others. *Keep your distance.*"

A hard knot of tension gathered in my chest. Forbidding me to see Jessa would only stoke the fire I had burning for her. He may be my father, and he may think of Jessa as his slave, but I was no slave. I would do whatever I wanted. No matter what, I would find a way. Until then, I'd just have to be extra careful. In the midst of my depression over Mom, Jessa was the only thing that mattered. He wouldn't take that away from me.

"I understand, sir."

•

I paced the length of my bedroom, rubbing my hands across my face. I stopped, tilted my head and gazed up at the ceiling. I needed to see her.

I wanted to talk to her, make sure she still wanted me as much as I wanted her. Two days had passed since her blue test, and I was a man obsessed. But in that time, I'd forced myself to stay away. My security team normally kept their distance when we were home. With palace guards and officers swarming the place, there wasn't a huge need for someone to tail me at all times. But ever since Richard had forbade me from dating Jessa, I'd noticed more eyes pointing my way than normal. More guards watching me, more officers around than ever. It was obvious that my father had sent out some kind of order to keep me under observation. At the rate we were going, there was no chance I could just pop into her bedroom again.

Forget it. I stalked from our apartment and out into the corridor. I was heading into the GC wing, even if it meant I only got to catch a glimpse of her. That is, if I was lucky. It came as no surprise that eyes followed me as I walked. If they didn't catch me actually with her, then they had nothing to say to Richard.

There has to be something I can do...

There were fewer watchful eyes in certain areas of the palace. The royal wing—but obviously that was out. The

47

gardens—but it was almost fall and there weren't many leaves left to keep us hidden. Not to mention, it was getting colder. And the servant areas had too many people.

No one seemed too bothered lately when I ate in the GC dining hall. But I went there again and again, just to catch a glimpse of Jessa. I couldn't help myself; I was seriously losing my mind over the girl. She was the best distraction I had to keep myself from thinking about…darker things.

I entered the dining hall, my steady gaze searching for her. Jessa wasn't anywhere to be found. The room was filled with alchemists and officers, paired off in their respective parties. I frowned and bee-lined to the one person who might have an idea: Jasmine. I sat across from the older woman dining alone and threw my hands up in the air.

"I need to see her."

"Hello, Your Highness," she said warmly. "How can I help you?"

"I'm sure you probably know this by now, but my father has pulled me off Jessa's training." She was one of the only alchemists who didn't bug me. She dressed her own way, moved to her own beat, and the officers let her because she was so good at her job. Plus, she was trustworthy. She'd never drawn an ounce of suspicion her way.

Jasmine nodded and pulled her gray braid back over her shoulder, stroking the ends before meeting my gaze. Her eyes were bright as she nodded, a knowing smile playing at her lips. "And this isn't okay with you, because?"

I coughed. "Because…" I didn't know what to say. I didn't have a good enough reason. I just wanted to be with Jessa. The pull to protect her was as strong as the need to breathe.

"Because you're in love with her?" She spoke like we were talking about the weather.

A zap of energy ran through my body at her question. I

thought maybe I was in love, but I wasn't ready to admit it out loud. It seemed so childish. I'd only known Jessa for a few months. There was still so much left between us to figure out, if we ever got the chance.

"I just…need to see her," I finally said.

She held my gaze, studying me.

"And since I've been tasked with her training now, you think I can help you with that?" she asked.

I nodded. Because I wanted to see her, yes. But I also wanted to talk to her about the Resistance some more. I hated that she was still working with them, whoever they were. I couldn't trust an organization shrouded in so much secrecy. That was exactly what had led me to distrust my own father in the first place. I needed her to understand, to get away from them so she could stay safe.

You couldn't save your mother. What makes you think you can save Jessa?

"Fine, you poor boy. I'll help you," she said, lowering her voice. A knowing smile lit her face. "I always was a romantic at heart."

"What do you need me to do?" I blurted the question.

"You two can meet in my classroom when it's empty. As you know, it has its own private greenhouse. You should find some privacy there. Not to mention, there are multiple entrances." She winked, and an iota of hope rose in my body. But the thought badgered me. Was she really willing to help us?

"I like you, Lucas." She smiled. "And I like Jessa. You two are good for each other."

"Thank you," I replied.

"Just promise me if you get caught, you won't drag me into it?"

"Of course not. And it's not like you're always in your

classroom anyway, right?"

"That's true. I always lock my desk. But sometimes, I forget to lock the doors." She winked again and eased herself from her chair. Her floral skirt sashayed around her as she shuffled away.

I followed her with my gaze and froze. Jessa had just walked in. She had that serious expression on her face that she got sometimes. I loved that look, but I loved her smile even better. I would do anything to see it again. I stood. Just as Jasmine was leaving, the two stopped to talk. They both caught my gaze for a moment. Jasmine leaned in to add something more, and Jessa's cheeks flared. Then they left together.

This was my chance.

I strolled casually from the dining room, careful to make sure nobody followed. After that, it didn't take me more than a couple of minutes to find my way into the greenhouse. Jasmine wasn't at her desk on my way in, but Jessa stood just under the cropping of tropical trees. She was leaning toward a flower, smelling it. Her hair curled down her back, her body relaxed. When she turned to me, her complexion glowed radiantly in the evening light. Then she smiled.

"Do you think they believed it?" Jessa asked.

"What?" I couldn't concentrate. The heat and her flushed cheeks were distracting me in a very good way. We walked farther into the greenhouse.

The room was massive, humid, and filled with colorful plants curated from all over the planet. I watched as her fingers trailed across them. Lucky plants. It was vital that alchemists had access to many colors so they could do their magic. They didn't have to have natural elements like these, but it made things much easier. Life held the most magic of all.

"With the blue test? Do you think they fell for it?"

I smiled, shaking my head in amazement. "You were incredible."

"I hate failing. The competitive dancer in me won't accept anything less than perfection." She laughed, and the sound drew me to her.

I grabbed her free hand, linking her fingers between my own, and pulled her even farther into the foliage. Once I was sure we were out of sight, I backed her up against a tree and stared down at her parted lips. Her eyes flitted from my mouth to my eyes and back down again. I took pity on us both and decided not to prolong the inevitable. I kissed her. Molding my lips to hers, all my stress fell away.

There was something different about this girl. Somehow I'd let her in, allowing her to peer into the hidden places of me. And miraculously, she didn't cower at what she saw. I came with heavy baggage, and she helped carry my load. No one had ever cared enough to do that for me before. Not beyond the surface of what I could do for them. She never asked me to do anything.

I wrapped her in close, while also restraining myself as much as possible. It wasn't easy. But she was young and innocent. I didn't want to add any more reasons for her to leave me. After losing my mother, I couldn't handle losing Jessa too. The break would fracture in too many places.

"So what do we do now?" she asked, pausing our kiss. I pressed my forehead to hers and breathed in her lilac and honey scent.

"Honestly," I said, "I'm not even sure myself."

"We have to keep this a secret, don't we?"

"Yes." I *hated* that word: secret. I groaned and stepped back, taking in every bit of her reaction. Was she upset?

"Okay." She smiled softly. "We can meet here until we

figure something else out."

Relief washed through me. The greenhouse was one of many on the property. It wasn't the most romantic or secluded spot in the palace, but it was cooling down now as the weather changed, and it was private enough with all the plants to hide us from view. And, most importantly, it was ours.

"But Lucas? Will you please talk to me?"

"About what?"

"About your mother. About Thomas. About *everything*. I'm really worried about you. I just...what is this between us? Am I just a way for you to numb yourself?"

I felt myself hesitate. When her face crumbled, I mentally kicked myself.

"It's not like that." I leaned in to hug her before facing her. "I don't know how to put it into words, Jessa. Are you a distraction?" I smirked, thinking about how good it felt to kiss her like I just had. "Absolutely. But a really, *really* good one. And not for the reasons you think."

"Is that so?" She let out a teasing laugh. "Not for any of *those* reasons?"

I played along. "Okay, maybe a little bit. But Jessa, I like you a lot. Ever since you walked into my life, you turned my world upside down. I used to be so lost. Hell, I'm still lost, especially now, but you, you make me feel like I can be found again."

I knew it was cheesy. Every word would have had me rolling my eyes just months earlier, but it was the truth now. She was my truth.

I stood back and studied her face. Her wide ocean eyes that pulled me in every time I looked at them. Her curly, dark hair that, in the last few minutes of kissing and the greenhouse's humidity, had managed to grow larger than it already was. But I loved it, and I loved that about her. Her cheeks lifted in her earth-shattering smile and there was just so much *goodness* in her.

"Say it out loud," she dared me.

I smiled. "My whole life I've been surrounded by darkness. My mother was sick for years. My father, well, you already know what kind of man he is. The officers can't be trusted. And the alchemists come in as innocent children and leave as brainwashed guardians. What few friends I have are more like acquaintances to me." My voice grew thick. "I'm an only child, and I've always just been so...alone."

She frowned.

"No," I said, putting my finger to her lower lip. "I don't want you to feel sorry for me. I didn't know any different. And I know I have it better in here than a lot of people have it out there. I'm not trying to throw a pity party. I'm just saying, I didn't know what I was missing. I didn't know there could be someone like you."

She blushed and swooped in for a quick kiss. I forced myself not to linger.   "I'm serious, Jessa. You love your family with a bigger heart than I've ever seen. You'll do anything for them. My family never worked that way. And somehow, in the middle of all this chaos, you decided to give me a chance. I'm so full of faults. I've made mistakes. And lost so much. And yes, I may be a prince, but I feel I have so little to offer you."

"I know you're doing your best. It's okay–"

"No, it's not okay," I spoke louder. "You don't deserve to be hidden away. But it's the best I can do right now. And I just...I don't want to lose you." I lost it then, my voice cracking on the last few words. I'd already lost too much. Truth was, if I lost Jessa too, I would fall apart for sure. But I also knew in my gut that I didn't deserve her.

"You won't lose me." She smiled and brushed her hand along my cheek.

I leaned into it, before moving into a hug. She burrowed her head into my neck, and shivers ran down my spine. It just seemed so illogical that I was here. That I was in this position, holding this girl, falling in love with this unattainable future.

"Lucas," she said, "I have to go now."

"Go where?"

She hesitated. "Resistance stuff."

I practically growled. That reminded me... "Are you sure you can trust them, Jessa? Maybe we don't need them. Maybe we can change things ourselves, without all the secrets and politics."

"You know I'm committed to this." She stepped back. Pain traced her features, and I decided to drop it for the moment. I nodded once and grabbed her hand, tracing the outline of her palm.

"Just promise me you'll be careful."

"I'll be careful, Lucas, I promise. It's okay, really, I'll be fine."

She kissed me quickly before disappearing. I was tempted to follow her, but decided against it. She would know. *They* would know.

I leaned against the tree, the same she'd used as her anchor moments ago. My thoughts turned angry.

She was too trusting. The Resistance could easily turn out to be just as dark and twisted as my father. What if they used her, hurt her, broke her spirit? She'd promised to be careful with them, but would they be careful with her? Not a chance. She was in danger. She'd willingly put herself right in the middle of a deadly situation, and there was nothing I could do to get her out.

That didn't mean I wasn't going to try.

The darkness rose inside me, blurring my vision. I gritted my teeth. She saw it in me, that demon. I knew she did. I needed to use it for something useful before it ate me alive. *Take down the Resistance. Stop your father. Save Jessa.*

I burst from my rigid stance and strode from the room, the demon hot on my heels.

FOUR

JESSA

Someone had been in my room.

When Jasmine told me where I could meet Lucas, she'd also told me to check under my mattress in an hour. So the whole time I'd been with Lucas, the back of my mind tinkered with the idea of what would be waiting for me. And who in the Resistance had access to my room?

I had few belongings: a high-tech slatebook with restricted access; a wardrobe of beautiful clothes Lucas had gifted me, of which I wore hardly any. Not when I needed to dress in the guardian outfits in order to fit in. I still had my lavender ballet costume from the night I'd been discovered, tucked away. And that was about it.

But still, my door was usually locked. So someone had used magic to open it. I wondered what color would do that. Or maybe someone had a key. That didn't narrow it down. I assumed many of the officers, guards, and even housekeeping staff had access to my room if they wanted it. It sent shivers all over my body just thinking about it.

But there was no doubt *someone* had come in, because sure

enough, as I lifted the mattress, a typed note was waiting for me.

Officer Wallace plans to work late tonight. There will be no one else in the office after 10 P.M. Get him alone and find out the status on New Colony and West American relations. Specifically, anything regarding the shadow lands. Don't let him remember your conversation. Someone will be in touch tomorrow. Destroy this message.

I reread the note twice, clutching it between shaking hands. *Are you kidding me?* My heart exploded at the thought of this mission. Even thinking I had a *mission* was beyond bizarre. Who had I become? My whole life had turned completely upside down in a matter of months. At any moment, I could be discovered, tried for treason, and executed. Was I really going to use alchemy on an unsuspecting officer?

Yes.

I wasn't here to back down. Whatever the Resistance asked, I would do it. I had to. Too many people were counting on me. It was time to be brave.

The first thing I needed to do was pocket a knife. That was easy enough, considering the dining hall had all manner of utensils available. A steak knife would be messy and wasn't my first choice. I'd have to get my hands on something smaller and cleaner, and soon. Especially if I was going to start using red alchemy on a regular basis. I took a deep breath and rubbed at my temples, squeezing my eyes shut. My magic could be the difference between the Resistance succeeding or failing, I reminded myself. My magic could be the difference between never seeing my family again!

I began pacing the room, building the resolve deep in my belly.

I wouldn't use red alchemy on any one person more than a couple of times. A little gray blood was harmless. Lacey,

Reed, and that officer girl in training had all forgotten what had happened to them because I'd made it so. But they'd all been fine. They hadn't turned out like Queen Natasha, who'd been abused for years with the magic.

I sat on my bed, anxiously waiting for the time to pass. When ten o'clock finally rolled around, I shuddered. I reread the note for what felt like the millionth time before flushing it down the toilet. Then I headed out to find a knife before I could talk myself out of it.

The note was right. This late into the night, there weren't any officers in the area. Not when I'd gone to pocket a knife. And not when I went to open the door to their office. It was locked. The guard at the end of the hall gave me a suspicious once over, shaking his head.

"It's locked," he said.

Duh...Well, now what am I supposed to do?

As luck would have it, a man rounded the corner. An officer. As he marched closer, I noticed he was probably in his early thirties. He eyed me warily. He was broad-shouldered and strong, with wiry, blond hair pulled back into a small ponytail. His dark eyes flashed as he realized I wasn't moving out of his way.

"Jessa," he said, stopping just feet away. "What are you doing here?"

So he knew my name. That wasn't a good sign.

"I came to report something. A crime."

His jaw ticked. "I was just grabbing my slatebook. I left it inside. Why don't I go in and call Faulk." It wasn't a question. "Stay here," he added, before swiping some kind of identification into the lock and walking through the double doors.

I peered back at the guard, who seemed to be distracted by a group of alchemists laughing as they staggered down the adjoining hallway. The sound of the polished floors tapped under their shoes. Now was my chance. I slipped through the door behind the officer, hoping to grab him before he got to his slatebook.

"What's your name?" I asked, gaining his attention.

He didn't slow. "Officer Wallace. You're not supposed to be in here."

My pulse quickened. "I know," I said. "I just needed to talk to someone right away." My hands shook as I gripped the head of the knife. I'd slid it into my pocket, but since it was a little big, I had to keep one hand on it at all times. Not suspicious whatsoever... *right*. I inhaled a steadying breath and relaxed my face; I could do this.

"I'll call Faulk for you."

"Actually, Faulk and I don't always see eye to eye, in case you hadn't noticed."

He turned then, a sly grin on his face. "I think everyone's noticed." He seemed stressed, but that grin transformed his features from ordinary to kind. For a moment, I didn't want to hurt him. I didn't want to do this, not to this man who seemed like he could probably be a friend.

I gripped the hilt of the knife a little tighter. What was I thinking? No way he was kind, not if he worked for Faulk.

"Yeah, well, would it be okay if I talked to you? Told you about the...crime that I saw. And then you can decide if we have to call Faulk."

"I really should just call her. And you really shouldn't be in here."

I followed him to his desk, a typical office cubicle at the back of the large room. All the monitors were off, the desks clean and locked up for the day. A quick glance up the open staircase to Faulk's large windowed office showed that it was also dark. We were alone.

"Please, I don't want to get yelled at again. Maybe what I saw wasn't a big deal. Last thing I need to do is drag Faulk away from whatever she's doing in her off time. You know what I mean? The woman doesn't like me as it is. I don't want to get in trouble." I poured as much trepidation and fear into my voice as possible. He frowned and studied me. With a slight nod, he pulled over a rolling chair from the cubical opposite.

"Sit," he said, gesturing to it. Then he settled into his own chair.

I sat, a few feet away, but still not quite close enough. I felt for the knife again, adjusting my position nervously to keep it from view. I peered around the space, double-checking we were alone. I also quickly assessed his person. He wasn't carrying a weapon.

"It happened yesterday," I said, catching his eye. "I saw some alchemists do something that I'm pretty sure is illegal."

"And what was that?" He held my gaze.

I tried to ignore the beads of sweat collected on my forehead. My story was a complete fabrication. Apparently, I hadn't thought this through. I dug my heels into the floor and rolled the chair closer to Officer Wallace, so our knees were almost touching. I leaned in as if to whisper my secret.

"You can tell me," he said, expression earnest.

"I wanted to say—" I shifted closer. "That I'm sorry about this."

I ripped the knife from my pocket and slammed it into his hand. Blood immediately squirted from the point of contact. The knife skittered to the ground. I winced at the sight, but determination ignited inside.

Wallace sprang into action, jumping away and up against his desk. His eyes darted to either side of me; he was about to make a run for it. I wasn't a complete idiot. But he wasn't an idiot either. He knew what I was capable of. I couldn't let him get away. My life depended on it. Just as he dodged to my left, I reached out and fumbled for his bloody arm.

"Stop," I said when I made contact. I felt the alchemy move between us. I didn't yell. I didn't have to. He did exactly as I asked. "Don't say anything. Don't move."

His features went blank as the red magic swirled violently in the air. His blood was already beginning to drip gray. I had to act fast.

"Log onto your computer, and print everything recent regarding West America." I figured that would be good enough. As he automatically did what I asked, I drilled him with questions.

"What can you tell me about the shadow lands and West America?"

"We're expanding," he said, his voice monotone. "The shadow lands are one of our best lines of defense. They keep us protected."

"What do you mean by expanding?"

"Right now they're mostly north and south. We're moving west." West? That didn't make sense. Canada didn't have much infrastructure anymore, nor people, and Mexico was in complete anarchy, controlled by the constantly warring gangs too busy to worry about us. But West America and New Colony had a nefarious history, and everyone knew it was best not to poke the beast.

"Going west, why? Just to keep us isolated?" I asked.

"To prepare."

Prickles of white-hot panic spread across my body. I had to lean up against the cubical wall to catch my breath. I feared where this conversation was going. "To prepare for what?" I asked, drawing out each word.

"War."

The mechanical sound of the printer stopped. Silence descended on the room. Thick drips of crimson fell from Wallace's wounded hand and splattered on the concrete floor. We'd need to do something about that.

I grabbed the thick stack of papers out of the printer. I flattened them between the waistband of my pants and abdomen, then pulled my shirt over to cover them. It was the best I could do. If I hunched just a little, no one would be able to see I was hiding anything. I hoped.

I reached out and grasped his bleeding hand. It was warm and slick, and rather large against my own. *All this power I have in my small hand.* I gulped.

"Let's go to the bathroom," I said.

Still in his trancelike state, he led me around the darkened offices until we found the bathroom. I kept my hand on his, even though it made me squirm. I had to make sure my alchemy was still working. But I also wanted to end this quickly. As much as I disagreed with what this man did for a career, I didn't want to permanently damage him.

We entered, and I instructed him to clean himself at the sink. I let out a sigh of relief when his separation from me didn't change the magic. I started searching the attached supply closet, rifling through the contents. There was a small kit in my dormitory bathroom, so I hoped there'd be one here too. I located a kit on the top shelf and pulled it down. I placed it on the counter next to where Wallace still washed his hand. The water ran over it, mixing in swirls of blood in the sink. I stepped closer. It looked pretty clean. Why was he still washing it then?

Oh, that's right. Realization hit me.

"You can stop that now," I said, guessing he needed a little more direction from me. "You're going to dry and bandage yourself, clean everything up, and forget this happened.

If anyone asks you about me coming here to talk, you're going to say I got spooked and never said anything. And if someone asks about your bandaged hand, you're going to tell them you accidently sliced it on a letter opener." Ugh, I hoped that story would be believable enough. It was the best I could think of with so little direction from the Resistance.

He just stared at me.

"Do you understand?"

He nodded, and I bit my lip. His head was drooping at an odd angle, his eyes glassy and dazed. I hoped no one found him like this or it would be obvious what had happened.

"Clean this up, then splash your face with some water, and go back to whatever you came here for tonight."

He began, and I didn't allow myself to hesitate. I rinsed the knife and replaced it in my pocket. Then I hurried from the bathroom and out into the offices. Luckily, the area was still deserted. I exited, light on my toes. I sucked in my stomach, the paperwork burning against my skin. I kept my head down as I passed the guard still in his same position. I felt his eyes trained on me, but I didn't allow myself to meet them. I stalked around the corner and made it back to my room in record time.

I slid the papers under the mattress into the same place the note had been left for me. I knew that would be one of the first places Faulk and her people would look if they decided to search my room, but where else was I supposed to hide it? I certainly didn't know any magic for hiding classified documents! Whoever was handling these items for the Resistance had better work fast.

I forced myself not to panic as I stripped off my clothes. Then I jumped in the shower to wash off any remaining blood. I'd already rinsed quickly back in the officer's bathroom, but still, it was better to be safe than sorry. Plus, the thought of having someone else's blood on me made my stomach turn. The feel of the warm water soothed my shaking body as the adrenaline melted away.

After finishing up, I wrapped myself in a plush towel and twisted a second around my dripping mop of hair. I padded out into my bedroom to grab some pajamas. I stopped. A vulnerable sense of knowing pricked at my senses. Someone had just been in my room. Was anything out of place? The bed was still immaculately made, the items on the desk untouched, the door locked. I lifted the mattress.

The papers were gone.

I wasn't surprised, but a gasp escaped anyway. Part of me was relieved it was over and the incriminating classified documents were no longer in my possession. But another part was freaked out that someone had been in my room *while I was in the shower.* I mean, seriously, I was naked in my bathroom and they'd broken into my locked room. Logically, I knew it had to be done. But that didn't erase the worst part: I had no idea who had accessed my room. I felt violated by that truth, the lack of privacy in this place yet again setting me on edge.

●

"I think it's time you joined the other alchemists for classes," Jasmine said. Over the last week, since my confession to the king, she'd completely taken over my training. Jasmine had become my constant companion in magic. The more I got to know her, the more I liked her.

I groaned. "Why would I want to do that?"

"It's not about what you *want* to do, it's about what you *should* do."

"And you think being around people who hate me is going

to help me?"

"I think it's time you at least tried to make some friends."

Oh no, I'd been afraid that this was coming.

As much as I hated to admit it, she was right. Since coming to the palace, I'd purposely separated myself from the other alchemists. And they'd done the same thing. At first it was because I didn't want to be one of them. And then it was because I wasn't sure whom I could trust. Jasmine was older, the strongest healer in the palace, and a teacher. I'd always felt comfortable with her. But I hadn't trained with any other teachers, and it didn't help that the one guardian I had befriended had turned out to be a terrible friend after all. I was still so mad at Reed for trying to persuade me to give up my secrets, but I had to let it go if I wanted to get anywhere with these people.

Still, even if I decided to play nice, it didn't mean they would.

"Okay fine," I conceded. I would *try*. But that didn't mean I'd have to like it.

"Let's start now, shall we?" Jasmine motioned for me to follow her from her office. I glanced back longingly at the space, with its clean modern finishes and attached greenhouse. Leaving the cocoon of this safe haven in the GC wing was not my idea of a good time. But, it was now or never. My heart kicked up a notch, unwelcome anxiety bursting to life.

As we walked down the hallway, Jasmine spoke, "We don't know when your last three tests are going to be. You could be done in a week, or you could be done in several months. You're being tested off schedule, so it's really just up to Faulk. As you know, everyone is tested in the five main colors. You have to pass three."

"And I'm currently one and one," I said, grumbling at my

failure with blue. Even though that failure probably saved my life, it still bothered me that I'd had to do it. Stupid tests.

"Yes. And we have to assume Richard will want to do something with red as well," Jasmine continued, "but that will likely come after your initiation. Of course, we won't know until it happens."

I swallowed hard, rubbing a hand through my tangle of hair. I was naïve if I thought that wouldn't come soon. But it still scared me to think about it. Every time I used red, it got easier. Or maybe I was just getting better.

"So what does this have to do with training with the other alchemists?"

"Everything. You need to make allies here. You need to better learn the other colors. I can help you, of course, but there are other teachers. It would only be expected that you would start working with those teachers as well."

She didn't say more, but I could read between the lines: Jasmine wanted several things from me. She wanted me to pass my initiation so I could get closer to the king. If the Resistance was going to use me against him, I needed to be a full-blown Guardian of Color. I also realized, if I made friends here, I might be able to build some alliances and bring more people into the Resistance. It would be dangerous, but in the end, if we succeeded, if we brought down the monarchy and allowed people to be free again, it would be worth it. I thought about my family in hiding, about all the families torn apart by this kingdom and its many laws, and strengthened my resolve.

"Okay, where do I start?"

●

I should've known better. Cowering awkwardly at the entrance of the large training gym, I nibbled my bottom lip. At the far end were weight machines and treadmills, but most of the area was open for sparring. And all around me, people were doing just that. The smell of sweat and grunts of combat saturated the gym. It was like there was an extra layer of testosterone in here. *Wonderful.*

"But you don't fight," I muttered to Jasmine.

"Why would you think a silly thing like that?" The old woman winked at me and then strode in like she owned the place. *Well, okay then...*

The gym was filled with both officers and alchemists. Apparently this was one space in which the two groups mixed well. Obviously, the alchemists would have the advantage in a fight, but the officers were strong, lethal even, and there were five of them for every one of us. Plus, many carried weapons.

I followed Jasmine to a beast of a man calling off positions to a couple of younger boys who were, for all intents and purposes, beating the ever-living hell out of each other. One landed a punch with a sickening crack. Blood flew across the mat. They both had light amber necklaces tied around their necks. Yellow. It made sense. The one who'd been hit barely noticed the impact. He jumped up and pummeled the other.

I turned away, shielding myself from the sight.

"All right, that's enough," the man called out after a couple more minutes of brutality. The boys instantly stopped fighting. One helped the other off the mat, where only seconds before he'd been punching him repeatedly in the face. They both acted as if nothing had happened as they limped to a door at the back of the gym. I briefly wondered where they were going.

"Are they all right?" I asked, unable to stop myself from asking the question. Fighting wasn't something that was tolerated by New Colony citizens. Violence of any nature was quickly quelled. Even the typical stuff that happened at school could end up in revoked privileges. Fighting was just not part of everyday life in New Colony. To see it so openly accepted, celebrated even, made me want to hide in a corner.

"Don't worry," the man laughed. "They like it. And there's a greenhouse out back. In a few minutes they'll be good as new." So they could quickly go heal their own wounds, I realized. I remembered the palace medical wing I had stayed in briefly, but I guessed that wasn't really for alchemists. It must be for everyone *else* who lived here. Alchemists could just heal themselves.

"Jessa, this is Guardian Branson," Jasmine said. The man was my dad's age, tall, but all hard lines and bulging muscle. Dressed in the typical black, he looked deadly. He probably could kill me with a single punch.

"Um, hi." I tried to steady my voice as I shook his hand. It was like shaking hands with a rock, his grip was so strong. "So I can assume you're good with yellow, then?" I asked. My voice shook.

He shot me a startled look and then cracked a warm smile. "You could say that."

I tried to hide my disappointment. I needed to work on orange, purple, and green, but I didn't say anything. Last thing I needed to do was make the guy angry.

"You're going to spend some time with Branson today, Jessa. Do whatever he says. Don't worry, he'll keep you safe," Jasmine said with so much confidence that I wondered if Branson was part of the Resistance too.

We'd be so lucky to have a guy like him.

"And tomorrow, I'll come find you again?" I asked, turning my attention on Jasmine. I bugged my eyes out at her, hoping she caught my meaning. I so did not want to spend days in this gym.

"Yes, we're going to start rotating you among all the best teachers here. Have you attend some of their classes, do private mentoring, and practice. You're behind on your training, and like I said, you could be tested at any moment."

I let out a squeak of anticipation.

She was right. As I watched her glide away, part of me was terrified to even think about what was next for me. But another part of me was excited for the opportunity. It was really happening. I was an alchemist.

"So, Jessa," Branson said, his voice gravelly. "I heard you passed your yellow examination with virtually no training."

I turned on him, smiling tentatively. "Yes, that's right."

"You got lucky," he said gruffly. *Oh shucks, thanks for the compliment.* "But luck won't always win. There's talent, and then there's hard work. Are you willing to work hard?"

"Of course." I meant it. This entire gym and everything that went on here terrified me, but I wasn't naïve enough to think I wouldn't need to know how to hold my own. These people could fight, officers and alchemists alike, and there would most likely come a time I would have to fight some of them. Maybe even for my life.

"All right then, I'm going to be teaching you some basic movements. But before we do that, let's see what level you're at." He handed me an amber necklace.

"I'm a beginner," I sputtered before I could stop myself. But he didn't acknowledge my embarrassing response. I followed him into the center of the gym, anticipation making me want to run in the opposite direction. That's when I noticed Reed had been hovering in the background. Just my luck, the second Branson motioned for him, he came running like a little puppy dog about to get his favorite bone. Remembering what Jasmine had said about making friends,

I held back my glare and met him with a huge fake smile.

"All right, you two, fight. Reed, go easy on her. I have a feeling she's never done this before."

"Hold up. What?" I turned on Branson. Was he serious? He wanted me to *fight* Reed? Right here? Now? But, before I could get an answer, the little weasel swiped my legs out from under me. I fell on my butt and scrambled backward. I may have been a novice, but I was smart enough to know that I needed to get back on my feet.

"Oh, so you want to play dirty?" I asked, venom in every word. Forget this, Reed wasn't getting my fake smile for another second.

He only laughed that infectious laugh that had made me want to be his friend in the first place. His eyes squinted mischievously. "Oh, I would love to play dirty with you, Jessa."

I groaned and rolled my eyes. *Such* a boy answer.

He moved in for an attack, but I dodged him. "When are you going to stop being mad at me?"

"When you stop spying on me."

"You know I regret that."

I swung a punch, but he blocked it.

"Oh, do I?" I swung again, but faked, and head-butted him in the chest.

He stepped back, not affected. *Dang it!*

"I was just following orders, but I didn't *want* to do it. You know me better than that." He shrugged.

I did know him better than that. He'd been my friend, and I thought I could trust him. Even though he liked me, he liked his boy-wonder status with Faulk more. And at the times when I was most vulnerable, he'd used his blue alchemy to get what he wanted.

But I apparently needed to make friends, to fit in, and

not to call suspicion to myself. Reed was the most popular alchemist in our age group. He was athletic, funny, outgoing, friendly, talented, and attractive. Anyone who was in with him probably had a better shot of winning over the rest of the group.

I swung at him again—missing, *again*.

"Geez, you're terrible at this." He smiled, brushing off the shoulder of his black uniform. "Use your alchemy, Jessa. Seriously, you're not even trying."

"I am trying!" I yelled. Okay, maybe I hadn't thought of using my magic. Not that he needed to know. I wiped away a bead of sweat running down my temple and connected with the necklace.

"Well, try harder." He lunged, bringing me straight down on my back. His solid body loomed over me, pinning me to the mat. He had the upper hand, the chance to break my face if he wanted to. But, his position didn't scare me. Reed wasn't on my side, but he still had that persuasive thing about him—probably to do with his gift for blue. There was just something about the guy that made people like him.

"Okay, fine, I'll forgive you," I said, "if you get off."

"Make me." He smirked.

I grumbled, pulling on the magic from the yellow. I allowed the feel of the rock against my throat to weigh on my skin, focusing. A moment later, the yellow alchemy connected and a surge of adrenaline shot through me. I catapulted him off me in a single shove, then jumped to my feet, cat-like.

"Good girl. Now, you're trying."

"Oh, shut up." I fought the smile lingering on my lips and stepped toward him, ready to go in for another punch.

"That's enough, you two," Branson hollered. "This is a fight, not a date."

Reed laughed. I shuffled back, taking in the crowd of

people who'd assembled around us. I'd been so involved in the task I'd hardly registered them. A pit of nerves landed in my stomach, and I bit my lip, sure my cheeks were flaming. It wasn't like that with Reed, but to the rest of the world, it sure looked like it was.

I caught a glimpse of stormy gray eyes at the back of the crowd. Lucas's expression held nothing. No evidence of jealousy. No amusement. Not even a peek of longing that I'd come to recognize whenever he looked at me. He was just... blank. We locked gazes for a heavy moment, before he took a step back and disappeared into the crowd.

FIVE

SASHA

The leaves crunched under my shoes as I headed down the path. The forest was alive today. I inhaled the fresh pine and welcomed the warmth of the evening sun as it caressed my face. I was alone at the moment, and I relished in that fact. Mastin and Jacob Cole were pretty much everywhere I went, and it would be a lie to pretend it wasn't bothering me. We didn't need them or anyone from West America to help us. We'd spent years getting to this point. Jessa was in the palace now, a red alchemist.

The Resistance had people who were either alchemists themselves or supported them. West America? They were anything but our allies. I didn't understand how we were suddenly buddies with them. But nobody seemed to care what I thought about it. If they did they sure had a funny way of showing it. Hank hadn't talked to me since the meeting in his cabin two days ago. Not that I was talking to him either. The sting of betrayal was too fresh.

My nightmares had started again. Dreams where the pain came in flashes, leaving me gasping for air as I woke. I'd been out running more than ever, dreading the snow that would arrive soon.

I continued down the path, smiling when a squirrel nearly ran into my foot. The little guy was probably used to us humans by now. I caught sight of Lacey then and sucked in a shallow breath. I'd been spending a lot of my time with her. It hurt, and was probably the source of my nightmares returning. Because as much as *she* didn't bother me, her parents certainly did. And it always seemed that one of them was hovering whenever Lacey and I worked. Granted, she *was* only six. But it wasn't like I was going to do anything to harm her.

"Hey, girl, are you ready to get to work today?" I approached her. She was sitting on a log bench—our usual meeting place. Her legs were crossed under her small frame. The crisp breeze caught a lock of her wavy hair, stretching it in ribbons across her face. It was probably one of the last hot days we'd have for a while, and she was enjoying it like any kid should be.

She smiled up at me, and I was struck again by her looks. She was a cross between Jessa and myself. Why people didn't question me about it had to be because few knew about my family history.

But our parents know. Don't they see the resemblance?

Of course Christopher, our father, chose that moment to grace us with his presence. Not surprising since Lacey was never alone. I really didn't want to deal with him.

Abandonment issues, anyone?

"Good evening, Sasha." He half smiled, but there was guardedness behind his hazel eyes. "How are you?"

"I'm doing all right." I wasn't. I was too distracted to care about things like happiness. It was depressing to see where I'd ended up emotionally after all this time. I needed to get it

74

together and suppress the itch to run.

We both stood awkwardly for a minute, neither making a move. What was I supposed to do? I could barely even look at the man. He brought up too many feelings of inadequacy. And much to my own frustration, longing was mixed with that pain. A ridiculous need to impress him, or something equally pathetic.

"So, how's our girl coming along? Everything…safe?"

I cleared my throat. "Absolutely. Safety is my number one priority."

Okay, that wasn't entirely true. I had pushed her hard a few times in the last couple of days. But it was only because I knew she was powerful. She had to be! Three alchemists in one generation, in one family like that? Unheard of. And with the West American guys hanging around, she'd need to know how to control her magic. I didn't trust them to care about her safety.

"Well, we'd better get to work." I smiled at Lacey.

Christopher fidgeted, shifting his weight. He was lanky, a typical middle-aged man. His sandy hair was threaded with gray, showing the signs of age. "So, Sasha, where are you from?" he asked.

Are you kidding me? My throat pinched as I fumbled for the right words. *Yes, Daddy, it's me, Francesca!* I banished the thoughts. I was Sasha now.

"New Colony. I was a GC kid who was lucky enough to get out and end up here. I've mostly been up here for years," I said. "That's all I know." I ended it with finality in my tone.

The pine needles crunched under my boots as I took a step back and turned away. If he figured out who I was, then what? We'd all live happily ever after? Yeah, right. No way was I going to forgive them.

This camp, this little misfit village we had here, it was

my home. The thick forest was my backyard. The morning fog, the ambient noise of small animals, the clear air, it all comforted me in a way the Capitol never could. These people who lived here were the ones I trusted. The only ones who cared about me. Hank and Tristan had gotten me out of the dark New Colony world, and I'd clung onto my new one ever since.

Christopher nodded, like he had an idea of what I'd been through.

I focused on the little girl who was beginning to follow me around with stars in her eyes. Hero worship, some might say. I guess that's what I got for training her. "So, what do you say, Lacey, ready to get to work?" I asked.

Christopher followed as I led her through the clearing of pines toward the nearest glittering lake. It was one of many that dotted the area. Small and docile, the lake was one of my favorite places to think. The rocky banks had been my friend and confidante too many times. I didn't mind bringing Lacey to my special place, but I hated that I couldn't tell her dad to bug off.

"So what color is your favorite so far?"

I matched her smile while she talked with animated hand movements.

"Well, I didn't know how to do purple. But I want to try again. Yellow was the most fun. But I really liked green too. That one is the best."

In time I would be testing all the colors on her, including red. And now that I knew about its capabilities, white as well. Red wasn't something I cared to relearn, but since I'd seen white in action, I couldn't stop trying to get it to work. So far I'd had zero luck. I hoped I could figure it out soon because *that* would be something valuable to have. White was a shield. It could be used for invisibility of all things. No wonder Lucas had been able to keep his a secret for so long. I wondered how many other alchemists knew about white, if any. I was dying to get it to work.

Red had been a brief ability for me, but it was gone now. My theory was that the horror of what I'd been forced to do with it had been too much for me, and I'd suppressed it. Good riddance.

"Would you like to try some other colors?"

A toothy smile spread across her face as she nodded excitedly, her blond curls dancing.

"All right, how about *orange*?" I laughed when she started jumping up and down.

"What does orange do?"

"Orange is passion."

She stared at me, a line deepening between her eyes, and I laughed harder.

"What's passion?"

"Well, think of it like this. Orange makes people happy." *Among other things.* "It lightens the mood, if needed. It basically takes a feeling someone is having and makes it ten times bigger."

Her eyes wavered, distracted by a couple of ducks floating idly on the water. Maybe I wasn't the *best* with little kids. I didn't know how to entertain her by *talking* about magic, but *showing* her would draw her back in.

I stepped closer to the lake, peering through the water until I found what I was looking for. My fingers slipped into the icy water, and I palmed a smooth orange stone. The lakes up this way were notorious for their colorful river rocks, and they came in handy more often than not. We didn't have access to the same crystals and exotic plants at the palace. I had my necklace, but I had to be careful not to use it up too fast. I mostly kept it on for safe keeping, just in case. I could find all the colors I needed in their natural elements. *So, take that, New Colony!*

"Are you going to show me?"

"You got it."

"And then can I try?"

"Absolutely."

Her gapped-toothed smile returned, and I mirrored it again. I had to be careful. She wasn't ever going to be my sister, not truly. The more I enjoyed spending time with her, the more it would hurt when she was gone. A rush of longing filled me at the thought.

"Tell me a funny story," I said, ignoring the feelings that threatened to overpower me. "What's something that made you laugh so hard that you couldn't stop laughing?"

I carried the rock as we made our way up to a tree to sit under. We both sat cross-legged, and Lacey wove a lock of her hair around her finger as she thought.

"Oh, I know!" Light sparked in her eyes, and she giggled. "This one time, Jessa told me the funniest joke, and I laughed so hard I peed my pants."

"You peed your pants?" I teased.

"I couldn't get my belt off in time. It was so funny!"

"Okay, silly girl." I shook my head, trying not to laugh too. I really didn't understand kid humor. That sounded like a mortifying experience to me, definitely not funny.

I waited for her to relax and the giggles to slow. Then, I pulled at my magic, allowing it to connect with the orange stone on my own palm. Thin wisps of color twisted into the air. With barely a thought, they found their closest entry point into Lacey—the tiny tip of her elbow.

"Was it like this belt." I pointed to my own.

That was all it took, and she shrieked into hysterics. This time, her enjoyment was tenfold. I watched, beyond amused, as the magic worked on her. I'd only used the tiniest amount, but it had been more than enough to keep her going for another five minutes. Finally she calmed, clutching her tiny torso, the pink shirt she wore rumbled around her belly. We'd probably have to get her into black soon. She was progressing so quickly. But the idea of taking away any ounce of her childhood, including pink clothes, could wait.

"Okay, now it's your turn," I said.

"Good." She smiled. "It's about time you're happy."

"Hey, I'm happy."

She shook her head, snatching the rock. "No, you're not."

"Okay, fine."

"Tell me a funny story."

Funny was a tall order. I didn't find a lot of things particularly *funny*. I didn't use it often, but when I did, I usually used orange to lighten up. Just to soften my mood and make my *shining personality* less grizzly. Not that anyone really knew just how depressed and angry I could get at times. I was a good liar. *Was* being the operative word lately. Lacey could see right through the illusion. Kids had a way of doing that.

"Well, let me think," I said, eyeing the rock in her hand. Small pulses of color were already beginning to filter out of the somewhat-muted orange. Was it really this hard to think of something funny? That was just sad. Footsteps edged around the lake, and my guard immediately shot up. I spotted the blue sweater vest and rolled my eyes. Christopher was walking around the lake, a little distance from us, making a ruckus as he did so, knocking rocks and weeds. He really didn't have the personality for roughing it in the wilderness. But at least he was far enough away that he couldn't hear whatever I had to say.

"When I met Hank, I was just a little girl," I said. "He

helped me and Tristan get out of New Colony."

"Like how you helped my family?"

"Yes, like that."

"Except you forgot Jessa."

I sighed. "No, Jessa came here, remember? But she chose to go back to help us from over there."

She frowned. "This isn't a funny story."

"I know, hold your horses, I'm getting to that," I said. "So when I first met Hank, he had this silly mustache. It looked so bad. It wasn't the scruffy man beard he has now. It was a corny mustache."

She grinned. "Like right here?" She pointed to her upper lip and made a face. I crossed my eyes at her and nodded, sending her into more giggles.

"Yes, and one time Tristan... Have you met him? Well, he's kind of a jokester. He's always playing pranks and making people laugh." I smiled. "Well, one time, when we first got out here, Tristan shaved off half of Hank's mustache while he was sleeping."

She erupted into laughter, and I joined in. Tristan had been a teenager then, always creating havoc wherever he went. But I'd been gone for a while, and I wondered if he still had those prankster tendencies—I had better watch my back.

"Then Hank got up the next morning and came to breakfast without even looking in the mirror." We had a lot of communal meal times back then. We still had some, but as our encampment grew into a village, those community meals had dwindled down. "You should have seen his face when he found out." I grinned. "He was so mad! And that only made it funnier. He had to shave it off. Which was actually a blessing in disguise."

I eyed the magic, still ready, and nodded for her to send

it to me. The second it attached I burst into tears. *Oh my stars, I still can't believe Tristan did that!* The memory of that morning mixed with the orange magic had my sides aching. I was doubled over in a fit, unaware of anything else going on around me.

I looked up to see Christopher had circled back, but he wasn't alone. Mastin walked with him, dressed in his typical combat gear. The man was kind of ridiculous. He stared hard when he saw us. Ugh, I didn't want him to see me like this. The image of Hank's half-'stache popped into my mind again, and I snorted and wiped the tears. *Awesome timing.*

"Is everything all right over here?" Christopher asked, a line drawn between his eyes. Always so serious.

"Yeah, Daddy," Lacey said. "Sasha is super funny. You should hear this story."

I shook my head. No way.

"Okay," he smiled at her, trepidation still in his eyes.

"It's the magic," I said through laughs, which were, thankfully, beginning to die down. "Your daughter has quite a strong affinity for orange."

"I don't get it." Mastin uttered the first words I'd heard from him in days. Since observing him, I'd found he had a way of lurking. It was annoying.

"No one expects *you* to understand alchemy, Mastin." I sighed, exasperated, my normal self returning.

"I know more than you think," he said, deadpan. Why was he always doing that bored voice? It grated my nerves.

"Well then," Christopher interjected, "I think that's enough for today. Lacey's mom has a meal waiting for her."

I held back an eye-roll and nodded as they wandered off together. The two were like peas in a pod. I noticed how close they were and tried not to let it bother me.

"What's your problem?" I turned on Mastin as soon as we

were alone.

"I don't have a problem." He glared at me. His blond hair glittered in the light. His face was *too* pretty. All high cheekbones and green eyes and full lips and… *Intense brooding nonsense!* I felt my pulse rise every time he was near, and it irked me to no end. He was equal parts off-limits and sexy. *Did I just say sexy?* I stomped my foot in frustration.

"Look, the orange alchemy is an amplifier of emotion. The emotion someone *is* feeling, not necessarily what they *want* to feel. We were talking about funny stories so we could see if Lacey could make them even funnier."

"You're training that little girl."

"Obviously."

"But she's only a child."

"Yup, all the best alchemists start young."

He shook his head, darkness flitting over his eyes and matching them to the color of the pines. "You think children can handle the…responsibility?" He said responsibility as if it were a synonym for sin or something.

Was this guy for real? He needed to back off.

"Actually, yes, I do. I was younger than her when I started."

"Oh, and you turned out great," he countered.

Prickly anger clawed at my hands, forming them into fists. "Haven't we already established that you can't talk to me like that?"

He didn't answer.

Someone that attractive and that mean was a lethal combination. I needed to distance myself from this man; nothing about him could be good. He shrugged and reached down to pick up the orange river-rock Lacey had left at our feet. As he flipped it over, we both noticed the alchemy that floated up. Lacey hadn't used everything she pulled. A trace of magic still remained, like an echo.

"Don't touch that," I said, grabbing it from his hands. A bolt of energy shot through both our veins. "Too late," I grumbled.

His eyes flashed again, alarmed. "What's it going to do to me?"

"Geez, no need to be afraid. A little orange never hurt anybody."

He furrowed his brow. Well, that was interesting. He was feeling afraid of me and only the orange alchemy had made it apparent. *Score one for Lacey!* Even with that panicked expression, I couldn't help but step closer to him. *Something about him, I don't know.* It was magnetic.

Oh wait, I *did* know. I'd been stupidly admiring his sexiness when I'd grabbed the rock from him. *Ugh, why?* Residual orange had made me lose all logical thought. Now all I saw was this gorgeous unreachable man, and that made me want to understand him even more. *What the...?* I breathed in, trying to calm the passion rolling through me, but all I smelled was his spicy scent.

I moved closer, closing the gap between us. His lips hardened. They were so...full. So soft. I wondered what they would feel like to kiss. A pulse of desire shot through me, and I dropped the stone.

"This isn't real," I whispered, stepping forward as he backed away. He pressed himself against the tree, and I continued until we were toe to toe. My emotions clouded my better judgment. It wouldn't be long before I turned the kiss in my head into reality, something that the back of my mind screamed at me to avoid. And I didn't care. That was only a small part of me screaming to *back off*. But, it was so insignificant compared to the burn of desire consuming me.

My eyes caught his, and I was done. I *had* to kiss him.

Just as our lips were millimeters apart, he shoved me away. Hard. I landed in a puddle of emotions on the dirt. Rocks pierced my palms. The pain was enough to pull me back to reality.

"Ouch! Geez, Mastin, what was that for?"

He shook his head, covering his mouth and stumbling backward. "Were you going to kiss me?"

Well, this is embarrassing. "No," I lied. "Are you afraid of me?"

"No." He glared.

Ha! He totally is. "I don't believe you."

"*I* don't believe *you*," he grumbled. "I know that look you gave me. I've seen it plenty of times before. You were going to kiss me."

"No I wasn't," I insisted. "You're so full of yourself!" Who was I kidding? I was such a liar these days. "And you *are* afraid of me," I said, changing the subject back on him. "I'm the big bad alchemist, out to get you, aren't I?" I laughed then, because it was kind of true.

"Orange is an amplifier of emotion?" he asked, eyeing the rock.

"It's not a bomb," I said. The thought brought me right back to the hysterics again. He was being such a baby!

"You people are so messed up," he said. "You're a crazy person."

"It takes one to know one."

"Whatever. I'm out of here," he said, stalking off into the trees.

I stifled my laughs and took a cleansing breath. *What just happened?*

●

A flash of annoyance rippled through me as I made my way down the path to Hank's cabin. It was dark, and I didn't use a flashlight. I knew this forest by heart. The chill had a bite, and I moved quickly, trying to keep distracting thoughts from entering my mind. Truth was, I didn't want to see Mastin again. Over the last couple of days, I had done everything in my power to avoid him. No doubt, he'd be at the meeting to go over whatever plan they were working on. When Hank had asked me to join them at dinner, I'd reluctantly agreed. I didn't want to associate with West America, but I also wasn't going to stop them from doing something stupid by staying away.

The lights shining out of the cabin normally were a comfort to me. Not tonight. I ambled up the steps and knocked on the door. No matter what anyone said, I refused to lose my cool. I was walking into a situation with people who hated me because of who I was. Because of something I couldn't change. That kind of ignorance wasn't my problem.

I inched taller as Tristan swung open the door. He pulled me into a hug before ushering me inside.

Mastin was draped across the couch this time, as if he didn't have a care in the world. At least that was a step up from hiding in the shadows. He wore some West America get-up, a kind of armed forces uniform. Most girls would probably take a double look at that. I refused.

"She's back," Cole nodded, standing to greet me.

"She's back." I smirked and joined him at the table. "But she still believes what she said before. She doesn't trust you."

"Let's not worry about any of that right now," Hank said as he maneuvered around the kitchen. He poured tea from the kettle, passing cups to everyone. The energy wasn't quite so tumultuous tonight, and I could tell Hank was making an

85

effort to keep it that way.

I caught Tristan's eye as he settled in across from me. He winked. I relaxed a little. I was glad he was with us again tonight. He always had a way of lightening the mood, no matter how dark. It was one of my favorite things about him.

Everyone settled in, and I noticed Cole motioning for Mastin to come and take a seat. When he slid into the chair next to me, he asked, "Are you going to attack me again?" His tone was dry and unaffected.

"I was only defending myself."

"Oh, is that what you're calling it now?"

"And what would you call it?"

"Attacking an innocent bystander with alchemy," he clipped.

I laughed. I couldn't help it. Why was this guy so bent out of shape about color alchemy? And of course, West America had outlawed it completely. What did he even know about the magic? More than likely, he was scared of what he didn't understand.

"All right, that's enough," Hank sighed. I glowered at Mastin, but held back my retort.

"Yes, *Sasha*. Settle down," Tristan smirked. His eyes flashed when he said my fake name. I was sure he was dying to call me *Frankie*. But I was holding onto this new identity, and I was grateful people were going along with it. I was pretty sure Hank had told everyone to keep their mouths shut on the name situation, on account of my parents' arrival.

I let out a long breath, deciding to get to the point. "Why am I even here? We all know these guys hate alchemy, so what do you want from me?"

"It's complicated," Hank muttered.

Cole straightened his uniform as I rolled my eyes. Military didn't intimidate me. "Is she always such a contrarian?" he asked.

"No!" I answered, at the same time as Tristan said, "Yes."

"Traitor," I growled.

"It turns out that as much as we don't agree with you and your lifestyle, West America needs your help," Cole admonished. He straightened his back and stiffened in the chair. I knew it was hard for him to admit it.

Let him squirm.

"So, that's why you're here… You need *our* help?" I averted my attention and focused on Mastin. Raising my eyebrows, I asked, "You need *our* help?" A smile followed, willing him to challenge me.

"So it would seem." Mastin met my gaze, his emerald eyes sharp.

The look triggered a flash of memory. The tension between us at the lake. The way the orange magic had amplified our feelings. Him, utter fear. And me, complete desire. I shook my head slightly, fighting the burn of embarrassment I was sure was exploding across my cheeks, and took a deep, steadying breath.

"What do you want from us?"

Cole cleared his throat. Mastin opened a folder that was sitting on the table. He retrieved a stack of papers, which he practically threw in my face. I glanced at the men briefly before making a show of stacking the papers neatly to read them. Not my most mature moment. Tristan laughed.

I should've been surprised by the words. I wasn't. Very little surprised me these days. It was on New Colony letter head: communications between Faulk, Richard, and a few other officers. There were even photographs.

"Shadow lands," I whispered. I stared at the landscape in the photos. They were prairie lands with sweeping fields and endless horizons. A rock formed in my stomach at the thought that soon this beautiful land would be dead.

"Richard has guardians all over New Colony, as you know," Hank said. "We have information that he's going to use those guardians, along with his military, to expand into West America. Very soon. And that includes destroying parts of our land."

I blinked, trying to wrap my mind around the situation.

"So? It's not like you'd let him get away with that," I said. "Don't you guys have armies? Weapons? Couldn't you just stop him?"

"It's not that simple," Mastin interjected. "Whenever we've tried to engage in any kind of combat with New Colony, your people's guardians are too strong. They're trained like soldiers, are they not? But what's worse, they have magic and can trick us or hurt us in innumerable ways."

"So you're too scared to even try?" I shoved the papers sidelong at Mastin. "Do you have any idea how bad the shadow lands are?"

"I never said we were scared," he paused. "We won't let him do this." His fist slammed down on the table, sending a vibration through the wooden surface.

"We didn't see this coming," Cole said. "These are areas of our country that are mostly empty. Some farmland—actually some very important farmland, but not near an urban city. As much as I hate to admit it, we're unprepared to fight alchemists. We need more resources, more soldiers, more everything."

"And that's why they're here," Tristan joined the conversation, his tone serious. The playful energy that usually accompanied him was nowhere to be seen. Tristan used to be an officer in training. Hank had gotten us both out together. He was fifteen and I'd been nine. I trusted him just as much as I trusted Hank. "You know I hate the royals as much as you do. If I'm willing to talk this over with these guys," he motioned to Mastin and Cole, "then maybe you should too."

As much as I hated to admit it, my friend had a point.

"All right, so you need alchemists. Don't you have your own?" Mastin ran his fingers through his stubbly hair, exasperated. I turned on Cole. His face had paled considerably. "Or did you murder them? Isn't that what you do over there?"

Cole sighed. "As you know, we run a democracy. And alchemy is illegal. But we're not animals. We don't kill them! We put them somewhere they can't hurt themselves or others."

I shook my head. *Not good enough.* I knew what that meant. Richard did the same thing with many of his less qualified alchemists. Did he kill them? No. But he took away their quality of life. Some were probably even institutionalized, too drugged up to perform magic. Medicate the alchemy right out of them.

"Let me get this straight. You've ruined your own alchemists, so now you've come here to see if you can wrangle up a few of King Richard's runaways?"

Tristan smiled. "She's perceptive, this one."

"Look, we need your help, okay?" Mastin said. "If you don't help us, a lot of people are going to die. Do you want that on your hands, Sasha?"

"He's right. The bug we put on Richard's slatebook stopped working about a month ago," Hank spoke up. He fidgeted in his seat, rolling his shoulders under his flannel button-up shirt. "We've since learned that he upgraded his software and got a new device. Our people on the inside knew something big was going to happen with West America, they just weren't sure what. Just a couple of days ago Jessa was able to infiltrate the officers' computers and get the rest of the information we needed."

"And what's that?"

"Richard has plans for war." The air grew thick as we took that in. "He wants to take back West America. In the process, he will kill anyone who resists."

"How is that even possible? West America is bigger."

"Maybe, but are they stronger? He's now in possession of two red alchemists, as you know. We're not exactly sure what research he's doing on them, but he believes he can use their power for mind control. If he succeeds, what's going to happen? You know. You've seen it for yourself."

He didn't have to elaborate. We both knew he was talking about when I was younger. I had access to the red as well and I'd been trained to ruthlessly use it. Luckily, the stars had smiled down on me, because I grew out of the ability. That rarely happened, but it did for me.

Either that, or I'd forced it out.

But it seemed Jessa had grown into it. And Thomas, the queen's killer, could also use the magic. If there was a way Richard could use that magic on a mass scale, or replicate it in other alchemists, then it was true. Richard would be unstoppable.

Maybe Lucas had been right. Maybe we should have kept Jessa away from his father. But it was far too late for that.

"All right, so what are you going to have me do?" I conceded.

"We've been informed that you already have about twenty alchemists living here and many more throughout New Colony. That doesn't include the citizens who have joined the Resistance," Cole said. "You have the people in the right places. And we have extra resources. We can combine and beat him."

"And what of alchemy? Let's say you win, do you take back New Colony? Do we become our own nation? And in this new world, is alchemy suddenly going to be legal?" I shifted, running my fingers through my hair, laying it over one shoulder.

"Our president has already signed an executive order to give any new alchemists immunity in our country. After all this is over, we'll take another vote. Things are changing. We're a very political country and people are beginning to be more open to the idea. If this actually works, and if the polls are correct, I believe soon we will make alchemy legal for everyone."

"Oh, so is this why Richard is suddenly so interested in you?" I asked, putting two and two together. I sucked in a breath, uncomfortable at the thought of Richard controlling more alchemists. If he had reason to suspect West America was going to create their own strong army of alchemists, of course he would want to retaliate. He always wanted to be the one with the most power. That would be a direct threat against New Colony and his tyrannical position.

Mastin added, "With the way things are going, you'd be welcomed right in." The way he said it made it clear that he did not agree with popular opinion. Loser. He still feared and hated alchemists. He probably always would. "But of course, if your king has his way, you certainly won't have a place. Being an outlaw and all."

"Oh, I assure you, Mastin, I take pride in my outlaw status."

He raised his eyebrows then looked away.

"Fine," I said, relenting. "What do you need me to do?"

"Remember those West American alchemists we were talking about?"

"Yes?" I asked wearily.

"The strongest ones are on their way as we speak."

I took that information in, frowning. This was all getting to be too much.

"You're the most well-trained and powerful alchemist we have at camp," Hank said. He still held his tea, which had to be cold by now.

"Let me guess, you want me to take a bunch of untrained, deadly, and probably angry alchemists and turn them into a magical army?"

Tristan laughed once again. I loved that sound; his laugh was like liquid happiness. But this time, it did nothing to lighten my mood.

I turned on Mastin, meeting his prickly gaze.

"That's exactly what we need you to do."

SIX

LUCAS

For the first time in two weeks I looked at myself in the mirror and stared at the person I'd become. I hated what I saw. The man staring back was partly responsible for his own mother's death. I knew it. Part of me wanted to forgive myself like she would want. But the bigger part refused to let go of the truth. I let it bore into me, disfiguring from the inside out.

I splashed running water over my face, watching the streams of liquid fall in rivulets. I wiped my face clean and groaned. I didn't want to go through this today. My royal uniform was especially restricting. The starched collar stifled my airflow, a snake wrapped around my neck, squeezing the life out of me. I finished buttoning up the gold brocade buttons of the black suit jacket and pulled at the sleeves. It trapped my body heat in with its thick and scratchy fabric. I lamented the traditional garment with the royal family insignia stitched on the lapel.

I hated funerals. Who didn't? Coming together to say goodbye to a person who was already dead as if it could provide any semblance of closure was a joke. What did the dead care of funerals? They weren't there. It was for the living, and it was unbearable, every time.

I took one last look in the mirror. I couldn't avoid it. I was who I was. The prince of New Colony about to attend his mother's funeral.

Mom is dead.

One of our most trusted officers had killed her. Thomas had used her, continually, to influence royal policy. He wasn't supposed to be an alchemist, none of the officers were. No one knew. That's what they said. And he'd been strong enough to pull the red from her blood and control her mind. He'd done it on and off for *years*, slowly killing her. She tried to get help. She even came to me. She didn't know what was happening to her since Thomas always wiped her memory with each event. But she knew something was wrong. I was too stupid and distracted to be of any use to her. I was a terrible son.

Time's up.

I stalked out of the bathroom and went to meet my father. He stood in the living room, in the exact spot she'd died. I wanted to look away but forced myself to stare. Bile rose in my throat. He was dressed to royal perfection, even had the crown perched on his head. He rarely wore it, only when he wanted to remind everyone of his power. His people surrounded him on all sides—officers, advisors, guards, and even a couple of alchemists. The actual members of his court would meet us there. They didn't live in the palace; they just attended the parties. And the funerals.

"Are you ready?" Faulk said, turning on me. Her voice sent a shot of hatred needling up my spine. How could she have missed it? How did she not see Thomas for what he was? She was supposed to keep us safe. It was her *job*, and her own number two had murdered my mother. She, too, was responsible.

●

The dome of the Capitol Rotunda stood like a beacon in the early September sky. Inside, Mom had been laid out for viewing for the last two weeks. It was tradition for the citizens to have an opportunity to come and pay their respects before the funeral. Our procession approached the building. Masses of flowers were piled outside the building—gifts from people who loved their queen. They were laid atop each other in systematic reverence. Most were already rotting.

Crowds lined the streets as our car pulled to the curb. Escaping the claustrophobic space, we were greeted with camera flashes. I blinked rapidly as the media captured our solemn expressions. Security was everywhere, but at an event like this, people had enough respect to stand back. They even kept their voices down. That made it real, and I momentarily longed for their usual noise.

Once inside, I sat next to my father on the front row— the row reserved for immediate family. Not that there was anyone left. It was just us. The room was filled with a limited number of dignitaries, just the typical influential crowd I'd grown up with. These were the court of New Colony, the barons and dukes and all those stupid titles that meant little to me. I thought of the crowd outside. No one forced any of them to come. It wasn't a social engagement, standing outside. They were here because they wanted to be. Something about that gave me comfort. Mother was loved by her people.

The black casket, surrounded by huge bouquets of white roses, was open.

As much as I tried to look away, the scene drew me to her. My eyes couldn't look away from her plastic-like body. She was ungodly pale, her lips and cheeks painted a sickly red. She was dressed in an ornate purple gown, dripping in diamonds. Such extravagance wasn't her normal style; she had more class than that. Except for her long, red hair, she didn't even look like the same person.

That's because she isn't!

As the funeral began, I couldn't look away from her body. Nor could I retain much of what was said. All the speeches and accolades and crying, it was completely washed out. It was like I sat behind a pane of soundproof glass.

No tears. No thoughts. Nothing.

A familiar face in my periphery pulled me back. Reed stood off to one side. What was he doing? A knowing look passed between him and my father. Then my father stood and headed for the podium. As he walked by Reed, he slowed and brushed shoulders with the boy. They paused for a moment muttering between themselves, and the little brown-noser nodded imperceptibly. Reed shifted in his suit, then touched my father's elbow. It happened so quickly, I was sure no one would have noticed anything unusual about the exchange. But if Reed was here, it could only mean one thing.

Blue alchemy.

Reed had quickly become the best in the kingdom at that brand of magic. And the power for persuasion was useful to someone like Richard. Leave it to him to find an opportunity to sway public opinion. Even at his wife's funeral.

Richard strode to the podium. All eyes and cameras pointed toward him. He wore the perfect expression of a grieving husband and an angry monarch. He almost *glowed* with it. I knew it then. He'd used some of Reed's magic to make whatever he was about to say as believable as possible. Even though Reed couldn't infuse his magic to the entire kingdom, he could certainly make anything the king had to say utterly believable.

"I am a man standing in front of you today with a broken heart. For thirty-two years I have loved and cared for Natasha, your queen. She was my soulmate and the love of my life. Today we remember the kind, strong woman she was. Not only in motherhood, not only as a wife, but as a monarch to this great country." He paused, as if to wait for applause. Being a funeral, the room stayed silent, but the emotion was thick. Her loss was felt by everyone.

"Many of you are wondering what happened to end her life so early. As you already know, her cause of death has been kept private as we investigated her early demise." He looked through the crowd, surveying their reactions. Everyone sat, most with backs stick-straight, leaning slightly forward. The crowd was enraptured by his velvet voice.

I found myself among them.

"The truth is, your queen, my wife, and the mother of my son, was murdered."

A hush, followed by a flurry of whispers.

Was he going to tell them what happened to her?

Finally. A wave of tension left my body as I exhaled a quiet breath, knowing that Thomas would get his punishment.

"After conducting a thorough investigation," Richard continued, "we have discovered that West America was behind the murder. Our only recourse is to declare war on our neighbor. We will not sit idly. We will avenge the death of our queen. It's time to take back what is ours!" The final words were said with such finality, that not one person in the crowd disagreed. Applause broke out. A completely inappropriate action for a funeral, but the magic was too strong to resist. Even I couldn't hold back a few claps. And I knew the disgusting truth.

He was using her *death* for his own political goals. I couldn't believe it. But then again, I could. I hated him more than ever for this. Anger pulsed through my core, and I squeezed my hands into fists.

He returned to his seat moments later, and the funeral continued, the last condolences said. A depressing song about loss and letting go was sung by the royal choir. Through it all, my mind raced, focused on the uncertain future. *War?* Richard had used this to rally the citizens for war? We hadn't had a war, not ever. Not since America broke apart and we became New Colony.

When it was time, I joined the other pallbearers. But even that experience was weightless. The coffin—a feather— and me, unable to process the moment. How could this be happening? My mother was nothing more than a decaying body. And my father cared more about his political gains than seeking justice for her killer.

Thomas needed to be held accountable.

I went along with the rest of the day in complete misery. It could've been minutes, or it could've been hours, but I endured it all. Forcing myself to feel every painful emotion, because I deserved nothing less.

At some point I found myself standing in the crowded cemetery. Headstones seemed to litter every square foot of earth. Most were worn and unidentifiable. Her body was sealed in the casket. The waxy shell, locked away.

Slowly, the men lowered her into the hole, the earth becoming her home.

It was a beautiful, sunny day, one of those rare fall days that still felt like summer. How was that okay? It should have been raining. Should've stormed! The clouds dark, the air bristly, wind and hail assaulting us. I joined the others in tossing a little pile of dirt on top of the casket, but I couldn't look. I didn't want that image burned into my memory. I couldn't handle any more.

After a few minutes, it was time to go. Relief washed over me, the strongest emotion I'd felt all day. I hated myself immediately.

We'd left the largest crowds back at the rotunda. Still, many people had come to gawk outside the cemetery gates. At least they had dressed in black. A couple of officers and several guards kept them at bay as we approached our waiting car. I was so ready to be done.

Pop! Pop, pop, pop!

Instinct flared. I flattened to the ground. Screams erupted. Bodies fell. More *pops* echoed around me. Little plumes of concrete and dust, grass and dirt rained upward. Acidic panic filled me. Then shock. Then *realization.*

"Get down!"

More shots fired.

"Your Highness," someone said, practically jumping on top of me. "We need to move." The guard snatched my arm and yanked me toward the car. The door was open, my father already inside, his eyes wild. I was shoved in, toppling over the seat. The door slammed. More bullets rained, a couple pinged off the car. One right against my window. The glass barely cracked. They clanged, louder than expected. We were safe. This vehicle was bulletproof.

Outside, the officers and guards took over. They fired back at whoever had attacked us. I stared, horrified, as bodies continued to fall, as people, some with children in their arms, ran screaming. Innocent bystanders had taken the bullets for us. But everyone knew who the true target was, who it had to be.

Someone had just tried to assassinate us.

"Has that ever happened before?" I choked. I already knew the answer.

My father looked at me then, his eyes wide. It felt like this was the first time he had really *seen me* in years. "Thank God you're okay."

I nodded, and he continued, "No, this hasn't happened before. Not in the capital."

"I know." My voice sounded far away.

A hush had descended outside, the occasional cry or shout cutting through.

"Our citizens shouldn't have guns," he said aloud, mostly to himself. Guns were illegal. They'd been illegal for decades and were extremely hard to get. Any citizen caught with one was severely punished. We tracked everything, and only officers and guards had guns. Even then, not all of them had the privilege. I didn't have a gun, though I had been trained to use one.

"That's a good point," I said, but had a sinking feeling I already knew. The Resistance. When I'd left them, did that mean they'd suddenly changed their plans? When I was helping them, they'd agreed to no assassinations. But I was right. It turned out I couldn't trust them. Who else could have done this? Maybe it was their plan all along, and they were just looking for a good opportunity? Get us out in the open, away from the palace. Catch us off guard.

"No matter who this was, we have to blame it on West America." Richard closed his eyes and brought his hands through his hair, lines crossing his face. In that moment, he looked his age. Older than he'd ever looked before. "We'll have to work it into the war effort."

"I'm not even going to justify that with a response," I said, shaking my head. West America had *nothing* to do with

Mom's death. Who was to say they had anything to do with this? Blame wasn't about justice, or even truth, but about political gain. And that was wrong.

A flash of darkness crossed his features, and he turned away. We would have this conversation later. He knew it. I knew it. But still, I found myself relieved he was alive. Guilt swept over me; he probably didn't deserve to be. It was confusing. I didn't agree with him. I didn't even like him. He was a terrible king. He hurt people. He was using Mom's death for his own ends.

But…I didn't want to be an orphan.

We sat in thick silence until Faulk finally banged on the car door. Blood was splattered across her white uniform, her face grim. Richard opened the door. "I have good news, and I have bad news," Faulk said, between panting breaths. "The good news is we got him. The bad news is he's dead."

"Who is he?" Richard said.

At the same time I responded, "I would think the bad news is all these other people are dead."

We slid out of the car to survey the carnage. It was worse than I imagined. Bodies littered the ground, carnage so gruesome I nearly vomited at the sight of it. Several more people were injured, either crying out or in shock. A few people were close to bleeding out, and they were swarmed with those trying to help. I had to look away. Luckily, the few alchemists we had on hand were already jumping into action. There was more than enough green in the graveyard to take care of those on the brink of death. The magic flowed through their hands into the injured. They would be okay. As for those who'd lost their lives, there was nothing anyone could do. Not even magic could save them now.

"And who authorized this?" Richard said, pointing to the healers.

"I did," Faulk snapped. For once, I agreed with her. She shouldn't have to defend this. *Alchemists should be doing this kind of thing every day.* If I were king, they would be much more public with magic. "It will be a blip," Faulk continued. "We'll get the media to sit down with some of our most persuasive alchemists. They won't report anything out of our control. But we have to save as many as we can."

And this was how it worked.

People like Reed would use their blue alchemy to sway a story in the direction the royals wanted. In this case, Richard would pin the deaths on whomever he wanted, whoever was most convenient. There would be no talk about the specifics. There would be no explanation for those who were healed. New Colony would be informed, of course, of something. But that something was not going to be the truth. They'd likely name the assailant as some West American assassin.

"Who is he?" Richard asked. We walked over to a man sprawled out on the sidewalk. He was dead, of course. Blood oozed from a hole in the center of his forehead, an assault rifle resting just beyond his gloved hands. He was dressed in black, probably mid-twenties, brown eyes glassed over. Nothing indicated his identity.

"We don't know yet." Faulk shook her head, kicking the heel of the dead man. She narrowed her eyes into slits. If looks could kill, he would be dead twice. No, he would be dead ten times over.

"I just buried my wife," Richard growled, "and we're about to start a war. The last thing we need are renegades running around. Find out!"

The metallic smell of blood and the faint assault of charred flesh was too much. I held back a gag. I needed to get away. I rushed back to the car like the coward I was. In silence, I waited until it was time to leave.

My mind worked through all the scenarios. Who would do this? Would the Resistance really kill innocent people? It was hard to believe. Rage burned a hole through me. I needed to say something about them, to tell Faulk and Richard what I knew.

But how could I do that? The truth would reveal way too much about myself. And it would put Jessa in danger. My mother was dead. Today should've been a day to honor her. I rocked forward and bit into my fist, my teeth ripping at the calloused flesh. A guttural scream erupted from somewhere deep inside, an ancient, foreign sound.

It was the inhuman battle cry of suffering. And I deserved to listen.

●

I stormed into the prison, ignoring the startled looks the guards shot my way. Locked in the bowels of the palace, it wasn't a typical area I frequented. But I had murder on my mind, and I needed answers.

I strode right to the door of Thomas's cell. "Open it," I demanded of the guard posted nearby. The hulking man shook his head for a brief moment before he caught my expression. "Now," I growled.

He immediately did as I asked, his hand swiftly opening the lock. I hadn't even bothered to change my clothing when we had returned home. I was still dressed from the funeral. I threw off the jacket, with its colorful ornaments, and strode inside. Only now in black and white, I had nothing to worry about.

Thomas lounged on his cot, meeting me with a lazy grin. "To what do I owe the pleasure?"

"Why did you do it?" I demanded.

"Do what?" he deadpanned.

"Don't play stupid with me." The old man was dressed in gray prison scrubs. His facial hair was beginning to grow into a white beard. His dark eyes assessed me, obviously catching the anger that radiated off me.

"You look upset. What happened?" he sing-songed and stood.

"I asked you a question. I expect you to answer it."

He laughed softly, the throaty sound filling the small space. "Faulk hasn't been able to get anything out of me. Even with her blue magic cronies. What makes you think you will?"

I stalked forward, pushing him hard against the wall. It was easy: his aging body was feeble without access to magic. His eyes darted from side to side. Did he think someone would save him from me? Not a chance. They finally settled on my own dark gaze.

"I still haven't been able to work out how you managed to evade my magic, Lucas. Your mother was always so...weak."

I shoved him harder. "Why did you do it?"

"I already told you I had my reasons."

"Did you work alone?"

"Ah," he scrunched his nose and winked. "Now that's a good question. One I won't be answering today."

"You're pathetic." I pushed him again, then stepped back. "You deserve to die for what you did to her."

"Oh my, so upset." He shrugged. "It was an accident."

"You knew she was sick because of it. You knew what you were doing to her, and you never stopped. You just kept going!"

"And what's your point? What's done is done."

"You're a disgrace of a human being."

"And you're hiding something." He smiled and returned to his cot, relaxing as if he didn't have a care in the world. "Why are you really here?"

Why was I here? Knowing that Thomas was still alive had been bothering me, that was true. But after witnessing what I had today, and seeing my father's reaction to it all, I had to come down here. To yell at the man? Make him feel bad for what he did? To find answers? It was pointless. He honestly didn't care. He was supposed to be a friend of the family, but his only regret was getting caught.

"You're going to die for what you did," I said, moving to leave.

"Maybe," he drawled, putting his hands behind his head. He crossed his legs and grinned at me. "Maybe not."

"What's that supposed to mean?"

"A red alchemist is hard to come by, you know. Richard may hate what I did to Natasha, but like I said, it was an accident. And well, now that he knows about my magic, do you really think he's going let it go to waste?"

A million nasty replies filtered through my head. The anger had each one ready to explode out of my mouth. But this man didn't deserve another word from me. I growled in frustration and left the room, slamming the door as I went. I didn't care what kind of magic he had. I didn't care if he was the most powerful alchemist the world had ever seen. He was going to pay for what he did to my mother. No matter what I had to do to make it happen, that man would not see the light of day ever again.

●

Hours later we met in our usual place, the heat of the sun pressing down, the thick plants hiding us. I was starting to love this greenhouse and the privacy it offered. With most of the alchemists wrapped up in the news, I was confident no one would find us here.

"Are you okay?" Jessa encircled me into a frantic hug, running her hands up and down my arms. She stepped back, her eyes searching mine. She wanted something from me. Validation that I was okay, perhaps. But there was nothing left to give. I looked away.

"Someone tried to kill me today."

"I heard. Everybody heard," she whispered.

"They failed."

"I can see that." She pulled me into another hug, her face finding the crook of my neck. A familiar anticipation ran through my body.

"Thirteen people—innocent people, *my* people—are dead."

Her body stilled. "I'm so sorry. Is there anything I can do to help?"

I paused, raking my hands through my hair. "How committed are you to the Resistance?" She moved away from me then. I studied her face as it paled.

"You already know."

"What if they were the ones who did this?"

"They weren't."

"How do you know?"

"I just know, okay?" She adjusted her body uncomfortably, her weight resting against the nearest tree. The lush plants surrounded us, tall and overbearing. They hid us from the world, but in that moment, they suffocated us too. She shook her head. "I just *know*."

"You just know?" I laughed, disbelieving. "How is that even possible?"

"It's none of your business."

"None of my business?" Was she kidding? She stood rooted to the ground with her arms crossed like a petulant child, unwilling to listen to reason. "How is a resistance group that's bent on ending the monarchy—*my* monarchy, I might add—not my business?"

"You were part of them!" she snapped.

"Not anymore. You didn't answer my question."

"I thought you wanted democracy too. I thought you weren't okay with what Richard's been doing."

"I'm not okay with what he's been doing. But I'm also not okay with murdering innocent people to remove him."

"And as long as there is a monarchy in this country, innocent people will be murdered." She was right about the past, and maybe about the future. Even if I somehow turned out to be an amazing king, there were no guarantees that future kings wouldn't be just like my father. Monarchy didn't work when it meant a small number of people got to control all the magic.

"I know that," I said. "But you didn't see what I saw today, Jessa. And to assassinate entire bloodlines; you think that's okay?"

"No. Of course I don't want *you* to die."

"Jessa, think about this for a second. Somebody, probably your precious Resistance, ordered a hit on my father and me. On the day we buried my mother! What about that is even remotely okay with you?"

She looked away, exasperated. What didn't she get about this? "I already said I'm not okay with that. But what I'm also saying is that you don't *know* it was them. And they already told me it wasn't them! And anyway, New Colony has loads of enemies. It could've easily been someone else."

I scoffed. Maybe. Maybe it was West America, or Mexico or Canada or any other number of enemies farther away. But we stayed out of their business, and they stayed out of ours. At least, we used to. With Richard's manipulation today, it seemed that wouldn't be the case much longer. But that still didn't answer the burning question. "Then how would they have come in without the help of alchemists? The only alchemist group I know of that opposes the crown is *your* Resistance. They are the most logical explanation, but you refuse to see it. You're part of a group who probably just tried to kill me, and you're standing there acting like it's nothing!"

"It's not like that, Lucas."

"Then what's it like? Please, enlighten me."

"You know I can't tell you anything. I'm not allowed to."

"See? This is exactly what I've been trying to say to you for weeks. First, they manage to pull on my heartstrings and recruit me. They get me to do a few things for them, all the while refusing to tell me anything. So I get out, but you turned into one of them, and now you say the same things Sasha always did. *Nothing*! And I'm supposed to just sit here and let them kill me? Let you be a part of all that? I won't do it!" The words flew out in a torrent of anger as I paced around the place. I couldn't believe I had gotten myself mixed up in all that crap. There had to be another way to stop my father. A *better* way.

"So what are you going to do? I'm the only Resistance member here, you know. Are you going to turn me in? Torture me for information?" she asked, her mouth set in a firm line, and the distance between us widened.

"Why do you have to be so difficult?" I paused. "Of course I'm not going to turn you in." She was the only good thing left in my life, but there would come a day when we'd have to choose the same path, or the space between us would suffocate our feelings right out of us.

I didn't want to think about the alternative.

She tentatively stepped toward me, the patterns of shadows and light flitting over her pained expression. Her eyes filled with tears. "I'm so sorry. I don't know what more I can say or do to make you feel better. I'm doing this for my family. For people like me, who need a way out. Richard controls me, Lucas. Or he will if I don't succeed. It's not about you. It's never been about you."

She was inches away. Her hair fell in curls, framing her face, ocean eyes filling. I wanted to reach out and wipe away the tear that rolled down her cheek, but I hesitated. "Then why do you keep meeting me? Jessa, why are you here?"

Trepidation crossed her features as she bit her lip. My gaze traveled between her mouth and eyes. A battle raged behind them, a dark ocean of fear. "Because I think… I'm pretty sure…that I'm in love with you."

Wait, she *loved* me? A wave of emotion pummeled me as I searched her face for hesitation. "You love me?"

My forehead fell to hers. She nodded. I shuddered, breathing her in. We were so screwed up. How was this going to work? We couldn't stop fighting, for one. We were opposite sides of the same fight. But I couldn't help it. I wanted her too. Desperately. She was the only thing that kept me going, the only reason I hadn't lost my mind completely.

"I love you, too."

I meant it. Every word, and I would mean it again and again. I'd never said that phrase to anyone who wasn't my mother. But the words just slipped out. So natural and heavy and *real*. Jessa, she was right there in front of me—all thin bones, warm skin, pumping blood and breath, and eyes, and hair, and lips…

I kissed her.

This girl, she might very well be the death of me.

SEVEN

JESSA

"I think your boyfriend is jealous," Reed said as he pinned me to the floor. I shoved him off and shamelessly glanced around the training gym for Lucas. He wasn't there.

"I don't have a boyfriend," I said. Okay, not officially. Lucas and I weren't supposed to be together. I still wasn't sure how we were going to find a way around that. Sneaking about could only last for so long.

Reed busted up laughing. He held his gut as he jumped to his feet. "You two are so full of it," he said. "If you don't have a boyfriend, then who are you looking for?"

"Oh, shut up and mind your own business." I laughed back.

"How's it going over here?" Branson came over, eyeing the two of us. I grabbed my water bottle. "I see a lot of flirting and not a lot of sparring."

I gagged, nearly drowning myself, and coughed. Reed just smiled. Reed was a flirt by nature, and it was hard not to get pulled in by his teasing. But there was nothing between us. There might have been an ounce when we first started hanging out, but once Lucas kissed me, I was a goner. Maybe it was foolish. Maybe I was naïve. But I loved that man, and there was nothing and nobody that would change how I felt. I kept going over and over the image of it in my mind. Me confessing my true feelings. His response.

He loves me too.

"Your boy is going easy on me again," I said to Branson. As a fighter, Reed was one of the best. Actually, all these people were so far ahead of me, it wasn't even funny. Not that I was laughing.

"You heard the woman. Do your job!" Branson huffed before stalking away to go chastise a group of unsuspecting students.

Reed came at me then. He was so much larger and stronger, so technically trained, and lethal, that I *shouldn't* stand a chance. But we'd been practicing for hours every morning, and I was finally starting to have a glimmer of confidence. One of these days I'd get him! Of course, it helped that I had magic to call on.

Reed toppled me in a matter of seconds. Again! I felt for the energetic connection with the yellow stone tied to my neck. I willed another burst of alchemy to flow into my veins. Seconds later, I pressed my knees into his chest. He rocketed off. I jumped up, landing gracefully on my feet, and threw myself into a combat sequence. I'd been practicing it so much I could probably do it in my sleep.

Block, uppercut, drop, kick.

I swept my foot out, catching him behind the ankle. As he fell back, I didn't allow a moment's hesitation. I pounced, pushing him to the mat. For good measure, I elbowed him square in the nose. The last part was something I added. But hey, he deserved it. A twinge of guilt grasped me as blood poured from his nose. *Oops.*

"What was that for? You play dirty, Jessa," he groaned, still smiling somehow. I ignored the double meaning—he was always doing that. I jumped off of him and back into a crouch.

"Nice one!" One of Reed's friends chuckled from across the gym. It didn't take long for all the other guardians to see what was going on in our corner. Since the shooting during Queen Natasha's funeral, the gym had become busier than ever. War was coming, and everyone wanted to be prepared. All I could focus on was how inadequate I was to fight. A flush of embarrassment ran through my body as I squared my shoulders and stood tall. In a real fight, I would break someone's nose if needed. Reed stood, shook his head, and then laughed as he ambled off to the greenhouse out back. A few nice green leaves, and he would be right as rain.

"How did you pin him?" Branson asked, returning.

"Using the sequence you taught me. Though, I might've gotten a little carried away at the end and elbowed him in the nose." I bit my lip and rocked back on my heels, trying to gauge his reaction.

The man's normally thin lips twitched up on one side. "Good girl."

Well, okay then...

I was getting stronger every day. As much as I hated to acknowledge it, I knew there might come a time I would have to fight for my life.

●

That afternoon, I followed Jasmine toward a new classroom. It was all work these days, training morning until night. She was happy with my fighting progress, and I would continue to work out in the gym every morning. But I needed to grow my abilities in *all* the colors—especially since there was no telling when Faulk and her lackeys would be calling on me to complete another test. I couldn't afford to fail again. Purple, orange, and green remained. I wasn't nervous about green—luckily it was one of the easiest colors to manipulate.

All I knew about orange was that it was used to enhance emotion. That's why the alchemists used it to replace alcohol—they could get a similar experience without the hangover. Made sense, and I didn't allow myself to get too worked up about the orange test.

I was too worried about purple.

Purple was something I could pull out, but what it *did* was still so elusive. I needed a lot of practice with that one. Jasmine assured me that if I could handle yellow then orange would be a cakewalk. So it was purple that needed my attention. I trusted her to be right about that.

●

It was one of the hardest colors. Very few alchemists used it. No one expected me to pass, because people rarely did. That was why I only had to pass three of the five tests. But I wanted to kick butt in every color! The few times I'd gotten purple out, the tricky color had split into primary colors—blue and red. That was another ability of mine that was apparently unique to me. I could separate the colors, but I couldn't do anything with them. And it made me way more exhausted than regular alchemy.

I rubbed my temples as I followed Jasmine. She knocked on a nondescript door.

A woman, not much older than me, flitted out of the room, her blond hair so light it was almost white. It was her defining feature, like it had a life of its own. It bounced around her shoulders in waves as if it was a translucent ocean. She was waifish, tall, with a way about her that didn't feel entirely grounded. Like she was half in this world and half somewhere else. Somewhere veiled in mystery. She had a carefree go-with-the-flow energy. Flightiness. Like trying to hold sand between your fingers.

"Jessa, I'd like you to meet Lily Mason. If anyone can help you with purple alchemy, it's her."

I stood awkwardly as Lily Mason glided over to me, her eyes calculating. They were such a disarming shade of light blue that I couldn't look away. I'd never seen this woman before in my life. She was a teacher here? Was she old enough for that?

"You're trying to guess my age, aren't you?" she asked in an apathetic tone, like she had zero attachment to my answer.

I nodded. It was true. So far all of the teachers I'd met were at least middle-aged. Sure, Lucas and Reed had assisted in my early training, and talent came in all ages. But the actual teachers who taught the alchemists weren't young. They were the most experienced, with years of training in the field before coming back to pass on their knowledge to the younger generation.

"I'm twenty-three."

"And she's been teaching for six years," Jasmine said. "Unheard of and impressive, I know. She knows. But there aren't that many people who are good with purple alchemy. And Lily isn't just good, she's renowned."

"It's my gift. And this way the king has better access to that gift." Again, she said things with no conviction. No emotion. It was as if she didn't care either way. They just *were*.

"Access to do what, exactly?" I asked.

Her eyes, which had been drifting, snapped back to meet

mine. A chill ran up my spine. "What do you know about purple alchemy?"

"Umm… I can pull it out of things, but I can't use it. I've been told it can help people find their life purpose. Connected to intuition, something like that. I don't really understand what any of that means…"

She smiled then. It lit up her entire face. "Come." She opened the door wide and strolled into her classroom, which wasn't like the others. It was smaller. And there wasn't a glass wall on the side of the hallway. There also weren't any desks or even any tables. There were a lot of comfortable-looking couches and pillows large enough to sit on strewn across the floor, with a worn oriental rug underneath. It was dimly lit, with purple practically everywhere. There were amethyst rocks placed around the space, some taller than me. And smaller ones were neatly tucked everywhere. A few plants with purple flowers grew precariously in ornate pots.

She sat on one of the pillows, crossing her legs. Feeling awkward standing above her, I sat on a pillow as well.

"You know it would be better if you left," she said to Jasmine without breaking our eye contact. It seemed that she didn't care either way what happened. The woman was unattached.

"I know. Jessa, there is nothing to worry about. You can trust Ms. Mason. The kind of magic she's going to show you works best one-on-one."

And with that grain of knowledge, we were alone.

"So, purple, huh? What is it that you do? Does it do multiple things like blue or just one like yellow and orange?" I couldn't help the questions from forming. When I was uncomfortable, I tended to do that.

Lily cocked her head at me, unfazed. "The purple wheel of energy is strong in you. The chakra is open. It's the third eye.

Intuition. You know so little, and yet you are so powerful. It's a dangerous combination."

"So I've been told."

She continued, "Do you want to know your future? I already know the answer. It's yes. They always want to know. But they shouldn't always know. And it isn't guaranteed. Prophecy is better. It has surer lines. It's rare. I can't choose it. It just comes when it comes. Fortunes, I can do those anytime, for anyone. But those lines move easily. They blur. Best not to plan your life around something so fluid." She said everything with a breathy voice, like she was talking to herself.

"You're a fortuneteller?" I asked. I'd heard about those people in old stories, but didn't know they still existed. A wave of excitement rolled over me.

"I'm an alchemist who can see fortunes…and misfortunes." She reached to one of the amethysts on the floor and held it in her palm. As expected the color leached out, dancing ribbons of purple magic. Then it split between us. I saw some of it flow into her and felt the color seep into me, calming my nerves instantly. The prickly sensation of trust swept through me. The magic was connecting us.

I met her eyes again, but this time she was wholly in the other world. A glazed, unseeing expression descended upon her.

Please let this be good news.

"You have dark magic," she hissed. "It will be used against you." She paused, nodding, as if listening to someone who wasn't there. "You're on a dangerous path, Jessa. There is heartache. Betrayal. So much suffering."

Lovely.

"So how do I change it?" I hated the fear in my voice. Did I really believe this? But it was magic, I saw the purple, felt it…

"Do not trust him."

"Who? Who's him? Reed? Lucas? The King?"

The door burst open. Light flashed across Lily's face. Her eyes filled with recognition and she was lost from her trancelike state almost instantly.

"Who shouldn't I trust?" I pressed.

"You know the rules." Faulk snapped as she interrupted, moving headlong into the small space. As always, she was surrounded by her hordes of officers. They filled all available space quickly, bringing a claustrophobic cloud in with them. I wasn't happy about the interruption, obviously. Lily, however, didn't seem to care one way or the other. Her impassive expression never seemed to fade, no matter the circumstances.

"You *teach* purple alchemy. You do not *use it on anyone* unless specifically asked to by the king or myself."

"Yes, I am aware. I sat down to teach Jessa about this magic. I picked up a stone, and it just happened. I'm sorry," she added, her expression serene. Uncaring.

She's lying. She'd wanted to give me my future, had asked me. If she'd broken rules to do it, what did that make her? Part of the Resistance?

"And what did your future hold?" Faulk turned on me.

There was no use in lying.

"She said I had dark magic. And it would be used against me. But you interrupted before she had a chance to explain." I tried to keep the venom from my voice. But it was no use. I hated her. The feeling was mutual.

Faulk glanced between us, suspecting. What was she going to do about it?

"One short lesson and you already got your fortune told. I think that's enough for the two of you," Faulk said. "Jessa, come with me, please. Ms. Mason, you can stay, I think you've done enough."

"Where are we going?" I stood. I knew better than to ask Faulk anything, but I always seemed to do it anyway. I caught Lily's ethereal eyes again, but they were impassive. Nothing could be discerned from them. *Creepy.*

Faulk didn't bother to answer as she stomped from the room. As I followed her out and down the modern GC corridor, I thought about what Lily had said. I'd memorized every word. *Heartache. Betrayal. Don't trust him.*

The king kept Lily in the palace under the pretense of training alchemists in purple. But really, purple was so elusive that few alchemists ever figured it out. So that meant she was really here to be his personal psychic. She'd said that the future wasn't set in stone. Things can change. But still, she had to be useful to someone as bloodthirsty as Richard.

That didn't bode well for the Resistance.

"If we can't have you around Lily without her spontaneously reading your future, and who knows what else, then it seems to me that we might as well get your failure behind us."

She walked so quickly I had to run to catch up with her. "Umm, excuse me? What are you talking about?"

"Your purple test. Let's do it this afternoon, shall we?"

"Um, no, we shall *not*," I shot back. She couldn't be serious! "That's not fair," I continued. "I haven't had a chance to study purple *at all*. You're setting me up to fail."

"It's the king who wants you to take your tests before you're ready. He's already growing impatient. If anyone is setting you up to fail, it's him. If you've got a problem with it, you can take it up with him. My suggestion, however, is to keep your pretty little mouth closed and do as you're told."

This was ridiculous. Where was Jasmine? She'd stick up for me, wouldn't she? But then again, Jasmine was only tasked

118

with training me. Anything more might look suspicious. I stomped my foot, annoyed as ever! I knew Lucas would help if he could, but he was supposed to stay away from me. His father wouldn't take kindly to anything Lucas had to say about me. Faulk could practically get away with anything where I was concerned.

There was no point. She always had the upper hand.

"Okay, so what exactly is this test? Am I supposed to read someone's fortune or something?"

Maybe I should just get this failure over with. There was only a small chance I'd miraculously know how to manipulate purple. I still would have green, which I knew was a sure thing. That left orange, and it was another easily accessed color. I would figure it out. I had to. There was no other choice but to pass at least three of these tests and be initiated into the Guardians of Color. Then I would get to work directly with the king and find a way to stop him.

"There's more to purple alchemy than looking for futures," she responded.

"What do you mean?"

Faulk stopped abruptly and gave me a hard stare. I was asking for her help, knowing full well how unlikely it was I'd actually get it.

"If you're lucky you'll be able to see the future. But there are more practical uses for the magic of intuition. You *may* be able to hear people's thoughts, telepathy even."

Umm…wow!

I stepped back and nodded. "Thank you." Now I was really curious. Mind reading? Telepathy? I hoped I would be able to do those things one day. Purple sounded amazing, but at the moment I was overwhelmed by it all.

She laughed. "Silly girl, don't count on it. Even *you* aren't that good."

Challenge accepted.

She turned on her heels, and I followed her out the ornate front doors of the palace. The cool air swept over me as I took in the sprawling, manicured yard. Where were we going? She stomped to the single black car waiting in the drive and motioned for me to get in. I didn't want to. I didn't trust her. But what choice did I have?

"The royal family *won't* be joining you on this one. With the recent attack, it's not safe for them to leave the palace grounds. So sorry your *friend* Lucas won't be there to cover for you." I had to force myself from rolling my eyes.

"Umm…okay." I smiled politely, sliding into the cool leather seat.

She threw a black blindfold at me. "Put this on."

●

There was a price to pay for everything, including magic. One of the most common prices of alchemy was energy. It made the user tired, especially if they'd been using a lot of magic. The day had been filled with alchemy already, and it was weighing on me. I might have fallen asleep in that car, had I not been so worried. With my next test looming, and the fact that I had no idea where we were going or what to expect, I wasn't sleepy. How long had we been driving? An hour? Two? Long enough that fat beads of sweat rolled down my cheeks.

"Hey, anybody up there? I know there has to be a driver in here. How much longer do we have?" No answer. I'd quickly figured out I was alone in the backseat. I didn't have anyone else to ask.

The smooth ride of the car changed as we drove onto some kind of gravel. That had to be a good sign, but the bumping vehicle only ignited my nerves. A few minutes later, the vehicle stopped.

I did a mental happy-dance, trying to hype myself up. I was probably going to fail, but I would try my best. I'd already decided that. The look on Faulk's face if I passed would be worth it. The car door swung open, and I took that as my cue to pull the blindfold from my face and get out.

I blinked as I adjusted to the filtered light.

There was no one there. *Actually,* there was no one *visibly* there. But I knew I was being watched as I stepped from the car and into a shady forest. The leaves were a hodgepodge of color. Some still held onto their green, but many were alight with the fire of fall. Brilliant orange, red, yellow, and pink surrounded me on all sides, interspersed with pine trees that gave off a comforting scent. I did allow myself to relax. I spotted a piece of white paper tacked to one of the trees. It contrasted so sharply from the rest of the scene that it stood out like water in the desert. I strode over, pulled it down, and read.

She's lost. You have one hour to find her. Take the amethyst at your feet and venture into the unknown forest. If you fail, she will stay lost.

The moment I finished reading the cryptic instructions, the car's engine turned on, and the vehicle backed out of the alcove and sped away. I peered around, and a chill prickled up my spine. *Maybe I really am alone.* I reached down to palm the crystal. The second it touched my fingers I heard it. A girl screamed.

I dropped the stone.

Frantically, I looked side to side. Nothing. My heart kicked up a notch as I picked up the stone again. Another scream pierced my ears. That's when I realized what was happening to me. *The purple alchemy is working.* That girl wasn't anywhere near, but I'd either heard her telepathically or glimpsed the future. I studied the stone in my hand, willing it to work again.

Nothing happened. *Seriously? Don't do this to me now!*

I stared hard at multiple hiking trails that led into the forest, wondering which to take. I squeeze the stone again. It was about the size of my fist, deep purple at the base and light purple at the tips, a jagged stone I could only describe as beautiful. Amethyst. The same stone Lily Mason used. I took a deep breath and pulled a wisp of color from it. It danced in the air for moment. I willed the color to enter my body. But it only poured back into the stone. Frustrated with little time, I picked the least worn of the three hiking paths and followed it.

I passed the stone back and forth between my hands and charged my way along the trail. Rocks jutted from the dirt floor. Weeds and tree branches brushed me on all sides. It was slow moving. I wondered if I should've chosen an easier one. This one seemed fruitless. I began to doubt I would find the person, the girl who needed my help, without the purple alchemy. I couldn't get it to work again. But what else was I supposed to do besides keep going? It wasn't like I was going to sit this one out. I had to try.

After a few minutes, I stopped to catch my breath and stared at the crystal again. I cleared my mind and relaxed as best I could. I tried not to imagine wild animals stalking me or what could be making all the cracking noises that came with the territory of a forest terrain. I allowed the sound of trickling water nearby to calm me. I focused on that and slowed my breathing. After a few moments of peace, I imagined the purple color of the stone seeping into my hands without opening my eyes.

An image flashed through my mind.

She was young, definitely close to Lacey's age. Her blond hair hung across her knees as she sat on the ground. Her face was buried against those knees, and she rocked with sobs. She sat against a tree trunk. There was nothing distinctive about her surroundings, other than that she was in this same forest. The image began to blur before fading to black.

I opened my eyes, trying to hold the image.

Who was she? A tiny voice of doubt rang through my mind. *Lacey?* But it couldn't be. Lacey was safe. She was with Mom and Dad, up north. New Colony had no clue as to her whereabouts. King Richard was only pretending to have them in his custody. He didn't know what I knew.

So who was this girl? Someone who looked like Lacey. A trick? My chest burned at the idea.

I pictured her sad little body, crying. It didn't matter who she was. I still had to find and help her. What had that note said?

If you fail, she will stay lost.

Would they really hurt an innocent girl, a girl who couldn't be more than six or seven years old, because of me? I wasn't sure, but either way, it lit a fire under me, and I started to run down the trail, hacking at the foliage in my way as I went. *Where is she?* I squeezed the amethyst so tightly the edges dug painfully into my palms. *Come on, please. Show me something!*

I was in the middle of nowhere, and so was this girl. She could be anywhere. I had to get this magic to work!

Please help me, a young choking cry sounded in my head.

"Where are you?" I whispered. Maybe she could hear me too?

Please help me.

Are you hurt? I asked, this time in my mind.

Please...

I listened to her thoughts, but she couldn't hear mine. I concentrated harder, pulling the images she saw into my mind. Trees. Just stupid trees everywhere.

I had an idea. *Water. Listen for water on her end.*

I stopped running and closed my eyes, hoping if I could see from her point of view, I could hear too. I could faintly make out the image of her huddled under a tree. But there was water. I could just hear it over the sound of her crying. It was close to her.

Okay. Sweetie, I'm going to find you. I said the words in my mind, hoping she could hear me. *My name is Jessa. I'm a teenage girl dressed in all black, and I have brown hair in a ponytail. If you see me, call my name. I'm here to help you.*

I need help. I'm lost. The voice an echo in my mind.

I'm coming, I responded. Maybe she'd heard everything I said and had responded? Part of me clung to that, convincing myself it wasn't coincidence, while the other part believed it was wishful thinking.

I took off, heading toward the sound of water. I wasn't sure how much of the hour I had left. I didn't know how far the girl was. But I had a fighting chance at saving her and passing the test. I'd give it everything.

Less than a minute later, I stood at the edge of the water. It looked almost the same here as it did in my vision. That was a good sign. How many streams could be up here that looked like that? I hoped for both our sakes there was only one. I took off at a run along the riverbank, half stumbling as I ran. I didn't trust Officer Faulk. Knowing her, that little girl really could be in danger.

Frigid water splashed, stinging my face, as I continued to trudge along the bank. Tree branches attacked my body as I pushed them out of my way. I squeezed the purple stone harder, thanking the stars I had figured out how to use it.

No, I wasn't an oracle or anything special. I couldn't do what Lily Mason did. I wasn't seeing the future. I probably wasn't having some telekinetic conversation with the girl. But I was able to reach out and read her thoughts, *see* what she saw.

Checking back in with magic, it was easier this time to find her. She still sat where I'd asked her. But it could be anywhere. Her head popped up, and I finally got a good look at her face. I already guessed she wasn't Lacey. But it was obvious they'd chosen somebody who came pretty close in appearance. She had blue eyes and blond hair and was about six years old. They must have picked her specifically to mess with me.

I'm coming to find you, I said, reaching out to her mind. No response.

I continued up the stream, heart pounding, breaths labored, determination pounding with each step. By this point, I could see her in my mind's eye and see my own reality at the same time. Like double vision, one clear and real image, the other hazy and in my imagination. *Incredible…*

How much time did I have left? I kept going, faster than ever. But I still had no real idea where she was, and the water had drenched me, sending my body into a shivering mess. I had an idea. Blue alchemy.

Frantically, I searched around for anything blue. My best bet was a river rock, so I started there. I all but jumped into the center of the stream and began lifting rocks, foraging for anything with even a blue tint. Holding onto the amethyst in one hand and searching for a new rock in the other was no easy task.

Finally, a flash of blue caught my eye. It shimmered under the moving water. I pried it out of the riverbed and palmed it. I willed the alchemy to work. I'd only done it one other time when Reed had shown me all those months ago in my old bedroom. But it had been easy then, so I could only hope for the best.

The hazy side-image of the girl began to fade as blue alchemy took over. She was still there, but this new magic was frenetic and excited. Standing still in the stream, I allowed it to take over me. The sound of the water magnified, but I pushed past that. Beyond was the scurrying of woodland animals: squirrels, birds, and even a few deer. It was as if my mind were a camera, flying over the forest, listening to everything with blue, viewing it with purple, and sending a signal back to where I stood.

It was easily the most amazing thing I'd ever done with alchemy. But I hardly had time to congratulate myself or get caught up in the wonder of it all because I found her.

And I was right. She was upstream. That was the good news. The bad news, she was much farther than I'd anticipated. At least another mile. I didn't have a clock, but I knew my timed test was nearing the hour mark. I dropped the large blue-tinted river rock, not wanting anything to slow me down. I ran.

Catching a glimpse of golden leaves, I grabbed a few in my fist, and willed myself to be faster. The yellow took effect immediately. I'd been practicing with it so much lately that I wasn't surprised. Pride warmed me at the accomplishment. I charged through the rocks, water, and aggressive tree branches at breakneck speed. Within a few minutes, I destroyed that mile. The little girl sat just on the horizon. I sprinted the final distance to her and wrapped her in what was probably a cold, wet, uncomfortable hug. I couldn't help myself.

"I'm here!" I exclaimed, joy bursting at all my seams.

She giggled, straightening her small frame into my embrace. "Good job, Jessa. The other initiates always fail this one."

"What?" I squinted. "You're in on this too?"

"Yes." She giggled again, as if it were the funniest thing in the world. It reminded me of when Lacey tried to pull her kid-pranks on us, always so simple to us but hilarious to her.

"It's okay." She stopped laughing and smiled at me. An adorable gap spaced out her front teeth, and dimples appeared on her freckled cheeks. "You did a good job. King Richard is going to be very happy about this."

Okay, this was just weird. I sat back and looked away, all adrenaline leaving my system.

She stood and waved at someone behind me. That's when Faulk appeared. Of course. It was all a test. *I knew that.* Still, the little girl being in on it too, that was beyond annoying. Maybe it was for the best. Even if my ego was a little bruised, it would have been much worse had the kidnapping been real.

"Lost forever, huh?" I said, glaring at Faulk, mentioning the words on the note.

"Halle is one of our youngest alchemists. She's been helping us out with this test for a few years now. Something about a little girl in trouble, lost and alone in the wilderness, puts a bit of skin in the game, don't you think?" Faulk smiled, her always-orderly appearance out of place in the wilderness. She walked to Halle and the two actually high-fived!

I didn't get why anyone liked Faulk, but it seemed many alchemists did.

"I guess," I muttered. Truth was, she was right. Halle had helped me gather the urgency needed to pass this test. I glanced at the girl, too young for this messed-up game. "Thanks for your help, kiddo."

"Too bad you failed," Faulk interjected.

"What?" I gasped. "I didn't fail!"

"Yes, you did. You are two minutes over the hour. Plus, this was a purple test, and you used several other colors."

"You've got to be kidding me!"

"Rules are rules."

"I was never informed of those rules. And two minutes? That shouldn't count. Why do you hate me so much? Why don't you want me initiated?"

She stared at me coolly, giving away nothing of her intentions. "It's time to go back to the palace."

"You *wanted* me to fail," I pressed. "Why? Isn't it your job to help me succeed so I can help the kingdom? Isn't that what King Richard, *your boss*, wants? Why are you trying to stop me? It doesn't make any sense, Faulk!"

My words fell on deaf ears as I followed her and Halle to a nearby path. I charged after them, anger fueling my entire body.

She turned on me then, meeting me nose-to-nose. "You cannot be trusted. Everything about you is defiant. You've lied on more than one occasion and I don't want you in my Color Guard. You are a stain on my reputation."

"You won't even give me a chance."

"Why should I? I am on to you, Jessa Loxley. I know you're hiding something. You'd be so lucky as to fail these tests and end up institutionalized, because if you join my ranks, I will find you out. And I will destroy you."

My mouth dropped open as she turned on her heels.

Did she know I was part of the Resistance?

Glaring daggers into her back, I vowed to do everything to best that woman. I'd passed one test and failed two. I had to make orange and green successes. I had to win. There was absolutely no way I would allow them to institutionalize me. I was a powerful alchemist, and I would use that magic to do what needed to be done. In the end, I would get what I wanted and she would just have to deal with it.

As we traveled back to the palace, a shadow of doubt followed close behind.

EIGHT

LUCAS

I sat back in my chair, my hands squeezing the base, and willed myself to keep quiet. Why must my father surround himself with idiots? We were in the main boardroom in the GC wing where the royal officers worked. His top advisers sat around the table with the king at the head and me at his side. We were going over strategy. War strategy. Papers littered the oval, wooden table, maps lit the screens on the walls, and multiple rounds of coffee had long since been finished.

"Do we have any more information on the assailant?" Richard asked, referring to the gunman—the dead gunman.

"No, sir, he is not part of our system. Everything he wore was untraceable, and his assault rifle did not come from here."

"So you're telling me an outsider got past the shadow lands?"

"It appears so, Your Highness. It shouldn't have happened. He must have flown in undetected."

"Are you surprised?" I interjected. "Whoever believed the

shadow lands to be a perfect line of defense? All it takes is an aircraft with radar-jamming capabilities to get over them."

"We have constant patrols," the older man replied, his face red. He was the officer in charge of our military. A military that hadn't seen much action in decades, and in my opinion, was mostly for show. Everyone knew the alchemists were the real threat. This guy was a clown if he thought the shadow lands were uncrossable. Maybe by foot, but not by air.

"Well, your patrols aren't good enough, are they?" I shook my head.

My father sat back, studying me, a small smile playing on his lips. No doubt he thought I was following in his footsteps. Subscribing to his twisted way of thinking. *It's not that simple.*

Of course I wanted to keep our people safe. And the terrorist attack had shaken me to my core. I wanted to find out who was responsible just as much as anyone else, but I wasn't willing to lie about it. And I certainly wasn't eager to head off to war with West America, something my father was obviously gunning for. He and I both knew he'd lied when he had said that West America was responsible for Mom's death. In fact, everyone in this room probably knew by now, for one simple and glaring fact. Their previous confidant, Thomas, was down in the dungeons, waiting to be executed.

"We will figure out who did this and make them pay, Lucas," Richard said. "Rebels, foreign enemies, a resistance group, or otherwise, we'll find them. Either way, West America or not, we will be going over there."

My breath caught at his use of the word "resistance". Did he know about the group of his own citizenry, alchemists included, working to take him down? Did he suspect Jessa?

"And what about Thomas?" I asked, changing the subject back to one Richard and I had been arguing over since the day of his incarceration.

"What about him?" My father met my gaze, his eyes matching my own challenge.

"When are you going to execute him?"

"Soon."

"That's what you keep saying. But *soon* isn't good enough. He murdered Mom. The queen! He tried to pull the same control crap on me. He doesn't deserve another day of life, and you know it." The words shot out of my mouth with such venom I hardly recognized myself. But I stood by it all. That man was a traitor, a murderer, and he needed to go away. Forever. The heat rolled through my body, and I longed to take off my suit jacket. But I'd dressed professionally for a reason, and I made myself settle down into my chair.

"Like I said, son, he will die soon. In the meantime, you can trust me when I say he is wishing for death."

Trust him? How many times had he asked me to blindly trust him, only to put his own needs before mine? I was getting tired of his antics.

I held his gaze. "Like I said, father, that isn't good enough. Mom deserves justice."

There was something more going on, and I knew it had to do with red alchemy. Why else would Richard keep the man who killed his wife alive? There was no other explanation. He wanted to keep Thomas around in case he needed him. That had to be it. Thomas spelled it out for me that day I'd confronted him. He had the magic my father has been so desperately trying to cultivate for years. And if Jessa didn't work out? Thomas would be waiting, a willing plan B. But Thomas was not to be trusted, nor could I ever forget what he'd done to our family. He didn't even feel an ounce of remorse.

"You need to do it now. For her..."

Richard caught his breath, his teeth grinding. I'd pushed too hard. I didn't care. He always seemed to play this game with me, as if he liked it when I challenged him. Almost like he saw it as a leadership quality. But there was a line at which he became territorial with me, a border at which I should agree to his every opinion. Kneel down to your king and father. I knew the line well. It showed up every time my lack of respect for him became obvious.

"That's enough." He slammed his fist onto the table. The mugs clattered, and cold coffee sloshed out of one and onto the mahogany surface. It spread, brown eating the edges of one of the papers. For a man who seldom yelled, I'd caught him off guard. It was stupid. I knew better.

"I apologize, Father," I said. "You know how passionate I can be."

"Don't we all." He smiled sourly. Turning to the room, charm warmed his features. Everyone nodded in agreement.

Oh, yes. Everyone knows how the prince can get.

Faulk, who'd been uncharacteristically absent from the meeting, chose that moment to interrupt. She strode into the room with the same air she always had, completely loyal to my father and her job. She was the type of woman who demanded attention with her ambition. There were no soft bits to her, only hard edges. I suspected she purposely chose to be cold because it gave her power.

Sometimes, I thought my father was in love with her because of it.

"I have some bad news to report, Your Majesty." She said *bad* as if it were quite the opposite. "We just returned from Jessa's purple alchemy test." My body tensed.

"And?" he asked.

"She failed."

My stomach formed into a hard knot. It took every ounce

of willpower to keep my face stoic. I wanted Jessa out of this world and safe somewhere else, but as long as she was here, she needed to pass the tests. If she didn't, nothing good would come of it. She'd most likely be institutionalized, or maybe even become a prisoner downstairs.

"What happened?" I asked casually.

Faulk never took her eyes off the king as she answered. "She came close. She did use purple alchemy, it seems. But she also used blue and yellow. And she took longer than an hour to find the girl."

"Did anyone tell her not to use the other colors?" I questioned.

She didn't answer.

"But she was able to manipulate purple?" Richard asked.

"Yes, the most common way. Not quite back and forward telepathy but she did get into the girl's head."

"Well then, I hardly count this is bad news."

"But she failed."

"That may be up for discussion."

"I agree," I said, interjecting on Jessa's behalf. "If an alchemist can manipulate purple, an alchemist can manipulate purple. That's all there is to it. What other question is there? And who cares if she used other colors? From your lack of response to my question, it sounds like you didn't tell her not to do it. That's hardly fair. Plus, guardians in the field do it all the time. Maybe that should be counted as a good thing. Counted toward a pass."

"But it's not the way things are done during the tests."

"Maybe the tests need to change then," I challenged.

Faulk finally turned her steely gaze on mine, her lips in a thin line. I cocked my head at her, not willing to back down on this. She had the common sense to keep her mouth closed.

"You know what, son? I think you're right," Richard said, meeting my gaze. "Maybe it is time to change how we run these tests." He said it with a knowing tone. A glimmer of an idea brewing, perhaps? My body went rigid. What was he planning?

"That's it for now," he continued. "We'll meet again tomorrow to discuss the first attack on West America. I don't want to wait much longer. Every day we wait, the element of surprise could be taken from us."

The men and women surrounding the table stood to leave, nodding their agreements as they went. I put my head down, thinking heavily, as I followed close behind. I felt a hand on my back, and I turned. Richard. We were alone.

"I think it's time you and I had a discussion," he said.

"What are you talking about?"

"You are mighty defensive of Jessa. Some might say overly defensive of her. Are you still interested in her romantically?"

"What do you think?" It was an impulsive way to respond. Sometimes, I just couldn't help myself. I was a grown man and tired of living under the thumb of my oppressive father. He expected too much from me and gave me too little. Shouldn't I be free to love whom I wanted? I hated how complicated it was to be a prince with a king like Richard judging my every choice.

"No matter," he said. "I have arranged a party for tonight. It's time you met some eligible women. Women who will put Jessa to shame." He winked at me.

"I'm not interested," I said, pushing past him on my way to the door.

"Get interested, or your little girlfriend will be removed from the palace." I stopped, slowly turning back to him. There were other places in the kingdom they could train alchemists. Other places she could go. Worse places. Was it worth it to challenge him?

Taking in his firm expression, I decided to back off. He reached a hand around me and against the door. He clearly wanted to talk candidly.

Give him this, I had to warn myself

"Fine." I smiled. Fake, of course. "Let's meet these lovely ladies and see what kind of woman you think is better than Jessa."

There wouldn't be anyone. He didn't seem to agree. Instead, he raised an eyebrow, clearly amused by the whole situation.

He pushed the door open and nodded for me to leave. "That's my boy."

I stormed into the hall, my heels clipping as I walked. The depression from the last several weeks descended on me then, thick and heavy. I hadn't saved my mom. I hadn't gotten through to Richard about Thomas. I hadn't convinced Jessa to leave the Resistance. And now I had to deal with my father's disapproval at Jessa being a part of my life. I couldn't win.

I ground my teeth, lost in tumultuous thoughts that only spiraled into darkness. I couldn't lose everything, but I was so close to that edge.

●

I didn't have a chance to connect with Jessa. I'd spent hours going over things in my head. I still didn't have any solutions. I needed to talk to Jessa, so I'd gone to our usual spot in the greenhouse, but she wasn't there. I'd even gotten desperate enough to knock on her dorm door. No one had answered. I resigned to the fact that she wanted to be alone, recovering from the purple test failure. I hated the image that conjured in my mind. I should be able to comfort the woman I loved. Everything was falling apart, and the fact that I was hopeless to stop it was destroying me.

Straightening my tux, I gritted my teeth and entered the ornate ballroom. Immediately, I looked for her. But there were no alchemists in attendance. Relief washed over me. Good. She didn't deserve to witness the ridiculous spectacle that was about to take place. I took it all in: the people, the white linens, and tables overflowing with flowers and food. This was the last place I wanted to be.

The room was filled with New Colony's nobility. Only the most powerful and respected families had been invited to this event. It made for a smaller party, smaller than what we were used to. But in light of recent events, it probably made us all safer. Many women sauntered around the room with glasses of wine and champagne. The service staff carried trays of hors d'oeuvres and drinks. Everyone was dressed to impress. The younger women wore more revealing dresses than their mothers—all legs and cleavage and open backs, showing skin to get my attention. They had high hopes of catching a crown with this prince. To them, it was status that mattered most. I was good-looking and women liked that. Still, that was only a bonus. The crown was what everyone wanted most.

My father sat on his throne overseeing the party. I hated that thing. He loved it. It was made of cherry wood and red padded seats, raised on a platform at the far end of the room. Laughter and music filled the space, and a line of people were at his feet, waiting their turn to greet him. He caught my eye, and the laser focus of his gaze issued a challenge: behave and do what he wanted, or else.

Better get this over with…

"I don't believe we've met," I said to the closest woman who looked like she was here to *get to know me*. She was dressed in a skin-tight, black halter-top dress with an open back that left little to the imagination. Sleek red hair was tamed to perfection and an ungodly amount of black makeup was applied expertly around her green eyes. She was gorgeous. So what?

"Your Royal Majesty," the woman replied with a coy smile. "I am Celia Addington, only child of the Duke and Duchess Addington. I'm embarrassed to say we've met before."

"I'm sure I would've remembered you," I replied politely. That wasn't always true. I was used to women throwing themselves at me. It had been a normal occurrence ever since I hit puberty.

"Oh, we've met." She winked.

"Right," I responded dryly.

I stopped returning the attention pretty soon after I realized what these women and their parents were really after. An unplanned pregnancy was probably top of most of their lists, but it was bottom of mine. Some of them would do anything to trap the prince. The nobility of the kingdom lived in better conditions than anyone else. They really didn't have room for complaint. But ambition ran in their blood—they were the descendants of the families who had helped put the Hearts on the throne, after all. For their service, they'd become the Dukes and Duchesses, Counts and Countesses, and all other forms of New Colony nobility. It was all part of the fun of living with a monarchy.

The woman was still hovering, expectant.

"I apologize. Please, dance with me and let me make it up to you." I caught the approving eye of my father as I pulled her into a waltz. Ballroom dance had been just another class with another tutor, but I was an expert. I held her close, her name already forgotten, and tried to ignore the envious looks. This wasn't a typical party like the alchemists had—theirs were a little more relaxed and fun. No, this was a parade for the court, to remind everyone how special we all were. It was also a total farce.

After the dance with the redhead, I found a brunette. Same dance. Same show. This one was named Harlow something-or-other. Then it was onto a couple of blondes and back to another brunette. Each dance started with a little bit of flirtation and ended with a swift kiss on the hand and a quick cold shoulder. Onto the next and the next I went. Only because my father was watching the entire thing. This was what he wanted. For me to meet the kingdom's most eligible bachelorettes. By giving them each a few minutes of my time, I could meet them all, prove I wasn't interested in any of them, and get on with my life.

Prince or not, I wasn't going to allow my father to arrange my marriage. I would do what he wanted, flirt with the right girls, maybe lead a few on until I figured out how to get Jessa in my life permanently. Until that day, I would stay "single" as long as possible. In my mind, all I ever saw, all I wanted to see, was Jessa. *She is the one.*

My father stood and the music slowed and then stopped. Everyone bowed as his bellowing voice filled the room. *Here we go again...*

"My friends, I am delighted that you could be with us tonight. I hope you are enjoying yourselves," Richard said. The crowd quieted at his voice, enraptured as he began his speech. "As you know, our great kingdom has been attacked. Twice. As we speak, our military and our Guardians of Color are gathering their forces and preparing to attack West America. We will take back what is ours!" The crowd cheered. "Keep your eyes open. Report anything suspicious to the proper authorities immediately. Traitors will be punished to the fullest extent of the law, and if found guilty, they will be executed." I clenched my fists, knowing full well that Thomas was below us as we danced. He was the biggest traitor of all, killing the queen, and he was not dead.

It made no sense. A flash of memory played in my mind. The way he'd tried to blame Jessa for his crimes. My mother's dead body. She'd been struggling with excruciatingly painful migraines for years leading up to her death! Heat poured over me just thinking about it. *He will pay. Be patient, Lucas. You'll find a way to end him.*

My father's playful tone pulled me back to the present moment. "I hope you and your beautiful daughters take this time to relax before the battle ahead. Please, loosen up my son a bit, will you?" Everyone laughed, and the girls of the court giggled and shot me their most flirtatious smiles. "I don't know about you, but I think it's about time we had some merriment in this kingdom. My late wife, God rest her soul, wanted nothing in the world more than she wanted grandchildren." I shifted, uncomfortable with where this was headed. "I'm an old man. I don't plan on ever marrying again. However, it is my hope that we shall celebrate a royal wedding very soon."

I didn't often blush, but heat blossomed on my cheeks. *What in the world does he think he's doing?*

"My son, so he has told me, is ready for a serious relationship," Richard continued, a mischievous ring to his tone. He was using my feelings for Jessa against me, acting like it was all a big joke. "It is my deepest wish that he finds a bride in this very room." A gasp of excitement rippled through the party as more applause broke out.

I glared at him for a brief moment before pasting a fake smile on my face and nodding. I was ready for a relationship all right—with a certain dark-haired, blue-eyed alchemist.

Not a woman in this room. This was low. "Thank you, Father." I laughed, going along with the game. For Jessa's sake, and her sake only, I needed to keep my mouth shut. Because he knew how I felt about her. Because he'd threatened to send her away from me. Instead, I said, "I am sure I will choose the most worthy girl in this *palace*." My words carefully constructed to dig back at him.

He paused for only a moment. "As you were."

With the flick of his wrist, the party resumed, the atmosphere now entirely different. There was nothing fun about the hungry scent of ambition suffocating the Godforsaken ballroom.

I danced with more women than I could count. Probably between twenty-five and thirty, all within a few years of my age. Most too young to be considering marriage. Even I was too young for that. It didn't matter. They didn't care about me. Not one person in that room bothered to ask me how I felt about it.

It was all for show. I wouldn't be making any of these girls a queen. My father may be good at manipulating people. He may even be good at manipulating me. But he could not force me to marry.

Hours later, the last of the guests finally shuffled out the doors. I retreated from the ballroom. *Forget this. I just want to find my girl.*

Not that I needed reminding of how I loved her and she was the only one for me. But something about dancing with others left a hole in my chest that only she could fill. The first place I checked was her dorm room, but once again she wasn't there. She must be feeling dejected after the purple test, but she couldn't hide away forever. I didn't think I could give her any more space. I needed to see her. To hold her and kiss her and forget about this night.

But when she wasn't in our regular greenhouse spot either, or anywhere else in the public guardian areas, I had no choice. Time to give up. Frustrated, I headed back toward the royal wing of the palace. It had been a long day and an even longer night, and the exhaustion was beginning to wear on me. All I wanted was my bed and my dark cool bedroom.

The usual guards were standing outside the doors to our suite. But the added sight of a girl dressed head to toe in a black guardian outfit made my heart hammer. *Okay, I'm awake!*

"Jessa." My body swallowed hers in a tight hug. She fit so perfectly in my arms, like she belonged there. She *did* belong there. "I've been looking for you all day. I'm so glad you're here. You have no idea the hell I just endured."

"Sorry. It wasn't my best day ever, but I'm over it now and I wanted to see you. I know it's stupid for me to come and find you here."

"It's fine. Do you know where I've been tonight?"

"No."

I hated telling her; it would hurt her. But she hated secrets more. "My father threw a party for me. Well, not *for* me, but because of me."

"What for?"

"He had all of the most important families parade their daughters."

"For you?" She stepped back, her nose scrunching in annoyance. She bit her lip, and I was about ready to end the conversation there.

"Yes. Kind of. I never asked for it. It was for everyone but me. It was for him." I took her hand and led her around the hallway corner and into a nearby alcove. It was after midnight and we were shrouded in shadows. It was dangerous, and, of course, those guards outside our wing could find us easily.

But I figured by now all of the families had left the palace. Richard was probably in bed.

I kissed her, long and hard. She returned the kiss, equally invested.

"What are you saying?" Jessa whispered in a low voice, pulling back.

I might as well come out with it. "He wants me to get engaged to one of them."

In the darkness, I could barely make out her face to gauge how upset she was. A small "Oh" passed her lips, and then she crumbled.

"It's not like that," I assured her, grabbing her hands. "You know how I feel about you. I won't go through with it."

"Are you ready to get married?" she whispered.

Was I? We were young, too young to be married. But it was different with royalty. There was a certain level of obligation to the country when it came to our marriages. I would be allowed to be a bachelor for a while. But before long I would have to have children. It was crazy to think about it, but it was the truth. It was how things were done. I wasn't ready for kids. And marriage also seemed wrong at only eighteen. But when I looked at the girl before me, I felt calm about everything. She made me feel like when the time came, if she were at my side, it would be a happy day. More than happy. She made me feel like maybe marriage wasn't such a bad thing.

A group of people approached, my father among them.

He walked down the hallway, talking to some advisor or other, laughing together. His laugh had an addictive quality. There was something about him that made people want to believe in him. A charisma that pulled others into his orbit. Made them want to follow him anywhere. Even into war. And if they didn't? Well, they had magic for that.

Jessa shoved me from our hidden shadow and out into the hallway before Richard could see me. He was engaged in conversation, and it took him a moment to notice me standing there. When he sauntered over, he was grinning like he'd done me some huge favor.

"Well done, son."

"Thanks," I replied coolly.

"You had those women practically eating out of your hand." He turned to his advisor, a mousy man I couldn't remember the name of at the moment. "He's always had a way with the ladies. Quite a scoundrel, this boy," he joked. "Time he settled down."

I grimaced, knowing this was the last conversation Jessa needed to be eavesdropping on. "I was only playing my part," I said between gritted teeth.

They both laughed. "You loved every minute."

"No. We need to talk about what happened tonight."

"You're quite right about that. Which one of those girls did you like best?" He smiled conspiringly. Who was this man? I was so unused to seeing him so...happy.

"Are you drunk?"

He bellowed, "Not at all. Okay, maybe a little. I'm just pleased with you, son. For once you didn't fight me on something. And with a looming engagement on everyone's mind, it will make the things we're about to do much easier."

"What things?"

"War. Among other things."

"What other things?" I pressed.

"I've decided to go ahead and expand the shadow lands. We'll see what the west thinks of us once we start draining their resources." He said it in the same tone he'd used when planning my future engagement. The thought of literally destroying land, *forever*, made him happy. What was wrong with this man?

I shook my head. "Are you sure you want to do that? It's such a waste. You know the shadow lands can't be reversed."

"It will be to our advantage."

"But if you really believe we're going to take over West America, then it makes for pretty inconvenient land for the future of New Colony."

"Sacrifices must be made. Don't question me, son," he continued. "Anyway, you never answered my question. Which girl do you prefer?"

"You talk of them like they are cattle. Of course I won't take any of them. You already know who I prefer."

We stood toe to toe. All joy drained from his face, turning it from red to white, then red again. He didn't scare me.

"What don't you understand, Lucas? You need to cut it off with that...*thing*. Alchemists are unnatural. Do not get attached."

"Too late," I challenged.

He shook his head. "I've been doing this job for a very long time. Trust me when I say I know what is best in the future queen. Leave the alchemist alone and date somebody appropriate. If you don't, I will do as I've said. I will remove her from your presence, from this palace. Don't tempt me any further."

With that final threat, he swept from the hallway, pulled the large set of doors open, and retreated into our home. His advisor scurried behind him and shut the doors before I could utter another word.

Worry washed over me as I moved back toward our hiding place.

Jessa stepped out from the shadows. Tears ran down her cheeks, and I nearly punched the wall.

"I have to go." She pushed me aside.

"I don't agree with him. You know that. I'll do anything for you."

"I can't talk about this right now," she choked.

"Please, Jessa. I'm with *you*. Don't you trust me?"

She didn't answer. She just rushed away, never once looking over her shoulder. Never once stopping to think that maybe this was hurting me just as much as it was hurting her.

My world grew a shade darker.

NINE
SASHA

They are still prisoners.

The new recruits were out of prison or wherever West America had put them, but they were not free. I eyed Mastin warily. Trying to ignore someone like that wasn't easy. He was so intense. Always watching as I trained the new alchemists, those green eyes never missing a thing. His posture appeared relaxed, but he wasn't really. He was always ready to pounce. And the worst part? He had a gun.

Guns weren't easy to come by out here, and they made most people a little more than uncomfortable.

"I don't get this," one of the recruits said loudly with a haughty pout. She was that preteen age that made her attitude *extra special*.

We were working on yellow and green the most. I didn't have time to teach them everything, so I'd prioritized the easiest colors—which also happened to be useful in battle. Even then, things weren't going that well. I wasn't a miracle worker. I couldn't teach inexperienced alchemists everything overnight. Most of them spent more time looking over their shoulders than paying attention to me.

"This is hard," the preteen girl continued. "Why does it even matter, anyway?"

I figured if these people were going to fight, they'd need to know how to have extra strength and speed and how to heal wounds. Everything else would have to wait. It was such a disadvantage, but what was I supposed to say to her? The whole thing seemed ridiculous to me too.

"Remind me of your name?" I asked as I walked through the clearing of trees to stand at her side. She was one of the alchemists having the most trouble. It didn't surprise me. I stared up at the sky for a moment, the problem grating on me. With the exception of Jessa, the older you were when you got started as an alchemist, the harder it was going to be. Most of the people here were adults, and truth be told, they weren't great. But there were teens and even younger ones as well, yet they weren't doing so hot either.

"Sam," she sighed. "I've never done this before. Never really had the chance to try."

"When did they catch you?" We both glanced over at Mastin.

"When I was seven. I'm thirteen now."

It struck a chord with me and I stiffened, meeting her gaze. I remembered those years of my life and how hard they were. I could only imagine what she'd been through in a country where her very existence was illegal. The girl was timid, with black hair hanging in her eyes and a lanky frame. I turned her away from Mastin, putting both our backs to him, and whispered, "What did they do to you?"

"They locked me up and threw away the key. What else? I was shocked when they brought me here. I'm not complaining, but when they took us from the prison, they didn't tell us where we were going. Part of me hoped I'd get to see my family again. I mean, we're not like your country. We don't have cruel and unusual punishment, so it's not like I *never* got to see my family. We get visits every couple of months if we have good behavior. But when they came to get me, I hoped that maybe I was going home. Not out in the middle of nowhere to train in alchemy." Her entire body deflated. "I'm so stupid."

"Hey, I don't ever want to hear you call yourself names again," I said, wagging a finger at the kid. "Do you understand?" She nodded. "You're not stupid. And being an alchemist is a gift. *They* are the ones who made your existence illegal. That's not your fault."

I suspected part of the problem this girl was having with controlling her magic was that she had a deep-rooted fear of being punished. Her country had isolated her for who she was. They did nothing to help her. So it was no wonder she was repressing her magic now. If my theory was right, it explained the issues I was having training these people.

"All right, everybody," I yelled, stepping away from Sam. "Who is struggling with these colors? Raise your hands, please."

A sea of hands shot up. The mutterings stopped as they turned to face me.

"You do not have to hide who you are here," I boldly declared. I stood tall, my straight hair swept back in a ponytail. Dressed in black, I hoped I looked fierce. Hoped they would believe I was the kind of person who didn't mess around. "The time for fearing your magic is over. We are *not* in West America anymore. And if we are successful in beating New Colony, you will not have to return to your prison cells."

An audible gasp sounded as, one by one, they took in the news. It had been my one requirement for training these people. The last couple of weeks hadn't been easy. When I'd first agreed to do this, Cole said that any New Colony alchemists would be welcomed into West America. It had taken some pressure, but I'd finally convinced the West American commander to extend that promise to his own people as well. He'd gotten the order signed from their president.

West America had better keep their promise or there would be hell to pay. It terrified me to think we could be going from one tyranny right into another. But I was learning to trust. And I was at the point where I didn't see any other options.

"Isn't that right, Mastin?"

We all turned to face the military man. He bristled. He hadn't wanted the deal to be made and had zero qualms about fighting for his beliefs. Alchemy was dangerous and needed to be kept away from regular society. That's how he felt, and he wasn't about to change his mind any time soon. Prick.

But their president was desperate and she was willing to see reason when he wouldn't. From what I gathered talking to Cole, the rest of their country was trending toward her beliefs as well. Everything there worked in a voting system. People voted for representatives who believed in what they did, and those representatives made the law. Apparently, the last election had caused some major upheaval, as many of those elected were outspoken in their sympathy toward color alchemists.

Mastin's firm line of a mouth twitched as I taunted him. "That's right," he said, eyes boring into mine. "It's been confirmed by the president herself just last night." He glared at me, because we both knew how much he hated that I'd won.

"And I will get the proof you need next time I see the commander," I said, taking in the many excited faces.

"The deal is, if you help us we'll pardon you," Mastin said.

"So here's the thing," I added. "You can help them and earn that freedom. You all can do this. I feel like most of you are holding back your powers because of your fear of the consequences, and the problem with keeping it in is the longer it stays inside, one of two things is going to happen. Your magic is either going to become weak and useless, or it's going to grow inside of you until it becomes dangerous."

I turned on Mastin. "I bet you didn't know that by keeping these people from their gifts out of your own ignorance, you've only made them more dangerous?"

He didn't respond. He didn't even move, his eyes narrowing to slits as he glared at me. But from the flash I saw there, I thought maybe he *did* know.

"Fine. Let's get back to work."

I had everyone using the yellow leaves to build up their strength. We'd gone farther into the forest than usual. There was plenty of space to do what needed to be done. The trees surrounded us on all sides, the sky bright blue and cloudless, the air crisp as an apple. I took in a deep breath before continuing.

"Take the yellow into your palms and imagine the color seeping into your body. Feel the adrenaline in your veins. Let it take over." I watched proudly when quite a few of them pulled the yellow and did as I'd asked. "We're going to try some things you've never done before. There's nothing to be afraid of. You're so much stronger than you imagine. Once you have the magic inside, I want you to pick a tree and climb it as fast as possible."

There was a moment of hesitation, and then one by one, they climbed. And they were fast. Smooth. Feline in their ascent, jumping from branch to branch, swinging upward, not a clumsy movement among them.

Not too bad, if I do say so myself.

I strolled over to Mastin and nudged him playfully with my elbow. "Well it's not nothing? Are you jealous?" I don't know why I taunted him like that. Something about this guy made me want to play the devil's advocate. I shouldn't even care. His jaw clicked, but as was his way, he stayed quiet and pensive. I turned back toward the alchemists.

"If you can still feel the magic inside of you, even just a drop, then jump to the ground," I called out.

"Don't do anything to hurt my people," Mastin growled under his breath.

"Oh, so now you're protective of them?" I folded my arms.

"You'll be fine! I promise!" I yelled toward the trees, ignoring him. After a couple of bodies flew down and landed in a safe crouch on the forest floor, the rest followed. His eyes widened, but he kept his mouth shut. If he was impressed, he certainly didn't show it.

"I know what I'm doing here," I said to Mastin. "My question is, what are you doing here?"

"My job."

I snorted and left him standing on the sidelines as I joined the new recruits. I clapped, beaming from ear to ear. We'd been at this for a while with little to no success. But I'd been right to press the issue on their freedom. Once they knew there weren't going to be dire repercussions for using their magic, *bam!* Magic in every last one of them.

"Okay, friends, I'm proud of you," I said, corralling them around me. "But that was just the beginning—child's play. Who's ready to get to work?"

●

I rolled the last bit of my dinner roll between my fingers and thumb, then plopped it in my mouth.

"Good job today," Mastin said, keeping pace with me as I skittered down the hill. "Looks like you finally got through to them."

"Yeah, no thanks to you." My stomach full, I was heading back to the cabin I shared with the other female misfits. The sun was already setting, casting a golden shadow through the woods. It was my favorite time of day.

"What's that supposed to mean?"

"Were you dropped on your head as a child?" I stopped to glower at him, and he almost careened into me. Was he serious? He really didn't know what the problem was? "They're scared of you, Mastin. Terrified! You come to all of our practices and stare everyone down. You've always got a gun on you. You're not one of them. You've made it clear you hate alchemy. I mean, hello? You're policing them! It would make anybody nervous."

"I'm just doing my job." He frowned, folding his arms. His biceps pulsed.

"Well, I'm trying to do mine. It would be a lot easier if you stopped coming around."

"Not gonna happen."

"So you're policing me too?"

He held my gaze, his green eyes catching the sunset, turning them the shade of a newly turned leaf in spring. A flame ignited in my chest, and I stomped away. *Forget him.* I was exhausted. I needed a good book and my bed. Fiction was hard to come by in New Colony. Most of the books the citizens had access to were state-issued propaganda. Here? It was a different story. A gloriously different story, no pun intended. I'd devoured everything in our makeshift library more than once over the years. Now with a paperback of

The Giver snug in my back pocket, I delighted in the fact I had the freedom again to read whatever I wanted. I took off down the hill.

"Hey, wait up," Mastin said, catching up.

"You're still here?" His normally stoic expression flinched, and I smiled to myself conspiratorially. It was fun toying with his emotions.

"I wanted to talk to you about something."

"Talk away," I said.

"It's probably best if we discussed this—*issue*—in private."

"I'm not inviting you into my room if that's what you're trying to get at." I eyed him suspiciously. He turned on me, his face incredulous. I shrugged.

"I don't like you like that," he said.

I shrugged again. "I'm used to men hitting on me," I replied. It came in handy when I needed to use my looks to my advantage. I'd certainly used it with Lucas—while I could, anyway. But there were many times that it drove me crazy. Tristan was my only male friend even remotely close to my age. He'd never once come onto me. Probably because he understood the same thing I did. There wasn't time for romantic entanglements.

"You think you're pretty special, don't you?" Mastin met my gaze.

I rolled my eyes. "Takes one to know one," I said and laughed, lightening the mood. "Fine," I added. "Let me grab a jacket and we can go to the lake." It was private enough that we could talk. There weren't many alchemists here with access to blue to the point of being able to eavesdrop. We'd be fine.

I ran into the cabin I shared with the other women, women who ignored my existence, and headed into my small private bedroom. I grabbed a black hooded sweatshirt from my drawer and sped right back out.

Mastin waited for me, always looking so out of place in his military getup. We walked for a bit until we found a patch of soft grass to sit on by the lake. The sunset was magnificent over the water, turning the sky a brilliant fuchsia and reflecting against the barrage of autumn-kissed trees. "I've been here for years, and I still can't get enough of that view," I said, sighing.

"It's amazing. But nothing compared to the sunset over the Pacific Ocean."

"Always trying to one-up me," I teased. He laughed. He had a good laugh. Hearty. It made his hard edges softer and he seemed less…untouchable.

He should do that more often.

"So the Pacific Ocean, huh? What's it like back home?"

"West America, as you call it, is beautiful. And big. We still call ourselves America, by the way. New Colony gave us that name. Anyway, it's not bad at all. Democracy slows things down sometimes, sure, I can admit that. But overall the people are happy, and we take care of our own." He leaned back on his elbows, lost in thought. "We're free. We can pursue whatever careers we want. We can vote. We can do a lot of things others can't."

I pondered that for a minute, picking at the grass. "I'm in hiding, obviously, but I'm more free here than I ever was before. New Colony is *not* free. The government controls everything. Where a family lives, what jobs they're allowed to have, schools, food, pretty much everything. Some people have a great life because of it. Most people have it okay. And then there are those few who are treated like garbage. Or, you know, those of us lucky enough to be forced into the guardian program."

"What happened to you?"

I paused. I wasn't ready to share my story with this guy. He was still a stranger, an unknown. "What did you want to talk to me about?" I asked, changing the subject.

He let out a slow breath. "We received word that King Richard is planning an attack on America soon. We're not exactly sure what or when. We do know, however, that he plans to extend more shadow lands into our territories. We need to act fast if we want to stop him."

It took me a moment to answer, the images of my childhood burned on my mind. "That's some bad news, Mastin. So what are your plans?"

"Take our alchemists and some soldiers into New Colony and fight him."

I sat back, gazing at him. He was serious. How could he be serious? "Are you kidding? That's suicide. They're not even close to being ready."

"That's why I wanted to talk to you. How long?"

I shook my head. "Too long!"

"You don't get it, Sasha. Cole is going to make the order with or without your support."

"Wow, he must really care about them," I said, each word dripping in sarcasm. I shook my head. "Fighting the GC would be impossible. They've trained for years, not only in alchemy, but in combat too. They're deadly. Your people are toddlers compared to that."

"But our soldiers are the best. And I'll be there too."

"It's still a terrible idea."

"Will you come with us?"

"On a suicide mission? No thanks. I think I'll keep my life, if you don't mind." I couldn't believe this. No way could a bunch of uneducated newbie alchemists take on an army of guardians.

"We really need your help. We're going in with or without

you. But I'm smart enough to know we don't stand a chance if you don't come. I've been watching the way they look up to you. They seek you out outside of training. They ask you questions. They trust you, Sasha. And I've seen what you can do."

I laughed because what he'd seen had barely even scratched the surfaced of what magic I was capable of. "Mastin, you don't understand, so please listen to me. I pale in comparison to some of those guardians in New Colony. They would kill me. They'll kill you! You have no idea what you're asking of me."

"Then at least help me delay the attack." His expression shifted, and he talked softly. "Help me convince Cole to wait a little while longer. At least so they can get some more training from you."

I jolted. Mastin always came off as so cocky. To humble himself in this way was disarming. I could tell he wasn't scared to fight. Or he at least had that soldier thing about him that kept it inside. But he was worried for his people and I found that admirable. Maybe he wasn't such a bad guy after all.

"I'll do what I can," I sighed.

He gulped, and I could tell he wanted to say more. "Out with it," I said.

"You have no idea how much I hate to ask." He sat up, running both hands across his buzzed hair. "But is there a way to use their magic to get Cole on our side of things? We're supposed to go meet him in a few minutes."

I sucked in a breath, considering. "There's two ways I can think of to make this happen. The first is red alchemy, which if used on someone's blood, can result in mind control." I met his eyes as they stared at me intently. "But I can't do red," I was quick to add. "If you aren't going to convince your boss to be reasonable, we'll have to do it the good old-fashioned way. I'll try the blue, which can be used for persuasion. No guarantees though, it's not my specialty."

He nodded. "Thanks."

"Have you ever been to the shadow lands?"

"I've seen the pictures."

"The pictures are nothing." I tried unsuccessfully to push the images from my mind. "They're dead. As in, no coming back. If Richard's going to do that to your country, you have to do everything you can to stop him. It can't lie in the hands of a few alchemists. You need to bring more than a few soldiers. You need an army."

"We're working on it."

"Good." I nodded.

"Have you been to the shadow lands?"

"You have no idea." I laughed, but it wasn't funny. "I helped create them." He let out a shuddering breath and bored holes into me with his crazy-intense gaze.

I looked away, unable to take the heat.

"It's not like I had a choice. But I was a kid, you know? It's messed up." I couldn't hold it in any more. Something about this moment had changed, and suddenly I needed to get it out. "They took me from my family when I was tiny. They trained me. And once they realized how good I was, they took me into the field. I was six years old when I went out there. I was there for four years until Hank saved me."

"I'm sorry."

"I don't want your pity," I said. "I just want you to know who you're dealing with. They care about their own agenda more than human life. Taking children from their parents is one thing. It's heartbreaking, but it pales in comparison to what else they do. The shadow lands had people on them. Poor people. Unwanted people. Uneducated outcasts… We didn't remove those people. They were part of a test."

"They died?"

"We killed them. I killed them."

"Thank God you got out."

"I don't know if God had anything to do with it," I scoffed. I was jaded, I knew it. "Hank and Tristan, I owe them my life. Did you know Hank used to be an officer? And Tristan was an officer in training. They defected and took me with them. I'd do anything for those men. They're my family."

Why was I telling him all of this? I needed to get a grip.

"It wasn't your fault." He said the same thing so many others before him had said. I studied his face, so earnest. He believed every word. If only I could believe them too.

"I know," I said. *Doesn't change what I did.* I'd learned a long time ago it was easier to agree on this point than to argue. We sat in silence as the sky turned dark.

Mastin stood. "We'd better get back."

He reached down and pulled me up. His hands were calloused, like he'd grown up working outside. We stood inches apart—the body heat between us suddenly electric. We were still holding hands when he squeezed mine before letting it go. He cleared his throat and took a step back. Looking for a way to break the tension, I grabbed the copy of *The Giver* from the ground. It must have fallen out of my back pocket. "Can't forget this," I mumbled before taking off down the path. He didn't say anything as he followed extra closely.

I had more important things to worry about than the weird moments between us. *Stay focused on the Resistance.*

Blue alchemy. Mastin understood and agreed, which I had to admit was kind of amazing. Blue was harder to find at this time of year, but, lucky for me, I had my stone necklace I could use. I quickly retrieved it from my room before heading out to meet the others. I slid it under my shirt.

"Lead the way," I said. Mastin led us to wherever we were meeting Cole and the others. If I had to guess, I'd say Hank's cabin again. Lo and behold, after a few minutes, we sauntered up his steps. I double-checked that the necklace was hidden as we entered the living room.

"Thank you for joining us," Hank said. He didn't have that usual twinkle in his eye or smile on his lips. His wrinkles were deeper than I'd remembered, and a few extra gray hairs had cropped up on his head. This must be serious. I steeled myself and took the seat next to Cole. I needed him close so I could work this magic inconspicuously.

"Well, there's no point in beating around the bush," Cole said. "Mastin told you what King Richard plans to do in America?" I nodded. "Then you understand why we have to act quickly. We need to get in there and take him down, take them all down, while we have the chance." He was so sure of himself. He was so clueless to the real risk. It was almost comical.

Except nothing about this was funny.

"Why haven't you tried something earlier? None of this would even matter if you could just deal with the problem with brute force," Tristan said, getting up from the couch and joining us at the table.

"We did. But we failed."

I wondered what that meant, but decided not to ask and draw unwanted attention to myself. I felt the stone against my neck and glanced around the room. It was just Mastin, Hank, Tristan, Cole, and myself. No doubt Hank and Tristan would recognize blue alchemy when they saw it. Mastin wasn't putting up any fights this time. I had to do it.

"And how would you suggest this is going to work?" I asked Cole.

"Some of our best soldiers and our alchemists, along with your people, go in and take over the palace. Take the royals and top people into custody. If they put up a fight, kill them. We can't allow war just because your king has decided he wants more land."

"He's not my king," I snapped. "And how exactly are you going to take down the hundreds of alchemists and officers who also reside in the palace?"

"We have weapons. We're smart. We'll hit them before they hit us, when they least expect it. We need that element of surprise."

I agreed that an element of surprise would be helpful, but enough time to prepare the people they were sending in was more important. And their alchemists were not ready yet, not even close.

"Give me more time," I said, making a last ditch effort to sway him without magic.

"There's no more time. As soon as I give the word, our soldiers will head this way. If all goes according to plan, we'll leave tomorrow night."

He stood. As far as he saw it, he was the one in charge here. But he didn't know whom he was dealing with. *We* were helping him, not the other way around. And we were the ones with alchemy. Whatever weapons he had at his disposal were nothing compared to magic.

I also stood. I reached out my hand and connected it with his arm. The blue alchemy was resting in my palm, barely the size of a button. Any visible trace was gone the second I connected the magic with him.

"We need more time."

He blinked several times and took a deep breath. "Okay," he conceded, "You can have more time. But we have to complete this mission soon." He appeared to be utterly

161

dazed but sure about his choices. Then, not saying another word, he left the cabin and strode out into the night. Mastin nodded at us, his eyes stressed, before he followed Cole.

The door closed and the room fell into silence.

"I'm just going to pretend I didn't see that," Hank said.

"What choice did I have? The guy is crazy. Now we have time to try to figure out how to stop this whole thing from happening."

"You shouldn't have done that," Tristan said. I turned on him, scrutinizing his words. He brushed a lock of dark hair out of his face, his expression angry.

"Are you for real right now?"

"It's time we stopped playing it safe. This is the chance we've been waiting for. If we don't take Richard down now, when will we?"

"I don't know. How about when it makes sense and doesn't put innocent lives in danger?" I couldn't believe this. Mastin, the anti-alchemist, hard-core military American soldier, saw enough reason to let me do what I just did. But my own best friend, the man who'd been through some of the same horrible things I had, the man who saw what they made me do as a kid, was siding with Cole?

"I'm going to take a little walk and let you two work this out," Hank mumbled before slipping through the door. *Coward!*

"You know as well as I do what the guardians are capable of," I sputtered, looking Tristan up and down. "You know what the king is like. How ruthless the officers are. This plan to somehow catch them off guard is stupid! Stupid, naïve, wishful thinking that will get us all killed."

Tristan pinched his lips together and glared at me. His high cheekbones and thick brows created an expression of indignation that I'd never seen him point at me before. A

162

lump formed in my throat, and I swallowed it down.

"Cole is on our side," he challenged. "You've always had a hard time with authority."

"Welcome to the club. It's not like you're any different."

He stalked closer, towering over me. He wasn't the teenager my kid-self was used to. I had to remind myself he was twenty-five now. And he was all dark. Dark eyes, skin, and hair. Add that with his Asian ancestry and a tall broad build, and he was the type of guy that made reasonable girls turn into bumbling messes. But I wasn't about to agree with nonsense.

He took a shaky breath, his voice low. "What I mean is, I feel like we can trust him."

"You're not an alchemist. That's easy for you to say."

"What other choice do we have? Honestly, sometimes—"

"What's that supposed to mean?" I cut him off. "There's always another choice. We were doing just fine on our own until those two showed up."

"Are you serious right now?" His eyes flashed. "Have we not been part of the same Resistance? Take a look around you, Sasha. Do you want to live here the rest of your life? Hiding? Is this enough for you?"

I didn't answer. The silence stretched between us.

"Because it's not for me," he finally said.

"It sure beats being a pawn. So what if we don't live in luxury? I don't care. We're free here, Tristan!"

"This isn't freedom," he grumbled. He ran his hand over the stubble on his jaw, shaking his head. I was just some idiotic, nineteen-year-old girl he'd babied all these years. He didn't see me as his equal. "What did you say?" he asked.

Oops. I must have said some of that out loud! "I'm not a child. I'm not stupid. I'm a grown woman with opinions of my own. Maybe it hasn't occurred to you, but it could be

163

possible that I have a better grasp on the situation than you do."

"And using blue alchemy on a West American general is mature?"

Heat flooded my cheeks.

"I'll have you know," I said, "it was Mastin's idea."

"Great! So you trust Mastin more than you trust me now?" A flash of pain ignited in his ebony eyes.

"It's not that I trust Mastin more than you," I snapped. "It's just that he happens to listen to good ideas."

He stalked toward me and his body filled every inch of my personal space. "It's not a good idea to sit on this opportunity. We need to move out as soon as possible. But I guess you and your new boyfriend decided to use magic to get your way."

"He's not my boyfriend. Don't be ridiculous."

"And you don't think your good looks have anything to do with him being so nice to you?"

"No. It's the fact that I'm an amazing alchemist who could teach the boy a thing or two about how to kick New Colony trash."

He laughed. "Whatever, Frankie, keep telling yourself that." He slipped in my old name, my real name, and I flinched. It brought back so much history, that name. History he was an intricate part of.

He paused in front of me, only inches away, and stared down at my face. The tension grew thick. "Just for the record, I like you for *you*, not for what you can do for me. Not for your looks. Not for anything other than for who you are on the inside." He stepped back. Just as he reached the door, he turned back. "And believe me, I know you're not a little girl anymore." His eyes bored into mine, searching for something. He must not have found what he was looking for, because a moment later, he stormed through the door, slamming it behind him.

I unclenched angry fists and fought the tears. I never cried, but I also never fought with Tristan. Sure, I hadn't seen him in ages, but we'd always been best friends before I left to assume my new identity. I thought we could go back to that. Now what were we?

Hank chose that moment to return. He stopped the second he entered, scratching his head and staring at me. I didn't want him to see the tears pooling in my eyes. I held up a hand to him. "Not now." I stormed past him and through the door, ready to get back to my room and end this night. "Be gentle with him," I heard Hank say, but I didn't look back.

It was too dark to go for a run, but my body itched for it anyway. It was my salvation, the thing that took the heavy thoughts away and gave me some space. What was going on? It almost felt like Tristan had confessed feelings for me. And there was definitely something going on with Mastin, too. I had to stop whatever was forming before something happened that I'd regret. I didn't have time or energy for this kind of distraction.

Forget it! I took off running, not caring what consequences would meet me if I fell.

TEN

JESSA

The heart-pounding exertion of combat training still wasn't enough to take my mind off Lucas. As I walked back toward my room to shower and change, I wiped the perspiration from my neck with a towel, lost in thought. Every heartbeat hurt, my chest filled with a silent dull ache. Was this heartbreak? It was a *physical* pain, and I couldn't take it anymore.

Lucas came around the corner, an expression of relief on his face when he saw me. I froze momentarily, then turned and high-tailed it toward my room.

I didn't even know if Lucas and I had broken up. A huge part of that was my fault. I was avoiding him for fear of what our next conversation would hold. For the last couple of days, anytime I saw him, I turned the other way. I didn't see the point anymore. The thoughts kept nagging at me. Why go through all the trouble to be together if, in the end, Lucas marries another girl?

The only solution put me right back to why I was in this palace in the first place. If I could help the Resistance take down the current system, then maybe Lucas and I could have a chance. Maybe.

He caught up to me just as I was about to slip into my room and lock the door.

"Jessa, we need to talk." He sighed. I turned to face him. His expression was guarded and a knowing sadness reflected in his charcoal eyes.

"Look, I really didn't want to do this," I said, beating him to the punch. "Your father will never let us be together. And the more we try to defy him, the harder it's going to be for us."

He looked away, shutting his eyes for a moment. This was dangerous, for both of us. He shouldn't be seen with me.

"Jessa, please just let me explain."

"There's nothing to explain. I get it, okay? We can't be together." I lowered my voice. "Your father is in control, and there's nothing we can do about it at the moment. He's made it crystal clear that you can't date me."

"I don't care what he says."

I peered around, exasperated. Of course there were people everywhere, stopping by their rooms between classes. They watched us curiously. What did he think he was accomplishing here? He was going to get me into trouble. "You should care," I whispered. "If you want to keep me safe, if you want me to be initiated so I can do what I came here to do, then you should care what he says."

"I'll talk to him. I'll figure something out. I won't date those women. They mean nothing to me, Jessa. You're the one I want."

I reached my hand behind me, gripping the door handle to my room with a tight fist. "While that may be well and true, it doesn't change the fact that the king forbade you to date me. You shouldn't be here right now."

"So that's it? You just give up that easily?" He leaned back on his heels, his face reddening. The skin around his eyes tightened as he stared me down, but I had to stick to my gut on this one. It was too risky for us to sneak about at the moment.

"I'm not giving up. You know how I feel about you," I said. "But what you don't seem to realize is that your father is the king, which means he's in control of my future. You heard him just as well as I did. If you don't stay away from me, then he's going to remove me from the palace. I can't let that happen. You of all people should understand why."

I didn't have to say anything more; we both knew we were talking about my mission with the Resistance. My parents were somewhere north, in hiding, and more than anything I wanted to be with them. They were counting on me.

We can't be selfish anymore.

I needed to think about the bigger mission, even if he couldn't. There was more than just my love life on the line. Lives were at stake. We were on the brink of war. If Lucas couldn't see the truth, then I would have to do it for him. Even though it ripped my heart in two. Even though it was the last thing I wanted.

"Jessa, just please meet me in our spot. We'll figure this out, I promise." He reached out to move a loose strand of hair behind my ear, and I hesitated for an excruciating moment. With a fixed resolve, I opened the door behind me and stepped back.

"I'm not giving up on us forever. Maybe one day the timing will be right for you and me. But I have to do what's best. I have to give up on us *for now*. I'm so sorry, Lucas." It took everything to meet his steel eyes and hold my gaze firm, keeping my love for him bottled inside. His face hardened, and his lips thinned, but he turned and walked away.

I slipped into my room and immediately collapsed on the floor. I allowed myself five minutes to cry. Five minutes, and then I had to be done. Then I'd find Jasmine and tell her why the Resistance couldn't put me and Lucas together anymore. I needed to move on.

●

"Another party?" I asked, gaping at the glossy invitation in Jasmine's hand. After the big to-do they just had for Lucas, I was surprised the royals were throwing another party so soon. This time it was for the alchemists. It had only been two days since the break up, and I wasn't ready to pretend to have fun. I was too busy feeling sorry for myself, I hated to admit.

"There are a lot of parties here, in case you didn't notice," Jasmine smiled. I had come to train with her in green alchemy, and we were just finishing up. "The alchemists have a gathering of this nature every few weeks." We collected the remaining pots and carried them back to the greenhouse as I listened. "It's part of the perks of living in the palace. Train hard. Play hard." Then she whispered conspiratorially, "Live in luxury and don't notice all the things we have to go without."

Like our families.

"I guess, but I don't want to go." I frowned.

"Unfortunately, this one is mandatory," Jasmine said. She'd understood my reasoning for ending things with Lucas. Once I'd explained Lucas was to be engaged soon and Richard had threatened to send me away if we spent more time together, she'd reluctantly agreed it was best to hold off on the romance. She talked about it like it wasn't real, like it was just part of the mission. But it was real for me, and I ached every day without him.

"Why is it mandatory?"

"I guess we'll have to go to find out." She smiled her usual warm smile, but I caught a glimpse of worry. "Go and get ready. I'll see you soon."

I mumbled my frustrations all the way back to my room.

After a long shower, I let my hair dry in its natural curls loose down my back. I took extra care with my makeup and even used the dark eyeliner and mascara I normally skipped. My reasoning was probably flawed and idiotic, but I figured if I had a bunch of black around my eyes it would incentivize me not to cry and ruin it. I fished around in the grooming kit that came standard in women's dorm rooms until I found crimson lipstick. I matched it to a form-fitting dress of the same color and donned black heels.

I was dressed to kill.

I'd dressed the exact opposite of how I felt on purpose. If Lucas was there tonight I didn't want him to know I was moping about, feeling sorry for myself. I couldn't risk him trying to fix things for us. As much as I wanted to be with him, I knew I had to be the smarter one in the relationship and focus on more important things.

I was late to the party. Fashionably late, I told myself. The alchemists knew how to have a good time. This affair was less polished than the first one I'd been to months ago. There wasn't food, for one thing. The lights were darker, the music louder, and the dancing a lot...closer.

Well, okay then...

Totally out of place and awkward, I made my way to the edge of the room to hide out. Why was this mandatory? Seemed like an excuse for people to indulge in too much orange infused drink and rub up against each other. Totally *not* my style. Especially not with people who hated me.

"You need to try harder to make friends," Reed said, sliding in next to me. "It will make it easier for you to be initiated if the guardians can see that you're one of us." I was trying, as per Jasmine's request. But so far, I'd not managed to make a single one.

"Easy for you to say," I groaned. "You don't even have to make an effort. People naturally want to be your friend. Everyone likes you."

"You don't like me."

I shifted to face him, noticing his tailored black suit and carefully styled hair. Maybe he did make an effort. "It's not that I don't like you, Reed. It's that I know what you did to me with the blue alchemy before. You tried to interrogate me so you could report back to your boss."

"I thought you wouldn't catch me and I could pretend it never happened," he said, eyes down casting shadows across his face. "I was selfish, and I'm really sorry about that. But I never didn't like you, just for the record. I would've gone after you whether or not Faulk had told me to befriend you."

"Sure," I mumbled.

"I swear. You don't know what it's like for us here. We have to do what we're told, even if that means hurting each other from time to time."

"That's not cool."

"No kidding." He nodded. We sat in silence for a moment, watching the crowd.

"Okay, fine, I forgive you," I said. "Tell me about something else, please? Like why is this stupid party mandatory?"

I caught his facial expression in the dim light as he chewed on his bottom lip. It was as if he was debating letting me in on a secret. "We're about to go to war. You already know that. Everyone does. My guess is this party will be the last in a while. No doubt King Richard will be out here soon to give us all a pep talk, maybe more. Faulk will be finding me in the crowd and asking me to help him with his persuasion. She always does. Like I said, I don't have a choice in these matters. I figured that out a long time ago."

"But if you did have a choice?" I asked.

"What do you mean by that?"

I shook my head and turned away. I'd said too much. Even if I could forgive Reed for his past, it didn't mean I could trust him with my secrets.

"Well, will you dance with me, or what?" He grinned.

At this point I realized I couldn't say no to that face. Or maybe I just needed to have some fun and forget about the heaviness of the last few days. "All right, show me what you got."

We moved to the dance floor, maneuvering through the crowd that pulsed to the thumping beat. I grabbed a flute of sparkling drink with an orange petal on top. I already knew what to do. I focused on building a happy feeling inside and touched the tip of my finger to the delicate flower. The orange alchemy danced into the drink, and I swallowed it in one gulp. The happy feeling swelled inside me, overpowering the pain. I welcomed it as Reed tugged me toward a group of his friends. Maybe I could have fun. It was better than crying.

I didn't allow myself to get too close to anyone. But I did dance my heart out. It wasn't the same as ballet. Nothing could beat ballet. But it felt incredible just the same. I lost myself in the thick crowd, the dark room, my eyes closed so I was cocooned from those around me. For all I knew they were glaring daggers at the weird new alchemist girl crashing their party. I didn't care. For once, I felt like myself, and I relished in that as long as I could.

"I think your boyfriend's here," a male voice shouted directly into my ear. I turned to see a dark boy with long black hair. I stepped away from him, not sure who he was. The kid just smirked and pointed behind me.

Lucas. He was brooding in the corner, looking gorgeous in dark jeans and a navy button-up shirt with the sleeves rolled up.

"He's not my boyfriend," I turned back to the guy; he was standing a little too close for comfort.

"Yeah right," he scoffed, and I shook my head before losing myself in the crowd.

What was Lucas doing here? Did he come here to check on me? Questions circled my brain. I tried to get back into the dancing, but I'd lost all the energy for it. I was officially done partying. I headed for the exit hoping my appearance at the party was enough for whatever higher powers had deemed it mandatory. Lucas caught up to me, pressing a hand to the door before I could leave.

"Please don't say anything," I said.

"Whether or not you care about me, there's something I have to tell you, Jessa. Because I care about you, and you need to hear it from me first."

I stopped. "Fine," I snarled. "Get it out so I can leave." I was being mean. But it was like some rude version of myself had taken over and was fighting back at Lucas for something that wasn't even his fault. What was wrong with me? Heartache did crazy things to people.

"I don't even know how to say this," Lucas said. He gulped as his face turned ashen in the dim light. "Things escalated very quickly this afternoon with my father. I did something I regret."

"What are you talking about? Look, Lucas, you need to stay away from me. We can't have this conversation over and over again."

He glanced around, clearly perturbed by our lack of

privacy and my response to his confusing words. Just as he was about to say something, the music stopped and a voice boomed from the other side of the room.

"Good evening, my color guardians," King Richard bellowed over the crowd. Lucas stiffened next to me.

"I have to go over there," he growled. "Jessa, why do you have to be so hard on me? I just wanted you to hear it from me first."

I didn't know what to say, but it didn't matter. He left. I watched, exhausted, as he rushed through the crowd to meet his father. His behavior reminded me of the man I'd first expected him to be, brooding and unreachable. I shook my head, frustrated at the constant battles in our relationship. No matter how much we fought for each other, there would always be some bigger reason why it wasn't going to work. I was tired of fighting.

"Oh, there he is, the engaged man himself!" Richard called.

My heart dropped as I nearly doubled over. *Did he just say engaged?*

"Aren't they a beautiful couple?" Richard continued as Lucas climbed the stage. Then he joined his son's hand with a gorgeous woman's hand and held them up to the crowd. My thoughts ran a million miles, in a million different directions. But they landed on one thing.

Was Lucas tired of fighting for us?

When Lucas glanced at the woman, he smiled his perfect smile, and I almost threw up. This was exactly why we'd broken up. Because sooner or later, I'd get hurt and he would marry some trophy socialite of Richard's choosing. I'd hoped ending things would have diminished that hurt.

Nope.

The crowed cheered, clearly excited by this news, many

of them still drunk on orange alchemy. From the blooming smile on Lucas's face, it seemed he was just as excited. Was he? I doubted it. Could it be possible that in giving up on us, he'd so easily moved his affections to a more worthy girl? I didn't want to believe it. Couldn't believe it. I knew him. Still, the nagging questions burned in the back of my mind bringing every insecurity I'd ever had to the surface.

Are we really done?

Maybe he doesn't love me anymore.

Maybe I'm too much work for him.

Maybe—

I pulled myself out of that downward spiral and focused my attention back on the stage. She was gorgeous, as to be expected. Porcelain skin and auburn hair slicked down her back. Big green eyes. Regal. She *looked* like a queen. Actually, she vaguely resembled the late queen, Natasha. I shouldn't have been surprised this was whom they picked. No doubt she came from a good family, was agreeable, well educated, and wealthy. *Not an alchemist.* All the things Richard deemed appropriate for his son.

Why had Lucas agreed to this? Surely he must be playing some other game here. I hoped…

"Thank you, Father," Lucas stepped forward to the microphone. That's when I noticed the camera crew at the front of the crowd. The media was rarely invited to the palace. And to have the alchemists and the media in one place was *extremely* rare. Practically unheard of. What was going on? "I look forward to our engagement and my future marriage to my lovely fiancée, Celia." He put his arm around her and kissed her sideways on the forehead, smiling his rakish smile. For all intents and purposes, he appeared to be a man in love. No doubt women all over the country would be mourning the loss of such a highly prized bachelor once the news broke out. I still couldn't believe it. Just two days ago we were still a couple, and tonight he was engaged.

No, there had to be a reasonable explanation. I needed to be patient until he came to me with the truth.

You should have let him talk, I chastised myself for blowing him off minutes ago. No way he'd actually go through with this marriage.

My heart ached. It was time for me to go. I pushed through the door when the king's steady voiced pulled me back into the moment. *Stupid curiosity!*

"The time has come for us to prepare for retaliation on West America. Not just for the death of our beloved queen, but for the deadly attacks during her funeral. Innocent lives were lost, and they will *not* have died in vain. I hope the news of an upcoming wedding will give us all something to look forward to as we begin the harrowing task of avenging those deaths."

War. He'd talked about it a couple of times before but never directly to the alchemists. There was no doubt about it now. We were his best weapons and this was our final warning. Get ready. The intensity in the room thickened as, one by one, the guardians stood a little taller. Sobering up, no doubt.

"It is with that happy thought," he continued, "that I must turn this conversation into something more somber." I bit back the annoyance at his use of the word "happy." Clearly, he was delusional if his idea of happy could resemble anything even close to what a war was going to look like.

"Bring him up," he said.

There was a scuffle on the side of the stage as someone was dragged onto it. At once, I recognized the man. He was dressed in gray prison scrubs and was handcuffed, his mouth gagged. Surrounded by way too many guards, there was no way for him to get away. Even if he could manage to touch the right color and use his magic, there were too many alchemists in attendance who could take him down. Still, he fought every step.

Officer Thomas.

Lucas and his fiancée had moved to the side of the stage. A thick hatred filled Lucas's eyes, almost consuming him. I'd never seen him look at anyone the way he looked at Thomas. I edged closer, around the crowd gathered at the front. First they made the party mandatory. Then Lucas announced his engagement. Finally, Richard brought Thomas out in public, in front of the media. Dread tingled up my spine. Something big was about to happen.

Richard and Lucas shared a knowing look, one I could easily read. I knew what Thomas did. But would it be revealed to the rest of the country when Richard had already announced something different at the queen's funeral?

"This man used to be an officer of the court," King Richard continued. "He was one of my father's most trusted advisors, and I admit that even I included him in my inner circle. But he is a traitor. We've discovered that he is the mole in our organization. For West America. It was only during an attempted murder on the prince that my brave son apprehended him and discovered the truth."

The crowd stirred, clearly vexed by the news. Journalists began calling out questions, but none were answered. A handful of officers knew the true story. But it seemed the truth didn't matter anymore. Not even to Lucas.

He was on the other side of Thomas from where I now stood, on the edge of the stage. He glared so intently at Thomas, it was unlikely anyone would break his gaze. But then, he met my eyes. I glowered back, not at Thomas, but at *him*. He startled.

I didn't care what his father had over him—this was too much, all of these lies. His expression softened, pained, fighting back at my own. Almost like he was willing me to understand. I shook my head and looked away. That's when I realized his depression over Natasha's death had clouded his judgment beyond anything I'd imagined. The Lucas I fell for wouldn't have let any of this happen.

"It's been ages since we had a public execution," Richard continued and the crowed hushed. "An attempt on a royal life is punishable by death. And the same goes for treason. This man has been found guilty of both. His only use to our country now is to be made an example of."

Thomas was squirming now, his old, bony body jerking. His white hair was matted to his head in perspiration. He screamed unintelligibly through his gagged mouth. The crowd mostly began to push back and out, but a few scurried closer to the stage. The cameras stayed where they were. That's when I noticed something horrible. A man dressed all in black with a mask over his face ascended to the stage. He carried a long blade. It glinted under the lights, sharp edges flashing death.

"Let this be a message to you all," Richard said, but he wasn't looking into the cameras anymore. He was staring out into the crowd, meeting the eyes of the alchemists. "This is no longer a time of peace. We are at war."

The men wrestled Thomas into a kneeling position. Someone yelled something into his ear, and he went still. I caught the words, "Or it will take more than one swing."

I clutched my stomach. I couldn't imagine the terror he must be feeling.

"There will be no mercy for traitors. If you betray this kingdom," Richard bellowed, his eyes bulging under his heavy crown, "if you betray *me*, you will die."

There was no time to turn away. Upon the king's final words, the executioner swung the axe wide. It was over in a moment, just one lethal movement. Blood splattered in a sickening arc. The body crumbled, the head rolled, then stopped a few feet away. Everything froze.

Bile rose to the back of my throat. I doubled over, sure I was going to either vomit or pass out. The message was clear. Somehow, some*way*, King Richard knew about the Resistance. He had to. And this was our warning. I'd assumed Thomas hadn't died yet because he was a red alchemist. But it seemed Richard valued loyalty more. And this? This was what his son wanted. What Lucas had been negotiating for… for weeks. When we broke up, had the pain been so intense that he thought *this* was the only way to feel better again?

Lucas still stood on the edge of the stage, comforting his bride-to-be, his lips set in a grim line, blood speckling his body. He didn't reach up to wipe it off his face. He remained motionless, glaring at what was left of Thomas.

Was it worth it?

His gaze landed on me then, as if he could hear my question. With an indecipherable shake of his head, he returned his attention to the woman at his side. He didn't look my way again.

ELEVEN
LUCAS

I applied pressure to my temples in a half-hearted attempt to alleviate the headache brewing. Celia and I sat awkwardly on the couch, our conversation stilted at best. She rubbed at the heavy emerald jewels draped from her neck as I fidgeted in my stiff suit. I cleared my throat.

"Did you want to say something?" she asked, perking up.

I shook my head, and she deflated.

Three parties in one week was not my idea of a good time. But here I found myself again, playing the role of dutiful prince. This time we were about to attend an intimate gathering to celebrate our engagement. I'd only met Celia earlier that week, even though she seemed to believe we had history together. Most likely we'd crossed paths a time or two, and while she'd held onto the memories, nothing remarkable had stuck around for me.

Couldn't everyone see that I wasn't interested, let alone *in love*, with this woman? Couldn't *she* see it? Sure, I was putting on a show for my father's sake, but even I wasn't that good of an actor.

"Come on," Celia said, snaking her arm around me. "You need to meet my parents."

"Goody." I smiled through gritted teeth.

We stood, and she led me to the door. Someone knocked politely on the other side. I pulled it open to two middle-aged people with hungry stars in their eyes. They looked just like Celia, both with red hair, pale faces, and green eyes. She was sent in right away to greet me while they were given a quick security briefing. Now that they were the parents of the future queen, they would be in the public spotlight. I'm sure they didn't mind. My father had already seen to it that Celia and her family were vetted, top to bottom. He'd chosen my fiancée, and I'd stupidly agreed in exchange for the execution of Thomas.

I am such an idiot.

I thought back to the events, still shocked that I'd been so impulsive. True, the fact that Thomas had been allowed to live had been keeping me up at night. But when Jessa broke up with me, something inside snapped. His execution become my sole focus, anything to avoid facing how bad Jessa had hurt me. A desperate part of me thought if I could just get justice for my mother, I'd feel better again. But I didn't feel better. Anger simmered just below the surface, threatening to eat me alive. I was out of control and would do almost anything to get it back.

"Ah, they're here." My father strode into the room. "I'll admit, I'm grateful you trusted me enough to give your daughter to my son. She's a wonderful girl. No doubt they will be very happy together."

They all blushed at the same time. *Who are we kidding?* We all knew every single one of those girls at that party had been dying to get my ring on her finger and a crown on her head. When Richard had proposed the idea of an engagement to me, he said he had a few girls in mind. I stupidly told him it didn't matter who he chose. In my mind, there was no way I was actually getting married to a stranger. Agreeing to an engagement wasn't agreeing to a marriage.

"I can hardly believe it myself." Celia winked. "I must have made a lasting impression." Little did she know that wasn't the case. "Lucas, I'd like you to formally meet my parents, Mark and Sabine."

I shook their hands. "Pleasure to meet you," I said.

"You'll be good to her?" her father asked. I could barely meet the man's eyes as I lied through my teeth.

"Yes, sir."

He continued, "Right, well, this all seems rather fast to me but as long as my princess is happy, then that's okay by me."

Princess... Yeah, I heard that. No doubt her father was just as thrilled as her mother despite his attempt to fulfill the role of the overprotective daddy.

"Let's eat, shall we?" I asked, focusing on the hearty smells wafting in.

We headed to my family's private dining room; extra guards lined the walls, their expressions stoic and searching. They were on edge lately. I couldn't say I blamed them. First their queen died, then a public attack, and then an execution. Not to mention my sham of an engagement.

I assumed dinner was delicious by the constant compliments of our guests. Mentions of "so tender" and "exquisite" filtered around me. But I could hardly do more than move my food from one spot on my plate to another. I wasn't the type to lose my appetite. With my morning workouts, and my age, I was always sneaking off to the kitchens for more food. But today my stomach was in knots. *How am I going to get out of this?*

Once again, Richard was getting everything he wanted

and I was stuck doing his bidding. If it came down to it, I'd refuse to marry her. I wondered what he would do to me then...

"Well that was the most incredible apple fritter I have ever had." Celia smiled, her overly made-up face beaming. "Thank you so much for dinner, Your Royal Highness."

"You're welcome," my father replied, wiping his face with his napkin in satisfaction. "Why don't us old folks retire to the sitting room and let the couple have some time alone." He winked at Sabine and Mark. "No doubt you remember what it was like to be newly engaged."

"Oh, do I ever." Mark laughed.

My body went rigid. They got up to leave, and I stayed like an anchor in my chair.

"Lucas." My father looked back at me. "Don't keep your fiancée locked away in this stuffy dining room. Let the servants clean up. Show her your bedroom where you can have more privacy to talk and to...get to know each other better."

I expected her mother at least to protest but she only nodded in agreement.

Wonderful. *How am I ever going to get Jessa back now?*

I bit my lip and stood. "Shall we?" As we walked to my room, I didn't even bother to look if Celia was following. Of course she was.

"Not many get to come back here," I mumbled.

"Oh, that's surprising." She followed me into my room and closed the door behind her. She was dressed in a short black dress and high heels. Her red hair was intricately braided down her back. She looked at me with expectant green eyes.

"Surprising?" I asked. "What do you mean by that?"

She smiled coyly. "You read the news. So do I." She was the picture of innocence. Delicate, yet brimming with confidence.

But I saw through the façade. She was dangerous.

I frowned and gripped my hands into fists behind my back. "The gossip columns love to paint me as a playboy. My father allows that to an extent because he thinks it makes me more desirable."

"So it's not true?" She smiled coyly.

I shrugged. "I won't lie and pretend there isn't a shred of truth to the stories. But overall? No, it's not true."

"Interesting."

"Besides, a lot has changed for me recently."

She nodded. "Your room is lovely," she said, walking around and running her finger over every surface. "Of course, I wouldn't expect anything less. You are the prince after all."

"And you're my fiancée," I said it as a challenge.

She squared her shoulders and smiled. "Yes. I am."

"Most women would be offended by the way that happened. I never even asked you." It was true. Once I agreed, Richard jumped into action and asked, or rather *told*, her parents to come to the palace immediately for the press conference. We'd only met again backstage. Some advisor hastily pushed a giant ring onto her finger and that had been that. My mother's ring.

I glanced at the rock, still planted on her finger, and a pang of regret shot through me.

"I don't mind unconventional," she mused. "We'll have plenty of time to get to know each other after we're married. Anyway, sometimes fast is more practical. And more exciting." She laced her tone with a level of innuendo as she approached me. Probably thought she was going to seduce me or something.

"I'm not going to sleep with you," I said.

She only smiled and raised a perfect eyebrow. "Of course not."

I shifted away from her, standing against the wall to put distance between us. She didn't seem to find it alarming in the slightest. The scenarios ran through my head. Should I try to push her away? Get her to break up with me? Was that even possible? Should I play along? Should I pretend?

But I can't cheat on Jessa. Even though we were no longer together, I wasn't stupid. Anything with Celia still felt like cheating, and I didn't want to hurt Jessa anymore.

"What's your endgame?" I asked, deciding to go straight for the kill. I needed the truth. I needed to know what Celia wanted most so I could use it as leverage. As bait.

She didn't falter. "I've been groomed my whole life to have an advantageous marriage. And, Lucas, *you* are the top prize. Not only are you the prince, you also happen to be rather attractive and intelligent. I couldn't do better. My endgame is simple. You."

"Well, at least you're honest."

"And you couldn't do much better either."

I eyed her confidence, skeptical. "You're rather sure of yourself."

"My father has a lot of influence in this kingdom," she replied simply. "And I will be a good wife."

"What if I don't want that?"

She sighed dramatically and placed a hand on her hip. "I'm not stupid, and I'm not romantic. I will let you do what you want if it comes to that." She paused, her expression grim. "Do you understand what I'm saying?"

I wasn't sure what to say. It wasn't like I needed her to spell it out for me.

"Don't be so obtuse. You can tell me you're not a playboy all you want, but like I said, we've met before. *I* remember

185

how you behaved as a boy. And honestly, Lucas? I'm okay with you as long as you stay discreet, stay safe, and most importantly," she paused, careful to get her point across, "nobody gets near my crown."

I pushed off the wall and stalked toward her. "Your crown?" I laughed. "Has anyone ever told you not to count your chickens before they hatch?"

She only batted her eyes. "I know what I want. Our marriage will benefit both our families. Don't fight the inevitable, Lucas. You won't win."

"Is that a threat?"

She inched closer and pressed a soft kiss to my lips. I didn't kiss her back.

"Absolutely."

●

"We had the response we were looking for," one of the advisers said. "The people are rallying around the idea of war. Men are volunteering to join the army in droves, and of course, the alchemists are prepared for anything."

It was the next morning, and I sat with my father around the same conference table I'd been at far too frequently lately. I squinted and pinched my nose, resigned to the fact that this war was really going to happen.

"I want to move up our timetable. With the national broadcast yesterday, it's probable something was leaked and West America will be expecting us."

"Then why did you do it in the first place?" I asked. "Of course Thomas needed to die. But why broadcast it for everyone to see? Why do it in front of the alchemists and the kingdom like that?"

He turned on me, his eyes sharp. "Because we suspect

there are spies and we won't have it." I held my breath, anxiety rooting me to my chair.

The men in the room nodded. "Not to mention, there is unrest," he continued. "The attack was performed by one of our own citizens. And Thomas lived in this very palace. I had to send a message."

"I think your message was received," I said, deadpan. My thoughts immediately went to Jessa. She needed to disassociate with the Resistance. I could only pray they didn't have her name written on some list somewhere. If Richard suspected an alchemist of foul play, it would only be a matter of time before he smoked them out.

"What's the prognosis if we launch our first attack tonight?" My father leaned in toward his highest-ranking general. The broad-chested man perked up at the attention, his military ornamentation gleaming. We hadn't been engaged in war in decades. Did this guy even know what he was doing?

"We're ready. We will need some of your best alchemists. Your fighters. And a few healers. But we have thousands of trained men ready to go and more who are preparing."

"We're going to send a message to West America. Going to suck them dry so they have no choice but to surrender."

"And why are we going to war again?" I interjected.

My father paused, his face sharpening. "Son, we've already gone over this. They killed your mother." *Lies.* "In all likelihood, they had something to do with the attack during her funeral." *Maybe.* "It's clear they want to start a war with us, so it's a war they will get. Besides, it wouldn't hurt to have more land. More resources. And to bless more people with our monarchy."

I gritted my teeth and nodded. There must be people in the room who didn't know the truth about my mother's death. War must be his priority because of his insatiable need for more land and resources. Lust for power. I tried not to think of the bloodshed that would happen because of my own father, but the reality of what was sure to happen haunted me.

He'd used his alchemists not only to destroy areas of our border, creating the shadow lands, but to essentially torture people. He'd used magic on them in so many unimaginable ways, most often ending in death. Maybe all those tests with magic had been his way of developing weapons. Maybe he'd been preparing for this war much longer than I realized.

"It's settled then. Round up your soldiers, and Faulk will deploy our officers. Together, we'll make a move on West America far worse than they can even imagine." A spark of excitement lit his eyes as the room burst into a flurry of action. The time for talking about war was over. It was time for action.

Richard had found a scapegoat in my mother's death and subsequent attack. He now had a reason to enact something he had long awaited. How many lives would pay the price? I left the room. I couldn't stand it anymore. This was not the way to lead the kingdom. This was wrong. But I wasn't king. And I was party to everything that was about to happen.

And there is nothing I can do about it.

●

I woke with a start. Sweat poured down my back as I caught my breath. I'd been so tired lately, but even sleep haunted me, turning dreams into nightmares. Images of my mother flashed through my mind, the blood pooling around her body, the smell of death, her eyes unblinking, the feeling of helplessness.

I jumped from the bed, changed into workout clothes, and

headed to the gym. There was a perfectly adequate gym on this side of the palace, but I found my way into the alchemist wing instead. I needed to make sure Jessa was okay. I wouldn't talk to her. I didn't deserve that. But I could at least see how she was holding up. I knew she spent most of her mornings sparring.

A few people sent odd looks my direction as I walked into the gym, but most seemed unbothered. I worked my way over to the area with weight equipment and began to lift dumbbells. My eyes scanned the room for Jessa, finding her sparring with another girl I didn't recognized. She laughed at something the girl said, her face lighting up.

I finished my set and moved over to the leg-press machine. I added more weight than normal and got to work. I focused on my shoelaces as I thought about Jessa. She needed to get out of the Resistance. At least while Richard was on his witch-hunt. The fact that I still didn't know who her handler was ate away at me. Who else knew about Jessa's involvement?

I got up from the machine and walked over to the water station. I swallowed a cup in one gulp and threw it into the trash. I didn't have to sit back and let the Resistance have Jessa. *I'm an alchemist*, I reminded myself. I glanced around the room, watching the mix of color guardians and officers for a moment. What would they do if they knew about me? It was my biggest secret. I'd revealed it once only because I'd had to. That day in the helicopter, I had saved my life, Jessa's life, and Sasha's. Sasha said she was going to tell the Resistance about my secret, but I suspected she never had. So far, no one had confronted me. I wished I could talk to Sasha and find out for sure. But she was hiding in the mountains north somewhere, and I had no idea how to talk to her.

My eyes traveled to Jessa again, and I saw her training with a man this time—some guy I didn't know. He came at her, pummeling her to the ground. Every instinct in me fired. I began to move toward them, but I stopped myself. She had jumped up and taken control of the fight.

She doesn't need you.

I ran a few miles on a treadmill, watching her. She never looked my way. She either hadn't noticed me, or she was deliberately ignoring me. I pressed the incline and speed buttons to max level for as long as I could possibly go. Exertion was the only thing that could distract me from the frustration that had been stealing every thought. When she caught my gaze and looked away just as quickly, I'd had enough.

I jumped off the machine and stormed out of the gym. I didn't have to deal with this silent treatment. If she wasn't going to see reason and distance herself from the Resistance, then I would find a way to do it for her.

I'd been working on my white alchemy for years. And I was good. I didn't have proper training in all the colors, but I knew I could be initiated if I had the chance. But white? That was my specialty. As a royal, I would never be part of the guardians. It would upset the balance. None of that stopped me from using magic when I had to. *Maybe I had to.*

I quickly showered and dressed myself in black, moving into action.

It was the same for all alchemists. Natural elements like plants and stones were easier to manipulate than synthetic elements. The best alchemists could still use the color from things like cloth, which was why everyone wore black. It was best to avoid any mistakes. And I wouldn't make a mistake again.

I would do anything to protect her.

Our royal quarters were private, and I was alone as I

walked into the dining room. I pulled the white rose from the large bouquet on the table, breaking its head from the stem. Nobody would miss it. It had been a while since I'd done this, and the thrill of excitement pulsed through my veins as I squeezed the soft petals. I calmed at the velvet feel between my fingers.

I watched as my body faded away, growing foggy at first, and then…nothing. I was invisible. I needed to be quick before I got too drowsy, as I knew from experience just how tiring this type of magic was on me. I took off running, careful to land softly with each step. I followed the corridors back toward the GC headquarters.

I'd noticed an extra level of anxiety at the gym earlier. I'd been too lost in my own cloud of depression to realize why. They must all be in a complete frenzy over the recent war announcement. Many of them would be leaving tonight. Faulk had been tasked to organize it and had immediately begun preparations. I had a strong suspicion Jessa would be connecting with her Resistance contact over the news. At this point, I hoped her initiation would be delayed. The thought of her being sent off to war wasn't something I could handle. But she wasn't ready, and Richard wouldn't risk losing her. She should be finished at the gym by now. I decided to follow her. If I was lucky, I could figure out whom it was I needed to blackmail.

Invisibility was an extremely useful skill. I balked when I rounded a corner, stepping into full view of a group of officers, but no one looked in my direction. I checked the gym just in case. She was still there. A few people came close to bumping into me as I went in, but I was able to dodge them. A small trickle of fatigue picked at my eyes, and I took a steady breath. I found a corner and watched impatiently.

Jessa, come on. Connect with your handler.

She was sparring with Reed. Again. She was always forgiving that guy. He grabbed her around her waist, and I was reminded why I didn't like him. He wasn't trustworthy, for one thing. But it was his obvious romantic interest in her that made me dislike him the most. He flirted ruthlessly, always worming his way into her life. He wasn't shy about what he was doing. I'd seen him around with plenty of different female alchemists. The kid knew how to get a girl. I never worried about it too much before, but now that we weren't together anymore, seeing Jessa with him killed me. The urge to go over there and rip the guy off of her consumed me. He had her pinned to the ground as she wriggled to get out of his grip. When they laughed, I almost lost it.

I stared at the wall as they did a few more rounds. Biding my time, I pushed off the exhaustion beginning to overtake me. I couldn't see the rose in my hand, since it was also invisible, but I wondered how much longer I had. A while, but not forever. I considered turning back.

If you don't keep her safe, no one else will. You owe her.

She knocked Reed to the ground and smirked in his face, letting out a whoop of victory. She helped him up, and he brought his arm around her as they walked toward the greenhouse out back, no doubt to heal their wounds. I followed, knowing this meant she was done fighting for the day.

I didn't anticipate that there would be so many people back there. I had to stop multiple times to let people pass, just in case. When I finally made it inside, I warmed at the sight. She had friends. The other alchemists weren't nearly so hostile toward her as they usually were. A few of them laughed with her over her knocking Reed out. I smiled. They would grow to love her if they just got to know her.

When she left, I followed close behind. It was most likely

that she was going to her own room for a shower. I may be invisible, but I wasn't a creep. I would have to wait outside for her and hoped she'd be quick.

But as she approached the corridor that led to her room, she passed it, and continued down the hallway. She stopped abruptly, every muscle tense and still. Then she whipped around. I didn't move an inch, holding my breath. She eyed the hallway but nobody was in this area right now except me. Of course she couldn't see me. But could she feel me watching her?

She hesitated for a few long moments and then opened the door to Jasmine's classroom and office. I wasn't sure what that meant. Jasmine had been training her, and I'd helped put the two of them together. Jasmine was older and kind, matronly even. Jessa had been so vulnerable in the beginning. She needed somebody comforting on her side, which was why I'd originally asked for Jasmine's help. I sighed, knowing it was probably a typical meeting with her mentor. I was running out of time!

Still, I pressed my ear to the door and looked in through the glass windows. But then something curious happened. The windows had a special feature to create privacy when needed. And that's just what they did. Jasmine walked over, and they nonchalantly switched from clear to opaque.

Why do they need privacy?

Mumbled conversation filtered from the other side of the door, but it was hard to make out the words.

"The war?" Jessa said. A scraping noise followed—most likely a drawer being opened. "Hold on…" Then there was nothing.

Absolute silence.

My heart rate skyrocketed. Jasmine. I'd trusted her. And clearly she was using blue alchemy to protect against eavesdroppers. There was no other explanation for complete silence on their end. She had to be Resistance, otherwise they never would have done that. It was dangerous to keep secrets here. That kind of behavior was forbidden.

How had I missed it?

I fought the urge to push open the door and confront her right there and then. I'd spent so much time with Jasmine while helping the Resistance. And all I'd wanted was some validation from them. If she was the Resistance's contact in the palace, why couldn't she have trusted me enough to reveal her secret to me? Knowing how close I'd been to her, and how easily I'd been deceived despite that, had me reeling.

I pressed myself against the wall, holding my breath, waiting for Jessa to leave. I had zero hesitation about what needed to be done.

Sure enough, a few minutes later, Jessa exited the room. Her face was reddened as she wiped a bead of sweat from her brow. She didn't hesitate as she ambled off toward her room. Once I was sure she was gone, and no one else was in the hallway, I took a deep breath and willed myself to become visible again. It worked, my body filling out into full color. The rose was only about half gray, divided down the middle by life and death. I pushed open the door.

"I know who you are," I said, slamming the door behind me. Jasmine sat at her desk, the blue stone still in her hands. "Don't try to deny it. I know you're with the Resistance. You're Jessa's contact."

She stood, her eyes widening. "It's not what you think."

"Save it," I said. "Let me make this brief. You're going to exclude Jessa from everything Resistance from here on out. She is no longer a part of your organization. Your only concern for her is her alchemy. And to keep her safe."

"You don't know what you're doing. We want the same

things, Lucas."

"You don't know the first thing about what I want!" I yelled.

She shook her head. "Where are these threats coming from? Lucas, this isn't you." I momentarily froze, confused by her tone. She meant what she said.

I shook my head, resolved in my decision. "Oh, it's not a threat. It's an order. And if you don't do as I say, then I promise you will be the next one on that executioner's stand."

I meant it. I moved in close, leaning my palms against her desk. "Do not underestimate me."

"And what if I told your father all of your secrets?" she responded, leaning back in her chair. I wasn't sure she was alluding to my short time with the Resistance or if she knew about my alchemy. I wasn't going to stick around and find out.

"You have no proof of *anything*. It would be your word against mine," I said. "And who do you think my father is going to believe? Some healer with a distaste for the rules?" I peered at her clothing. She was the only guardian who didn't dress in black. She got away with it because she'd been one of my mother's only alchemist friends. I still didn't know why she went against the grain; self-expression had always been my guess. "Or is he going to believe his own son?"

Something threatening traced her eyes, as well as something else. Tiredness. Both were emotions I hadn't seen on the woman before. Either way, I seemed to have the upper hand. She nodded, lips pinched.

"Oh, and one more thing. Don't you dare tell *her* anything about this conversation." I headed for the door. We both knew whom I was talking about.

"You don't understand what you're doing, Lucas. You'll only put her in more danger by doing this," she called after me.

I didn't dignify that garbage with a response as I shoved the rose that had been hanging limp in my hand into my pocket. I slammed the door behind me.

TWELVE

JESSA

About a quarter of the guardians were gone. When they left the night before, everything went from chaotic to downright silent. Nobody wanted to talk about it. And nobody wanted to admit it, but worry followed us around like a dark shadow. Breakfast was a solemn affair as we all waited to hear news, knowing it was likely we wouldn't hear anything for a while.

I wasn't the only one pecking at my food as I sat at one of the tables surrounded by my new friends. It was weird, how far I'd come. Not to say I was friends with Brooke or her crowd. But ever since the last party, it was as if the other alchemists decided to stop hating me.

Over the last couple of days, the others my age had started talking to me. Inviting me to eat with them, spar with them, sitting by me in the few group lessons I attended. It was as if everyone was worried about bigger things, and I was suddenly invited to the party. It was part of what Jasmine wanted, so I wasn't complaining. As much as I hated to admit it, it felt good. I guessed deep down maybe there was a part of everyone who wanted to be accepted. Some of us just knew how to hide it better than others.

•

"I wonder when we are going to be called up," one of the girls said. She'd gone out of her way to be nice to me, which I appreciated. "Usually those of us under eighteen are stuck in training, with the occasional mission," she finished. I'd recently learned her name was Callie. I didn't question why she'd befriended me, because I quickly noticed she was one of those people who made friends with everyone. There were four of us: a boy, me, Callie, and a blond girl who sat across from me.

"Not this time," the girl across the table sighed, her brown eyes heavy. "Reed and Brooke have both gone, as well as about twenty others under eighteen. There were even a couple of fifteen-year-olds and one fourteen-year-old." She snagged a hair tie off her wrist and began pulling her hair on top of her head.

"Fourteen?" I frowned. "That's so young."

"It just depends on how good they are," Callie responded, spooning her grapefruit. "Reed's been going out on stuff for a long time. There are others who go even younger than that."

"But that's different, isn't it? This is an actual war. It's not like they're in New Colony territory. They went over to West America."

"That's true." The other girl nodded eagerly. "I can't wait until I get called up. I've been training like a mad woman. I need a real fight."

I sighed and looked back at my buttered toast, picked up a piece, and plopped it into my mouth. It tasted like cardboard, but I made myself swallow. I took a big drink of water, trying to dissect the conversation in my mind. It seemed they were all *eager* to get in on the action. Nervous, of course, but more excited than anything. Did they know what they were really asking for? Fighting or not, this preparation wasn't for an initiation test or a sparring round. This was war, and that meant to the death.

And I can't change their minds, so don't mess this up.

"What about you?" Callie asked. "Do you want to fight?"

"She's not ready." A guy piped in. He had shaggy blond hair around his ears and glasses. He shrugged from across the table. "No offense."

"None taken," I responded, though I was a bit put off. "Honestly, you're right. I'm not ready for battle like that. Plus, I haven't been initiated yet. I still have to pass two more tests."

"Which ones?" Callie asked. "If you don't mind me asking?" She blushed, but I got the feeling she liked to know the latest gossip.

"It's okay. I passed the yellow. But I failed the blue and the purple," I said, a little embarrassed. "Even though I can do a little bit with both. It wasn't enough, apparently."

Callie's friend, who I hadn't really met, smirked. "It's harder than it looks, isn't it?"

I bit my lip. *You're here to make friends, Jessa.*

"It's okay," the boy said. "*Nobody* passes all five tests. And you only have to get three. Green and orange are pretty easy. You'll do it."

"Are they the same tests for everyone?"

"Sometimes," Callie said. "Not always. But we can't give you any hints. It's against the rules," she was quick to add.

I nodded, already knowing this to be true. The element of surprise was part of what made the tests difficult. "I'll be fine with green," I said. "I just haven't used orange all that much."

"Everybody can do orange. It's going to be fine. You'll see."

I smiled at my new friend. She had caramel eyes, wiry blond hair, and thick glasses, but she pulled it off in an adorable smart-girl way. "Thanks."

"I wonder when her next test will be," Callie's friend said to the other two at the table, basically ignoring me. *Umm, hello? I'm sitting right here.*

"What's your name?" I asked the brazen girl in my friendliest tone.

"Tessa," she said, turning on me.

"Hi, Tessa, I'm Jessa." I laughed. Our names rhymed and something about that was funny. I guess she didn't think so. I decided to be nice. "I'm wondering when my next test will be just as much as you are. Truth is, with this war stuff happening, I have no idea anymore."

"Well, King Richard definitely wants you for something."

I bristled. "What do you mean by that?"

She shrugged. "Just that you're here because you have something he wants. So my guess is your initiation is going to happen sooner rather than later."

The shaggy-haired boy nodded. "Yeah, Tessa is right. I'm Nate, by the way." He reached out a hand across the table, and I shook it. "I wouldn't say the same thing for most alchemists. Anyone else would probably have their tests postponed."

Callie chimed in with a smile. "But you, my dear, are extra special."

"Lucky me."

"You should consider yourself lucky." Tessa got up with a huff and strode away from our table. What was with that girl? I had been nothing but nice.

"Ignore her," Nate said. "She'll get over it."

I realized something then. No matter how I acted or

what I did, there would always be someone who didn't like me. Maybe that was a fact of life. Stand for something, and people hate you. Stand for nothing, and hate yourself. Plus people would still hate you. I decided to take Nate's advice and ignore Tessa's behavior. It wasn't my problem.

"I'm sorry, you guys," I blurted. "This is hard for me. I didn't grow up here, and I still have a family. I miss them so much. Don't get me wrong, the magic is amazing, and I can see how it can help a lot of people. And I like doing it. But war? I didn't sign up for that."

"No one signs up for it." Callie sighed.

"You'll get used to it here," Nate added.

I smiled. "Thanks. I'm sorry, I haven't introduced myself." I reached out a hand. "I'm Jessa."

"I know." He laughed, shaking the hair out of his eyes, but it just fell right back into place. He met my handshake with a firm one of his own. "Everyone knows who *you* are."

"You really have a family?" Callie whispered. She pushed her plate away and leaned in. Part of me wanted to hold back, but making friends wasn't about keeping secrets.

"Yes. It's me, my mom, dad, and my little sister, Lacey. She's only six. I *really* miss them."

"You're so lucky. I don't remember my family. I'd give anything to even have one memory."

"You can't think about it, Callie," Nate said.

"It's not as easy as that." Callie stared down at her plate.

"Nate might be onto something," I said. "Don't get me wrong. I'm doing everything I can to have some kind of connection with my family again. Let's just say the king has…leverage. And I would never choose not to remember them. But I can see how you guys have the advantage."

Maybe I said too much.

"You're right," Nate agreed. "The king doesn't have as

much leverage over us." He blushed, cleared his throat, and got up from the table. "Forget I said that. I have to go."

Callie stared after him. "That was weird."

I shrugged. But actually, I didn't find it that weird for Nate to question the king. Maybe he would join the Resistance? What was weird was all these talented people going along with everything Richard wanted. Couldn't they see there had to be a better way? To see Nate behave that way signified that, perhaps, there were more people like me out there. More alchemists who weren't happy with the current state of things. And if that were true, maybe the Resistance really did stand a chance.

What was going on with Lucas? Was the boy I'd fallen in love with under the summer stars turning into his father's son? I didn't want to think like that, but I couldn't help the questions from turning over and over in my mind.

When I'd met him, he'd taken me completely by surprise. I'd thought I knew who he was. That he was just what the media presented him as: a handsome, spoiled, playboy and duty-driven prince—nobody I wanted to know. But then he'd showed me someone *completely different*.

And now we weren't even talking.

I pushed the remaining food around on my plate, lost in thought. He was clearly moving forward with his life. Forward in a completely different direction than what I wanted. It hurt to think about my future without him; the wound constantly reopened. When push came to shove, would Lucas stand with his father? Would I have to fight against the man I loved in order to save not only my family and countless others, but myself? Those were the questions that haunted me.

"Earth to Jessa?" Callie's voice rang out. "Are you in there?"

I shook myself out of it and smiled. "Sorry." We stood

together and threw the rest of our meager breakfasts away.

The day continued—training, meals, whispered conversations, and anxious glances between the guardians. We all assumed the attack had happened and watched the newsfeeds on our slatebooks eagerly. But there was never any news.

●

I woke to sharp pounding on my door and catapulted myself from my bed. The gym training must be going better than expected because I landed expertly on my feet. I fell into a defensive crouch. My heart thundered as I glanced bleary-eyed around the room. Darkness filtered through the drawn shades on the dormitory window. Another series of booming knocks sounded. There was a cry and a shuffling noise. What was going on?

I didn't hesitate. I leapt for the door and pulled it open. The hallway was dim. Nobody. I peered from side to side, my ears trained in the direction I'd heard something. The shuffling sounded again, around the corner. "Help," someone mumbled, before the cry broke off.

I darted toward it, down the hall and around the corner, ready to jump in and aid whoever was in trouble. My instincts kicked into high gear. The hair on my arms stood on end. I was only wearing shorts and a tank top but hardly noticed the cold air as I swooped into action.

Again, nobody was there. *What in the world is going on?*

Then a blood-curdling scream erupted though the space. It sounded farther down. I squinted into the darkness. A figure was crouched down, much farther up the corridor. A few of the other dormitory doors flung open, but I took no notice as I sprinted down the hallway. Just as I reached the figure, it stood to full height. A man, much taller and much older, loomed over me. There wasn't a trace of emotion on his face.

"What's wrong?" I asked, confused.

"Sorry," he muttered.

A ripple of pain blasted through my side, followed by a clipped boom. He stepped back, lowering a gun into his holster, and disappeared into the darkness.

I gasped, the icy pain turning to tormented burning. I fell to my knees. Blood blossomed around the wound, forming a circle of crimson. *He shot me!* My mind grew dizzy. A few people surrounded me in a wide arc. What were they doing? Why were they just standing there?

"Help me!" I screamed, but the sound came out all wrong.

Someone moved forward. "Don't," one of them said. "She hasn't been initiated yet, remember?"

"Oh, sorry," another replied. Was that Nate?

I tried to respond. Only a low moan came from my mouth. What were they talking about? All at once, they retreated to their rooms. When the last door closed, panic ran through me. How could they be so cruel? I tried to piece it together—why someone would shoot me, why others would walk away—but I couldn't make sense of it over the pain. My mind wasn't clear.

I held my side, shocked at the blood. There was so much! If I didn't do something, I was going to bleed out. I struggled to look around the hallway, trying to figure out where I was. That's when I realized what the tall, darkened shadows in the room next to me was—one of the greenhouses. I gritted my teeth, pushing with both my hands against the wound and willed myself to a standing position. I shuffled to the room, gasping as I opened the door. I fell, grunting, crawling into the room. I reached out a bloody hand for the closest green

I could find.

It didn't take long to get ahold of a plant, but the time it took me to reach my magic felt like an eternity. Finally, the green alchemy flowed through my body, penetrating the source. The healing was familiar. It was icy, tingly, as it wove through the wound. I kept one hand on the pain and another grasping desperately at the poor plant crushed between my fingers. Something solid oozed out of the wound and into my palm. The bullet. Relief swept through me as I stared, shocked. But the pain still held on as my eyes fluttered. A wave of tiredness overtook me, exhausted from both the magic and the wound. I managed to lie down just as the darkness took me.

●

"That was a harder test than most get," someone said, perturbed. "You didn't need to go to such lengths as to *shoot her*."

"We had you on standby," someone else responded coolly. "She was never in any real danger. And look? She passed. She's *fine*."

Where am I? What is happening? My thoughts were hazy. A wave of adrenaline pulled me to the surface. My eyelids fluttered, and a needle of light found its way into my vision. I opened my eyes, blinking repeatedly up at the women standing over me.

"Good, you're awake," Jasmine said, frowning down at me. I wanted to cry out and hug her. She brushed a bead of sweat from her forehead. She looked tired. Worried. I blinked a few more times, trying to gauge the situation and failing. Faulk was with her. A glint of disappointment flashed across her face before she stepped back. Why were they standing over me, and why was I lying on the floor?

"What happened?" I asked, sitting up, but the memory came flooding back just as I asked the question. "I was shot!" I hissed.

"Clearly. She's observant," Faulk remarked.

"You passed the test," Jasmine said. "I'm sorry, I wasn't allowed to warn you. I didn't know they would go to such lengths."

"You had me shot?" I gasped, glaring at Faulk.

She only shrugged and scribbled something down in a notebook. She and her people were clearly done with me as they began to exit the greenhouse. Well, at least I'd passed the test.

Jasmine knelt down next to me and brushed the loose hair from my face. I breathed a sigh of relief, allowing myself to be comforted. She'd become not only my mentor, not only my contact to the Resistance, but probably my best friend in the palace. It sounded weird to be best friends with an old lady, but it was the truth.

"The king wanted to see what you were made of," Faulk said, standing in the doorway. "We usually shoot a few other people for you to heal. But sometimes, the lucky ones get to be shot and heal themselves. You should be grateful; this will only raise your esteem in the palace. I, of course, didn't think you'd be able to do it. You're a more powerful healer than I gave you credit for." She stared at me for a moment, almost torn by her statement, her jaw tense. She slammed the door behind her.

Well, okay then…

"She's right," Jasmine said. "What you did was remarkable. I was in here the whole time. I would have stepped in if you needed me, but you passed that test with flying colors, Jessa. You should be very proud of yourself."

"Thanks. But geez, a little warning would have been really nice," I said, reaching for Jasmine as she helped me rise to my feet. I was a little unsteady, so I leaned against the woman for support. "That was terrible."

"I know. I'm sorry." Jasmine sighed as we moved toward a couple of chairs. "Believe me, it wasn't my idea." We sat. She faced me so her back was to the glass wall along the hallway. She opened her palm to reveal a blue stone. It was risky, doing that here. She must have good reason. A wisp of magic danced in the air before it split, going into me and then into her. In the darkened room, no one from the outside would have seen it. And with the magic now flowing, we'd be silent to the outside world. If someone looked in the window, it would appear we were just sitting here, resting for a moment.

"Don't say anything," she said. "You're facing the hall, and I don't know if someone is watching." I narrowed my eyes at her and nodded imperceptibly. I understood what was at stake. Normally, she used the switch to turn the glass wall opaque, but that was too dangerous with officers lurking outside.

"Your initiation is being moved up quickly. The king plans to pass you in the orange tomorrow no matter how the test goes, so there's nothing to worry about with that." She got up, tending to the plant I had used in my recovery, her back still to the hallway. "But it means he needs you to be a guardian sooner than we expected. He must want to use your red alchemy in the war, especially now that Thomas is dead. It's the best explanation."

I shuddered, but it made sense. I had to gain his trust. And then when the moment was right, I would turn on him. I would find a way to bring him under my control, under the control of the Resistance. That had been my mission all along. I was terrified of what it would mean for me, but I could do it. I fidgeted in my chair, pulling my shirt up to look at the mess of blood.

"There's more. Your initiation is set for just two days' time. You're not supposed to know this, but they're always similar. There will be another party, a nice dinner, and you will be asked to use your magic publically to do something for the king. There will be a large crowd of the alchemists and officers there to watch it all happen—bring you into the fold, so to speak."

This was news to me. But I could handle it.

"There's one last thing." She paused, coming back to sit down, grim-faced. "You're out of the Resistance."

"What?" I sputtered.

"Shhh," she said. "Don't talk, remember?" She leaned over, appearing to look at my wound.

I stared into her eyes, willing her to read my thoughts.

"Look, I can't explain what happened, but it's not good. For the time being, we need to lie low. No more missions until I'm sure it's safe. No more talking to me about *anything* other than normal guardian business."

I bit my lip, hating what she was telling me. The Resistance was the one lifeline I had left to my family. I was not okay with being cut off from them.

"I'm really sorry about this. But it can't be helped. I promise to bring you back in as soon as I can." *Fine.* "There's one last thing," she added. "I probably shouldn't be saying this, but you deserve to know. We have plans to use your initiation to stage an attack. You'll be fine. But you must stay out of trouble." My eyes were probably as large as saucers at this news. "There will be a lot of high-level people in one room at the same time. And with most of the best fighters gone, we can't miss this opportunity. But you, Jessa, must *not* reveal your alliance to the Resistance under any circumstances. I too will be sticking to the background, keeping my cover."

With that information-bomb, she slipped the blue rock into her pocket and gave me a quick hug. She left the room in a flash. "Get some rest," she said, disappearing around the door.

I soon followed, heading back to my room, the shock sinking into me with each step. So much had happened in the space of one night. I still couldn't believe it. First, I'd been shot, then I'd passed another test, only to find out that the Resistance was ditching me, even if it was temporary. It still hurt—the memory of the bullet wound *and* the news about the Resistance. And now my initiation into the Guardians of Color loomed. I was scared of everything that it entailed, but an attack? What would it mean? Who would they go after?

But this was what I'd wanted. I needed to chill and move forward. There was no turning back. No matter what, I had to make sure I passed tomorrow's orange alchemy test. I had to shine at that initiation ritual. Whatever it was, I would excel and earn my place.

I shuffled into my room and landed with a thud on my bed. I stared at my ceiling, going over every possible scenario the rest of the night. My mind couldn't stop spinning, but deep down it didn't matter. I couldn't control what Richard did to me, but I could control my own effort. And I would do everything in my power to impress him.

It wasn't until much later when my whole body had finally relaxed that I opened my hand. The bullet still rested in my bloody palm.

THIRTEEN

SASHA

"I heard it's your birthday," Mastin said. "Why didn't you tell me?"

"I hate birthdays," I moaned. It was a matter of fact. I didn't get what the big deal was. And I didn't want to celebrate. "So what? I'm another year older, who cares?" I shrugged.

He smirked and sat by me on the fallen log—currently my favorite thinking spot.

"How old are you?"

"Twenty."

"A new decade of life. What's not to celebrate about that?" He laughed. "I'm also twenty," he added.

I rolled that fact over in my mind for a minute. "You're young to be working so closely with a general, aren't you?" I tried not to sound impressed. His ego was big enough as it was—no need to inflate it more.

He shrugged and changed the subject. "So, do you come here often?"

I let out a laugh. Living in close quarters with other people meant I had very little privacy and space. I spent most of my time outside during the warmer months. Once winter came, I would get super cooped up. I watched a leaf as it fell in the wind, resting on the hard earth. A breeze blew my hair out of my face, and I pulled my collar up around my ears.

"How did you find me?" I asked.

I was a little off the beaten path, higher up on the mountain. Or "hill" as Hank called it. There was a clearing with a view of the whole camp, and now that there were more people here than ever, I'd needed to find a new alone spot.

"I found you by accident." He shrugged. "I was just looking for somewhere to get away." He held up a book. I smiled and held up the ratty paperback that I clutched in one hand.

So he wants to be alone and yet when he saw me, he chose to sit right next to me. I filed that information away as I peered over at him. He shifted closer and his warmth brushed my arm.

"You know, Hank has been to the Rocky Mountains. He acts like they're so much better than these. Is that true?"

Mastin laughed. "I wouldn't say better. It's beautiful here too. But yes, they're a lot bigger."

"I'd like to see that."

"You will."

I nodded, placating him. But I wasn't sure if it was true. I'd spent the better part of a decade hiding out in Canada. I was used to this place. To think I'd ever go to West America was almost unfathomable. What would it even be like? Would it be better than what I had here?

I looked over at Mastin, studying him. He was wrapped up in a coat and scarf, unperturbed by our proximity. "Why are you being so nice to me?" I blurted. Sometimes, I wondered if he forgot I was an alchemist.

"I don't hate you, if that's what you think."

But he hated alchemy.

Cole said laws on alchemy in his country would be changing soon. I knew better. It was probably a lie, a manipulation to get what they wanted from us. I didn't like feeling backed into a corner, and the truth was, maybe the Resistance actually did need their help.

"I don't know what I think anymore," I murmured as we fell into silence.

We sat for a while. I was more and more comfortable around Mastin every day. He wasn't my type, so rigid and by the book. But I couldn't pretend I wasn't attracted to him. I was. The accident with the orange alchemy had proven it. But at the end of the day, it was foolish to get close to a guy like Mastin. We may be from the same planet, but we were from totally different worlds.

And you don't have time for that right now. It was the truth I clung to.

"Do you still hate alchemy?" I asked, feeling brave.

He stood, pacing, but silent. I wasn't sure he was going to reply when he looked back at me. "I was raised to be a soldier my whole life. I was always the top of my class."

"And what does that have to do with alchemy?" I asked, pressing the question again.

"Our soldiers are trained to maintain order." He stopped, taking me in with his eyes. "Our job is to not only protect our country from outside invaders, but to protect our citizens from the alchemists that pop up. It was something I personally worked on."

"What do you mean?" I stood too. "Just tell me."

"If an alchemist was reported, I would go and apprehend them."

"So you're basically telling me that you were not only trained to hate alchemists, but you personally saw to it that they were put away? Awesome, Mastin. I think that answers it." I shook my head.

He squinted at me, jaw tense. "What I am saying, Sasha, is that I was trained that way. Magic doesn't fit in my world."

"So that makes it okay then?"

"I saw a lot of dangerous people."

"Most of them were children, though, weren't they? How can you hold them accountable for that?"

He didn't answer.

I studied his eyes, looking for something that would make it okay. But the green eyes staring back at me were unreadable. "Got it."

"No, you don't get it, Sasha. I was trained to hate alchemy. And I thought I would hate you. I knew I would…" He paused. "But I don't. I should, but I don't feel what I should feel for you." He shook his head. "I have to go."

He stalked off down the hill. I let him leave, somewhat relieved that he had. The last thing I needed was to get mixed up with a guy whose job was to put alchemists in prison. I needed to forget whatever weird feelings were building between us. Besides, if I wanted a relationship, there was someone else who would be a much better fit for me.

My thoughts traveled to Tristan.

He'd been my rock growing up, my best friend for ages. But in the last few years, Tristan had grown into a man. And I had grown up too. He was older than me by five and a half years. And for most of my life, he felt like the brother I never had. But lately, things between us had shifted. It had all started that night he'd confessed some sort of feelings for me. I hadn't been able to get him out of my mind since.

He is good for me. He brings out my best qualities. And I do feel something for him, too.

Mastin was like the forbidden fruit. And that was probably

why I was suddenly crushing on him. I pushed all thoughts of romance out of my head, determined to be done with it once and for all. My focus needed to be on preparing these alchemists for the battle ahead.

I sighed and began to make my way back to camp.

Much to my annoyance, I found myself at Tristan's door. Our recent argument had been weighing on me. I needed to make things right with him. In hindsight, I could see why he was more comfortable going into New Colony as soon as possible. He'd been ready to fight years ago, and only now had the opportunity finally presented itself. Of course he wanted to take it. He was also ready to live a free life outside of this camp.

I knocked on his door, sucking in a breath.

The man had actually built himself his own small cabin with his bare hands. Being stuck up here for years on end caused the guy to be extra resourceful, and it was impressive. Even though the cabin only had a couple of rooms, he'd installed electricity and running water. It was just him; what more did he need?

He opened the door, running his hands through his wet hair. When it was dark and wet like that, it nearly reached his shoulders. I watched a drop of water fall onto his shirt. The blue cotton clung to his body. There were a few more wet spots, and I was pretty sure he'd rushed from the shower to answer the door.

"Hey," I said, smiling up at him. He towered over me, lean and athletic. "Can I come in for a minute?"

"Always," he said, making room as he stepped inside.

I sat on the worn, puffy couch and patted the seat next to me. "We need to talk."

He sighed. "I'm sorry about our argument before."

"Me too."

"I just…really want to get this over with, you know?" The couch dipped as he sat next to me. He smelled of soap and citrus, and I closed my eyes momentarily as I took it in. "It's only a matter of time before we have to attack. I'm ready."

"I know." I nodded. "And maybe you're right about everything. It's just hard to think about sending those people in there. They aren't ready, Tristan. But the truth is, they may never be ready. I don't think even I'm ready to face that place again."

He laughed and leaned over, giving me a side hug. It felt good to be close to him, comforting. A moment passed and then he relaxed with his arm around me. "You need to give yourself more credit. You're good enough to beat them."

"Thanks," I mumbled. I was never any good with compliments.

"I mean it. You're extraordinary," he whispered, his voice scratchy. "I've never met anyone like you."

I swallowed hard. My heart pulsed, and I stood, breaking the connection. I was so confused by all these feelings. I almost couldn't believe myself. It wasn't long ago that I was attracted to Lucas. Sure, Jasmine had ordered me to get close to him, but he was easy to like. That didn't work out for obvious reasons, namely him falling for my sister. But it seemed that the second I got over Lucas, I'd found myself gravitating toward Mastin—the guy I most definitely needed to stay away from. And now Tristan was appealing to me in ways he never had before. He was my best friend. I wasn't supposed to feel this way because it would ruin that feeling of safety that we had together. How was it possible that someone who'd never been that person to me was suddenly…more?

Clearly, I didn't know what I wanted.

"I think we need to stay focused on the mission, you

know? Overthrow the monarchy. Start a new life."

"Agreed."

Tristan's eyes flashed before he looked away, and he stood and headed to his kitchenette. He opened a cupboard, pulled out two glasses and filled them with water. Handing me one, he cleared his throat. We both gulped the water, as if trying to keep ourselves from saying anything stupid. From the strained look on his face, I would guess he was as uncomfortable as I was, but I wasn't sure. He was harder to read than most men.

"Are you okay?" he asked, his left eyebrow rising in a familiar gesture. Just one of the many things I loved about him.

"Yeah, why?"

"You look like you're trying to do a math problem."

I hated math. *Yup, I am obviously over-thinking everything.*

"Hey, I wanted to wish you Happy Birthday." He smiled.

Oh, here we go. My birthday. I didn't celebrate.

"Thanks."

"I got you something." He slipped into his room and came out with a box-shaped gift wrapped in brown paper. I was never good with stuff like this. Presents. Birthdays. Holidays. Being abandoned by a family did that to a person like me. But Tristan was the opposite. He'd always found a way to make everything special. And his homemade gifts were the best. They were the one thing about my birthdays I looked forward to.

I unwrapped the gift carefully to find a tin filled with brownies. The smell of chocolate made my mouth water instantly. "How did you pull this off?" I gasped. Cocoa was nearly impossible to get out here. We traded with the closest Canadian town, but they were just under a hundred miles west. Not very convenient trip; plus, we didn't like people thinking about us too much.

"I traded with one of the new families. Helped them with their plumbing. They smuggled it in from New Colony, and then I convinced Mrs. Riley to bake them for you. I helped clean out her garden."

My eyes burned, and I pushed back the tears. He had done all that for me. He was always doing nice things for me. I didn't deserve him. I felt my eyes brim with tears.

"This is so nice." I smiled up at him as we stood close, the tin between us. "Thank you. Here, you have the first one."

We both plopped a square of the chocolate cake into our mouths. I moaned. I caught him staring down at my mouth, and I blushed again. I swallowed, licking the chocolate from my lips. He moved an inch closer.

"You've got something…" He reached up and brushed my lips with the pad of his thumb. Then his hand stopped, traveling to cup my cheek.

I decided to be brave and met his eyes. There was so much there. So much unsaid, burning in the darkness. Longing and torment…and love.

I wasn't sure if I was more afraid or less afraid by what I saw.

"I don't think I can do this right now," I whispered. He let out a breath and stepped back.

A heavy knock sounded at the door, and I jumped. He held my gaze for a heated moment and then left me to open the door.

Mastin stood in the doorway. They stared at each other for a beat and then turned to look at me. Agitation crossed Mastin's brow. Tristan had shut down again. Nobody moved.

"Hey, guys," Mastin finally said. He sounded a bit winded. He also appeared a bit flustered. "We're having an important meeting down by the fire pit at eight o'clock tonight.

Everyone's invited. Spread the word. You both need to be there."

"Is this about what I think it's about?" Tristan asked.

Mastin nodded slowly. "It's time."

●

"We all have an important decision to make," Cole said. "Consider your options carefully. The choice you make will determine your future."

About a hundred and fifty men and women stood around the large fire, crowding the area. It crackled as the night settled over us. Almost every adult and teenager who had defected from New Colony at some point were in attendance, a handful were alchemists like myself. Some were ex-officers like Tristan and Hank. But most were just regular, everyday people who'd caught word of us and fled here for one reason or another. The flickering of the fire danced off their faces, their eyes shining in the darkness.

"New Colony has attacked America. This is what we were worried about. King Richard has accused us of not only the death of Queen Natasha, but for aiding in a recent terror attack. His claims are completely false, but that doesn't seem to matter to him. We believe he's been preparing for this opportunity for a long time now."

"How many dead?" someone shouted from the crowd.

"We don't know an exact number yet. He struck a military base as well as the surrounding town. The reports coming back are…disturbing."

Which was to be expected with anything that man touched.

"His strongest alchemists and military leaders are out of the palace at the moment. We've decided to strike while the iron is hot. West America has helicopters on their way now to pick us up, armed with many of our own soldiers. Anyone who wants to fight is invited to fight with us. We'll be dropping in on the palace tomorrow after nightfall. But we're vulnerable to the alchemists, and we're asking for any alchemist who is willing to join us."

"But we're barely trained," someone protested.

"Don't take the children," another person yelled. I agreed, of course the kids had to stay behind. Lacey popped into my mind and my breath caught.

"I have an executive order straight from our president herself. To our alchemists sixteen and older, if you come with us, no matter what happens to you, your family back home will be excluded from the military draft, should we need to use it." The crowd was silent, apparantly considering. A draft meant they would force people to fight this war. No one wanted that. "And once this is all over, should West America be the victor, all your crimes will be pardoned." He then looked over the audience, catching my eye. "And to those of you who aren't citizens of West America, if you help us win this war, we will grant you citizenship and a good life. You will be free to enjoy our prosperous society."

A hush ran through the crowd, coupled with the buzz of excitement. The news infuriated me. *What?* These poor people. Alchemists punished for being themselves. *Crimes pardoned only if they agreed to fight. Ridiculous!*

The draft was new information. How many people were in their military? And how many more would be joining? Was it possible we could win this thing? I couldn't stop the images from popping up. The thought of having a better life ahead caused a ripple of excitement to burst.

"Sign me up!" someone called.

"We're in," a couple said, stepping forward. A man, holding

a toddler in his arms, placed his son in his wife's arms and spoke in a calm voice, "So long as I can act on behalf of my family as well, then I'm ready to fight."

Cole nodded.

After a few minutes, about half the crowd had agreed to the mission. If we had a hundred volunteers from this camp, plus special-ops soldiers coming in, maybe we could do it. Maybe we could end this war right now. It was wishful thinking, but the hope bubbled inside just the same.

"For those of you who are in, meet us back here at first light tomorrow. We have a lot to go over in preparation. One last thing," Cole continued. "Thank you. Thank you for stepping up. We won't let you down."

It was a promise. But not one he could keep. We all knew the risk, but did the people around me really know how difficult this was going to be? Did these people have any idea what the alchemists at the palace were capable of? And forget about the officers. They might shoot first and ask questions later. Plus, there were the palace guards—not quite officers, but they still knew how to fight. And they were crawling all over the palace...

Not everyone is going to make it.

I peered around at the stoic faces glowing in the firelight and realized the truth. These people weren't stupid. They knew they might die. But they were willing to take the risk anyway for something they believed in. That was true bravery. I looked at Tristan standing to my left. He caught my eye and nodded.

"You're coming with us?" Mastin asked, joining Tristan and me as we observed the frenzy of conversation.

"I wouldn't miss it for the world," I said, my words dripping in sarcasm.

A head of blond curls squeezed through the crowd. Lacey.

She shot through the people and dashed over to me. "You're going?" she asked. I nodded, and she hugged my legs. "You're going to kick their butts!" I reached down to rest my hand on her head. "Please be careful," she added, quietly. She sounded so grown up, so afraid. This stupid situation was stealing her childhood and there was nothing I could about it. She deserved so much better.

"Kind of a crappy way to end your birthday, huh?" Mastin said, frowning.

"The worst," I agreed. But hey, it wasn't like I expected much.

"It's your birthday?" a woman's shaky voice asked, moving in behind me. It was Lara. *Oh no...*

"Yup, our girl is twenty today," Mastin said, oblivious. But Tristan reached out to squeeze my hand. He knew my secret was dangerously close to being revealed.

"You're twenty. *Today...* Oh my God," Lara breathed. She was technically my mother, but I didn't consider her as anything other than a passing acquaintance these days. I wasn't ready for some happy reunion.

"Christopher," she called, her voice unnaturally high. "Come here."

Oh no. Double no!

"What is it, honey?" he asked, the shadows of the fire extenuating the lines on his face. His hair was graying and he looked...defeated. Tired. He was a completely different man from the one I remembered. But his smell...it was the same. It was leather and grass clippings and everything that broke my heart.

"*Sasha*," she said, drawing out my name, "is twenty years old. Today."

He blinked, his gaze moving from me to Lacey and back again. "I thought it might be. The resemblance... But I didn't want to get my hopes up," he whispered.

"All right, well, you two have a good night," I said, stepping back farther. I needed to get out of here immediately.

"Wait," Lara said. "Please. Don't go, Francesca."

I stilled, my whole body numb.

"Frankie, please," Christopher added. "We've been waiting for this moment for years."

"What are they talking about?" Mastin glanced to Tristan, who only shook his head imperceptibly. "Who's Francesca?"

"She is," Lara said, pointing to me, her hand shaking. "She's not Sasha. That's not her real name." Tears formed in her wide eyes. "She's Francesca, our daughter."

"Frankie," Christopher gasped, rushing and pulling me into a hug. Frozen, trepidation filled every cell in my body. *What do I say?* What was I supposed to feel? I wasn't happy. I wasn't sad. I wasn't angry. I was just…*nothing*.

"All these years, we prayed to find you again," Christopher whispered into my hair. His voice cracked. "We didn't think we would ever see you again."

"And all this time you've been here?" Lara asked.

At some point, she had also started hugging me. I was in the middle of two people grabbing onto me for dear life. Fight or flight response was firing through me. *I need out.*

"Why don't you let her go now?" Tristan said, resting a hand on each of their backs. His tone wasn't asking; he was telling them what to do. They caught the meaning and stepped away from me. Everything went hot and cold and hot again. I watched the ground, unable to look anyone in the eye.

"But…" Lara sputtered, turning to Tristan. "You don't understand. They took her away from us when she was only a child. We had no choice."

That's when I finally got my mouth to work again. "I

remember it. I saw it all, okay? You didn't even fight. *That* was a choice." Indignation filled every word. Anger. Regret.

My head popped up, letting her see all the pain my eyes had held onto for years.

Tears began to cascade down my mother's face. "We made a mistake. We were in shock. Total shock until it was too late. And you were just…gone." Her voice broke and she sobbed.

I shook my head. Something wet caught my attention, and I wiped at the sensation moving down my cheeks. I was crying too.

"Please," Christopher begged. He was shaking. "Please forgive us. Please, let us be a family again. We've missed you more than you could ever imagine."

I glanced at Tristan, not knowing what to do. *He* was my family. My rock. He would know what to do, what to say. I willed him to do something. *Get me out of here!* He caught my sense of panic and grabbed my hand, squeezing it before nodding.

"I think this is a lot for all of you to process right now. Why don't you let Sasha go to her cabin and you can all talk about this later?"

"After the mission," I said. *I can deal with it then. Just, not now.*

"You can't possibly go on that now!" Lara continued. She had Jessa's hair, dark and wild, and it danced around her face in the firelight, causing something painful to rise in my chest. I didn't want her concern. I didn't know what to do with something like that.

"It's too dangerous," Christopher agreed.

"But we need her. She will save a lot of lives if she goes," Mastin said, the light of the fire igniting his features, making his cropped hair shine. Apparently, he'd caught up on the situation, but his mind was focused on the mission ahead, as it should be. *As mine should be.*

"I'm going," I said, finally feeling a moment of confidence and grabbing on for dear life. "I'll be fine. I'm really good at what I do."

"It's true," Tristan confirmed. "She's the best alchemist we have."

"Then I'll go too," Christopher said calmly. His back straightened.

What? No way!

I shook my head. "No, we promised Jessa we'd keep you three safe."

"Please don't go," Lara tried again.

Lacey had been standing on the edge of the conversation. She didn't seem to get everything that was being said, but she was smart enough to understand her father had just volunteered to go and fight. She crawled into his arms and hugged him tightly around the neck. Her little body trembled with fear and confusion, but she didn't say a word.

"I'm going," Christopher said again. "And I'm getting you and Jessa out of that horrible place." He turned to his wife. "And then we're all going to finally be together."

I cursed inwardly. There was already enough riding on this mission, and now I had to keep my estranged father safe as well. As much as I told myself I hated my parents, deep down, I *wanted* to forgive them. I wanted the hole in my heart to be filled. I wanted to be loved by a mom and a dad and siblings, just as any normal girl was. And if I was ever going to get the chance, I had to keep him alive. A man with no military training, no magic, and no advantage except an overpowering will to reunite his family. He was a liability, but from the conviction in his voice there would be no convincing him otherwise. I didn't want him to die.

Why can't I just say that? A small part of me longed to

reach out and wrap my arms around him just like Lacey had. I squashed that part.

"It's a bad idea," I said, giving them both a pointed look. "You will probably die."

"I have to try," he shrugged. "Frankie, please understand, we *love* you."

I smiled half-heartedly, attempting to placate them, but I couldn't do it any longer. "It's Sasha," I said. They only blinked at me, confused. "Like I said, it's a bad idea. You can't come. We can talk about what's next when I get back." Then I pushed through the crowd and took off running. I ran like the devil was chasing me, and then I ran faster.

FOURTEEN

LUCAS

"She's what?" I exclaimed, clenching my fists at my sides.

"She's moving in," my father said.

I practically growled as I stared up at the ceiling. "You can't be serious."

He'd called me into his private home office, a place he didn't spend too much time in. Except lately. He worried about there being a spy somewhere in the network of the officers and had started to keep his plans even closer to his chest. Some I knew he even kept from me.

"I don't see what the problem is," he continued. "You barely know her, and she's going to be your wife soon. This is a great opportunity for you both."

I didn't know how to argue with that. He was right, but it still didn't want Celia anywhere near me.

"Besides, you two have wedding plans to make," he shrugged.

I stilled. "We have enough to worry about right now without adding a wedding."

"You're not trying to get out of this, are you?"

Obviously...

He stood, pressing his palms into his desk. "Lucas, we made a deal. Thomas was executed even though he was our only reliable source of red alchemy."

"At the moment," I spat. "Don't pretend like you won't pounce on Jessa the second she's initiated. I know why you're pushing her through."

"You're too protective of her."

"Someone needs to be!"

"It's not your place to be her protector!" He stalked toward me, his face losing its usual calm demeanor. "You are *not* her boyfriend. You are engaged to Celia. She is the daughter of an influential family, a duke and a duchess, charming, beautiful, and more importantly, she's a suitable bride." His voice quieted. "Jessa is and will always be an alchemist under our rule. She will get in line, just like everybody else. Just like *you*, Lucas."

I glared, matching his steely gaze with my own. We both knew I wouldn't back down so easily.

"You cannot be with an alchemist!" he pressed. "We have an established hierarchy here and order must be maintained. The royals. Then the officers. Then the guardians. That's it. We will not allow those lines to be blurred."

"Or what?"

My father sighed exasperated, like I was beyond reason. "Or we will lose our power," he said. "The alchemists already have more than they know. If they get too much power, it won't be difficult for them to overthrow us, eradicate us, Lucas. I know you don't understand it, but it's the way things have to be. Believe it or not, I do love you. And as much as I want you to be happy, I want you to have a promising future."

What kind of future was it to be married to someone against my will? He could tell me how much he loved me, but I didn't see him doing much to show it. "And an alchemist on the throne would ruin everything?"

"It could," he said. "Is that a risk you're willing to take? Because I'm not."

"Yes," I said. "For Jessa, it is. I love her, Dad. Don't you remember what it was like to marry Mom, the woman you loved? Please, don't make me do this." I'd never been so vulnerable with him before. It was probably a lost cause, but I couldn't help it. I had to try. I was a goner when it came to Jessa. I'd been lost to her for months. The thought that I would actually be married to another girl soon was something I couldn't swallow.

"The people need a distraction," he said. "A royal engagement and wedding will keep their eyes off the gritty details of war long enough for us to do what needs to be done."

I stared at the oak-paneled wall for a moment. And at the family portrait taken years ago centered there.

"So this is all about you then, isn't it?" I should have known. It always came back to what he wanted, even if he was twisting it to look like something else. "You're faking the motivation behind this war. We don't know that West America ever did anything to us. So why are you doing this?"

It was true. He could lie about it all he wanted, to the media, the country, the alchemists, himself…but he couldn't get past me.

"I don't expect you to understand," he said, moving for the door, but I stepped in front of it, holding it closed. This conversation wasn't over.

"Try me?" I said.

"We're confined. Our population is growing. Our people

depend on us to provide for them. Millions of people depend on me. We need more land to grow our crops. We need more coal. It's about resources, Lucas. I don't expect you to understand."

"Okay, we need more resources. So you feel justified to just go and *take them*."

"We're the superior nation. Our kingdom is special. What we have here is special. Everyone is taken care of. Everyone has a place. New Colony has thrived because our people chose to go back to the monarchy instead of bickering over every law. And every day that American democracy exists is a day we have a threat to our way of life. They're *bigger* than us! They have more people. It's only a matter of time until they come for us. I would rather be the one to do it first."

"And what makes you think we'll even win?"

"We are stronger than we've ever been. And they're weak right now, having just gone through a politically divisive election. Their people are in turmoil, and ours are united." Crazed excitement filled every word. "We're ready for this. The Guardians of Color are incredible, don't you agree?"

I nodded reluctantly.

"And it's only a matter of time before they see the goldmine they're sitting on and begin to train their alchemists too. Their people have feared magic for generations, but a shift is happening. The new president is sympathetic to alchemists. It was a big part of her platform, the "untapped resource" as she called it. People want change there, and that might just be the change they get. We have to defeat them before they get smart enough to mimic what we've created here."

His reasoning made sense. But his lies? They were wrong and manipulative. His people trusted him, and he would keep that trust with lies and smokescreens. My engagement was just the latest proof of it.

"Father, there has to be a better way," I said.

"Lucas." His eyes held mine. "There is no better way. Get on board. Marry the girl. Please the people. Win the war. That's the plan, and you need to embrace it. It's your future."

"No," I said simply. I didn't accept it. I couldn't.

"I didn't want to have to do this…"

"Do what?"

"Get on board or Jessa will be joining the soldiers and alchemists in the field. We could use her out there anyway."

"She's not ready for something like that! You could get your only red alchemist killed."

"I know," he said. "I'm well aware of how new she is. But I'm also aware that her red alchemy could help us win this war!"

"So that's it, that's all that matters to you? She's a real person. She could die, and then what would you have left?"

"And that's the one thing keeping her here. She's here for her training, to grow strong, to become an asset to this kingdom. She's not here to be with you."

I'd heard enough. I slammed my way from the room, angrier with him than I'd been in ages. I knew what this meant. He was using my feelings for Jessa against me. And he would continue to use her as leverage over me, threatening her safety with my obedience. It only made me hate him more.

There had been moments since Mom's death that I felt myself growing closer to him. Wanting to trust him. Trying to make up excuses for his behavior. Looking for the logic in his seemingly insane choices. But that was over. If he was willing to trade my happiness to better deceive his own people, to win more power, then he didn't really care about me.

I had half a mind to hook up with the Resistance again,

but it was foolish. I'd already gone down that path, and it didn't lead anywhere good. And now with this looming threat about Jessa over my head, I felt too nervous to seek her out. What if he saw an interaction with her as reason to send her away? No. I was alone, with a stranger for a fiancée as my only foreseeable company. I needed to find a way out of this. If he could find my weaknesses and use them against me, then I would just have to return the favor.

●

By that afternoon, Celia had moved into the palace.

And no one put up a fight.

I'd hoped her parents would decline the offer, wanting us to date more or something remotely close to normal, but I wasn't so lucky. This was probably their biggest dream come true, as if their only child couldn't amount to more in life than marrying into higher status. If her father really was as influential as she'd let on, then having his daughter at the palace would only increase his sphere.

The palace sprawled across acres of land, leaving plenty of room for residential living, despite all the government offices that operated here. The guests of the royal family were placed in our area of the estate, so Celia was now living just down a hallway from the entrance to my family apartment. If I wanted to avoid her, it would probably mean more white alchemy. And I didn't want to take the risk. The reason I'd kept my ability hidden as long as I did was because I only used it when absolutely necessary.

But if it got out? There was no telling how my father would react.

Suck it up. I knocked on the door to Celia's suite. *You did this to yourself.*

She smiled coyly as she opened it, stepping back to let me in. She was dressed in a simple, blue gown with a low neckline. "You're just in time, darling," she said. I noticed a crimson flush run up her cheeks, matching her hair. Her eyes widened when they met mine. Maybe this was just as awkward for her as it was for me? "Our wedding planner just arrived."

"Thank God." I smiled and winked. She smiled back earnestly. *She knows I'm being sarcastic right?*

"I hope you don't mind," she said, motioning her hands airily around the suite. "I brought some of my own furnishings."

And that she had.

These suites were all pretty similar in their overstated grandness. She'd replaced everything with frilly and feminine pieces, a lot of white, and way too much pink. Even the main couch was a pale shade of pink. It didn't fit her personality in the slightest. She pretended sweet innocence, but had a hidden side to her, like a viper. I had a feeling her mother had a hand in the decorating. "Of course, I was thrilled when my father suggested that I move in early. I know it's only temporary until we occupy our own suite as newlyweds, but this way we can get to know each other much faster."

So, her father had made the suggestion. *Figures.*

She stared at me expectantly.

"I like what you've done with the place," I said. Her lip quirked skeptically.

"Lucas." A woman I hadn't paid any attention to stood near the table. She matched the room. Unfortunately, that was the best way to describe her. I couldn't put my finger on her name, but I knew her. She'd been planning events at the palace for as long as I'd been alive. Her face was overdone, circles of pink painted on her cheeks. Her hair was styled in a huge yellow poof on the top of her head. And when she smiled, a small smear of lipstick stained her teeth. "I'm so pleased to be your wedding planner for this wonderful occasion," she gushed. "It's been a while since you've had any part in planning the parties here, but of course I expect you to have many things to say about this special day."

Sure.

We all sat, and she jumped into an array of options. My head spun as I half listened. I didn't care what flowers were chosen, or what food we served, or what music we played, because as far as I was concerned, none of this was going to happen. Celia, on the other hand, stepped right into the role of bride-to-be. She had a strong opinion on each and every detail.

I counted my breaths in and out while pathetically attempting to look interested.

"With a winter wedding, our flower options are going to be limited…"

"Wait, what?" I sat forward. "We're having a winter wedding?"

The wedding planner, whom I still hadn't paid enough attention to in order to remember her name, stopped mid-sentence. Celia smiled calmly, not the least bit fazed. "Of course, silly," she said. "The first of December."

"That's only a few months away."

"Yes." She reached out and wrapped her hand in mine. It felt wrong, calloused and cold. "It's very exciting. I can hardly believe it myself. A winter wedding will be so romantic. We'll have white roses everywhere, and I'll wear a fur cape over my dress for the outside photos."

"We can only hope for a storm the day before," the wedding planner added. "A white, untouched backdrop."

"Oh, that would be amazing!"

"There's so much to prepare with this short engagement." She returned to her normal tone. Back to business. "The ceremony will be televised, and the king has already told me to spare no expense. He wants to give the people something they can talk about for ages." She smiled, as if tickled by the thought. "He said that himself, you know." She winked at me.

Wow, lucky me.

How could I be so stupid? In my haste to see judgment served against my mother's murderer, I'd agreed to an engagement. *An engagement.* I'd never said I would be married. I figured I could draw the engagement out long enough to find a way out of actually marrying someone. But what I'd taken as one thing, my father had turned into something else: an arranged marriage.

Who was I kidding? An engagement *meant* a wedding, which *meant* a marriage. But I had to wonder. Why so quickly? And why *this girl?* It couldn't really be about saving face. There had to me more.

As the women continued on with the planning, my gut told me to bolt. But I stayed rooted; I was going to have to figure out Celia. There had to be some deeper reason why she was here. Of course becoming queen was good enough reason for many women in the kingdom, but there was something about her father. And the way she *talked* about her father.

He would be my exit out of this marriage.

If I could get enough dirt on him, could I use it as leverage to break off the engagement? I had to try. Part of me felt bad for Celia. She was just as much a pawn in this as I was. But she didn't see it that way. Our earlier conversation in my bedroom, the one where she'd all but told me it was okay to sleep around as long as I was discreet, said as much.

She was not in this for love, but she was not in this for money.

She was in this for power. For herself. For her family. And most definitely for her father. I needed to find out why.

After the wedding planner left, I stayed. Celia expected it; I could tell by the way she never let go of my hand, her fingers crushing mine. We sat on the couch and she immediately moved in closer.

"You know—" Her green eyes fired up. "You could have offered your opinion."

"About what?"

She scoffed, "With the wedding plans. It would help the situation for everyone if you at least tried to enjoy this."

I needed to tread lightly. She wasn't going to call off this engagement. That much was clear. And if I didn't play nice, she'd likely go tattling to her daddy, who would in turn go to my father. And I didn't want to deal with another of his threats. Jessa couldn't afford it.

"Sorry," I said. "I'm just…in shock, still, I think. It's not your fault."

Okay, it kind of *was* her fault.

"You can't be a bachelor forever," she said. "Eventually this was bound to happen. But marriage won't be that bad, I *promise*." I wasn't sure I liked the way she said *promise*. Any promise she made came attached to strings I didn't want to pull.

"What aren't you telling me?" I asked, pushing for a weak spot.

She paused. "I'm going to be your wife. You need to trust me."

"How can I trust you? I don't even know you."

"Then get to know me." She stood and strode to the window. This was a game of cat and mouse. The problem she didn't seem to understand? I didn't want the mouse.

I changed tactics. "Let's have dinner with your family again." I swallowed, careful to keep my tone playful. "I didn't do a very good job last time, I'm afraid."

She turned, a smile back on her lips. "That's a great idea. I'll call and arrange it for tonight."

So soon...

But with a wedding date in less than two months, I didn't have a lot of options left. If I was going to get something on this family, I couldn't waste a day. The sooner, the better.

"I'm looking forward to it." I joined her at the window, kissed her gently on the cheek, and left her to daydream about a wedding that would never happen.

●

"We have news." My father strode into my room without even a knock. He rarely did that. My large bedroom—with a sitting area, bathroom, and adjoining office—had always been my own private space. But there was a light in his eyes tonight, an excitement, and he couldn't help himself from sharing it.

"Good news?" I said, standing from the couch where I'd been trying to distract myself with a book. I was meeting Celia for dinner in a few minutes, and the very thought of it made my stomach squirm.

"*Great* news," my father said.

He closed the door behind him and smiled widely. I stepped back. I couldn't remember the last time I'd seen a genuine smile on the man. Of course, Mom's death hadn't been easy for anyone, but even before that, he'd held a permanent scowl while around me. It was only in the presence of cameras that he seemed to transform into the charming king the people thought they knew.

"We've received more reports back from the attack. It appears that even though West America was expecting something, they weren't very well prepared. In just a few short days, we've taken over *thousands of miles* of their eastern territory."

My gut twisted in knots, but I nodded. I was stuck, unable to side with any end result the attack could have gone.

"Of course, there's work to be done. Their most populated areas is the west coast, but we've cut them off from a lot of important farmland."

His smile was magnetic. Gleeful. I was kind of disgusted to think he was excited about cutting people off from food.

"That's great, Dad. I'm glad things are going your way." I hated it. I hated lying. I wanted to go back to the days where I could tell this man off without such harsh consequences. But with the forced engagement and Jessa's safety on the line, I needed to play nice.

He was a fool too because his face lit up when I called him Dad. It was manipulative. I'd been using his first name for years.

"I'm glad to see you're starting to understand, son." He put his hand on my back, leading me to the door. "I want you to keep attending briefings with me. It seems it's doing you good."

I wanted to laugh. *No, it's called blackmail. That's why I'm playing nice.* I clenched my fists.

"I heard you're having dinner with your beautiful fiancée tonight and her parents," he said. "I would join you, but I'm going to be helping Faulk select which alchemists to send out next."

I stopped. "Not *her*."

"A deal's a deal. Keep up your end, and I'll always keep up mine."

Relief washed through me.

He walked me to Celia's suite, because I was apparently *picking them up* to come back to our dining room. They were waiting eagerly, dressed stylishly and regally. The women wore extravagant gowns and the men wore tailored suits, as was customary for a royal dinner. Not that I expected anything less. It's how we did things at the palace. It wasn't like when I was with Jessa, when I could wear jeans and a t-shirt. When I could just be myself.

The family exchanged pleasantries with my father before he took off toward the officers' wing, and I led them back to our home. I was distracted, barely paying attention to the conversation. I needed to focus. If I was going to get something on Mark, I had to get serious about what I was doing.

As we approached the royal suite, I almost missed a step. Jessa.

She stood at the door, biting her bottom lip. Our two guards glared at her. Her expectant gaze seemed to indicate she was hoping to talk to someone on the other side of that door. Me?

"Jessa." I narrowed my eyes, and Celia squeezed my hand. I'd forgotten we were even holding hands. It wasn't like I'd initiated it—or like I even would. "What are you doing here?"

"I was…" She faltered, taking us in. "I was hoping to talk to your father."

Of course. She knew to stay away from me.

"He's with Officer Faulk, dear," Celia's mother, Sabine, said.

Jessa nodded and skirted past us. I tried not to follow her with my eyes, but I failed miserably. In a second, she was gone.

As we gathered in the dining room, my mind wouldn't

stop thinking about her. I wanted to talk to her so bad. I wanted to explain. I'd stayed away because she'd told me to. But maybe that was a mistake. And now she'd seen me holding Celia's hand, going to dinner with my fiancée's family.

"Was that girl an alchemist?" Celia asked coolly as I pulled out her chair. The table was dressed with silver domes at each setting, our first course waiting for us to dig in. She eyed it with an apparent lack of interest.

"Yes," I said, careful that my voice sounded indifferent.

"Dangerous little things, aren't they?" Mark said, adjusting his large frame in his chair. "But I suppose I should be thanking them."

"Why's that?"

"Without them we couldn't possibly face a foe like West America and expect to win. But with them? Well, it's good for business."

"Business?"

"Your father and I have an agreement," Mark continued and cleared his throat. "What's good for the war is also good for me."

Who was he? I wracked my brain, trying to remember what he did. At some point, someone must have said something. Celia caught my confusion because she added, "Daddy manages the food supply for New Colony. He's very good at getting the farmers to do what they're supposed to. And now, we'll have more for everyone."

Not more for everyone. More for New Colony.

It made sense. We didn't live in a traditional economy, far from it. Everyone was given a job according to their station, schooling, and skills. If someone wanted to move up, they had to apply to do so. The highest-ranking officials controlled everything, under the direction of the monarchy, of course. Mark must run the farming sector, controlling what seeds went where and who was paid what. It was an important job. One I'd paid little attention to.

Fortunately, dinner didn't last too long. When the plates had been cleared, I insisted Celia leave with her parents, pretending I had a headache. "They run in the family, you know," I said, rubbing my temples. They nodded, probably having heard about my mother's mysterious migraines before she died.

The staff cleared out as they said their goodbyes quickly. Celia even kissed me gently on the cheek. Then they left me sitting in my chair. The second they turned the corner, I grabbed a white rose and pinched the petals. The magic filled me in a rush of prickly heat. I watched as my body faded away. Yes, I was going against my normal way of conducting alchemy—which was not to do it at all. But was the risk worth it to follow Celia's father?

I intended to find out.

I held my breath and followed the Addington family out the door.

FIFTEEN

JESSA

I lay on my bed, counting all the reasons why I hated the tests. But I was starting to understand the purpose of them. All this magic was forcing me outside my comfort zone. And I was getting better with each one. Even though the tests themselves were pretty screwed up, so were the people who created such extremely dangerous scenarios.

First the water, then the interrogation, then trying to save the girl in the forest. They'd grown in intensity with each one, the worst of them being the experience with green alchemy. I still had the image in my head. The pain still fresh in my memory. And the blood, it had taken a scalding shower to get it off me. I'd had to throw my pajamas in the trash.

Would orange possibly be more terrible?

I trusted that Jasmine would tell the truth. I held onto that trust, because I was too terrified to imagine the worst. *No. Orange will be fine. It won't be so bad.*

I had gone about my day as normal on the outside, but inside, I was full of jitters. I kept expecting to be taken away for the test. Nothing happened. I couldn't handle the anticipation. The waiting.

Sitting up for a second, I plopped my pillows back into place and fell back with a huff. I couldn't believe how dumb I had been!

I'd gotten it into my stupid head to go and talk to the king directly. He wanted me initiated. I had reasoned that another test wasn't even necessary. I would pass since orange alchemy wasn't that hard for anyone. But pass or fail, I was confident I'd be joining the guardians. King Richard wanted my red alchemy. That was what everyone had been saying for weeks. So I figured I could just go right up to him and ask for my initiation.

Besides, I had an even bigger reason to get it over with: the Resistance.

Jasmine said I'd be tested in the morning, and the next day would be my initiation. Well, nothing had happened this morning. The Resistance was ready to attack. I didn't want there to be any delays. I was ready for this. Ready to help the cause.

I had sat outside the royal wing, waiting—hoping to catch the king and praying I didn't see Lucas. My heart was shredded because of that boy. But of course life being awesome, he walked right up to me with his fiancée's hand tucked perfectly in his own. I had scurried away as quickly as possible. So angry for putting myself in that situation.

I never should have dated him.

I groaned and rolled over. My pillow was all wet and pathetic. Of course after seeing Lucas and his new fiancée, I'd locked myself in my dorm room. I had thought for sure Lucas would have come to me with some explanation for his engagement, but he never did. And seeing the two of them like that? The tears I'd been holding inside for days came bursting out. More than anything I just wanted to go home.

You don't have a home.

I curled up into a ball, so sick of feeling sorry for myself. This wasn't me. I needed to get past this.

A loud knock sounded on the door. I held my breath. I was so not ready to face anyone. Maybe if I was extra quiet, they'd go away.

"Open up," the unmistakable voice of Faulk said. "It's time for some orange alchemy."

"One second," I called.

I quickly ran to the bathroom to wash and dry my tear-stained cheeks. I ran my brush through my hair at record speed and called it good.

I opened the door.

Once again she was surrounded by officers. Was she ever alone? I was pretty tall, even taller than most of them. But from the way they assessed me skeptically, I felt small. I spotted the man on whom I'd secretly performed red alchemy at the back of the group and looked away. *No need to stare, Jessa.*

"How can I help you?" I tried to keep my tone level. Lately, I suspected Faulk was warming up to me as much as an ice queen could. She wasn't so suspicious around me. Nor was she so angry. She didn't snap at the things I said or watch me with cool contempt. I'd take any improvement I could get! Still, I didn't want to ruin it. If there was one thing she hated it was defiance, something I had in spades.

"It's time for your last test," she said. "This should be easy." Then she turned and marched down the hall. I followed behind, my thoughts flying in a million different directions.

"It will come as no surprise to you that this last test is in orange alchemy."

I rolled my eyes at her back. "Yup. Thanks for warning me this time." If she caught the indirect complaint about the green test, she made zero indication.

Deep breaths.

"So when I'm initiated, then what? Will I be able to talk to my family?"

I really hated asking the question I already had the answer to. I knew for a fact the Resistance had my family and they weren't even in New Colony anymore. But Faulk and Richard didn't know where they were. They'd lied to me. They pretended to have them in custody. Leverage. I couldn't give away what I knew, so that meant acting like I believed their stupid story.

"Everything in due time," she said over her shoulder.

Liar!

"Well, I've worked really hard to prove my loyalty to you," I said. "But I can't help it. I'm worried about them. I just want to make sure they're being treated okay. They never did anything wrong."

She didn't say anything.

"I know you're not afraid to put people in prison," I pushed, "but you've got to have good reason to do it or it's just cruel."

I'd been detained in holding cells twice. Once when I was first discovered, and again when I'd been questioned about Sasha's disappearance after I'd run away. The places I'd been were completely gray, not a shred of color anywhere. Nothing an alchemist could get their hands on and manipulate to their advantage. I wondered where they put non-magical people.

She stopped abruptly, turning to meet my gaze. Hers was cold, calculated. She watched me carefully, scanning for something. A break. A lie, perhaps? Shivers ran up my body. I had to play into this game of theirs. If I didn't, I'd appear even more suspicious.

"They're fine," she finally said. "You have nothing to worry about. We'll talk about it more *after* your initiation."

I nodded and looked to the floor, no longer able to meet the eyes of someone who'd done nothing but lie to me. Her job wasn't to protect me. It was to protect everyone else from me, and use me to do it.

We began walking again. I kept my mouth shut.

One good thing had come out of our conversation. She'd basically confirmed it. I was going to be initiated! This final test was just for show, a customary event. The king wanted what he wanted, and even though I'd failed blue and purple, I could still do them. I was more than good enough. Besides, it was the red he cared about...

I tried to imagine what would happen tomorrow during my initiation. They would have their attack, and even though I couldn't participate, I could still pray they accomplished what they came for.

What if they hurt Lucas? That thought had been running circles in my head for the last twenty-four hours.

No. They won't.

Would they?

He used to be one of us, but lately, he'd gone so far in the other direction. He was spending more time with his father than ever and was engaged to the exact type of woman his father expected. He'd even been on the stage when they'd executed Thomas and when Richard had made his threats. *There will be no mercy for traitors.*

I shook the thought from my head. Lucas was all over the place lately, and it pained me to even think about what would happen to him.

"Tell me something, Jessa." Faulk turned. We now stood outside a closed door in the same wing of the palace I'd first stayed in. I had a feeling that I wouldn't like whatever was

245

on the other side. "How much do you know about orange alchemy?"

"Umm." I faltered, eyeing the door. "It's an enhancer, used for emotions."

"And what else?"

I wasn't sure. My mind traveled back to when I'd spent weeks studying the color wheels and all the different attributes of each. "Creativity."

"Very good," she said.

"But I don't know how to use it for creativity," I mumbled.

"Orange can help you figure problems out. It can help you see solutions that you might not normally see," she said. "You just have to use it the same way you would for emotions, with the focus of trying to understand something."

That was interesting news to me. Useful.

"Why are you helping me?" I asked. I had every right to be skeptical of her sudden interest. What was in this for her?

"Because passing this test will not only guarantee your initiation, something I tried to fight but now see as inevitable—" She frowned. "But it will help your kingdom. More specifically, it will help me."

"I don't understand…"

"Of course not." She stepped closer. "Your test is simple enough. On the other side of that door are two people who may or may not be sympathetic to our enemies. They don't know what you can do. They don't know the nuances of alchemy."

"And what do you want me to do?" My voice cracked.

"Use orange alchemy to enhance their emotions. Help us figure them out, Jessa." She smiled ruefully, the skin around her mouth tight. "I already have a good idea they're against us. Your job is to prove it. It'll be easy."

I nodded as she placed a corded necklace with an amber

pendant around my neck. Then she pushed open the door, and we entered a sitting room. It was much like the one I'd been brought into months ago when I'd first arrived here. Cozy and welcoming; everything about the space appeared safe. But I knew better.

A fire crackled in the wood-burning fireplace, and plush leather couches faced each other in the intimate space. A dark burgundy, plush rug covered some of the polished wooden floor. Orange pillows rested on the couches, and orange succulent plants were placed in a woodsy centerpiece on a large coffee table.

A young man and woman stood by the window, talking in low voices. They jolted when they saw us, but turned and smiled. Their nerves rolled off them in waves of fear as their eyes shifted between us. I didn't blame them. It seemed Faulk had brought them in for interrogation. But first, she wanted to see what I could do. Orange test, huh? I had a feeling this was a little different than a typical alchemist's test. I ignored my resentment and strolled into the room.

"Hello again," Faulk said. "How was your dinner?"

"It was great." The woman smiled weakly. "Thank you."

Faulk nodded. "Please, come and have a seat."

The couple moved to one couch, and Faulk and I took the other. The frantic energy was palpable; it wasn't just coming from them. *I can do this.*

Now would not be the time to use the orange alchemy. All I would get from anyone would be more of the same. And nervous didn't tell us anything.

"Jessa," Faulk said, smiling. Her face turned into the picture of joy, and she looked nothing like her normal self. I bit my lip and stared. "I'd like you to meet Jane and Parker Abbot. Remind me, you two are newlyweds, aren't you?" Faulk's charm was nothing but creepy!

247

"We've been married a year now," Jane said, reaching for her husband's hand. "But I guess you could say we're still new to this whole marriage thing."

He looked at her with fixed adoration, and she blushed. What they had was real. They loved each other and had gotten married for no other reason than that. It was how marriages were supposed to work!

"Wonderful," Faulk said. She turned to me. "These two were invited to the palace for a little tour. Isn't that wonderful?" I nodded, a little confused. People didn't just get invited for palace tours. "They were both there that day, you know? Terribly tragic."

"What day?" I asked. Jane's and Parker's faces flushed simultaneously as they looked at the floor.

"The day of the attack, of course," Faulk continued. "These two were rather heroic, I must say."

"Oh, I wouldn't say that," Jane said.

"We just did what anyone else would do," Parker added.

"Oh, nonsense." Faulk laughed amicably. "When everyone else was running away from the gunman, you two were running toward him. Tell me again, why on earth would you do that?"

There was a long pause. "Instinct, I guess," Parker said. He shifted, running a hand through his dark hair. "I had to take him down, and Jane came after me." He shrugged.

Jane nodded, her chin shaking. "I shouldn't have, but I couldn't help it. I love Parker. I wasn't going to let that terrorist kill my husband."

"Like I said, very brave."

So that's why Faulk had these two here. It was odd that two citizens would run after a gunman like that. But that hardly proved anything, right? At the very least, it was an act of bravery. Still, something about the discomfort between them told me there was more to the story. I briefly wondered if they were part of the Resistance and whether I should try to protect them. But if they were involved in that attack somehow, no way they were Resistance. A trickle of curiosity wormed its way in.

"You're very brave," I said. Putting my hand over the necklace so no one could see the magic, I allowed the orange to filter into me. Faulk was right. By using the magic during that moment, I had enhanced my feelings of suspicion. Suddenly, every rise of an eyebrow or held breath or shared look was part of a puzzle. I wasn't sure who these people were. My initial instinct was to like them, but that didn't mean I should. And it didn't mean they were innocent. Maybe they really did have something to do with the shooting. Maybe they knew the shooter.

"Did you ever figure out who the shooter was?" I asked Faulk. Officially, King Richard had said it was a spy with West America. Maybe that was the truth, but what if it wasn't?

"Oh, that information is still classified," Faulk purred, then pointed to a tea trolley in the corner. "Jessa, will you do us the honors?"

I stood and wandered to it. I began pouring hot tea into cups. This was my moment; Faulk had set me up on purpose. I pulled a little of the orange magic into my hand while my back was turned and deposited it into the cups. It only enhanced the dark color of the tea and was pretty much unnoticeable. This would be easier than actually touching our guests, but it would work the same. At parties, orange magic enhanced true feelings. It would work here too.

"Well," I said, "you two are wonderful for doing what you did. You probably saved lives that day."

"They did," Faulk said. "They took the man down before

we even got there. Of course, it would have been nice to keep him alive for questioning, but beggars can't be choosers, right?"

So that's what happened.

"You took him out?" I gasped, handing them the teacups at that exact moment. "How brave! You should be so proud."

They both looked down and then took sips from their cups.

"I'm not proud," Jane muttered.

"Why not?" I asked, placing my hand on her shoulder. A little more orange wouldn't hurt, would it?

"He didn't deserve to die," she said.

Guilt.

It was guilt they were both immersed in now. It was so heavy it clouded their better judgment. But I was sure it wouldn't last long.

"Why not?"

"He wasn't a—"

"She only means that it would have been better to question him," Parker jumped into the conversation, cutting his wife off. He was right back to nervous. I would have to focus on his wife.

"Of course." I smiled as I walked behind them, taking the long way back to the trolley to return the tray.

"He was a bad man, wasn't he?" I asked. On the way back to my seat, I lightly touched both of their shoulders, leaning between them for an answer. If that question elicited them to hide something, to disagree, we would know.

"He wasn't what you think," Parker said at the same time as Jane said, "He wasn't one of us, sure. But not bad. He was *good.*"

I stepped back and caught the satisfaction on Faulk's face. "Is that enough?"

She nodded and licked her lips.

"What's going on?" Jane mumbled just as the door burst open and guards swarmed in. I moved to the side to make room for the guards, and Faulk joined me. She seemed pleased with me for once, and I didn't know how I felt about it.

"We already suspected they were working with the gunman somehow."

We watched the couple, still in a daze as they were put into handcuffs. It all happened so fast that they barely had time to protest.

"No worries." Faulk continued moving toward them. Her tone was back to the pleasant one from before. "Now that we're sure, we'll get all that we need from you during interrogation."

"But…" Jane sputtered. "What just happened?"

"Take them," Faulk ordered. It only took a minute, and we were left alone in the room. The teacups sat on the coffee table, still warm. I picked up my own and studied it. The liquid warmed my fingers. I squeezed my eyes tightly shut for a moment, hoping I had just done the right thing.

"That was impressive," Faulk said, moving to the door. "Can you imagine how easy it will be once we use red to do it?"

I gulped. *What have I done?*

I followed her out to find none other than King Richard waiting for us. He was talking lazily with Celia's parents in the hallway. My eyes darted between the three as they looked over at me. They seemed unfazed by what I'd just done. Maybe it wasn't a big deal to them, but my heart exploded in my chest just thinking about it.

"I knew you'd pass." Richard beamed at me. "But that was fast."

"Uh, thanks." My tentative happiness at completing the task evaporated.

"Good job, dear," Celia's mother said. Her eyes moved down me with contempt. It was clear she wanted nothing to do with an alchemist. Her husband did a better job of hiding his feelings, but even he held a grimace on his face. *Or maybe they don't like the way Lucas looks at me?*

Nonsense. He'd moved on. If he hadn't, he would have come to me by now. I hesitated, ready to leave.

"We'll make the announcement," Richard said. "Tomorrow night, there will be a banquet to celebrate your initiation."

"Wow," I said, my smile faltering. "Thanks."

"Your initiation will follow immediately after."

I nodded, the words no longer able to form on my tongue. I didn't know how I felt about all of this. The group left, and I rushed to my room.

As I walked, my heart thumped in my ears like the heavy beat of a drum. This was happening. I was being initiated tomorrow night. I was *in* with the king. I would be one of them. And at the same time, the banquet would allow for an attack. The odds of taking out Richard were pretty slim. The palace was crawling with people sworn to protect him. But an attack *would* weaken his forces, and it would send a message to all the alchemists: *there's another choice. Join us.*

No one had told me the specifics, and true to her word, Jasmine had closed up on all things Resistance.

Be careful. Stay out of the way. We need you to appear loyal.

That's what she'd asked. That's what I would do.

I rounded the corner to my dorm, eager to take a shower and get to bed. I needed to wash away all images of what just happened. I was terrified I'd done the wrong thing, but that gunman had stolen innocent lives. How could anyone sympathize with that?

Sleep. That's what I needed. Not that I expected much of it. I was too nervous. This was happening. Really happening! One day closer to seeing my family again. One day closer to freedom.

I stopped abruptly.

"The guards told me where to find you." Celia was leaning nonchalantly against my doorframe. She still wore the extravagant dress from earlier, appearing as relaxed in it as I was in my pajamas. She yawned. "Let's get this over with, shall we?"

She was in GC territory. Was she not afraid of alchemy? No, if she was anything like her parents, she just hated us. Her hard gaze shifted over me, a question forming.

"Can we talk, woman to woman?" She reached out her manicured hand. I nearly stumbled as I stepped forward to shake it. I was a ballerina for crying out loud. When did I suddenly have two left feet?

She made me nervous. That was why. Everything about her reflected my own insecurities back to me. She had what I wanted. Pure and simple. Her grip was firm as she smiled.

"Sure, come in." I opened the door.

"It's...cute," she said, her gaze roving over the small, sparse room.

"It's fine," I said. "It's not like I chose it."

"That's funny." She smiled. "I thought being an alchemist was an honor. I'm certainly honored to have the opportunity to live at the palace."

"Such an honor," I quipped.

She raised an eyebrow, and I ran my fingers through my messy hair and bit my bottom lip. I needed to relax. This girl wasn't my enemy. Lucas had made his choices all on his own.

I sat on the bed and motioned for her to take a seat at the desk. "Why did you want to talk to me?"

"How long have you known Lucas?" she asked.

Of course she wanted to question me about him.

"Not long," I said. "I've only been here about four months."

"And in four months, you managed to get him to fall in love with you?" She didn't say it defensively, as a fiancée would. It came out more as a matter of fact. A question even, like, *how did I do it?*

My stomach twisted. "What? Why would you say that?"

Her lips twisted and she rolled her eyes.

"If he loved me, why would he be engaged to you? Lucas and I aren't even talking anymore."

"Then why were you waiting outside his door earlier?"

"I was trying to talk to Richard."

"You're on a first name basis with the king?"

"Kind of," I frowned. "I was going to ask him about a test I had to take tonight, okay? Why is that any of your business?"

She smiled, and it lit up her entire being. My heart ached as I realized that maybe she could find her way into Lucas's heart after all.

"You don't have to get upset. It was just a question," she said, kindness in her voice.

I shook my head. I wanted to ask her to leave, but I had to remember my place, and I didn't need to make any more enemies. She was the fiancée of the prince, and there was a real possibility she would become the next queen. I felt like puking and crying at the same time.

"Listen, your name is Jessa, right?" she asked. I nodded. "Listen, Jessa, I'm not here to tell you to back off my man, if that's what you're thinking."

My jaw dropped—like literally dropped—at the laugh that exploded out of her mouth.

"I know, not what you expected the second you saw me waiting outside your door, right?" she said. "But the truth is,

I hardly know Lucas. And he hardly knows me. It's not fair of me to lay claim to his heart."

"Umm…okay." What was I supposed to say to that? It was so weird. Was this some kind of reverse psychology? Some kind of game?

"But I *am* laying claim to the crown."

"And there it is." I sighed.

Of course that's what this is about…

"And there it is." She nodded. This woman was bizarre. She had to be close in age to me, and she cared more about a crown than about marrying for love. A little jaded for someone so young.

"How old are you?" I asked.

"Eighteen."

"Don't you think eighteen is a little young to be married?" In New Colony, most people paired off in their mid-twenties, but younger marriages weren't unheard of. But still, I certainly didn't feel quite ready to get married. She was only two years older. And I could honestly admit I was *in love* with Lucas. How could she be ready for that level of commitment when she'd just admitted the opposite?

"He's a prince, Jessa. Come on, you're smarter than that. It's a monarchy, and he's an only child. The. Only. Heir." She smoothed her red hair, fingering a piece at the end, before turning her eyes back to me. "No doubt his parents tried for more. Just in case. But as it stands, Lucas needs to have children."

"And you're going to do that for him?" I was going to be sick. My body tense, I breathed in slowly as I waited for her answer.

She shrugged. "I am."

"So that doesn't explain why you're here."

"It's simple." She almost looked sorry for me. I didn't want her pity. "I'm not stupid enough to expect him to stay away from you. I saw the way you looked at each other, and I knew there had to be a reason why he's been so aloof with me. Men are never that way with me." No doubt; she was gorgeous and sophisticated. She was the type of girl to get her pick, no matter which men were on offer. "I'm just asking you to do me the courtesy of keeping things private. And safe, if you know what I mean."

Okay, now I really was going to puke!

I stood. "I don't know what you think is going on, but Lucas and I are over."

She studied me and finally shrugged. "Well, I thought I would ask. You know, woman to woman. Just in case it isn't *really* over."

"That boy has put me through so much, you have no idea. I refuse to be someone's second choice."

She stood, nodding. "All right. I guess I underestimated you."

"You did."

I'd had enough. I jumped off the bed and stalked to the door, wrenching it open. "Have a good night."

"Thank you," she said over her shoulder as she left. "I think I'll do that."

I had to keep myself from slamming the door.

I stomped to the shower. I ripped off my top, screwing it into a tight ball until my knuckles turned white. Peering down for a moment, I threw it at the wall and practically growled as I finished undressing. How could Lucas be engaged to that woman? She was truly sadistic if she thought I'd be her husband's mistress. That's what she'd alluded to. I would keep him happy, love him, and she'd run the household, give him children, and most important to her, she'd be queen.

It was wrong on every level!

It broke my heart to be away from him. I missed him so much. I missed our easy conversations and the way he challenged me. I missed the looks he gave that were only for me. I loved him. But I wasn't willing to share. I wouldn't stick around and be his side-woman. I had more self-respect than that. Besides, after the experience with Sasha last summer, my heart couldn't take it. Whatever had happened to cause his engagement was *their* business. Let him deal with it. I was staying out of it.

The water scalded my skin, pelting hot irons with each drop. I didn't turn the shower heat down. I wanted the distraction. *Don't think. Don't feel.* But for the second time that night, it happened anyway. I cried.

This time, my tears washed away instantly.

SIXTEEN

LUCAS

As I stood pressed against the wall, I realized that invisibility was a blessing and a curse. It was exhausting. Dangerous. Tailing people at a distance and silently slipping through open doors behind them was less than enjoyable. I didn't know what I expected to discover taking off after the Addington family. Would I have to follow the man *home*? And then what?

They first took Celia back to her new room, going in together before I had a chance to follow. I waited outside, trying to keep my eyes open as the minutes ticked by. It would've been a lot more useful to have an affinity for blue alchemy. But it wasn't my forte, and grumbling to myself wouldn't solve anything. I willed the conversation to filter through the door but couldn't make out a word.

Just when I'd about given up, thinking about where the closest and safest place to make myself visible would be, the thick door swung open. Inertia nearly landed me flat on the ground, but I was able to jump back and out of the way. I studied the family, but they didn't seem to notice anything.

They headed toward the GC wing—a curious choice, considering normal people didn't venture over that way.

Celia broke off, heading toward the guardian dorms. Her parents didn't go with her. They kept going into the heart of alchemist territory. They didn't seem to be bothered about what they saw, not even cautious. Occasionally, a guardian would give them a funny look, but mostly they were ignored. I think everyone had the war on their minds: wondering what it all meant, if they were next, if their friends were okay. The whole palace was turned upside-down so apparently a couple of citizens taking a stroll down their hallway didn't seem out of the ordinary. The palace wasn't the same place it used to be. Not for any of us.

We continued down the hallway and when they met up with my father, I shouldn't have been surprised. I mean, really? But I was.

"How is she doing in there?" Mark said.

"She'll pass." My father nodded calmly.

The next moment, a door opened and a bunch of guards pulled a handcuffed couple from the premises. They looked a little confused, but definitely agitated. They were quickly whisked away. A second later, Faulk and Jessa exited the room. Jessa was pale as a ghost, but a wisp of accomplishment tilted her smile. At odds, to say the least. I wanted to help her. To touch her. Something.

I stood back, listening to their conversation, waiting for something out of the ordinary. My father placed a hand on Jessa's back. "We'll make the announcement," he said. "Tomorrow night there will be a banquet to celebrate your initiation. Your initiation will follow immediately after."

She smiled and responded appropriately, but I could sense something else behind those eyes. Worry? A few more words were exchanged, and Jessa headed back to her room.

I stuck around. Just as she was out of earshot, Richard rounded on Faulk. "I told you she was good."

She shook her head. "It was never a matter of Jessa's power, it was always a matter of her loyalty."

I sucked in a breath as my whole body went numb.

"You and I both know we can't *really* know who's loyal anymore, can we?" Richard's face flashed. My mind conjured an image of Thomas; my father was right. "It's not a matter of *if* we have more executions, but *when*. The least we can do is use up these alchemists' powers while we can."

Would he have done that with Thomas? Faulk shouldn't have missed the signs, and she had to know it. They could have used his red alchemy years ago.

Faulk pinched her lips and nodded. "We need to be extra cautious."

"Come." Richard patted Mark on the shoulder. "Let's get out of here, and we can talk more about our plans."

I followed the group, and the security detail that was my father's constant shadow. They went to the officers' headquarters, which were in another part of the GC wing, so it was easy to slip into the selected office with everyone else. When my father asked the security team to leave, I ducked into a corner. No one batted an eyelid in my direction. After a minute, it was only the four of them remaining.

Sabine stood aloof on one side, an older version of her daughter. The resemblance was uncanny if not a little bit disturbing.

"What have you found out?" Richard asked.

"We've been interrogating people all along the borders. Anyone who lives near there, asking them if they've seen people, helicopters, airplanes, anything," Mark said.

"And?" Faulk raised an eyebrow.

"So far we only have a few leads but they didn't pan out."

Richard narrowed his eyes. "That's not good enough."

"I know," Mark said. "We're not giving up."

"And what about that one helicopter? It was heading north the same day Sasha went missing."

"We're still investigating. It must have been going to Canada."

"How did it disappear like that?"

"We still don't have the answer to that."

"Magic!" Richard began to pace.

"It's obvious they have alchemists," Faulk said. "The question is how did they use magic to get away from us like that? Invisibility is not something we've ever seen before, and we need to find out how it's done. What do their alchemists know that ours don't?"

That this was still under investigation was a problem. I realized I was utterly juvenile to believe the incident had been forgotten. Of course it hadn't been. It was still the forefront of my father's worries, and apparently Mark wasn't who he said he was. These people weren't in charge of managing farming and food resources. Or if they were, it was only part of the job. He was an investigator for my father. Someone undercover?

"Keep looking," my father said. "Keep interrogating."

Mark nodded.

"And what of your efforts here?" Sabine asked. She'd been standing off to the side, seemingly innocuous, when she turned to casually join the conversation.

"Like I said," Faulk interrupted, "we're being cautious."

"There must be a spy in the palace somewhere," Mark added.

"We know that," Faulk replied. "We're working on it."

"You think it's Jessa," Sabine purred, her green eyes focusing on Faulk.

"I think everything started the moment she showed up," Faulk replied defensively.

"Or it's merely coincidence," Richard said. "We've gone over this again and again. The girl is only sixteen. She was a dancer before coming here. What could she possibly know?"

"Her parents are missing."

The room fell silent.

"It is curious," Mark offered. "But it's not proof of anything. It could be that her parents were the spies and she knew nothing of it."

"Does she know about her older sister?" Sabine asked.

"We don't know," Faulk said.

"But the two were put together unwittingly," Richard accused.

"We've gone over this," Faulk said. "There *must* be a spy in the palace because otherwise Sasha never would have been able to infiltrate our system. Her cover was carefully planned out. I still want to know why she left."

They quieted for a long moment.

"You've combed through every person here, every alchemist? Every servant and guard and officer? You're sure of their history?" Mark asked.

"I'm positive," Faulk said. "No more false identities. We won't let that mistake happen again."

Richard shook his head. "She was Francesca, wasn't she? That girl who got stolen from us years ago?"

"We believe so," Faulk said.

"It was a blow to lose her. I can't believe she came back, and we missed her." He directed his words at Faulk, and she shrunk back. "It makes sense now that Jessa would be a red alchemist like her older sister. Talented family. Dangerous…"

"Then the damage is already done." Mark rubbed the back of his neck.

"Maybe," Sabine said, walking over to place a hand on her husband's shoulder. "Or maybe it was a blessing in disguise."

"Explain." Richard motioned to her, a flicker of hope crossing his features.

"Now that you know the parents have disappeared, and about Sasha, or should I say, Francesca, you know that someone is out there trying to get Jessa back. You can keep her close, protect what's yours." Sabine smiled. "Not to mention, now you know there's a mole in the palace in the first place."

"We need to start interrogating the alchemists." Richard nodded.

"I wouldn't alert them just yet." Mark relaxed. "If we can find the Resistance leader, we can cut them off at the knees."

They stood in companionable silence for a few minutes, possibly going through all the scenarios in their heads, weighing the options. They knew about the Resistance, that much was clear. From what I gathered, my father had called in extra help after Sasha had turned out to be a fake. Now they were searching for answers, trying to find her as well as Jessa's parents. And, of course, they were watching Jessa closely.

"How's Celia doing?" Richard asked, breaking the silence.

"She's unsure," Sabine said.

His eyes narrowed.

"Your son is obviously in love with Jessa. Even you know that much. But Celia isn't sure if it's just that or if something else is going on."

"Like what?"

An icy chill ran through my entire body.

"Richard," Mark interjected, "you already know Lucas went from dating Sasha to dating Jessa. It is suspicious."

"You don't think I know that?" Richard challenged. "What

263

is Celia's take on it? Does she think Lucas is the spy?"

"She's not sure." Sabine shrugged. "But she's leaning toward no. However, it's likely your son knows something. Being involved with Sasha, did he really have no idea who she was?"

"The girl was gorgeous and mysterious," Richard said, defensively. "Not to mention being an alchemist and off limits. My son has always dated that type. He wants what he can't have."

Anger coursed through me. Celia was reporting back to her father about me! I knew I didn't like her, but this was taking things to a whole new level.

"How do you know Sasha wasn't just using him?" Sabine asked.

"She probably was," Faulk growled. "I just wonder how much that boy gave away to that traitorous filth."

"Celia will know more soon," Mark said. "She's talking with Jessa now, as a matter of fact."

Celia was with Jessa? I imagined my cold fiancée cornering the girl I loved. That was not okay. I wanted nothing more than to storm through that door and go and find them. Celia seemed to be some kind of spy with her parents—that much was more apparent than ever. She was a snake in the grass, and now she was toying with Jessa too. The whole thing had me dying to punch a hole through the wall right then and there!

"Celia had better make a decision soon," Richard said. "I need to know that my son is loyal. That's the only reason I agreed to this engagement!"

There it was. The real reason I was engaged. So my father could keep a closer eye on me. I swallowed angry words that needed to be released. He got the daughter-in-law he wanted, the one who kept me in line. The one who *worked for him.* And I got nothing.

"The engagement is beneficial to everyone," Mark said. "Your son will be lucky to have my daughter for a wife."

"Oh, don't get all fatherly on me now." Richard laughed, his voice filling the space. "We all know she gets a crown out of the deal."

"It's true." Sabine smiled. "She's very happy about that."

"Is there anything else?" Faulk asked. They shook their heads. "Then if you'll excuse me, I have some work to do." She headed up the stairs to her private office, her heels clacking loudly with each step.

"The minute you catch wind of anything, you tell me," Richard said, pointing at Mark.

"Yes, sir." He nodded.

They left in a rush of activity. I followed closely behind, my heart hammering. *I'm a suspect!* I should have never worked with the Resistance. Not because I didn't believe my father was a terrible king—he was—but because I didn't know enough about the Resistance to agree to do their dirty work. And now, not only was I in danger, but Jessa was too. I'd made a mess of everything, and she was bearing the weight of that.

I needed to find out what Celia was saying to her. I tried to clear my mind as I squeezed the rose in my hand tighter and rushed toward Jessa's room. Taking deep breaths as I went, I willed myself to be rational about my next action. If I was going to get out of this engagement, I had to prove my loyalty to my father. I needed to give him something he wanted more than marrying me off to that awful family. *What does Dad want more than anything?*

Control.

He wanted to dominate me by choosing whom I married. But it was more than that. He wanted to control more people and resources by going to war with West America, and getting in his way was the Resistance. He was searching for answers. If there was a way I could give enough answers to satisfy him, maybe I could protect Jessa at the same time.

I had an idea. But I needed to think it through. In the meantime, the need to comfort Jessa was overpowering. She needed to understand that this was all so much bigger than just our relationship. She shouldn't be afraid of someone like Celia. I would find a way out of this, for both our sakes.

I ambled up to her room, waiting a few minutes until the hall was clear. I tapped at the door. A long minute passed before she opened it, in wet hair, no makeup, and pajamas. She peered around, seeming half annoyed and half relieved not to find anyone. Red rimmed around her eyes, and her cheeks looked shallow.

"Jessa," I whispered. "Please let me in."

She paused, her face lighting with recognition before darkening. I hoped she wouldn't be upset I'd come using white alchemy. I expected her to slam the door in my face, but she nodded and pulled it open just enough for me to squeeze through.

Once we were alone, I breathed out, dropping the rose from my grasp. After over an hour of being invisible, I was not only exhausted, but the rose was almost completely gray when it fell to the floor.

"You're sure no one else can do that?" she asked, picking it up. She studied the rose between her finger and thumb, twirling it, no concern for the thorns.

"Not that I know of."

"Hmmm…" She nodded. "You're engaged."

"I'm sorry."

"I met your fiancée tonight. She came here to talk."

"I heard." I shook my head, running my hands through

my hair. "Whatever she said, please don't listen to her. It's not what you think."

"She basically asked me to be your mistress," Jessa whispered bitterly. She moved to sit on the edge of her bed and narrowed her eyes on me. "I told her no, by the way. Just in case you're wondering."

"I didn't know she was going to say that," I said. "I don't get her."

"She doesn't care about your heart, Lucas. Only your crown."

"Well, that I did know." I sighed. Then I laughed.

"It's not funny," she said, her eyes flashing.

"Believe me, I know."

I tentatively sat next to her on the bed. She scooted away. Only a couple of inches. A small amount, but it felt like so much more. She was communicating something with that motion: stay away forever.

"I spied on her family. They're working with my father. Celia is too," I said. "Believe me when I say that this mess is bigger than I imagined."

"Celia is spying on you?"

"And you," I said.

"Wow. She's bold." She ran her hands through her hair, and more drips of water soaked into her black, cotton top.

"Don't get me wrong, she wants that crown. But her father is trying to sniff out the Resistance. Plus, Richard and Faulk haven't given up on figuring out what Sasha was doing here, how she got in and out... all of it."

"I guess it makes sense." She nodded. "But why did you have to get engaged, Lucas? I've been trying to understand it. I'm sorry. I just...don't."

I hated this. She said the last few words with so much sadness. And it was my fault. "I was an idiot. My father was having second thoughts about executing Thomas. He wanted that red alchemy, and when you broke it off with me, I kind of lost my mind. You were right, Jessa. You're always right about me. I should've just talked to you about my grief, but I wasn't thinking straight. I thought the only thing to make me feel better would be Thomas's death."

"And do you feel better?"

"No."

"And you're engaged because of it?"

"My father made a deal with me. He'd execute Thomas if I agreed to an engagement. I *never* agreed to an actual marriage. I figured I'd call the engagement off or something, I don't know, I was stupid. But when I went to talk to him about it, he threatened to send you away."

"So I was right." She frowned. "I didn't want to be, you know."

"You were right. You broke it off between us because our relationship bothers my father. It's not what he wants, but Jessa, it is what *I* want." I reached out and grasped her hand. It hung limply in my own. More than anything, I wanted her to squeeze mine back, but she didn't. "You're all I ever wanted."

A tear ran down her cheek, and I shifted closer, catching it with the tip of my index finger. She turned her cheek. "I would do anything for you," I said. "Don't you see that? I love you."

"I know." She sighed, more tears absorbing into my palm. "But you're *engaged*, Lucas. I can't."

"I didn't choose Celia. She was chosen for me. I barely even know her. And what I do know about her tells me I can't trust her."

"So what are you going to do about it?"

"I can't marry her, Jessa. I won't do it. I'll refuse."

"So what's your plan then, huh?" She was jaded. It was my own fault.

I gathered every ounce of passion and looked her dead center in her eyes. "I'm going to find a way to convince my father to call off the wedding, to let us be together."

She laughed. "And how are you possibly going to do that? There's no way."

"There has to be a way. And I will find it. I promise."

She shook her head.

"Jessa, look at me." I carefully placed my hands on her cheeks again, moving her face to my own. We were only inches apart, and I stared into her ocean eyes with everything I had in me. I needed her to believe in me. In us. I needed her to fight for me as much as I was fighting for her. She was the only thing left. The darkness would consume me without her.

But I'd messed up. And I didn't deserve her forgiveness.

"Nobody else matters to me anymore but you," I said. "Please, I've already lost my mother. My father doesn't care about me, not really. You're all I have left that matters. Don't give up on me. I will find a way out of this. I'll do anything. Whatever it takes for us to be together, I promise I will find it."

I searched her eyes, waiting for the spark to come. The one I knew so well, the one I'd seen so many times before. It had to be in there.

"Please, Jessa," I said. "I love you."

It was the truth. It was everything. *I love her.*

"I love you too," she said, the words a sweet breath on her lips.

"I am not going to marry Celia," I said, my spine turning to steel. "I won't do it." It was true. I would do *anything* to be with this girl before me.

She nodded, hopeful.

"I'm going to marry *you*, Jessa."

A spark lit in her eyes, and she gasped. Surprise. Longing. Love.

I couldn't hold back. I kissed her gently, waiting for her response. Her lips felt like coming home. They were hope. They were passion. They were everything coming alive in one touch.

Our foreheads touched as I continued. "You will be my wife," I breathed. "When you're a little older, and when you're ready. I'll wait for you. I promise." She kissed me harder, her arms moving to wrap around my neck, and I came home.

I didn't know how long we went on that way, kissing to fill the void that only each other could fill. I'd always thought "butterflies" was a dumb expression. But that's what I felt with Jessa. Only more. It was so much more than butterflies.

"I know we're young. You especially," I said, pulling away, "but there's no one else for me."

"I know it too." Tears rolled down her face.

"Don't cry," I begged, kissing them away, the salt wetting my lips.

"I'm happy," she said, her smile making her cheeks move against my mouth. "I'm just scared, Lucas. I'm scared I'm going to lose you again. I don't know what it will do to me."

"I promise, we will be together." I laced her hands in my own and stood her up. Then I hugged her tightly to my body, ignoring the struggle to kiss her again. Right now, she just needed to be held.

I gripped her hands in mine. "Jessa, I don't know when, and I don't know how, but I *will* marry you. That is..." I coughed, nervous. When did I become this romantic guy? "That's if you'll have me." I kneeled before her. This was how a proposal should be done. I would do it again properly one day, with a ring and everything. But for now... "Jessa Loxley, will you marry me?"

Her eyes widened. A smile lit up her entire being. That alone told me everything I needed to know. But I waited for her to say yes.

She did.

I kissed her again, losing myself. I hated that my *real* engagement had to stay a secret for now. We'd have obstacles to overcome. But I would make it happen. Too many times, I'd rolled over, allowing my father and his people to tell me how to live my life. But not on this one. Not with Jessa.

We lay in her bed for most of the night, holding hands, kissing, but mostly talking about the future. We never brought up our problems or how we could potentially overcome them. Instead, we imagined what it would be like to be married. We saw a world without obstacles and talked about it like it was real. Where would we live? Would I become king or would we run away together? If I was king, what would she do as queen? Would we have kids? Yes. And what would our kids look like? We laughed over some of the options and held our breath over others. But we held nothing back, and it was the best night I'd ever had. I kept her safe in my arms, as if that was somehow all it took. Just a boy holding a girl he loved, and deciding not to let go.

●

Time moved despite our best efforts. Reluctantly, I got up to leave, knowing I had already been gone far too long. She grabbed my hand, fear lining her eyes.

"What is it?"

"Lucas, tomorrow. Do you know I'm being initiated tomorrow night?"

I nodded. "I heard you passed your final test. Congratulations."

She stared up at me, the moonlight casting a blue glow across her face.

"You'll be okay," I said. "You're a champ. It's easy."

"It's not that," she whispered. Her face closed off for a second, as if considering something and deciding better of it. But then just as quickly, she opened herself up again. "Something is going to happen tomorrow night...with the Resistance."

I stilled, holding back the resentment that bubbled up at the mention of them. "What? What it is?"

She paused, eyes darting from side to side. "They're going to do something during my initiation. I don't know the details. Just promise me you'll be careful?"

I nodded, fear spearing through me. Of course they were going to do something during her initiation. It would put her in danger, but they didn't care about that. They never did!

"You too, Jessa," I said. "You can't fight."

She shook her head. "I won't."

I kissed her one last time. Then I snatched what was left of the gray and white rose from the floor, went invisible as quickly as possible, and returned to my room.

●

The next morning, I woke early with complete clarity. I knew what I had to do.

SEVENTEEN

JESSA

I floated on dreams all night and well into the morning. Dreams about Lucas and growing old together. Dreams about reuniting with my family. Dancing again, always, the dreams had dancing. Every time my consciousness pushed me toward waking, I was pulled back under. Back into the weightless surrender.

●

Lacey is learning to walk. Her chubby fingers grip onto my index fingers. They feel warm, sweaty. She toddles between my legs as we shuffle across the living room.

"Look, Dad, she's doing it." I laugh.

She peers up at me, startled by my laugh, I think. Her blond hair is curly around her face, like a halo. It reminds me of a wig because it's only a few inches long. Her blue eyes mirror my own.

"My girls." Dad smiles, and we walk toward him. One step. Two steps. Three. Four.

When we're only a couple away, I slip my fingers from her grip. She hardly notices, finishing the final few on her own before plunging into the safety of Dad's arms.

●

Mom stands over me as I sit on the bathroom counter.

"Let me see," she says, motioning to my feet.

I have big socks on, and after a moment, I peel them off one at a time. There are blisters on almost every toe, above my heel is rubbed raw, and the whole foot is beet red. "How long has it been like this?" she asks.

I shrug. I don't want her to get mad because I don't want her to make me stop.

"I'm going to talk to your teacher," she says. "See if we can get you a better fitting pair of pointe shoes next time." I exhale a sigh of relief. "You didn't think I was going to make you quit, did you?" she asks. "I would never do that to you, Jessa. I know how much you love this. I'm proud of you, honey."

I stick my feet in the sink, running cold water over the sores. I know the pain might not be temporary. Battered feet are part of ballet. Still, it's so worth it.

●

The dreams continued. Fragmented memories mixed with hope. Some made no sense and then perfect sense in the way dreams often did. What mattered was the right people were there. What mattered was how it felt. The sunlight started to pitter-patter across my face. I could feel the warmth pouring in, asking a question—but I wasn't ready to answer it.

I rolled over.

I run along behind her, my bare feet smoothing the dewy grass. The light filters between the trees, catching her blond hair. Her laugh has a way of calling to me. I want to play. She is taller than me, so I have to hurry to catch up. My legs are still chubby. Hers are sticks.

"Show me," I say, grabbing at a dandelion. She looks around, back at the house, at the fence.

"Come," she says, taking off again.

We go to our favorite spot: the trees where no one can see us. The place where it's safe to play.

"Show me," I ask again. Does she hear me? Does she know what I want? I push the flower at her, but she already has one in her hand. She smiles, and we sit, our knees touching.

"Don't tell anyone," she says. She squeezes the dandelion; the yellow comes off in her hand. It floats into the air, hovering just between us.

"Magic." I giggle.

"Shh…" she says, blowing it toward me.

When it hits, I erupt into a fit of laughter. I suddenly have the best idea. "Let's climb the tree. I go, up, up, up."

"No," she says. But I've already gone. It was easy. I'm high. So high. Too high. I'm scared to come down. I start to scream. "Frankie! Jessa!" Someone calls. Mom? I scream again. I want down.

"What is she doing all the way up there?" someone says. "How was that possible for her to move that fast?"

It's not Mom.

•

I sat up, my breath rushing out of me. The dreams were all so vivid, so real, but that last one was something else. And it wasn't the first time I'd had it, either. I climbed out of bed and I attempted to tame the mane that is my hair after sleeping on it wet. I couldn't rid my mind of the images. The dandelion. The girl.

Was it a recurring dream or a memory?

I tried to grab onto the last fragments of it, but with every minute, the dream slipped farther and farther from my mind. I held onto the memory of my mother calling my name. That was right, wasn't it? And whom else had she been calling for? I couldn't quite remember well enough. But it felt important.

I stretched my body for a moment, then flopped out of bed. Next, I opened my closet and dressed in the same thing I wore almost every day. At least it was comfortable. Checking the time, I groaned when I realized I'd slept through breakfast. I had combat training every morning and needed to get moving. Combat didn't scare me nearly as much as it used to, and today would be no different, even though most of the best fighters had been whisked away for the war. Plus, Branson was gone.

I went through the motions of training in a bit of a daze. Slumped against the wall, I sipped at my water bottle and took in the remaining alchemists who populated the gym. Part of me was training, going to class, going through the motions. The other part was wondering where Lucas was, wondering how we were possibly going to make it work. And I was absolutely giddy about last night, which was foolish. But I couldn't help it.

I sighed and wiped at the sweat on my neck with a towel.

I trusted him; he would figure it out. I couldn't wait until the day when we didn't have to hide our relationship anymore. And then another part of me was solely focused on the night to come. The initiation. I would swear my allegiance to the monarchy and perform a task in front of my peers. And then? The Resistance would do…something.

It was almost time, and whatever happened, I was ready. Throwing my towel and bottle to the side, I pushed off the wall and strode forward with confidence.

●

I brushed at invisible wrinkles in my satin gown. The dress was midnight black and hugged my torso in a sweetheart neckline, leaving my shoulders bare. It tapered out at the hips and ended just above the knees. Delivered in a velvet box, it had arrived courtesy of the king, along with strappy black heels and a gorgeous diamond necklace. I'd put the ensemble together and even spent an hour painstakingly straightening my hair. After applying smoky eye makeup and red lipstick, I'd been pleased when I'd left my room. And more than a little nervous.

I clutched the invitation in my hand, once more checking that I was at the correct entrance. I allowed myself a moment to breathe, then pushed open the doors and walked inside. Blinking, I stared wide-eyed at the scene before me. It was more than I expected. The place was packed, the ballroom filled with round tables and a sea of faces. White tablecloths adorned each one and a colorful floral centerpiece was placed identically in each center. All the guardians in residence were already seated, as were the officers.

In tandem, the whole room turned to face me.

I grimaced but quickly recovered with a smile. I quickly realized that since the invitation had been so specific about when and where I entered, I shouldn't be surprised to see everyone already seated, expecting me.

"And here is the guest of honor," King Richard's voice

boomed through the speakers. Applause rang out, and I gave a little wave. Richard stood at a podium on top of a stage that appeared to be set up just in front of me. I quickly moved to join him and he continued. "Please, join the royal family for our meal, and then we'll get started. A little magical presentation during dessert, anyone?" The crowd tittered; I was going to puke.

Apparently the initiation meant I had to perform magic in front of everyone and swear my allegiance to the royal family. I could do it. *Breathe.* I scanned the crowd, frozen to the spot, when Lucas caught my eye. He nodded to me, smiling. I scurried off the stage to join his table below, sitting across from him and his fiancée. She smiled warmly at me, and my stomach seized. Richard joined us at that moment, taking the seat next to mine.

"You know, Jessa," he said, "you're a very special girl. It's usually the case that alchemists are initiated into the Guardians of Color once a year. We put on a big production that they all get to share. But you get the spotlight all to yourself tonight."

"Congratulations," Celia purred.

I quickly glanced her way, muttering my thanks, before turning back to my food. Her hand wrapped around Lucas's upper arm didn't go unnoticed.

"She *is* a special girl." Lucas smiled. My gaze shot to him, and I was unable to speak. His eyes glowed as he stared at me. He didn't try to hide it, even in front of Celia or Richard. My cheeks flamed, and I bit back my smile. He was gorgeous, of course—he always was—but dressed immaculately in a tux with his hair styled to messy-perfection and a cleanly shaved face was a *really* good look on him.

We ate a four-course dinner but I hardly swallowed a bite. I contributed almost nothing to the conversation. I was too nervous. Nervous to be at this table. To do the magic. To even *be here*. Whatever I was asked to do, I prayed I wouldn't make a fool out of myself. I couldn't even think about what would happen with the Resistance afterward; it sent my nerves into overdrive.

"Time to go," King Richard said into my ear before standing and heading to the podium.

I took a deep breath. Lucas nodded, and I allowed myself to be comforted—if only for a moment. Then I followed Richard onto the stage.

"My friends," the king said, "it is a special occasion that we get to initiate Jessa into our family. The Guardians of Color have long been a pillar of this kingdom, serving in a variety of important roles. It is because of you that we are so strong. Though you may stay out of the public eye, you are the cornerstone of our society. Thank you for all that you do."

The crowd applauded.

"And a big thanks as well to the officers." He motioned to their tables. Only a small fraction was in attendance, which sent a little wave of shock through me. I assumed the rest were helping with the war effort. But the palace was normally swarming with officers, and there were only a few tables of officers tonight. "Without your steadfast commitment to the law, none of this would be possible." More clapping. "Jessa came to us in less than desirable circumstances. As most of you know, she accidentally manipulated color during a ballet performance. Luckily for her, we were able to bring her in and train her like one of our own."

I climbed the five steps to the stage and stood next to the king. I smiled, hoping my discomfort was well hidden. It seemed the way he remembered how I was "brought in" and the way *I* remembered it were two different things. Typical.

"Now, I think it's time we dim the lights and get started,

don't you?"

More clapping, even a few cheers from the alchemists. I blinked, somewhat amazed at the sound. Turned out, I'd come a long way with my peers over the last few months.

As the lights dimmed, a spotlight illuminated the stage. I was dizzy. Momentarily blinded. A longing burned in my chest. Memory. In my life before the palace, this feeling was accompanied by a ballet performance. The lights created a cocoon around the stage, shrouding the audience in darkness. It used to be a comfort for me, made it easier for me to relax. This time, the nerves didn't go away; they only increased. Everyone was watching, and I couldn't watch them back.

"Jessa passed green, orange, and yellow alchemy." Richard's voice vibrated around the room.

Someone must have removed him from the stage, because I was alone now. Frozen. Dazed under the lights. Alone on the stage. But not *alone*. Hundreds of eyes blinked back at me.

"She also showed signs of strong aptitude in purple. But what is most curious about her is a couple of unique abilities. Abilities we hope to study and replicate in more guardians. You see, when we first met her, she had inadvertently pulled the purple from her dress—a feat not uncommon, even though it wasn't the organic materials that come easiest with magic. No, it was the fact that the purple separated into primary colors: blue and red. Now *that* was rather impressive."

The crowd broke into whispers. They'd heard the rumors, of course, but this confirmed it.

"We haven't since replicated the act, but we will," Richard continued. The way he said it wasn't in disappointment; it was calm, assured. As if he was bragging about me: I was his possession, a new toy, and he'd almost figured me out.

An icy chill trickled down my spine, but I stood taller.

"However, we were able to conclude that she *can* manipulate red." More whispers followed his words. "Would you like to see it in action?"

They cheered, a thrum of nervous excitement rushed through the room.

Oh, no. I don't know if I can do this.

Part of me had wondered if Richard would continue to keep my red alchemy a secret.

Guess not.

Still, something nagged at me. He wanted to replicate it in others, sure, but that didn't mean he *could*. If it were true that he'd had access to this magic on and off over the years, he'd have already done that. Right? So why this big show? I fought the urge to run.

"Jessa, darling girl, are you ready?"

No! But I nodded. I had to do whatever he wanted. I ignored the ocean of panic that was rising, pushing it down.

"Now, I think her favorite *teacher* would be a wonderful help to us today. Who better to help demonstrate this than the woman who has taught you so much?" Richard purred. "Jasmine, please join us on stage. That is if you don't mind."

I gasped. I wanted to shake my head, to refuse, but my entire body was frozen to the spot. I had to play along.

Someone shuffled from the back of the room, and molten fear rolled through my body, creeping and hot. No! I couldn't do this to *her* of all people, it was too dangerous. What if I hurt her? What if she revealed her true identity?

"Ah, here she comes," Richard continued. His voice sounded as charismatic as ever, but I couldn't bear to look at his expression. "Please give her a round of applause."

The crowd clapped, but the applause was stilted. Slow.

Nobody knew what this meant. Even *testing* red alchemy on someone felt wrong to me. Did they think so too? But this? Jasmine was one of the most respected alchemists in the community.

She ambled to the stage, a warm smile lighting her face. When she finally looked at me, a flash of something crossed her eyes. Something controlled. I didn't understand. What was I supposed to do?

"Please, Jasmine, have a seat."

A chair was brought onto the stage. I barely noticed as someone placed something in my palm. I looked down at it, my stomach turning. A small knife. The blade glistened in the spotlight.

"Red alchemy has long been sought after. We know that red is connected to belonging, family, and *loyalty*," Richard said. I finally glanced over at him, taking in his animated gestures as he spoke. "What's interesting is we haven't been able to do much with red materials, flowers, plants, rocks, and such. But blood, on the other hand, for some that is a different story."

I bit my lip, sucking in a breath.

"Jessa, please show us."

I stared at Jasmine, willing her to do something. *Tell me what to do!* She reached up and took the knife from me. I was barely holding it. Then she smiled at me, her eyes sad, and she cut herself across the arm. "It's okay," she whispered. "Just do your best and everything will work out."

The knife clattered to the floor.

I fought back tears and reached for her arm. The blood wet my hand, slick and metallic. I cleared my mind, took a deep breath, feeling as the magic weaved its way into her blood. It pulsed out in tendrils of red magic and then shot up her arm. She jerked.

The crowd cheered, once again, as red alchemy swirled into the air. I expected Richard to interject and order me to tell her to do one thing or another, but he didn't. I wanted to get this over with as quickly as possible. I needed to show them what was possible with red alchemy. The more I pulled the red from her blood, the more side effects she would have.

I pushed the red magic farther into her, felt the power surging through me as well. "Dance!" I called.

Immediately, she stood and began to move to a beat only she could hear.

"Freeze!"

She did, one leg balanced in the air.

"Sit down."

She sat right there on the floor.

"What's your name?"

"Jasmine," she replied, calm.

"Where do you live?"

"The palace."

"Go and sit in your chair."

And now we're done, right? I looked out in the crowd, took a little bow, and made my way toward the edge of stage.

"Not so fast, Jessa," the king sing-songed. His voice echoed through the room. I stopped. "That was a charming little presentation of red alchemy. As you can see, manipulating the color out of a person's own blood and then using it on them allows for mind control." The crowd was utterly silent. The room even had a faint echo. "Now, I'm curious. Do you think we could control someone enough to tell us the *truth*?"

Terror gripped my entire body. No. I couldn't do this. I shook my head. "It's used for actions. Blue is used for communication," I protested.

The king laughed as he strolled over to me, carrying the microphone in his hand now. "Blue is very useful, that is

283

true. Persuasion, listening, trying to figure out if someone is being honest. But red, now, I think red takes it to a new level, don't you?"

"I don't know," I breathed. What was I supposed to do? Run?

"I think you do know," he said. "But no matter, let's find out. Go to Jasmine, put your hand back on her wound, and repeat what I tell you. Got it?"

I stared at the room, blinking rapidly. Would someone save me? Where was the Resistance? Shouldn't they be here by now? Something was wrong.

I walked back to Jasmine and did as he said. Her blood was thick under my fingers, and I longed to make it go away. Just make it all stop!

"Ask her if she's loyal to the monarchy."

I gulped. She stared off into the crowd, dazed, her eyes empty orbs. She wasn't in control. This was wrong! I prayed she'd be able to fight this magic, but it was futile. The magic would work. It had every time before. I wouldn't be so lucky. Jasmine wouldn't be so lucky.

"Are you loyal to the monarchy?" I asked, my eyes filling.

She paused, her eyes moving from side to side. I hoped that meant she was gaining control again. But I felt the power coursing through me, felt my question fighting with her mind.

"No," she said, her voice steady and sure.

The crowd, so silent before, erupted in noxious whispers.

"Now that's a shame," Richard said, his voice flat. "I had hoped my suspicions were wrong."

Officers lined my peripheral vision. The heat of panic burned hotter.

"Ask her who she works for."

I paused.

"Ask her who she works for!" he bellowed, stalking toward us.

"Who do you work for?" I forced the question from my mouth, fighting tears.

"The Resistance."

I dropped my head in shame.

"Well, even I could have come up with a better name." Richard laughed, but he moved to put his face between Jasmine's and mine. A blood vessel pulsed in his forehead, and he gritted his teeth. "Now tell me, Jasmine, are you working alone?" He looked at me, eyes bulging.

Terror ignited through my entire body. What was I going to do? I stalled for a second.

The king yelled, "Ask!"

I started. "Are you working alone?"

"No."

I needed to stop this. I needed to help her!

He growled, dropping the microphone now. He moved in, his face only inches from Jasmine's languid expression. "Who are you working with? Tell me?"

I forced myself to speak. "Who are you working with?" I asked, the tears now free, running down my face. Any minute now, everything would be over. She would tell. And I would probably be dead because of it.

She fought, shaking her head, yelling nonsensically. She put her hands to her ears. Blood started to drip from her nose.

"We're hurting her," I gasped.

"Ask again!" Richard boomed, then straightened. I choked on a sob as he moved in behind me, squeezing down on my bare shoulders. Officers surrounded the stage, ready to intervene.

"Who are you working with?" Terror gripped me.

"I…I…" Jasmine sputtered. She ripped at her hair. "Get out of my head!"

"Ask again!"

"Who are you working with?" Tears ran down my face. I hated myself for it. My grip loosened momentarily as I fought the urge to vomit.

Her mouth opened and closed in rapid succession. She dove. It all happened so fast. One second she was in the chair, the next she was on the floor. More blood. The knife gleamed between her fingers. There was no hesitation as she ripped it across her throat. *No!*

There was erratic screaming. It was me, sobbing, falling to my knees, reaching for her. I was wrenched away by meaty hands. I clawed at them. Thick arms wrapped around me, restraining. Jasmine was slack. Richard screeched words I couldn't understand. What was happening?

"Heal her," I yelled. Or maybe it was Richard. I looked around, frantic. I needed to help her. Several alchemists jumped to the stage. Someone dragged a green plant with them.

So much blood. Everywhere.

Alchemists surrounded her, pushing the green magic into her again and again. It wasn't working. It wasn't doing anything. I tugged at the arms around me, needing to try for myself. Nothing.

"We can't save her," someone said.

"She's gone."

Someone was sobbing.

It was me.

●

"Snap out of it!" Faulk shook me, minutes later. "It's over, done with. Jasmine is gone."

I didn't know what to say. I had nothing. It was empty inside. I looked around, finding myself in a ball on the floor off to the side of the stage. The ballroom was still filled with people. They buzzed, talking loudly over each other.

"You did a good job," Faulk said, her blond hair shining in the light of the stage. The room was still dark, the spotlight still lit. "I didn't think you had it in you. But Richard was right."

"What?"

"Come on, you have to finish your initiation."

I shook my head. I wanted to save Jasmine. I wanted to see Lucas. I wanted to get as far away from the palace as possible. I wanted to go home. Tears began to spring to my eyes again.

She slapped me. My head jolted to the side.

"Ouch!" The sharp pain cooled across my skin, focused me.

"Stop it." She stared at me, her eyes sharp. "Suck it up, Jessa. You will finish this initiation *right now.*"

I nodded this time. She was right. I was in this thing whether I liked it or not. And now Richard had the weapon he needed. Me. I stood, deep breaths filling my lungs, and wiped away the tears. And I did what she said. I sucked it up.

Faulk held my arm and led me back to the front of the stage. I tried not to look at the blood. The urge to gag was too strong.

"Sit down!" Richard called out to the crowd over the microphone gripped tightly in his white knuckled hand.

The room quieted immediately, everyone finding their seats. I could make out Lucas, just barely through the spotlight. His eyes were wide, staring at me.

"I hope I've made myself clear," the king continued. "*There will be no rebellion!* We are at war. We will win that war. This kingdom, my alchemists, my officers, you are all loyal to me! And if anyone shows even a moment of hesitation, I will use whatever means necessary to root you out and *end you.*"

The room was blanketed in complete silence.

"Now," Richard said. "Let's finish this initiation, shall we? Jessa, I know that was hard for you. Thank you for your loyalty."

I nodded, hands trembling. I closed them into fists.

"Repeat after me," Faulk said, taking the microphone into her slender hand. She wasn't dressed up as everyone else was; the officers had stayed in their white uniforms. Hers was stained in blood. "As a member of the Guardians of Color, I hereby swear my allegiance to New Colony and to my king. I will defend and protect the royal family with my life. I will be true to my word and swear myself to His Majesty."

I repeated every word.

"Long live the king!" she finished.

"Long live the king." I repeated that too.

The crowd cheered, less eager than earlier in the night. Fear had replaced me as the guest of honor.

"Now, somebody clean up this mess," Richard said, "and let's finish our dessert, shall we?"

EIGHTEEN

SASHA

I concentrated on the thumping rhythm of the rotor as we zipped through the night sky. True to their word, West America sent helicopters, guns, and soldiers. We had a troop of about twenty of their best men, and combined with our own, there were about a hundred willing and able to fight. Their helicopters were much larger than ours, each fitting twelve bodies plus the crew. We flew out after dinner, knowing it would take about four hours to get to the capital. My stomach in a knot, I hadn't touched much food all day. I absentmindedly picked at the hem of my long-sleeved black shirt and adjusted my combat boots under my weight.

I was strapped into a rudimentary chair, the two rows close and facing each other. Among us were Hank, Tristan, Mastin, Cole, and Christopher, much to my frustration. He had insisted on taking the trip and nothing would dissuade him. It was awkward, and every time I looked his way, I caught him staring at me. We'd all done our best to outfit ourselves in black, durable clothing and sturdy shoes, but the military men really looked the part. I sat quietly, going over every scenario in my head.

The palace was weak at the moment. Most of the best alchemists and officers were in West America trying to gain ground. King Richard had declared war, and in the process he had not only begun stripping areas of West America of color but had also taken over multiple cities. New Colony had a bigger army than West America expected. It seemed King Richard had been planning this for years.

"You don't have to do this," Christopher said, speaking loudly over the whoosh of the chopper. "You and I can stay in here until it's over." He pleaded with such sad eyes that it was hard to meet them. This man was my father, but he was a stranger.

I sighed and turned away. He already knew my answer was no. All day, he'd been hounding me to back down. But we were already on our way, no backing out now. I shot a glare his way, jutting my chin. "And what about Jessa? Are you going to forget about her now too?"

He frowned. "It wasn't like that. It was never like that."

"Fine. Explain it to me then. What was it like?"

"We would've kept you hidden." He rubbed his hand along his jaw. "We even did for a little while. If we'd known they'd take you away forever then we would've found a way to get out of there sooner."

"But you did know about my magic?" I asked.

The body of the chopper was lit with a red light. It shone on his face in the darkness, casting long shadows. I could just make out the whites of his eyes before he closed them briefly. "Yes," he said.

"Don't you get it, Christopher? I remember what happened!"

"We didn't know what to do." His voice shook. "When they came for you, it was because a neighbor had told on us.

She saw something, I guess. They wanted to take you both. You and Jessa."

"So you let them take me to protect Jessa? Or to protect yourselves?"

He sat, quiet for a minute. "I am so sorry, Frankie. We made a mistake."

"Don't call me that. I don't use that name anymore."

He nodded. "I'm sorry, Sasha. You didn't deserve this. There wasn't a day that went by when we didn't think about you."

"I find that hard to believe," I muttered.

The other ten passengers had grown silent during our exchange. Some stared openly while others looked away, their faces taught. We were free entertainment. *Just line right up and see the cast-off daughter and estranged father put on a show.* But part of me wondered if he was telling me the truth. What if they really had tried to help me?

"I know we met before but just in case you forgot my name, I'm Hank." Hank reached out to shake Christopher's hand. "I'm sorry your family had to go through that. It's not right."

"Thank you," Christopher said, returning the handshake.

"I hope to get your other daughter out of there." Hank didn't say what I knew. Getting Jessa out wasn't the mission. Jessa was exactly where she needed to be, and no one was taking her out tonight. Not unless this mission went so well there was no New Colony at the end of it. Not likely. "I'll help you make sure Sasha stays safe in there," Hank continued.

They nodded at each other, like they understood what it was like to love me. To be my dad. I ground my teeth, refusing to be swayed by the warm, fuzzy feelings exploding in my heart.

This was too much for me.

"Let's go over the plan again," I said, changing the subject.

"All five choppers will land at the same time, and we storm the palace together," Tristan spoke up. He sat forward in his seat. "All of the major operatives will be busy for a few hours in the main ballroom, the royals too. So that's our target. Of course, we still expect guards and patrols. But we will move quickly."

The idea of landing five helicopters at once sent me into panic mode, but I didn't show it. This was how war worked. It wasn't supposed to be safe.

"Our targets are General Faulk and King Richard. We want them dead," Mastin said, his voice cutting through the darkness like a knife. "We'll give everyone else a chance to surrender."

"Jasmine is confident that most of the alchemists will be sympathetic to us," Hank nodded. "We can expect the same of the officers, but there shouldn't be as many of them there tonight."

"You're sure about that?" I asked.

"Faulk and Richard have been sending more and more people out every day," Cole's steady voice jumped in from the far side of the chopper, low and sure. It was the first I'd heard from him all night. "The king has left himself vulnerable for attack. It's the perfect opportunity."

It made sense. But still, not everyone signed up for this was equipped to do the job. Most of the alchemists were newbies, and even though we had trained soldiers too, I had yet to see them in action.

"Your boys any good?" I asked.

Mastin laughed. "We're men. And we're the best."

"I hope you're right about that."

●

We dropped quickly. The inertia did little to calm my nerves as I bent over to see out the back window. From my position, I couldn't see much. When I caught sight of the palace, lit up like a beacon, blood rushed through my eardrums. I felt my face get hot, and I inhaled a deep breath. We unstrapped our safety restraints and got ready, knees slightly bent, our bodies close together at the edges of our seats.

The alchemists had gemstone necklaces wrapped around their necks.

Everyone else had guns.

A lot of guns. And I worried many of those gun-touting men didn't actually know how to use them. Maybe West America had thought of that and some of those weapons held tranquilizers instead of bullets. But I knew that it was probably wishful thinking…

The second the helicopter landed on the grass, Cole slammed the doors open. We jumped out, crouching low. We all ran as silently as we could, arcing out in a fan across the palace lawn. More helicopters dropped in, and more people spilled from inside. We continued to fan out, low and quiet. It was so dark, and the heavy cloud cover blocked out any stars. The moon was only a faint glow.

I looked to my left and noticed Mastin taking off in a different direction. I could tell Tristan was staying close to me on purpose. So was Christopher. He wasn't trained for this. He should have stayed back, but heaven forbid that stubborn man listened to reason.

"Hide out here," I told him, pointing to a darkened cropping of trees. "I'll come back for you." And I would. Even though I didn't consider him my father, he was still Lacey and Jessa's father. I didn't want him to die.

"I'm not leaving you," he said, pushing forward to keep pace with the others. I sped up but he matched it. He must have been a runner. I wondered what it would be like to exercise solely for health. For me, it had always been a matter of training.

A matter of life and death.

The soldiers had walkie-talkies. One of the devices crackled, and a man muttered a reply. Then there was a yell and the snap of a gunshot. It sounded like a silencer.

"Let's go," Tristan said. He grabbed my hand, and we high-tailed it to one of the lower level windows.

Christopher followed on our heels. I jumped when my father picked up a rock and threw it through the glass. Then he reached in and unlatched the lock. "I'll go in first," he muttered.

Maybe I get my impulsiveness from him.

The plan was pretty simple. Everyone had already been briefed on where the main ballroom was located. We were to go in from all angles. There were several doors leading into the room so it would be easy. The alchemists were to fight the other alchemists and officers. The West American soldiers were the ones going in for Richard, Faulk, Lucas, and anyone who got in their way. If I was given the chance, I would do the same. I wanted to end the king. But it would have to wait. The plan was to kill Faulk and Richard. Lucas and the remaining officers and alchemists would be arrested. Anyone who put up a fight would also get arrested, and if we had to kill some of them to make that happen, we would.

As we scrambled through the window, a few others followed. The room was dark. Empty. I knew where we were, having spent so much time here. We were in a parlor right across from the ballroom. As soon as we left this room, it would be time. About ten other people crawled in through the window behind us. We all kept quiet, waiting for the signal.

It felt like an eternity. Every breath was like a full minute. I was hyperaware of each movement, each excruciating second that we sat there like sitting ducks. I wrung my hands out, fighting the urge to jump into action. I looked around the room instead, taking in the familiar palace decor. Being in this place brought up all kinds of mixed emotions. I had made friends here. Some would be on the receiving end of what was about to go down.

Then the walkie-talkie sounded. The voice coming through the other end was scratchy low, but I knew it was Mastin. "The fox is in the hole."

A soldier threw open the door, and we sprinted across the hallway. The door to the ballroom burst wide just as quickly. There was a second of hesitation. A moment of suspended belief that this was *really happening*. A couple of shots fired. A woman screamed.

And then it was chaos.

I raced into the room, my hand pushing my necklace under my shirt. It didn't matter if I held all the colors at once; I knew how to use each one as needed. Intention was enough. I willed the yellow into my system and felt the rush of adrenaline spread through my limbs.

"Get them!"

I startled at the king's voice as it bellowed through a loudspeaker, filling the room. Just the sound of it again ignited more adrenaline in my bloodstream. He was going to pay tonight for everything he'd done.

The alchemists hesitated, but the officers jumped into action immediately. A couple more shots fired off.

"Don't kill my guardians!" Richard bellowed.

The thudding sound of fists hitting bodies rang through the room. I made my way between the tables of alchemists; most were standing now but some still sat in shock. I ignored them and sprinted toward the action up front. I couldn't help but move in that direction. I spotted Lucas and a redhead sitting at a table next to Jessa.

My sister.

Dread overtook me as I took her in. Blood was smeared all over her arms and chest; her face white as a sheet. What happened?

"Jessa," Christopher shouted just over my shoulder. When he took her in like that, his expression completely crumbled.

"Don't go up there," I said, reaching out to calm him. "There are officers." It was true, they were swarming the royal family's table, desperate to protect them. Some of them formed human barriers. Others were locked in combat with our soldiers. But I noticed there weren't very many of them...

Somebody grabbed me, yanking me to my left and throwing off my center of gravity. I stumbled but quickly caught myself and turned. A middle-aged alchemist crushed a yellow flower between steady hands. A brief cloud of magic, and then they threw a punch. I ducked out of the way, barely grazing their knuckles, but even that would bruise. I caught a glimpse of the centerpieces on all the tables. Oh no! Why hadn't I realized this immediately?

They were filled with *all* the colors in floral arrangements and were easy access to anyone. We were on an even playing field. I fought back blow for blow. I didn't personally know most of the alchemists fighting around me, but I recognized most. It unnerved me, but I focused on the woman in front of me. I felt for the yellow alchemy inside and kicked her hard. She flew against the table, breaking it down the center. I leaped into position, ready to take her out, when another alchemist pounced. This one was a teenage girl and she was lethal in her movements. She ripped my ponytail back and kneed me in the kidney.

"What do you think you're doing, Sasha?" she growled in my ear. Hearing my fake name motivated me to fight back.

I head-butted her from behind. I felt the cartilage of her nose shift and break. She screamed. We turned toward each other and erupted in combat, our movements strong and catlike. The magic worked its way through our blood, enhancing every movement to dangerous levels. Tables broke. Chairs went flying. Table settings clattered to the floor, dishes splintering into glass shards.

I lunged for her, taking her down and bashing her head into the metal leg of the table. A sickening crunch sounded, and she passed out. I sighed and shot some healing green into her, enough to save her life, but not enough to wake her up anytime soon.

I glanced around the room and saw others engaged in combat. A lot of the newly trained alchemists that I had worked with were not as bad as I had first feared. The youngest had stayed home, obviously. But these people seemed to be holding their own against the guardians. Pride swelled as I watched them. And still, it helped that many of the color guardians stood back in shock. And even more pushed *away* to the edges of the room. A few darted out of the ballroom completely. But that didn't make up for the fact that there were guardians willing to fight any threat against their king. I needed to get back in there!

"Stop them!" I heard Richard boom again, his voice still attached to some microphone.

Why haven't they gotten to him yet?

More than anything I wanted to get up there and get in on the action. But I growled as I began to fight off yet another of these alchemists. If they knew why we were really here, what our mission really was, would they turn and join us?

I managed to get away from my attackers, immobilizing them both, as I headed farther into the ballroom. All that training was paying off, but this was taking too long. Then I glanced at my father. *Christopher.* He was stronger than he looked—a man on a mission. He had more motivation than most of these people had, and he was going for it, blow for blow.

This king had taken two of his daughters, and he was hell-bent on getting us back. But I watched in horror as he began hand-to-hand combat with a hulking officer. The man had a gun in a holster, and it would only be a matter of time before he used it. I veered in their direction, cursing Christopher. I needed to stay on task! I'd known he was going to be a distraction.

The officer had him in a tight headlock; the wrinkles around Christopher's eyes were deep as his eyeballs bulged. His face turned beet red as he struggled to breathe. I screamed and jumped on his attacker's back, beating my fists into his head. He didn't see it coming, and he didn't match my magical strength. Only a few hits were needed before the body beneath me went limp.

Christopher gripped his wrist. "I think it's broken."

"Come," I said. Quickly, I edged us to the corner of the room.

"Here." I reached out and gently held his wrist. During the fighting, my necklace had begun to press deeply into my skin under my shirt. The gems felt warm, and I knew they allowed me access to the magic instantly. I was lucky to be skilled enough not to mix the magics accidently. I'd coached the newer alchemists to keep their necklaces on the outside of their clothing for that reason.

I thought about the green gem and instantly sensed the magic coursing through my veins. It twirled out and into

Christopher's wrist. He sucked back a shocked grimace as his wrist righted itself with a sickening crunch.

"That's amazing," he whispered.

"For someone who has three daughters for alchemists, you sure don't know a lot about alchemy."

He grimaced.

Welcome to the truth, old man.

"Please," I chastised. "Stay out of everyone's way. I've got to get back."

"But I want to help."

We turned to watch the action going on all around the room. We were gaining ground! Richard was not only surrounded by our people, but most of the officers had been taken out. Only a few alchemists still fought. The mood in room was shifting—on the verge of surrender.

"You did well. The best thing you can do now is to stay safe."

I didn't wait for a reply this time. I took off running. Cole held a gun against Richard's temple. It was all about to be over. I caught up to Tristan who stood on the edge of the action. Sweat dripped down his face as he huffed.

"I can't believe we did it," he said.

I laughed. "Now he tells the truth."

He shook his head, smiling. "Your friend is one hell of a fighter." He nodded to Mastin, who had one of the officers in a headlock. With expert skill he flattened the man twice his size.

I scanned the crowd until I found Faulk. She was handcuffed between three of our guys. I narrowed my eyes, studying her. She looked strange; a knowing smile pulled at her face. A wicked glint lit her features as she glanced around the room. I froze. I knew that look. What was going on?

Something was wrong.

"Put the gun down," Richard calmly said to the man who had him. Cole.

"You attacked my country, unprovoked. You've killed my citizens. You've destroyed vast amounts of our land. Tell me now why I shouldn't just kill you." Cole spat at Richard's feet, anger rolling off him.

Richard began to laugh. The laugh of a maniac, high and mechanical.

The room froze, all eyes trained on him. Had he lost his mind?

An echo popped through the room. A gunshot. A spurt of blood sprang out the front of Cole's head. He startled and collapsed in a heap. I stepped back just as screams echoed through the room.

Richard dove to the floor as more shots broke out. More people fell. Were they dead? I flattened myself against the ground. Then I frantically reached up and pulled Tristan with me.

"Get down!" someone shrieked. More screams. More shots.

Tristan and I crawled under a table. It was one of the only remaining tables that hadn't been completely destroyed from the fight. The tablecloth hung low, covering us.

"It's a trap," Tristan growled. He grabbed my hand and fixed his gaze on me, unease in his eyes. "We have to get you out of here."

Feet pounded across the floor. More bullets sounded.

"I said don't kill the alchemists!" Richard yelled again. No microphone this time, his voice howling from farther away.

I peeked under the tablecloth. Officers swarmed the room, securing the perimeter. Where had they all come from? There had only been a few tables of officers when we first came in the room. But now? Their numbers had practically quadrupled.

"Go!" Tristan said, forcing me in the direction of the closest unmanned exit. It was our only chance.

We crawled across the floor, dodging bodies at every turn. Most of them were alive, thank goodness. Many people were still lying flat on the ground for safety. Some had tranquilizer darts embedded in their skin and were unconscious. But I knew some were dead the second I laid eyes on them.

I recognized too many of their faces.

Tears stung my eyes. How could we have been so eager to rush into this place? Of course it had been a trap. We couldn't expect anything less from a man like Richard. We'd been led like lambs to the slaughter. I had willingly led people who weren't ready for this kind of combat into the situation. I should have trusted my instincts from the beginning. I should have never listened Mastin and Cole. Or anyone else.

We were all going to die. Innocent people were going to die.

"Go," Tristan hissed, pointing again to the unmanned door.

We jumped up, sprinting toward it. Just as we were about to push through, Mastin popped up at our side. He nodded, huffing quietly, his face grim. "Go!" he mouthed. We erupted into the hallway.

"Wait, where's Christopher?" I skidded to a halt.

The men exchanged a glance as they both shook their heads. "He's probably out already. We'll sort that out later," Mastin said. "We have to get out of here now."

Four or five of our people sprinted down the hallway from the same direction we'd just come in.

"The choppers are out here," one of them called, motioning to us. They didn't wait for us to follow.

"You go," I said, pushing the men in front of me. "I'll catch up."

"I'm not leaving you," Tristan said. Of course, it was only to be expected. He'd been my protector since we were kids. "Fine," I huffed. "But, Mastin, you need to help those people get out of here. We'll be out soon."

He hesitated.

"I'm serious, Mastin. If we're not there, you still have to go. Tristan and I know this city. We'll be fine. We'll get out. You have to get out of here. You have to get home and get reinforcements."

I could tell he didn't want to leave me, but he had to.

"I mean it," I said, nodding at him, then turning back to the ballroom. When I heard him take off, I exhaled, momentarily relieved.

Christopher! If he's not dead then I'm going to kill him.

Tristan and I edged our way along the shadows, peering into the doorway. There were too many officers. Several stood just beyond us now. It was hopeless. We couldn't go in there.

The moment I was about to give up on Christopher, I saw him.

He was crawling on the floor, along the back of the room—in the *wrong* direction. He was moving toward the action, not away from it. He slowly crept nearer to Richard and Faulk, both of whom were now standing over Cole's body. Others were littered around them. The soldiers who'd been caught, I didn't think any of them had even been given a chance or a second thought. Bullets into the heads of each. Our alchemists had been spared.

I gripped my hands into fists. Magic...

"We need to go," Tristan whispered into my hair, his body against mine, tugging me away. "We can try to make the helicopter if we leave now." He needed to get out of here. We both did. We were traitors to our kingdom, and if we were caught, it would be an instant death sentence.

I nodded, and we began to back away. We'd already wasted too much time. There was nothing I could do for Christopher. He was in the thick of it and there was no way I could get him out without getting caught myself. That was a suicide mission. Impossible. They might save me, but Tristan would be killed on the spot. I just hoped they took mercy on Christopher, or that maybe, by some miracle, he got himself out of that room before someone realized who he was.

"This way," Tristan whispered, as he pulled us into a room and shut the door.

The window was open, but it wasn't near the ground. It was at least ten feet up. I didn't know this room. We hastily found a table to move and give us a leg up. The thumping of one of the helicopters starting back up sounded through the room. More gunfire.

"We need to move it," I hissed. Tristan was ahead of me, already on the table. I grabbed at my necklace, feeling for it under my shirt. "Yellow alchemy," I said. "I'll boost you up and then come over."

It only took a second for the magic to connect, igniting my veins and filling me once again with that burst of power and adrenaline. In a flash, I wrangled Tristan up and out of the window.

I crouched low and readied myself to jump.

"Are you lost?"

I shouldn't have looked. I should have just jumped through the window. Run. Moved. *Anything!*

But my curiosity got the better of me. I turned to the voice.

"We've been looking everywhere for you," Faulk said.

She pointed a gun. Everything burst into a flash of white.

And then there was only darkness.

NINETEEN

JESSA

As soon as the chaos started, Lucas grabbed me. He *never* let me go.

When the first gunshot erupted, I thought we were going to die. It was a mess of bodies and bullets, and we huddled together in shock. There was no way we could overcome the attack sitting at this table. But they knew me, right? Even though I was sitting at the table with the royal family, had Jasmine told the Resistance about me? Did they know I was one of them? So much about the Resistance was secretive. People didn't tell me anything, so how could I expect her to tell them? That thought circled my mind over and over, bringing me to sheer panic.

I had allowed hope to come in once that man had Richard. But then that man was shot through the back of the head and the screaming started again. More blood. After Jasmine's death, I didn't think I could take it. The fear was exhausting, and it just kept coming. I focused on my breathing, letting the minutes tick by as Richard directed the room.

We lost...

"It's okay," Lucas said. He wrapped me in his arms, kissing the side of my face. "It's okay. It's okay."

I'd lost track of his fiancée. Not that he seemed to care, but I did. She had appeared to be just as terrified as me, if not more. And no one had been there to comfort her. "Where's Celia?"

"Some of the officers already took her away." He breathed into my hair. "She'll be fine. She's a big girl."

Guilt swept through me. If I'd been in her shoes, I certainly would have wanted Lucas to hold me instead of another girl. I must've said something out loud because Lucas squeezed me tighter.

"It's okay. I'm not with Celia anymore. I'm with you."

I didn't fully understand. Well, I kind of understood since we were secretly engaged. I couldn't believe that it had been less than twenty-four hours since Lucas had come to my room, begging for my forgiveness. Maybe that was what he was talking about.

"Things are starting to calm down now," Lucas said. "Why don't you close your eyes for a minute?"

I just wanted to get out of there, more than anything. I was sure he could see that. I looked at my hands. They couldn't stop shaking. "Can't we just go?"

"We shouldn't leave until the officers say it's okay."

"I really thought…" I mumbled, trying to sort through the events in my mind. It was all a mess. "I really thought the Resistance was going to win this time."

Lucas didn't say anything, his expression grew somber as he took in the scene around us. Too many people had died. Pools of blood circled the bodies. Alchemists, officers, and even some of the waitstaff had lost their lives. I glanced at the face of a waitress who had tended to me at dinner, and I grimaced. Tears filled my eyes as I took in the bodies of soldiers. Where were they from? And the Resistance? They had either fled, been shot, or been captured.

The wounded cried out around the room. Luckily, enough alchemists were helping out with that, green magic circling.

"I should go," I said, pointing to some of the wounded. "I can help them."

Lucas nodded his agreement. "But I'm not leaving you."

I stood on shaky legs and walked to some people who still needed to be healed. Even for those who seemed to be gone, we still stopped to see what we could do.

"Check for pulses," I told Lucas.

Then we began making the rounds—him checking for wounds, and me healing where I could. Even in my frazzled state, the magic came more naturally to me than ever. One after another I healed wounds, extracted bullets, pulled out tranquilizer darts, and even mended a few broken bones. It felt good to do something to help others. Right.

For once in my life I was actually making a difference.

The king yelled through it all, but at this point, I'd tuned him out. He'd gotten what he wanted. He'd won, and in the process probably squashed the Resistance. Jasmine was gone, as were most of those who came in to fight. It was a devastating blow, one I didn't imagine the Resistance could come back from.

I didn't know where I fit in anymore. The ache of loss threatened to tear me apart, but I just kept moving.

At least I had Lucas. I looked up at him, catching him checking more pulses. He handled everybody with care. That look of pain, it still held strong on his face. He was sweating, and blood was splattered across his suit. His hair was a mess, and he strained to lift somebody up into a chair. An officer. They cried out, and I rushed over to administer magic.

Technically, the officers were my enemy. I was Resistance.

But I couldn't see somebody with that look on their face, the pain so terrible that they were on the verge of passing out, and *not* step in to help. That wasn't me. I'd learned that my magic could be a gift. Or it could be a curse.

I chose the gift.

The officer was coated in blood. His hazel eyes fluttered as I sent a pulse of magic into him. "Thank you," he croaked.

We finished up in our area. I scanned the room, sighing. It looked like everyone else had been tended to. So with the small bit of relief we allowed ourselves, we moved back toward the front of the room. The shock began to wear off as the reality finally set in. Deep into my bones.

We lost. The Resistance had *lost*.

"That was horrible," I whispered, sitting down at what was left of our table. Flowers were scattered about, dishes lying in shards, and everything was covered with splatters of blood.

Lucas reached out and squeezed my hand, before releasing it. "It's over now," he said.

Something tickled my ankle, then grabbed. I jumped! I almost let out a yelp, but I saw whose hand was attached to my leg. I sunk to my knees. Everything came into focus as I stared at the man before me.

"Dad?" I breathed out, shocked. Then I wrapped my arms around him and sobbed into his shoulder. I couldn't help it. "It's really you. What are you doing here?" The pain of missing him had dulled over the last few weeks, but now that he was here, it ignited, waking me up.

"I need you to help me get us out of here," he whispered.

Of course! He couldn't be here. I didn't mention that I would be staying.

We looked around, it seemed nobody had noticed us. Lucas sat still, staring down at us. His eyes were wide. A horrified expression had crossed his features, and he clutched his stomach.

"I'll help you." The words came out like a promise. But how was I going to help? The room was swarming with alchemists and officers. "Hide under that part of the table." There was a bit that was still standing, toppled to one side and covered by the tablecloth. It was plenty big enough. He nodded, and I stood.

I met Lucas's eyes. "You have to get him out of here."

He knew what I was talking about. His frown deepened, but he nodded imperceptibly. He needed to use white alchemy. If he went under the table where no one could see, he could make himself invisible and make my father invisible too. He could get him out. It was dangerous, but this was my dad.

We stared at each other, Lucas and I. He was thinking too much, I could tell. But so was I. My father was *not* trained. He should never have been here. The Resistance shouldn't have allowed it. How could they? They'd promised to keep my parents safe, and then they went and did this!

"Please," I whispered to Lucas. *You love me. I know you love me. Do this for me.*

Lucas glanced around the room. The king was still making the rounds on the other side. No one was looking at us.

"You can do it," I said, my voice low, and reached for one of the white lilies strewn across the floor. "You've done it before. You can do it with this, Lucas." I handed him the flower. "You're more powerful than you give yourself credit for. No one will know. It will be fine."

He nodded again. "Okay."

He shifted, about to go under the white tablecloth with my father. No one would notice. I had to believe it. Someone patted me on the back.

"That was impressive," Richard said.

A rush of hatred covered me from head to toe. How had he gotten over here so fast?

Moments ago, he was on the other side of the room, and now he was standing inches away from my father. My father, the man he had pretended to have in custody. The man who was officially part of the Resistance. The man who had raised me. The man who had left the kingdom!

"Thank you?" I questioned. Everything that just happened was horrific.

"You're one of us now."

"Father, not right now," Lucas said, his body stiff.

Richard laughed. "So fickle. One minute you're begging me to call off your engagement with Celia to be with this alchemist, and the next you act like nothing is going on."

I glanced between the two men.

"I don't understand." I turned to Lucas. A small voice of doubt sounded in my mind. *Something is off.* "What's he talking about?"

Lucas only shook his head. "We'll talk about it later."

"Is your engagement to Celia called off?"

"It wasn't," Richard said. "But I keep my word. Lucas did what he was supposed to do, so I'll hold up my end and reconsider."

"Reconsider what?" My voice cracked.

"Reconsider you, my dear." He frowned. "Not the brightest, are you? I was always very clear with my son that he wasn't to get involved with an alchemist, let alone marry one. But I suppose, under the right circumstances, with the right woman, I could allow it."

I still didn't understand. What was happening?

"There's someone under this table," an officer said. In horror, I turned to find the hazel-eyed man I'd helped just minutes ago. Those eyes were fully awake now. He lifted up the tablecloth and pointed to my father.

"No!" I cried. "Don't hurt him."

"Who's this?" Richard ripped the tablecloth away. The remainder of the centerpiece and dishes flew in an arc. A clattering of broken pieces rang out, followed by a moment of silence.

"Please don't hurt him," I begged. "None of this is his fault."

Faulk appeared. I hadn't seen her in a while, and she strode up as if she had conquered the world, all confidence and pride. She sneered down at my father. He still hadn't said anything. His hands were up, but his eyes were trained on me. They never broke from me.

"That's Jessa's father," Faulk confirmed, flicking her wrist at him.

Richard laughed. "Are you brazen enough to think you could come back here?" But he got no reply from my father.

"Jessa." Dad's gaze held steady on mine. "No matter what happens to me, I love you. Do you understand? I love you. You are stronger than you know."

I had no words. I reached out to grab him, but someone restrained me.

"Get off me!" I screamed, clawing at the hands. The same officer whose life I'd saved with magic. I looked to Lucas. He would help me, wouldn't he?

"Traitor," Faulk spat at Dad. "We ought to execute him right now."

"Please, think it through, we can't just kill him," Lucas said, his voice somehow calm. "He's Jessa's father."

"Yes," Richard said. "You make a good point, son. As Jessa's father, he makes great leverage, doesn't he? Not to mention he could be full of valuable information about that disgusting Resistance."

I struggled against my captor. "Please."

"Don't you worry, my dear," Richard said. "We'll only put him back where he came from." He winked.

I couldn't say anything to that. It was a test. I wasn't supposed to know that my father had ever gone away from the kingdom. I was supposed to believe he'd been in holding this whole time. So I just nodded. I felt he wanted me to thank him or something. But I couldn't. I just couldn't! In prison, my father would not be treated well. And to use him as leverage against me? Now that Richard knew what I was capable of, he could use my father to get me to hurt more people.

I was so tired. I was so sad. And shocked. I needed to either puke all over Richard or claw his eyes out!

But mostly, it was anger running through me.

When was I ever going to get away from this awful king? When was I ever going to get to live a life on my own terms? And how in the world had the Resistance attack ended so badly?

It was almost as if Richard had known it was going to happen...

"Take them away," Richard said.

They yanked my father up. He didn't protest as they led him away. He was too smart for that. He couldn't win, everyone knew that. But in that moment, watching them take him away from me, I vowed to find a way to free him. To free all of us.

●

No one knew what to do with themselves the next day. Classes were canceled. The infirmary was filled with officers and waitstaff, sleeping off the last of their injuries. But with enough alchemists helping out already, they didn't need me.

I didn't know what to do.

Mostly, I stayed holed up in my room, trying to sort out the details of the previous day. I couldn't piece it together. It seemed that Richard knew Jasmine was a spy. How? Or he'd at least suspected as much and then used my ability to find out the truth. That seemed more likely. But I still wasn't sure. I felt her loss like I was missing a limb. I kept looking for her, expecting her to be there, and she wasn't.

She was gone.

And those friends I thought I had? Every alchemist I'd come in contact with since that night avoided me. They were afraid. I could see it in their eyes, the way they shifted gazes when I looked at them, and then shifted back to me when I looked away.

They were afraid of the red alchemy.

They were afraid to be the next Jasmine.

They were terrified I would somehow do something to make them suffer at the hands of the royal family. And I didn't blame them. I'd proved what was possible, so they should be afraid. I was dangerous. Lethal. As much as I hated it, it was true. Red alchemy destroyed lives.

I was alone in this burden. But at least I had Lucas. I got up and wandered around the palace, looking for him. He would know what to do. Except, I couldn't seem to find him. I didn't dare go to the royal wing, but I went to our greenhouse, to the gardens outside, and I looked for him in all the usual places. He was nowhere. I even went down to the kitchens and asked the staff if they'd seen him. Nothing.

I finally retreated back to my bedroom. That small dorm room was my safe haven. Even though it wasn't actually that safe, I could pretend. I would avoid the truth—that I was sleeping in the belly of the beast. In the most dangerous place of all. With the most dangerous people.

And I was one of them.

Another invitation greeted me when I walked in the door to my room. I shuffled around the small space, eyeing it suspiciously.

Really, again?

Someone had slid it under the door, like all the ones before it. I should be getting used to this by now. But I wasn't ready for another party, or dinner, or dance, or execution, or whatever the hell this was going to be. I just wanted a night off.

Please join the royal family in their private quarters for dinner. Formal dress. 7 P.M.

A wave of nervous tension rolled over my body. I wanted to see Lucas, but Richard was the last person I wanted to spend another dinner with. Last night's had seriously scarred me for life. And he was holding my father prisoner because of it. Jasmine and many others were dead because of it.

What would this one do?

But I did as I was told. I styled my curly hair on top of my head, pinning it into my best version of an up-do. Then I zipped myself into a gold velvety gown I had yet to wear. It clung in all the right places, and I groaned, tired of being on display. I fixed my makeup and slipped my feet into nude pumps.

●

"Doesn't she look regal?" Richard purred as I entered the elegant dining room.

Lucas and his father stood upon my entrance. They were as handsome as ever. It was just the three of us. *Okay, I guess this really is an intimate dinner.* And it made my stomach curl.

"Thank you," I said, my voice flat. I hated this man. I hated what he had done to me. And I hated most of all what he would do to my father. What he *was* doing! But he had all the power at the moment, so once again, I had to smile and pretend like I was the leader of his personal fan club.

"Please, join us." He motioned for me to sit next to his son. His son, whom he had forbidden from me. *Okay, this is weird.*

"I'm dreadfully sorry about last night," Richard continued. "Horrific business, isn't it? But sometimes what must be done must be done."

I nodded. My neck felt stiff, and I rubbed at it, pressing hard.

"Father," Lucas said, his face blushing. "Why don't we talk about something else?"

Lucas rarely blushed. I eyed him, once again getting the feeling that something wasn't right. Why was he blushing?

"Of course. Where are my manners?"

Good question, Your Royal Highness!

We talked about the weather. The upcoming holiday. The war, though that was mostly Richard's doing. We talked about anything we could besides what was really on everyone's minds: the night previous and all that it meant for us.

I pushed the food around my plate, hardly able to eat despite the warm texture of the potatoes and the juicy flavor of the seared steak. I'd grown used to the decadence of palace food. The novelty was growing old. I longed for a simple meal of pasta and vegetables, or even bread with cheese would suffice. The type of food I used to eat regularly with my family.

"I hear congratulations are in order." Richard turned his charm on and pointed it right at me. His eyes twinkled, but they'd never lost that calculating shine. I was beyond the point of ever caring what this man thought of me.

"Congratulations on what?" It was possible he was talking about joining the guardians, but I doubted it. He'd already congratulated me on that multiple times. This was something more.

"Your engagement." Richard smiled. He took a sip of his wine, studying me.

"What are you talking about?" I sputtered, sucking in a sharp breath.

He knew about me and Lucas? There was no one else. But everything between Lucas and I wasn't official. No, it was a secret. He had to figure out how to end it with Celia first. He had to convince his father…

"Yes, Lucas told me all about it. Your…love."

I turned on Lucas, incredulous. He paled and reached out to grab my hand. "It's okay," he whispered into my ear. "He's okay with it." I breathed in and out, but the oxygen just wasn't filling my lungs fast enough.

"I thought we mentioned this last night?" Richard asked. "Oh, but last night was all such a blur, wasn't it? Well, in any event, I've decided to be supportive of the union. I think you'll make a wonderful queen, certainly an asset to our kingdom."

What. Is. Happening? A ringing sensation began to sound in my ears.

"I'm sorry." I shook my head. "I don't understand. Lucas is engaged to Celia. Isn't he?" I stared down at our clasped hands. Mine didn't look right in his anymore.

"I'm afraid not," Richard sighed. "Of course, we had to keep that appearance up last night. I just had to make sure Lucas would hold up his end of the deal. That he was telling the truth. Of course, you understand."

Lucas squeezed my hand again. I ripped it away.

"No, I don't understand." The room began to spin.

"When Lucas came to me offering information about the Resistance's little assassination attempt in exchange for your hand, it was a deal too good to pass up."

The whole world crashed. My heart sputtered, then stopped. I gasped, and I also couldn't breathe. I stared at Lucas, taking in every inch of him. I needed an explanation. This couldn't be. He smiled, but it didn't reach his eyes. They were dark. Regretful. And also…hopeful. No!

I tore my gaze away and doubled over.

"Anything for love, isn't that right?" Richard laughed. "It turned out my son had heard a thing or two around the palace and had caught wind of the timing of that little attack last night. So, it was the perfect opportunity for me to end the Resistance, as they called themselves. Such poor souls. They never stood a chance. I really don't know what they were thinking, teaming up with West America like that. No matter. They're gone now."

I sat frozen. Numb.

"Well," Richard said, patting his mouth with his napkin. "I'll leave you two lovebirds alone." Then he met my gaze, winked, and stood. "If you need me, I'll be with the officers. We have quite a bit of planning to do. Not to mention, interrogations to continue."

He left.

We sat in silence.

"I'm sorry," Lucas finally said, his voice scratchy. "I never meant for it to get that far out of hand."

"How could you?" I whispered, anger clawing at my throat. "I trusted you." And that was what hurt the most.

Lucas turned on me then, gripping my hands again. "I love you. I was desperate. My wedding was only months

316

away, and I had to be with you. I never expected that many people to show up. I had no idea your father would come."

"But you knew he was with them. You knew there might've been a chance!"

"No. He shouldn't have been there. He wasn't trained. It was stupid of me to do it, I know. I'm so sorry. I just thought that I would help my father get the upper hand in *one* attack. And I used that as a bargaining chip for you and me to be together."

"And then what?"

"Then we would figure it out. I would figure out how to fix everything, but we'd be together. And that's all that matters, right? That we're together now."

Nausea bubbled in my stomach. "No, that is not all that matters."

"Don't you love me? I did this for you, Jessa."

"Our love killed twenty people last night. Our love killed Jasmine! Our love is disgusting. I can't love you anymore. It's poison." I shot up so fast my chair crashed to the floor.

"Please Jessa." Lucas stood, his tone accusatory. "You're being unfair."

Betrayal ripped through me. Unfair? He had a lot of nerve talking to me about unfair. He had ruined everything!

"Don't you trust me? I'm telling you the truth," he continued. But I knew there was nothing he could say to fix this. "I'd have never done it if I'd known it would've ended like that. I didn't know they were going to send in all those people. I didn't know that was going to happen."

"But you did it. You still did it!" The words exploded from my mouth. "You betrayed my trust. Everything I told you, you took it to your dad."

"No! Not everything!"

"You said enough," I said. "Enough for Jasmine to be dead."

"I never mentioned her."

Lies...

"Enough for others to have died, in vain. Enough for my father to be in prison. Probably under interrogation right now. Probably being tortured!"

"We will help him," Lucas growled. "We can do anything together. Don't you believe in us?" A blood vessel pulsed in his forehead. He looked like Richard.

"You don't get it," I snapped. "You don't get anything I'm saying. If I can't trust you, then we can't be together."

His face darkened. "Nothing I ever do will be good enough for you."

"My father is probably going to die because of you. Others died because of you. I'll probably never see my mother or my sister again because of you, because you're so selfish, because you're so blinded by what you want. Because you're just like your father!"

He stilled. "Fine," he said. "Consider us over. You can go now."

"You don't need to tell me twice," I snarled, stomping out of the room and slamming the door behind me.

A fire ignited within me. The rage. The anger. How could he betray me like that? He was supposed to love me, and yet he could take something I'd told him in confidence and turn it over to his father. He knew how much the Resistance meant to me. He knew that was the only reason why I was still at the palace. I'd told him about the attack only out of concern for his safety. And he'd used it against me.

I would take this love and turn it into revenge.

I would burn it.

Bury it.

And no matter what, I would never trust him again.

"**Come with me,**" Faulk called, pounding on my door.

The night had been spent in a fire of rage, and I'd woken to an inferno. I'd gotten dressed and then stomped around my room in circles. I didn't leave it. What was the point? The palace was a mess, and I wasn't going to willingly participate in the clean up. I was done playing nice.

I climbed off the bed and stormed to swing the door open for Faulk.

"What?" I spat.

She raised an eyebrow. "Come." Then she took off down the hall.

I followed, hot on her heels. People stared at me as we passed them. I didn't care. Let them stare. I may have appeared broken to some, but I was stronger than ever inside. I'd spent the night thinking through everything, going over every angle in my head. I had painstakingly accounted for all the pain the people in this palace done to me.

Reliving it all, again and again.

Driving the heartache in.

Drowning in the anger.

And I was resolved. I was going to end the royal family, even if it ended me.

I followed her to a lift, and we descended. I'd been this way before. We were going to the dungeons. Well, I guessed it was technically called the prison. In my mind it was "the dungeons" since this was a deplorable palace. Even the very land it sat on was tainted by greed. Maybe they were going to lock me up? At this point, I wouldn't even care.

We walked down a hall and a rotting scent filled my nostrils. It was covered up by antiseptic, but not well enough. A female moan echoed from the far end of the hall.

"We have somebody we want you to meet."

"Okay." I nodded. *Let's get this over with…*

I noted that we were in the vicinity of the gray rooms. These were the sorry places the officers used to keep alchemists away from their own magic. I had been in these rooms. I felt a nudge of guilt for the alchemist I was about to find behind the door. Resistance, no doubt.

We walked inside.

The girl's blond hair hung heavily in her face. She was handcuffed to a chair, and, as expected, dressed in black. She peered up at me. Recognition lit her eyes.

It was Sasha.

"I already know her," I said to Faulk, sounding bored. "You said you wanted me to meet somebody. She is nobody new. So why am I really here?"

"Oh." Faulk laughed. It wasn't a pretty sound. "I guess I should've said meet *again*. In a new light. Under different circumstances."

"Fine," I said, striding into the room.

Sasha had bruises forming on her cheeks, some yellow and others a shiny, dark purple. There were a few cuts as well. The one that cut across her eyebrow looked deep enough to scar. Her eyes still revealed the friend I knew, though. Maybe I could help her.

Once inside, the door closed, and I turned back on Faulk. "What do you want?"

"Jessa." Faulk smiled. "I'd like for you to meet your *older sister*, Francesca. I think it's time the two of you were properly reacquainted."

The words rang in my ear, taking a moment to settle in. This made no sense. I shot my gaze to Sasha.

She just stared back at me, not a glimmer of surprise in her face.

Her blue eyes reflected my own.

I stumbled backward.

Francesca? A dream assaulted me. Not a dream, a flash of memory. A girl running through the grass. Blond hair streaming behind her. A dandelion in her small hand. Yellow magic twinkling in the air between us.

My sister.

END OF BOOK TWO

CONTINUE READING

Thank you for reading The Color Alchemist series.
If you liked this book, please leave a review on Amazon
or Goodreads. Word of mouth is the lifeblood to an
independent author and it only takes a moment.

Thanks again!

Join my newsletter for news on releases, giveaways,
advanced reader teams, and more. I'm also working on
a short novel to release exclusively to newsletter readers.
Among Shadows will reveal Tristan's backstory and will be
ready by the end of 2017.

Visit **www.ninawalkerbooks.com** for more information.

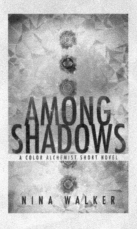

The series will continue with book three, *Blackout*,
coming Spring 2018.

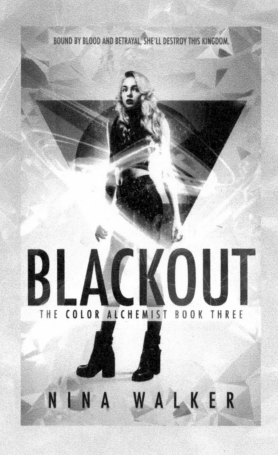

ACKNOWLEDGMENTS

When I released *Prism*, it was with a lot of excitement and fear. As a new author, doing this publishing thing on my own, I was completely terrified. I have to say, the reception blew me away. To my readers, thank you very much. You have no idea how much you helped me. It took me years to find the courage to release *Prism*. You made the experience wonderful and I can't thank you enough.

Thank you to my husband for putting up with my crazy, for supporting me every step of the way, and for feeling every up and down with me. You are my world and I am so grateful to have you in my life.

Thank you to my family for your support. I love you!

I have to send a huge thank you to my developmental editor, Kate Foster, for not only believing in this series, but for doing such a fabulous job with the manuscripts. You helped me take my writing to another level with *Fracture*, and I am eternally grateful for you. I can't wait to work on the next two books together.

Thank you to the world's best cover designer, Molly, at *We Got You Covered*. Your eye for design blows me away, not to mention your ability to work with picky authors. Thank you for all your help.

Thank you to Madeline Dyer for the copy edit. And to Stevie, Ailene, and Kate for the proof-reads. I love you ladies!

Thank you to my ARC team, to my readers, and to everyone who took the time to reach out to me or to write a review. I appreciate it more than you could know. To all my friends who share my books, even if YA Fantasy isn't your thing, you are amazing.

Stu Thaman, launch strategist extraordinaire, thank you so much for your help on *Prism*.

Thank you to everyone in the Indie community who reached out to congratulate me, to answer a question, or to teach.

And last, but always first, thank you to God. Thank you for carrying me through this entire experience and for answering my prayers.

ABOUT

NINA WALKER is an emerging author of young adult fiction. She lives in Utah with her husband, children, and two ornery cats. *Fracture* is her second book.

Connect with Nina:

Facebook at fb.com/ninawalkerbooks
Instagram @ninawalkerbooks

www.ninawalkerbooks.com